LEGACY

A Raptors MC Novel by
Elle Rease

Other titles in the Raptors MC series:

Original Cin
Hero

Cover Design: Wendy Bow, Apple Pie Graphics

ISBN 978-0-6397-8211-9

Dedicated to the Raptors MC fans:
Knowing how badly you wanted to read Logan's story kept me going.
Thank you for your unwavering support!

PART I

THE BOY

CHAPTER ONE

THE MAN WITH the shoulder-length auburn hair and ice blue eyes peered into the camera. He had a strong jaw, plump mouth. His lips—the bottom one with a ring in each corner—twitched as if he wanted to smile, causing slight dents in his cheeks. Dimples.

Logan unknowingly touched his own cheeks, where he sported the same.

"Cin, what're you doing?" The man's voice was low, gruff, yet in no way rude.

"Come on, babe. Just say it once."

"I've said it plenty."

"Bren!" Cinnia laughed. "I need proof!"

"Not a fuck."

"Please?"

That icy gaze became warm as he grinned broadly. "Okay, fine. I'm a softie, but only for you." And then the man dragged Cinnia into the frame to fuse their mouths together.

Logan pressed pause.

He's seen this, and other videos, so many times he's lost count. He has inspected each one of them, frame by frame, and overanalyzed every word, every emotion. He knew them by heart.

He still didn't get it.

Glancing at the photos on the side table, he focused on one: his parents beaming at each other. *That* made total sense. Byron and Cinnia were inseparable, always have been. His first memories included them being overly affectionate and clearly in love.

His head turned back to the screen. How had his mother loved someone else?

He's your father.

Logan shook his head, denying that voice. He was so deep in thought that he didn't hear the front door opening, and therefore had no time to reset the room.

"Hey, Lo."

Logan's eyes widened as he gazed at his *real* father, even though other people used the prefix "step" to describe Byron's relationship to Logan. "Hey, dad."

Byron absorbed the freeze-frame on the television for a moment before striding into the room, sitting next to Logan. "This again?"

Logan flinched and reached for the remote. "Sorry."

"You don't need to apologize, punk, but what's going on? Did something upset you?"

He suppressed a sigh. "There were kids talking smack at school yesterday."

"Oh? What kind of smack?" Byron prompted.

"Just… How I'm not a real person, because mom wasn't pregnant with me. It doesn't usually bother me."

"But this time, it did."

"I guess. I mean, they don't even make any sense: I'm physically as real as they are. I shouldn't care what they think."

Byron was quiet for a moment. "Logan, it's normal to second-guess yourself because of what someone else says. It's part of the human condition, unfortunately." He bumped his shoulder against Logan's. "Then again, your life has been incredible. You have plenty of friends, you're top of your class and you're a phenomenal athlete. Yes, there are aspects of your life that are unconventional, but they're part of what makes you, *you*."

"I don't want to be different."

"I understand. I was the same when I was your age."

Logan observed the faraway expression on his stepfather's face. "Really?"

"Sure," Byron chuckled dryly. "I was a skinny, awkward boy too smart to be popular. It didn't help that I had feelings for girls *and* boys. It wasn't as acceptable back then as it is now. I just wanted to fit in."

"When did you grow out of it?"

"Honestly? Your mom helped with that. She was one of the first people that accepted me the way I am. Ryan, too."

Logan knew the story of his parents' love like the back of his own hand, and yet he never tired hearing about their mutual adoration. He hoped that he would be lucky enough to have a relationship like theirs one day.

"You'll find a way to make peace with your life, punk. I have faith in you."

"Sometimes I feel like your faith is misplaced."

"Nah," Byron said, "there's no way that you'll ever let me down. You're already someone that I look up to."

Wow. Logan refrained from blinking, afraid that the tears in his eyes would fall. "Thanks, dad."

"Why don't you go hang out with your friends? I don't think you should be alone right now, and I know you wouldn't want to talk to your mom about this."

Logan winced. "Does that make me a bad person?"

"No, it makes you a teenager."

Laughing, Logan jumped to his feet and held out a hand to help Byron to his. "I'll go to Sophie's. She knows how to deal with me when I'm like this."

"Sure," Byron said, raising an eyebrow.

Logan felt his cheeks heat up. "It's not like that."

"Sure." Byron squeezed Logan's shoulder. "Be safe."

"Always."

Avoiding eye contact, Logan strode to the front door, grabbing his keys and leather cut along the way. Even though he's been riding since he was four, he had acquired his motorcycle license when he turned sixteen. He wasn't legally allowed to ride anything over 150cc, but the Chief trusted the Raptors MC implicitly and gave them a free pass. At seventeen, Logan couldn't think of a better mode of transportation than a Harley Davidson.

Logan had a smile on his face as he straddled his vintage Blackline. He was aware that Brennan had preferred this model, too, but didn't linger on this shared trait. He donned his helmet and ignited the engine.

Ah, freedom.

The ride to Sophie's dance studio gave Logan the opportunity to process the confused rattle in his brain. It was difficult to look beyond the fact that his family, which included the broader Raptors community, saw him as the club's golden boy. It made him feel like he had the weight of the world on his shoulders simply for being a Drummond heir.

Brennan.

Logan's sigh was drowned out by the rumble of his bike. He had no recollection of his biological father and, therefore, no real connection to the man. To Logan, Byron Johannson always has been, and always will be, his father. Byron had raised him, taught him how to ride his bicycle, and been there to take him to his first day of school. Byron had helped with homework; had gone to all of his football games; had bought his first Harley. Byron had drilled the Raptors' traditions and responsibilities towards the community into Logan's head.

Most of all, Byron loved Logan's mother.

Logan had grown up in a home wrapped in love, the affectionate kind. The *true* kind. The type of connection that Byron and Cinnia had… How was it possible for that to come around twice in one lifetime? Brennan and Cinnia's love, so different from Byron and Cinnia's, also seemed all-encompassing. It was confusing.

I'm just confused.

But what if it wasn't about that? Sometimes, Logan hated the reminder that Byron wasn't the only man his mother loved. A part of Logan loathed the mere mention of his deceased father. Brennan had been spoiled: given everything simply because of his surname. One of Logan's biggest fears was turning into an entitled brat, like Brennan had been. Worst of all, he couldn't talk to anyone about it, because referring to Brennan as a "brat" would only upset his loved ones. They worshipped him.

Can't compete with the legacy of a dead man. Why bother trying?

He parked at the curb and sat staring into nothing for a moment, hoping these conflicting views will quiet down. With another unconscious sigh, he headed up to the studio. There were several girls his age leaving as he walked towards the door. He didn't fail to notice their lingering looks or flirty giggles. He raked his own gaze over their bodies. Hot damn, the female form was gorgeous!

Distraction: successful.

He stepped over the threshold with a smirk. Sophie, at least a head shorter than him, was busy drying her face with a towel. Her light blonde hair was braided down her back, the fringe straight despite having worked up a sweat. She wore a loose-fitting lavender T-shirt that was so long that it didn't appear as if she was wearing any pants. Her toned legs were a sight for sore eyes.

He's always followed Sophie around like a lovesick puppy, although their feelings for each other were platonic. Several years older than him, she's been his babysitter, the older sister of his good friend, Connor, and ever since he lost his virginity to her, the person he went to for advice.

"I should've known there was a reason for the commotion outside," Sophie remarked dryly, her gaze meeting his. "Did you flash them your dick?"

Her blunt nature was one of his favorite things about her. "Considered it, but no. They must have X-ray vision."

She rolled her eyes. "This is a large room and yet you still manage to fill it with your ego."

"What can I say? You created a monster."

She bit her bottom lip to keep from smiling at their inside joke. She turned to the counter to grab her water bottle. "What can I do for you, Lo? It's not like you to come here."

"I remembered that you work until four on Saturdays. Wanted to chat."

"What happened?"

"I…" He raked his fingers through his hair and let out a breath. "Can we build up to that?"

She eyed him, gauging his mood. She pulled her shirt over her head, proving that she was, indeed, wearing clothing underneath. A sports bra and boy shorts, but still. She walked to the sound system. "Dance with me."

He groaned. "Soph—"

"Nope," she interrupted firmly, tapping the screen of her iPhone. "You came here to lament about your life, so I need to get something in return. There's a routine I've been dying to try out." Happy with her selection, she faced him with a smug grin. "Besides, you haven't been my guinea pig in a while."

"For good reason," he muttered as he stripped off his leather cut and boots. He had a feeling he should be grateful that his jeans weren't too tight. "I suck."

"You don't suck at anything unless expressly asked."

He chuckled, peering at her while the sound of an accordion filled the air. "Is that a request?"

She shook her head with a laugh and held her hand out. "Come on, Lo. Let's get you warmed up."

He would never admit it aloud, but he secretly enjoyed dancing with Sophie. He liked to believe he wasn't half bad at it, despite his earlier comment. She's never asked him to be her partner in competitions, though he suspected it had more to do with the fact that she was older than him and aware of his passion for sport than his lack of technique.

Within minutes, she'd loosened him up enough to forget his reservations. She always lost herself to the rhythm: it transported her to another world, one that she never shared with anyone. He loved doing something that brought her joy. Not everyone understood that and often confused their friendship for an inevitable love connection.

In another life, maybe.

He easily learned the choreography, which made him confident to take the lead. Her breath snatched as he moved her across the floor, tugging and pulling and pushing. His core and arms strained from the effort it took to make each spin or lift as seamless as possible.

They broke apart after the third attempt of the routine. Sophie chucked a bottle of ice-cold water his way, taking a long drink of her own. "That was good."

"But?" he panted.

"Something's missing." She swiped her bangs back, thinking. "The whole theme is that we used to be lovers—"

"No shit."

"Shut up," she said good-naturedly. "We haven't been together in years, but then we see each other, and you try to get me back into bed."

There was a large part of him that wanted to sleep with her again. They've been on and off on that front for three years. *You never forget your first.* "You need to get laid, Soph."

Her gaze went to the ceiling again. "Let's go, Drummond."

He shed his shirt, which was already drenched. Whoever thought dancing wasn't real exercise had no idea what they were talking about. "If you're sure you're ready, Tyrell."

"Please." She smiled sweetly as she pressed play. "You're tame."

She'd purposefully taunted him to get his head in the game. He slowly circled her, knowing she expected him to start the dance, yet intent on taking her off guard. Behind her, his fingers curled around her biceps and he pulled her flush against him.

"Lo—"

"My turn."

Before she had a moment to think that through, he was spinning her across the floor, his footwork not as graceful as hers but still giving her a run for her money. He only introduced her choreography halfway through, after she became pliable, relaxed. Their movements, mimicking the act of sex, increased his heart rate and the blood flow to his cock.

He wasn't at all surprised when they eventually stumbled to the mirrored wall, tugging at each other's clothes. He'd hoped, *known*, this would happen the second he saw her. He yanked the boy shorts down and she kicked them off, her fingers gripping his hair as they kissed. She wore a lacy G-string underneath and he pushed it to the side to gain access to her hot, drenched center.

Logan shifted his mouth to her ear, where he nibbled on the lobe. "Soph, should we stop?"

"We need this."

He slipped two fingers inside, pressing the tips against the spot that drove her crazy. *Fuck, yes.* She was wet and ready. "Don't have condoms."

She unzipped his jeans and released his cock from the confines of his underwear. "We're safe."

Hooking a leg over his arm, he pulled his fingers out and sheathed his cock in her warmth, shuddering when she did. He was already teetering on the edge. "Soph."

"No! Want this to last." And yet she rolled her hips as if her sole mission was to get him to unravel as fast as possible.

He's only ever had unprotected sex with her and the clenching around his dick reminded him why he didn't chance it with someone else. His thrusts became shallow to hit her G-spot. All the while, he did his best not to cum. "Soph," he warned again.

"Logan!" she exclaimed once her pussy began pulsing.

He withdrew to prevent himself from spilling. "Finish me off, Soph."

She slithered down his chest to kneel in front of him, taking his cock in her mouth and applying suction immediately. She swallowed him down her throat, something she'd practiced on several occasions before she first managed it.

Gripping the back of her head, he pumped inside once, twice, and exploded on the third. He leaned his forehead on the cool mirror. Spent, he gently pulled out and dropped to the floor next to her. Their breathing gradually returning to normal was the only sound in the large room.

They glanced at each other and burst out laughing.

"I can't believe we just did that."

"I can. We both needed to unwind." She wiped her mouth and sighed. "Rough week."

"What's wrong?"

"Victor and I broke up."

Logan frowned. "Who the fuck is Victor?"

"Someone who wasn't worth introducing you to." She stretched her leg out and used her toes to grip her discarded boy shorts. "We dated for three weeks. He seemed interested until he saw me naked."

The frown deepened. "I don't understand."

"Lo, you're my friend so you have to be nice to me, but not all men want flat-chested, no-ass type of women."

"Soph, there is absolutely nothing wrong with your body. *Nothing.*"

She pecked him on the cheek. "You're sweet."

It seemed crazy that they were having this conversation. She was the quintessential confident woman, and for good reason. Wasn't she? "Did you not feel how hard I was? That was because of you."

She blushed and moved away, putting those shorts back on. "What upset you, anyway?"

He let the other topic go. For now. "It's stupid."

"Tell me anyway."

He reluctantly recounted the guys at school cornering him and spewing bullshit that, in retrospect, shouldn't have affected him as much as it did. He tried incredibly hard to keep bullying in check and was successful when it came to protecting *other* people.

Sophie kneeled in front of him, putting her hands on his legs. "Logan, let's run through your list of good qualities for a moment."

"Let's not."

"You're tall, gorgeous, a phenomenal athlete, and a bad-ass biker. You're stupid smart—"

"That's an oxymoron."

"*You're* a moron if you think, for one minute, that what they said was true! You're the most thoughtful and kind person I've ever met. That means you're *real.* More real than any of those small-dicked jerkoffs ever could be. Speaking of, did I mention you have the biggest dick I've ever seen?"

Laughing softly, he glanced at his lap. He was still unzipped. *Whoops.* "Thanks, Soph."

"People are just mean sometimes."

He leaned forward, making sure she couldn't look away. "You're beautiful. Your *body* is beautiful. Whatshisface doesn't deserve you if he can't see that."

"If I'm so great, why haven't *you* ever made a move?"

He blinked, momentarily taken aback by the question. "Because we promised we'll always be best friends, even if we occasionally screw each other's brains out. You're precious. I don't want to mess up the relationship we have."

"You're that sure you'll mess up?" she asked, giving him a watery smile.

"You need a bear of a man who's going to cherish you forever, not some punk who's trying to figure out why he hates his real father."

"Maybe because you're afraid that loving him would betray your other father?"

His heart stuttered. "Maybe."

She hugged him tightly. "I love you, Logan. We'll always be friends."

"Always." He shifted her onto his lap. "Tell me what else is bothering you."

"I'm almost twenty-five." Sophie sighed. "I want to meet the man of my dreams and start a life together. I don't want to be single anymore."

"Ah, so that's why you suddenly want me to make a move."

"I don't, not really. You're an awesome guy, Logan, and you'll make some girl super happy one day. But you're not *my* awesome guy, you know?"

He pressed a kiss to her forehead. "Yeah, I know."

They sat like that for a while, each lost in their own thoughts. Logan's never been able to explain to his parents—heck, to anyone—that he wasn't in love with Sophie. In some ways, he felt like a protective brother. She made him hard because she was hot and female, not because she was his true love.

He knew she felt the same.

She turned to straddle him, resting her hands on his shoulders. "Wanna come to my place?"

"Still feeling lonely?"

"Yeah. You?"

"Yeah." He cupped her ass, already hardening. "Have you got condoms?"

"Yup." She leaned forward to kiss him. "I want to fuck until we're both raw."

His cock twitched. "Let's go, then."

"Can I ride with you? I walked today."

"Get your things, Miss Tyrell."

She slapped his shoulder with a laugh and got up. "Quit that. Makes me feel old."

They got dressed and he helped her lock up. They headed downstairs to his bike, where he handed her a spare helmet and mounted. She got on behind him, her strong thighs gripping him tightly. He pulled away from the curb and rode in the direction of her apartment, which was only a couple of blocks from the studio. He parked and cut the engine.

Sophie led the way to the second floor of the building. She unlocked her door and dumped her bag in the entryway. "Shower first?"

"Definitely." He stripped as soon as they were in her bedroom, happy to be out of his sweaty clothes. "Can I crash here tonight?"

"Only if you make dinner," she quipped, disappearing into the ensuite.

"Deal." He followed her into the cubicle, savoring the feel of warm water washing away the grime of that tango.

She handed him a towel afterward and they ended up in the kitchen, where she looked inside her mostly empty fridge. "Beer?"

"Please."

"We might have to order pizza. I don't have many ingredients for dinner."

He did a thorough inspection, extracting the items necessary to make spaghetti bolognaise. He gulped down half of his beer and raised an eyebrow at her. "Soph, we could just hang out. We don't have to have sex."

"No, I want to." She swiped her thumb over the label of the bottle in her hand. "Can we, uh, try anal?"

Damn, he thought, struggling to hide his surprise. His dick certainly liked the idea, if the twitching under the towel was anything to go on. "Seriously?"

"Yes. Is that something you can handle?"

"I've never… We're each other's firsts this time."

"Don't make this cute."

He smirked. "Then stop talking and get on the bed."

"Since when are you so demanding?"

"Since I started tying girls up." He motioned to her bedroom and finished his beer. "Get going, Soph."

"Are you gonna tie *me* up?"

Raising an eyebrow, his gaze followed her onto the bed. "Is that what you want?"

"I don't know," she mumbled, breaking eye contact.

He knew that facial expression: she was curious but giving him the power to make the final decision. Her trust in him did wonders for his ego, pushing past the possible embarrassment he would have felt at the dominance he was about to display.

"Take off the towel."

Her eyes widened at his tone. She slowly parted the towel.

Logan stared at her, taking her in from head to toe. Her body was lean, lithe, supple. She might not have a distinct dip in her waist, but she had long, shapely legs and a toned stomach. His favorite part about her body was her lower back, where she sported two dimples at the base of her spine. He had no idea why whatshisface had rejected this beautiful woman.

He moved until his back connected with the wall opposite her bed. "Get lube and a condom."

She obeyed, reaching into her pedestal's top drawer, and dropped the items on the bed next to her.

"Touch yourself, Soph. Make your pussy nice and slick."

"Touch yourself, too."

He shook his head. "You'll get my cock when I say so."

Sophie wasn't usually one to hesitate. The fact that she did emphasized how out of her comfort zone she was when she gave control to someone else. They both knew that he would stop if she asked. That she was willing to carry on proved how brave she was.

She shifted to lean against the headboard, her hands trailing from her neck to her small breasts. Her nipples were standing at attention, ready to be squeezed. She shut her eyes on a sigh, tweaking those hard points with one hand while the other made its way to her pussy.

"What're you thinking about?" he asked, keeping his tone hushed.

"Your tongue." She spread her legs, as if to give him a better view of her fingers gathering liquid. "Damn, Lo, no one's ever eaten me out like you."

When she began rubbing her clit, he had to hold himself back from joining her on the bed. He watched, transfixed, as she masturbated. He remembered the day he'd gathered enough courage to ask her to be his first, how he'd wanted to try everything. She'd let him. Where his friends' first times had been awkward, his had been glorious, and it was all because of this woman.

"Are you close, Soph?"

"Hmm." Her fingers dipped inside to gather more lubricant before she picked up the pace on her clit. "So close."

He could tell by the way that she arched her back that she wasn't going to last much longer. "Your pussy better be soaked by the time you're done."

"Or what?" she whimpered.

"Or I'm going to pull you over my lap and spank you."

Her thighs trembled. "You'd do that?"

"You bet."

She cried out as she came, slumping into the bed. "Fuck, Lo!"

He stepped away from the wall and joined her on the bed, dropping his towel and grabbing a pillow. "Lift your hips." He pushed her legs to her chest and opened them as far as her flexibility would allow—which was pretty damn far, considering her occupation as a dancer—while his eyes remained glued to her glossy center. "Hold them there. Don't move."

She hooked her arms under her knees, effectively exposing every inch of her core and ass.

Some of her liquid had trickled to the puckered hole. Logan swiped his fingers through her folds, clenching his jaw once he felt how wet she was. He pressed the tip of a finger against her anus, finally making eye contact again.

"You want my cock here?"

She swallowed and nodded. "Yeah."

He lowered his mouth to her pussy, sucking on her clit. He groaned at her taste and swirled his tongue over her. Once she clutched his hair, he halted. "I'll stop if you touch me again."

"When did you get so intense?"

"When you told me to fuck other girls."

"Right. Thank me later."

He grinned, glad that she enjoyed this side of him. Then he got back to business, slightly increasing the pressure against her virgin ring while he jabbed his tongue inside her. His nose prodded her clit and it wasn't long before she rolled her hips to get more friction.

Inflamed by her response, he deepened the open-mouthed kisses he gave her pussy, sliding his tongue up, inside and around. He raised his free hand to one of her tits to pinch her nipple in time with the suction on her clit. She cried out and he smiled inwardly: time to turn up the intensity. His mouth shifted down to lick and suck her puckered hole.

Sophie's body nearly came off the mattress and the noise she let out conveyed her surprise, her pleasure. "Oh God, yes!"

He didn't fail to notice that her pussy was dripping from the attention he gave her anus. His grip on her sensitive nipple must be painful, yet she didn't seem to mind. He glanced at her, his toes curling at the uninhibited expression on her face. He was making her forget where she was. Was there a bigger ego boost than that?

He alternated between her pussy and the tight ring below, slowly introducing his finger again. She took him to the first knuckle before she even noticed he was invading her ass. Her breathing snatched at her chest as he went deeper. His thumb breached her pussy at the same time and his lips sought out her clit.

She screamed as she flew over the edge, her inner walls gripping his thumb and her clit pulsing against his mouth. "Fuck, Lo!"

He scraped his teeth over her stomach as he moved up to her unclaimed breast, sucking the slight mound into his mouth. "Feel good?"

"Shit, Lo, I can't…"

He grinned against her skin. "Gonna add another finger."

"Oh-okay," she stuttered, her hips bucking when he followed through. "Shit, need you in me."

He got onto his hunches, careful not to remove his fingers. "Condom, Soph."

With jerky movements, she sheathed his cock. Her pupils were wide and the look on her face…

Carnal.

He flipped the cap of the lube bottle with his free hand and squirted a generous amount on the fingers that pumped into her ass. He leaned forward to replace his thumb with his cock, watching her eyes roll to the back of her head. The evidence of her pleasure inflated his ego to crazy proportions because he knew no one else has ever done this to her.

He thrust into her pussy, amazed that she was tighter than before. Her hips jerked, fucking him back. "Fuck, Soph. Slow down."

"Can't," she moaned, out of control. "What're you doing to me?"

"What you want." While she was distracted, he pulled out of both orifices and then slid his cock inside her lubricated ass, hearing her call out his name. A shiver went down his spine at the sensation. He had to take a moment to regain composure, so close to releasing he may as well be a virgin again.

Her legs automatically went over his shoulders, the angle allowing him to sink deeper. She gazed into his eyes, her lips parted and her cheeks red. "Don't stop!"

He gripped her thighs as he stretched her back door. He let instinct guide him, pumping into her repeatedly. Her hands roamed over her tits before settling on her pussy, rubbing her clit in furious circles.

"Shit, I'm coming," she rasped.

He raced her to the edge. She broke first, mere seconds before he tipped into orgasm. Their cries and harsh breathing filled the room while he pushed in as far as she could take him. He shut his eyes, his heart threatening to burst out of the confines of his ribcage.

She laughed breathily. "That was fucking fantastic."

Logan inhaled deeply and gripped the base of his cock to make sure the condom didn't somehow get lost. He retreated slowly, eyes fixed on her. "Sore?"

"Not..." She trailed off, biting her bottom lip as his tip got closer to the ring. She shuddered when he slipped free. "Holy shit, feels like I can go again."

He chuckled. "Give me ten minutes. That was... a lot." He pulled the condom off and chucked it in the direction of the bathroom; then he collapsed on the mattress next to her.

She grabbed a discarded towel and wiped the mess he'd made of her pussy. She closed her eyes. "I can't move."

"Me neither." He turned on his side and kissed her shoulder. "You're so sexy, Soph. That guy doesn't know what he's missing."

Her blue eyes twinkled when she smiled. "Thank you for reminding me."

"No problem."

Within seconds, she drifted off.

So much for going again.

He watched her while she slept. He could probably be with her, without messing it up. They'll be happy, to some extent, but it wouldn't be the kind of love either of their parents had and that aspect was too important to them both to settle for anything less.

He hoped that she'll find the man of her dreams. It would give him hope that he'll meet the woman of his.

Do you even know what kind of woman you want? With such an incredible one right here, how can you be convinced you'll find someone better?

Logan sighed deeply. With thoughts like those, he wouldn't get any rest tonight.

CHAPTER TWO

TODAY WAS THE fifteenth anniversary of Brennan's death.

The local MC was gathered at the lake, celebrating the man's life and, to a lesser extent, the Raptors' legacy. There were other people around, but they kept a respectable—and somewhat fearful—distance from the bikers.

Logan sat on his own, removed from the festivities, staring at the tranquil body of water and lost in his own thoughts.

"Lo."

He glanced at Byron. "Yeah?"

"What's going on with you lately?"

"Nothing," he sighed.

"That's not nothing."

Logan hesitated, as always. He never knew how Byron was going to react to his true thoughts. Byron was fiercely loyal to Brennan's memory and Logan didn't fully understand why. It was one thing to be there for someone when they're alive, but those promises were surely moot once they died? At what point was it okay to carry on as if the dead never existed?

"I'm just thinking of him."

"Ah."

Logan clenched his jaw. "I don't understand why we still do this. It's been so long."

"The others remember him." Byron ran his fingers through his dark hair. "It's important to your mother and grandparents."

"You're too understanding."

"Lo, we've been over this."

"I just don't get it," Logan insisted quietly. "I look at the two of you and I don't see how she ever had that with someone else."

The corners of Byron's mouth tilted up. "Thanks."

"Doesn't it hurt that she's doing this for him?"

"I loved him, too. Your father was a great man."

"My father *is* a great man. He's still alive, right next to me."

Byron's facial expression softened and he draped an arm over Logan's shoulders. For someone who was less than a year away from turning forty, Byron looked incredible. He was tall and strong, his hair didn't have a spot of grey in it and, except for a few laugh and frown lines, he didn't have many wrinkles.

Whatever fountain of youth Byron was drinking from, he'd given some to Cinnia as well. Logan often had to hear his friends talk about what a MILF his mother was. He supposed he couldn't really blame them: she was beautiful, even with the few streaks of silver in her ebony mane.

"It's an honor to be called that," Byron murmured.

"You should've had more kids."

"You're such a fucking handful already, punk."

Logan smirked. "Chicken."

Throwing his head back, Byron laughed loudly. He squeezed Logan for a moment. Then he let go altogether, becoming serious. "Your mom thought I wanted another one. It took a long time to convince her I don't."

"But *why*, dad?"

"I didn't grow up with all of this," Byron replied, gesturing to the large extended family behind them. "My life was very different. I was scared that I'll screw up a child's life beyond repair."

"You didn't screw up mine."

"Happy coincidence." He bumped his shoulder against Logan's. "Besides, you can't improve on perfection, right?"

Logan rolled his eyes, although he was glowing with pride. "Smooth."

"Your mother's coming." Byron leaned forward, resting his elbows on his knees and smiling thoughtfully. "Act happy."

A quick perusal behind him confirmed that yes, Cinnia Drummond was indeed on her way over. "Seriously, how do you do that?"

"I honestly don't know."

"I wonder if I'll ever know what it's like."

"If you gave Sophie or Rory a real chance, maybe you will."

"Rory? Please." Logan snorted and launched a pebble, watching it bounce on the surface of the lake. "She's like a sister. An annoying sister."

"She's always hanging around you."

"I've tried telling her to stop, but she won't let it go."

"That's 'cause you have your father's charm."

"I know. I heard you were quite the player before mom."

Byron's brown eyes twinkled as he shook his head. "You know I meant him."

"What're my boys talking about?" Cinnia asked as she joined them.

"Girls," Byron responded, to save Logan from an argument.

Logan shot his stepfather a grateful look.

"Well, I used to be a girl, so I can give you some pointers," Cinnia teased. "Who would you like to charm, Lo?"

"Who says we were talking about me?" Logan joked back. "I was telling dad that he should always wear protection. Some STDs might be curable, but it's just not worth the itch."

Cinnia's green eyes grew stormy. "Not funny, Lo," she muttered, stepping closer to the boulder as if she was going to tackle Byron. "I'm an old woman and get jealous very easily."

Logan's heart melted. "Aw, shucks, I'm sorry, mom. I was kidding."

"You're not an old woman," Byron told her softly.

"Right, this is about to get awkward," Logan said brightly, jumping off the boulder. "If you decide to have sex, please keep it down this time."

Cinnia pulled her son into a hug. "I love you, Lo."

"Love you, too, momma," he mumbled, pecking her on the cheek and letting go. He glanced at Byron. "Thanks for the chat, dad."

"Anytime, punk!" Byron called after him.

Logan meandered back to the party, looking over his shoulder. Byron had his mother pinned to the boulder while he kissed her. Anyone could tell that he only had eyes for her. There wasn't a doubt in Logan's mind that Byron would rather cut off his own balls than ever cheat on her.

He was happy that they were finally getting married. Cinnia was a tad insecure now that she was nearing fifty. Logan often thought that she might be going through the early stages of menopause, something she vehemently denied. Her reaction, in and of itself, was partly why he suspected her hormones were making her crazy.

Shaking his head with a soft laugh, he turned his attention to the Raptors.

Both sets of grandparents were seated in the shade of a large tree with content smiles on their faces. Haye, the Prez, nodded at something grandpa Reade was saying. Mysie, with her wild grey curls, was chatting to Loraine and James, gesturing so animatedly it was a wonder how she kept her drink from spilling.

There were men crowding around the barbecue, beers in hand, while the women worked diligently to get the rest of the food ready at the nearby picnic tables. Kids played under the watchful eyes of a couple of teenagers, and in the distance he could see the convoy of Harleys and SUV's in the parking lot. Life was good.

"Finally!" That was the only warning he had before Sophie jumped on his back. She giggled when he struggled to keep his balance. "I thought you were going to sit there the whole day, being mopey and depressed!"

"I'm back for you to abuse."

"Good, 'cause I brought the ropes for our climb."

"You know what I like. Who's joining?"

"Tess and Teagan," Sophie answered, slithering off his back and hooking her arm around his as they walked to the cars to get the rock-climbing gear. "Jesse."

Logan suppressed a groan. "That means Rory's going to be there."

"Probably."

"Fuck, she's always so weird around me."

"That's 'cause you have a tight ass," Sophie said saucily, spanking him. "What girl wouldn't drool over you?"

He leered at her. "You've done that."

"Damn right I did, before you had all of *these*." She squeezed his biceps. "You should stop exercising with your dad."

"It's way too much fun. Besides, chicks dig it."

She sent her gaze to the sky for a brief moment. "Thank God I had you before you got all cocky. This is not an attractive attitude, Lo."

"C'mon, Soph, it'll be fun," he whined theatrically.

"I'm twenty-five now. Shouldn't I be the responsible one?"

"Hate to break it to you, but you should've thought of that when you were twenty-two," he said, his tone lower. "Technically, you had sex with a minor."

Sophie's cheeks turned pink. She grabbed her backpack and made eye-contact. "Four times in one day? Jesus, you were eager."

The air shifted between them and Logan got hard from the memory. "You were sore after the first time, so maybe *I* wasn't the eager one."

"Yeah, well, you're huge," she countered, her eyes dipping to his package. She licked her lips once she saw his bulge. "I'm surprised you don't pass out every time you have an erection."

"Have you had bigger?" he asked as he moved closer to her. Her back flattened against the vehicle and he pressed his hips forward to anchor her there. He had to lean down to whisper in her ear. "Has anyone bigger ever been in your pussy, Soph? In your ass?"

Her breathing was shallower, but she wasn't going to back down. She never did. Jemma raised her to be a spitfire. "I haven't been with a black guy, so no."

"Do you want to feel me again, Soph? Feel my cock stretch you?"

"That depends. Think you can hold out if I squeeze your cock?"

"Maybe not the first time, but you know it doesn't take long for me to recover," he murmured, placing his hands on either side of her head.

She pretended to be undecided. "Hmm, from what I remember, I had to teach you everything."

"Not everything." They stared at each other in silence for a while, reminiscing. "Besides, I've had more practice since the last time."

"I doubt you can handle all of this."

Logan ducked his head and caught her earlobe between his teeth. "Think you can hand over control again, Soph? I could keep you on the edge for hours. How long do you think it'll be before you beg me for an orgasm?"

She gasped. "You'll never make me beg."

"Maybe not verbally," he agreed, dropping one hand to her hip, "but your body's begging me, even now."

"Wait, Lo." She pressed her hand against his chest, blinking when he gazed at her in question. "Stop."

He retreated immediately. If there's one thing the Raptors men have hammered into him since he was old enough to understand concepts, it was to back off the second someone asked you to.

Sophie's breathing leveled out. "Jeez, sometimes I forget you're only eighteen."

"Age is just a number."

"I took you too soon."

He raised an eyebrow and picked up his own bag. "I'll never regret it."

"Sadly, me neither." She fell into step with him. "I thought virgins were supposed to be premature, but you were something else."

"I'm glad it was as good for you as it was for me." He placed his arm over her shoulders, pulling her closer. "I'd hate it if you went to your friends and said how embarrassing your time with Logan Bean Drummond was."

She burst out laughing. "Narcissist."

"Cradle-snatcher."

"Egotist."

"Cougar."

"Fine, you win," she cackled, poking him in the ribs. She hesitated as they reached the crowd, holding him back. "I did meet someone. That's why I stopped you back there."

He nodded. "When do I get to meet him?"

"He…" She blushed a fiery red. "He's not a biker, so I have to make sure first, you know? He's a cop."

"Have you told your parents?"

"Not yet."

"I won't say anything." He squeezed her for a moment. "As long as he treats you right."

"He's sweet. He makes me laugh."

"I'm happy for you." He looked up at the sound of his name and blanched once he recognized the expression on his mother's face. "Uh-oh."

"Fifty bucks says she doesn't want you to climb today."

"No deal. We both know it's true."

Cinnia's green gaze was electric as she caught up to them. "Where are you going?"

"Climbing."

She pinched the bridge of her nose. "Can this wait? We're about to have lunch."

"I just went to get my bag. We'll climb afterwards."

"Can't you—"

"He'll be fine," Byron chipped in, wrapping an arm around her waist. He shared a look with Logan. "Let's eat first."

"It's just my luck that I have a daredevil son," Cinnia remarked, making everyone laugh. There was nothing but love coming from her, though, so Logan didn't take offense. He knew he put her through hell every time he did something she deemed reckless, but he was addicted to the adrenaline rush. She often told him that he was exactly like Brennan, forever testing the limits. She was afraid that she'll lose him, too.

He sat down with his family and thanked his mother for the huge plate of food she handed over. Aurora took a seat next to him and he suppressed a sigh. "Hey, Rory."

She pushed her strawberry blonde hair over a shoulder and smiled. She was gorgeous and sweet, yet he didn't have any romantic feelings towards her. She's always fought for his attention or tagged along to things that didn't really interest her. He had no idea why she insisted on being around him when he's made it clear they're never going to be more than friends.

"You've been distant today," she commented.

"Just thinking."

"About?"

He paused. The one time he'd attempted to explain his feelings about Brennan to her, she had made him feel as if he was ungrateful and bitter. Byron and Sophie were the only two people who actually got it.

"Not important. You ready for your final semester?"

She pouted, toying with her food. "A part of me doesn't want to start working, you know? 'Cause then I'm a grown-up for real."

He couldn't relate. His parents had raised him to be independent, to grab as many opportunities as he could, which was why he helped out at his grandpa's customs shop to earn extra cash. He's already submitted a portfolio to a local architecture firm, and they've agreed to help pay for his studies if he manned their office when he graduated from high school.

A large part of him was hoping to further his football career, but he knew that was a pipe dream. He couldn't leave the club: he was next in line to be President of the Raptors. There was no escaping that responsibility.

Aurora and Jesse, on the other hand, were spoiled rotten by their parents. Haye couldn't say no to his daughters and whatever rules Dawn put in place to compensate for that were blatantly ignored, especially by Aurora. Jesse was too focused on her writing to care about breaking rules.

"Must be quite stressful," he offered.

"You have no idea! Everyone in my group is freaking out because we don't know what to do with ourselves and…"

He zoned out. Aurora had the tendency to chatter on and on about herself, and he's probably heard most of it already. He peered at those around the table, smiling at how happy they were. Perhaps this *was* better than a day of mourning, after all.

His light green eyes—apparently, they changed to ice blue when he was angry—halted on his mother and stepdad. Byron was whispering something in her ear that made her blush and lean into him. To Logan, it was a familiar sight and, even though he mocked them often, beautiful to behold. He wanted that kind of love. Something that was pure fire, burning from the inside out. Not the easy companionship he had with Sophie, and not the superficial infatuation that other girls represented.

He craved to be irrevocably changed by love.

His gaze shifted to Tessa. When he was twelve, his parents had sat him down to explain why there were no pictures of Cinnia with a baby bump, why Brennan and Cinnia had had to go the surrogate route, and why Cinnia had then made Tessa his godmother. Logan had taken it in stride, since he'd seen Tessa as his mom-away-from-home already and loved spending time with her.

"Do I have something stuck in my teeth?" Tessa asked teasingly.

He shook himself, only half-aware that Aurora shut her mouth when she realized he's lost interest. "Yeah, you've got this weird green dot right here," he replied as he demonstrated scratching between his two front teeth. "Must be spinach."

"You've got a little something, yourself." She wiped her top lip with her middle finger. "I think it's from all the bullshit."

"Nice, Tess," he laughed. "Where's your girl today?"

Tessa pulled a face. She was in love with a flight attendant. "Seven-day trip."

"I'm sad she couldn't make it."

"She's got a three-day layover in Tokyo, so she'll be okay."

"Lucky fish." Logan wanted to travel the world and jump off a couple of skyscrapers, and Japan had the type of skyline that tickled his fancy. "Tell her I said thanks for the invite."

Tessa winked and turned her attention back to his aunt Piper.

This reminded Logan that he was being terribly rude to Aurora. "Sorry, Ror," he mumbled, finishing up his lunch and swallowing it down with soda. "You were saying?"

She launched right back into her tale of her university experience.

Logan was probably going to be punished for pretending, but it was better than listening to her endless drivel. If he'd seen her as more than someone who talked about things that don't matter to him, he would've tolerated her better.

Once everyone was done eating, he helped clear the table and added a bottle of water to his backpack. He hurried to the bathroom to change into more comfortable pants and climbing shoes. Then he headed to his mother. "We're off. We'll be back in a few hours."

"Lo, please be careful."

"I always am. Try to stop worrying."

"Never. Have fun."

Rolling his eyes, he strode to the tiny group going with him. Tessa and uncle Teagan loved climbing with him and Sophie, but Jesse was still a beginner. She was generally quiet, more withdrawn than her sister, and curvier. Her freckled skin and red hair were due to Haye's genetic influence and made her stand out from the crowd, though she seemed to hate it.

Logan briefly wondered why Connor wasn't tagging along. He was infatuated with Jesse and usually found a way to involve himself in everything she did. When Logan glanced over his shoulder, he couldn't spot his friend anywhere.

"Ready to go?" Sophie asked him. She, like everyone except Aurora, was now dressed in tighter clothing, which wouldn't get caught on the rocks.

"Born ready," he replied, taking the lead.

"Born two weeks premature, you mean."

"The only time I've ever been premature."

"Ugh, Logan!" Tessa exclaimed dramatically. "We did not have to hear that!"

"I beg to differ, seeing as you invested nine months of your life in me," he joked.

Tessa burst out laughing. "You're one of a kind, kid, that's for damn sure."

"Lo, take it easy," his uncle panted, further back. "I'm an old man!"

"Yeah, right!" Logan called over his shoulder. "Not when you and aunt Piper go at it!"

"Too much info!" Sophie and Tessa chorused, cackling right after.

The banter continued as they headed further up. It was the most beautiful scene: clear water in the valley, surrounded by rocky hills and cliffs. When Logan had first showed an interest in rock-climbing, the Raptors had got in contact with park officials, surveyed the area, and set up a few climbs. The site was open to the public, although indemnity forms had to be signed at the entrance.

Logan scanned the sky as the sun beat down on them. It was about two o'clock in the afternoon and sizzling hot, but the temperature was bound to drop when the sun slipped behind the mountain. Although it would've been more ideal to climb in the morning, this shouldn't be too tough.

"I think we should go for number seven!" he called over his shoulder. "Who's in?"

"I haven't done that one yet!" Jesse argued nervously.

"You will today!" he encouraged. "We're all here for you, Jess!"

"Okay!"

Their voices echoed back as they worked their way into the valley. They'd passed the fifth climb. Seven was quite steep, about fifteen meters high and, at the pinnacle, connected to a viewpoint on the side of the winding pass that led to the lake. Most of the climb would be in the shade, which was why he'd thought it was a better idea.

He grinned once they arrived, eyeing the trail of pitons that led to the top. He felt like it's been years since his last ascent when, in fact, it's only been a week. If he could do this every day, he would.

Well, this and football.

"Alright, let's get cracking." He put his bag down. "Soph, are you gonna go first?"

"Hell yes," she replied as she got into her safety harness. Her chalk bag dangled behind her, within reach. "Tess, be my belay?"

"Sure thing."

Sophie, with a whole bunch of carabineers attached to her belt, was roped and ready to go. She rubbed chalk on her hands. "Let's do this!"

Logan absently noted that Aurora was taking a bunch of selfies while he helped Jesse set up. He stood between Jesse and his uncle, a few steps behind Tessa, as his eyes followed Sophie's lithe body. She easily reached the first bolt, but that was to be expected. She hooked a carabineer and then added the rope.

"Nice, Soph!" Tessa cheered. The person belaying was much more than an anchor: they also had the task of keeping the climber motivated and alert. "Which way are you going?"

Now that she was safely clicked in, Sophie leaned back to observe. The next bolt was out of reach. She'll have to find a way to get to it first. "I'm thinking left."

Logan's eyes drifted over the area she was referring to and he nodded to himself. He'd go that way, too.

Tessa braced herself. "Sounds good! Ready?"

Steadily, Sophie made her way upwards, leaning back every once in a while to calculate her next move. Tessa was a damn good belay, too, since she never got distracted. Logan's fingers itched with the need to feel the rocks, but he would have to wait his turn.

Sophie reached the top and gave out a whoop as she dangled from the rope. She threw her fist in the air while the rest of them applauded. Then she abseiled to the bottom, clearly willing to take a few risks now that the adrenaline has kicked in.

"Jess, you *have* to go next!" Sophie encouraged. "It's such a great climb!"

Jesse eyed the route. "Can we leave the rope like that, just in case?"

"Of course," Logan nodded. He untied it from Sophie and fastened it to Jesse's harness. "You've got this."

She stepped up to the starting point. She was two years older than him and Logan found it funny that he was the one comforting *her*, but that seemed to be a regular occurrence. People looked to him for strength and advice, often forgetting that he was still in high school.

"Wow, that was amazing," Sophie breathed, taking a few gulps of water and rinsing her hands. "Seven was a great idea, Lo."

"I always have great ideas."

She glanced at Jesse, who was past the first bolt. "Do you think she's going to make it this time?"

"I never know for sure." He eyed Sophie in a wolfish way. "Nice ass, by the way."

"Logan," his uncle chuckled.

"You're incorrigible," Sophie informed Logan.

"Such a big word!"

"I'm aware it's above your level of intellect, yes."

"Ooh, ouch, Soph. Warn me about the claws next time."

"Please don't," Teagan laughed, "I love seeing his face when you diss him!"

"Who's the adult here?" Logan asked dryly.

Tessa's next exclamation made them all focus. "You've got it, Jess! You're about halfway there!"

"It's too far!" Jesse said, panic in her voice.

"What happened?" Logan asked Tessa as he leapt forward.

"Her hand slipped and she stumbled down a bit," Tessa murmured quietly. When she addressed Jesse, her voice was firmer. "You're completely safe, Jess! Why don't you fall back to remind yourself?"

Jesse was clinging to the rock face, stuck in one spot. She was about eleven inches away from the next bolt, but Sophie had already secured this climb. She had nothing to fear. "I can't!"

"Jess, listen to me." He felt bad for not paying attention earlier. "The rope's there, all the way to the top, remember? So lean back a little. On the count of three!"

"O-okay!"

"What a baby," Aurora muttered behind them.

Logan shot her a look of warning before giving her sister his full attention. "One, two, three!"

Jesse let go with a small squeal. Then, feeling how safe she was, her shoulders slumped and she giggled. "I'm sorry, that was stupid! I forgot about the rope!"

"So why don't you finish this climb?" he challenged.

That got through to her. She began gripping the edges of the rocks with renewed vigor.

"You know, sometimes I think your talents will be wasted as an architect," Tessa chuckled. "You should be an instructor or a teacher."

"I only have this kind of patience with my family."

"Still, you're very good at it."

He shook his head and fell back to stand with his uncle and Sophie. He glared at Aurora, thinking: *the next time you call someone a 'baby', do it because they couldn't do something you did, at the very least.* It was easy for her to pass judgment. She's never taken a risk before.

Jesse made it all the way up. They whistled and clapped as she slid back down with a spaced-out smile on her face. Once her feet touched the ground, she blushed. "I did it!"

"Good job, Jess," Logan said, high-fiving her. "Next time, you're doing it without the rope."

She nodded. "Definitely. But listen, I think I heard a car when I was up there."

"The road's right—"

"No, it stopped," she interrupted. "I heard men's voices."

"They're just looking at the view, dumbass," Aurora snapped.

Jesse's pleading eyes found Logan's. "It didn't *feel right*. They sounded violent."

He frowned. "Okay, I'll go next and see if they're still there." When she seemed relieved, he glanced at his uncle. "Will you be my belay?"

"Buy me dinner first," Teagan grinned.

Teagan and Tessa swapped places and he pulled the rope down, knowing that Logan didn't like or need assisted climbs. It was bad enough that the carabineers were still in the bolts: Logan loved the fear that went along with hooking them in, but that'll have to wait until the next climb.

He jumped up and clung to the rock, using his core muscles to stabilize while he ascended. A part of him felt like skipping every second carabineer, but he didn't want to alarm anyone, so he stuck to the rules and hooked his rope through each one he passed. His body thrummed from the exercise and he paused halfway, looking over his shoulder.

God, this place was beautiful: about sixteen miles out of town, far enough that the scenery changed, and the vegetation became lusher. He wasn't sure if he'd trade this for the city life.

Except maybe Liverpool, if I could play for Everton…

"Lo, you okay?" his uncle hollered.

He snapped out of his daydreaming. Like he'd ever get the chance to join his favorite football team. "Fine!"

The rest of the climb was uneventful and he wished he'd picked a more difficult one. When he got to the top, he reached further for something to hold on to, eager to check out what Jesse had heard. She wasn't the type to cry wolf. He peeked over the edge.

The car was long gone, but there was a suspicious lump in the middle of the small parking lot. His eyes focused and, with a start, he realized it was a body.

"Holy shit," he puffed.

"Lo, what's going on?"

His uncle's words were faint. Logan got a better grip and pulled himself over the edge. He knew the rope wasn't long enough to get to the body. *Shit,* he thought. He got on his hands and knees, glancing down to his family.

"Call my dad and get up here!" he shouted. "I'm loosening the rope!"

"Logan—"

"Just *do it!*" he insisted firmly. He untied it and, after hesitating at the look of panic on their faces, let it drop.

CHAPTER THREE

LOGAN APPROACHED WITH caution, his gaze darting around to make sure it wasn't an ambush. Things were relatively calm between the Raptors and rival motorcycle clubs, but what if someone intended to kidnap him, and hold him for ransom? Worse, kill him in broad daylight?

How did they know that you were going to climb today? That you would choose to climb number seven? Stop being paranoid!

It was a young girl lying in a fetal position. Jet-black, dirty hair covered her face. She was wrapped in a worn sheet and her bare feet, peeking out from under it, were muddy. Upon closer inspection, Logan realized it was dried blood. His eyes stretched wide and he dropped to his knees, pushing her hair out of her face.

He couldn't stop his gasp.

Her right eye and cheeks were swollen, a trickle of crimson running down from the corner of her mouth. Her lips were split and he had no idea if they were naturally that full, or puffy from the abuse. He was tempted to look under the sheet, to see the extent of the damage done to this poor girl, yet he held himself back.

Where the hell were his brothers?

He placed his hand on her shoulder and gave her a soft shake. "Hello?" No response. Shit, what if she was *dead*? "Miss?"

This reeked of gang activity, but surely she was too young to be involved in illegal drug trade? Fuck, what if she was a victim of human trafficking? But why would someone dump her body here?

He let out a breath of relief once the rumble of Harleys coming up the hill cut through his thoughts. He was going to drive himself crazy, trying to figure out what this meant.

Soon, he found himself transfixed by her face: the features beneath the injuries. Her skin was bronze and she had long lashes. High cheekbones. A stunning arch in her eyebrows, and a cupid's bow on her top lip. She was beautiful.

"Logan, what the *fuck*!"

Jumping in fright, he glanced to his left, seeing his dad marching towards him. Eight men accompanied Byron and half of them were already spreading out, guns drawn.

"Do you want to give your mother a fucking heart attack?" Byron's gaze dipped to the ground and his face went pale.

"I'm sorry I made you worry," Logan said levelly, "but I'm sure you can understand why I didn't abandon her."

"Jesus Christ, it's like Cinnia all over again." Byron held a hand in front of his mouth as he hunched next to Logan. There was a haunted glimmer in his eyes, something Logan's seen only a handful of times before. "Is she...?"

Logan reached for her throat to feel for a pulse but, as his fingertips made contact, her good eye flipped open and she scrambled away, panicked. The sheet dragged down and exposed the fact that she was, indeed, naked underneath. And she was headed right for the edge of the cliff.

He lunged after her, pegging her to the ground.

"No!" she screamed, thrashing against him.

"Miss, please calm—"

"*No!*"

Going with his instincts, he sat up with her in his arms, rocking her back and forth. She was surprisingly strong for someone so small, but he had more muscle and easily kept her from escaping. He made soothing noises, hoping to calm her down, and looked up at his dad.

The VP of the Raptors was already barking orders into his phone, pacing back and forth. Two of the men got back on their Harleys, having inspected the tire tracks on the dirt-covered parking lot and calculated the direction her abusers must've come from. They shot off without delay.

The girl went limp in Logan's embrace. He didn't ease up on his hold, in case it was a tactic to run away. "What's your name?"

She didn't respond, and she wouldn't look at him.

"Jemma's on her way with a first aid kit," Byron told them once he'd hung up. "Thank fuck she's a doctor. I don't think…" He cleared his throat and gestured to the beaten young girl in Logan's arms. "It would be better if a woman got her cleaned up."

This had to be hard for Byron to see. Logan knew about his mother's attack and that Byron had been the one to save her; that the experience had driven Byron to hard drugs and alcohol. Heck, *Logan* would like a drink right about now. It was horrible to witness what happened when men didn't believe in keeping women safe.

The girl was shivering in his arms. Logan pulled the sheet up carefully and kept swaying her while they waited for help.

His mother's SUV arrived and Jemma jumped out of the passenger side. She took one look at the girl and declared: "We need to get her to the club. Can you move her?"

He shifted under the girl and, like a scared animal, she clung to his sweat-stained shirt. "Let's get up, sweetheart," he whispered, rising to his feet while holding her as gently as he could. He leaned down and hooked his other arm under her legs, then carried her to the SUV.

Cinnia was holding the back door open, her green eyes wide once she took in the girl's face. "Jesus Christ."

Logan would've found it amusing, in any other situation, that his parents had identical responses to this situation. He slid onto the backseat, his arms tightening a fraction as the door shut.

"Why aren't we taking her to the hospital?"

Jemma gave him a look from the front passenger seat. "Why do you think?"

"We don't have proof."

"My boy, listen to your gut," his mother mumbled, steering the SUV to the road and accelerating as soon as the tires hit the tarmac. Harleys fell into formation behind them. "Does this feel like a run-of-the-mill incident to you?"

"I just want her to be okay."

"She will be. Jemma's got this."

The girl shut her left eye. The right was more swollen. These had to be recent injuries, but why on earth would the perpetrators drive out here to dump her body? Where had they attacked her, and when? On the side of the road, while Jesse was climbing?

"It doesn't make sense. Did they know we were in the area?" he asked through clenched teeth. "Is this a threat?"

"I don't know, Lo."

"What does dad say?"

"He hasn't told me anything."

The girl stirred in his arms, her fingers digging through the sheet and his shirt. He stroked her hair softly and she stiffened, jerking in his grasp. "Okay, okay," he murmured quietly. "I won't do it again."

She remained tense, as if she didn't believe him. He wondered how many people have said things they didn't mean to her. It made him feel sick.

His mother's phone rang and she pressed the button on her steering wheel to answer. "By?"

"Oz thinks he found something."

Cinnia hesitated, glancing in the rear-view mirror at her son. "Will you be home tonight?"

"I'll keep you posted. Haye's meeting you at the club."

She sucked in a breath, probably wishing she'd kept this conversation private. "Please be at the club by seven. I don't want to worry that you're… that you've…"

Byron's tone was patient, calm, when he spoke again: "Cin, I'm not going to break fifteen years of sobriety because of this, okay?"

"Seven, By."

Climb number seven led us to this girl. Maybe it's not such a lucky number…

"You've got it, boss. I love you."

His mother blushed. "Love you, too," she said and ended the call.

"That was annoyingly sweet," Jemma teased.

"Shut up."

"Seriously, I was gagging," Logan piped up.

Cinnia rolled her eyes, turning onto the road leading to town. "We've got other things to worry about."

"Yeah, true. Has she got a name, Lo?" Jemma queried.

"She hasn't said anything." He glanced at the girl in question. "Are you ready to tell me your name?"

She pretended she didn't hear, keeping her eye screwed shut.

He refrained from sighing in exasperation. She's been attacked and she should be mistrustful of anyone at this point. It didn't matter that his intentions were pure: he was most likely the same gender as the ones who've hurt her.

By the time they arrived at the clubhouse, he'd become used to her weight in his arms. He waited for Jemma to open the door and got out of the car, carrying the girl into the clubhouse. He wasn't imagining her violent reaction once they were inside and instinctively knew that she's had bad experiences with a motorcycle club.

"Come on," Jemma urged, going down the hallway to the emergency room. As soon as she had completed her medical degree, the club had converted one of the bedrooms into a consultation room to remove bullets and stitch up knife wounds without having the victim questioned by nursing staff and, more importantly, the police. The cabinets were well-equipped with apparatus, disinfectant, pills and the like. Only the more serious cases were referred to the hospital.

"Put her on the gurney."

He lay the girl down, jaw clenching when she refused to let go. "Jemma's a doctor, sweetheart. She'll take care of you."

The girl's good eye went from Logan to Jemma. Hesitantly, she released her hold on him.

"I'll be right outside." He strode into the hallway, closing the door behind him, and breathed out. He was edgy, angry. He wanted to be with his brothers, to kill the sons of bitches who'd laid their hands on this defenseless girl.

His mother found him pacing and handed him a cup of coffee. "I'm sorry I assumed the worst." They sat down together. "When they told me you climbed up and left the rope with them, I had all these terrible images running through my head."

"Can't imagine what's worse than this."

"*You* being kidnapped, or killed."

He sipped on his coffee and gave her a sideways hug. "I'm okay."

"I know." She snuggled closer to him. "I'm worried about By."

"He'll be fine."

"He relapsed once."

Logan frowned. "What?"

"After your father died," she explained slowly, "the MC got help from a drug lord, but the favor was too big. Byron cut a deal to work off the debt. Everything went according to plan, at first. By and I had just admitted we're in love with each other when he was abducted. He says he cracked a few weeks in." Her body went rigid. "When I saw him again, he was passed out on the porch, beaten up and high on morphine."

"You never told me." Logan silently dissected the information. "He did that?"

"He knew Georgie would want the MC to start selling drugs as payment. By didn't want that for us, after everything we've been through."

He shook his head, once again amazed by the force that was Byron Johannson. "No wonder they call him Hero."

"He's a wonderful man." She lifted her head and wiped her tears away. "I guess I associate traumatic experiences with his drug use."

"Fifteen years sober is a long time, ma. Plus, he's got the guys. They'll look out for him."

"I can't help worrying. I don't know what I'll do without the two of you."

He grinned broadly. "For starters, you won't worry this much."

She smacked his chest. "Careful, boy. Today was stressful enough."

"You take this day way too seriously."

She peered at him while she tried to figure out what he meant. When the penny dropped, her full lips pressed together in a line of anger. "He is your *father*. Why do you hate him?"

"I didn't say I hated him." The last thing he wanted was to argue with his mother, especially about this. "I just *don't remember him*. How am I supposed to love someone I don't know?"

Shaking her head, Cinnia leaned back against the wall. She let out a short, humorless laugh. And then, suddenly, she was sobbing with her head in her hands. So many different emotions in so little time… Can anyone blame him for thinking she was going through early menopause?

"I wouldn't trade my time with Byron for anything in the world, but sometimes…" She hiccupped, her body trembling. "Brennan was such a good man and he loved you more than anything. It's hard to hear you say you don't feel the same. I wish you'd known him, or that you could remember the smaller things, like how *he* was always the first to hold you when you cried. I had to fight to have you to myself for a few minutes because you were the apple of his eye."

Logan swallowed past the lump in his throat. He put his cup down and embraced his mother. "I don't mean to sound insensitive. I'm sure I would've loved him. I just can't wish for a better dad than the one I have."

"I know. I got so lucky, first having Bren and then Byron. I think I was in love with Byron even while Bren was still alive."

"You hussy," he teased, eager to hear her laugh again.

She didn't quite manage to conceal her giggle. "Logan Bean Drummond, you can make me so angry and happy, at the same time."

"Guess that's what being a mom is all about."

"Your gran did try to warn me."

He finished his coffee. "Thanks for the cuppa, momma."

"You're welcome, Lo." She eyed him curiously. "What's with you and the girl?"

"What do you mean?"

"I saw how protective you are."

"Jeez, ma, she was attacked and left for dead. I have a heart."

"There's more to it than that," she insisted. "I know you prefer talking to your dad about girls, but I want to know what's going on."

"I'm not sure." He ran his fingers through his black hair. He has been told it had a copper hue in direct sunlight, a fact that made his mother very happy, since it was another thing that reminded her of Brennan. "I'm probably crazy. I mean, it's not like she's looking her best. Bruised women don't turn me on."

"Glad to hear it."

It was too weird discussing this with her. "If she doesn't tell us how to reach her family, we'll have to keep her here until she's ready to leave."

Cinnia smiled. "You're starting to think like a Prez."

Feeling awkward gave way to guilt. No one, not even Sophie or Connor, knew that he wasn't convinced that he should be the next President of the Raptors. He had bigger dreams: he simply wasn't certain how they were going to become a reality, or if they even could be.

Jemma stepped out of the room, unwittingly—*thankfully*, Logan thought—interrupting. They both got to their feet, eager to hear the diagnosis. Jemma pushed her light grey bangs out of her eyes and sighed.

"Nothing's broken, but she has a lot of deep bruising on her stomach and chest. There are a few cuts on her back, as if she was whipped. The swelling will go down in a few days, but I think she'll have scars." Jemma hesitated. "She was raped, too. Based on the tissue damage, I'd say repeatedly, by more than one man."

Logan was simultaneously furious and nauseous.

"She relented to my examination because she knew I'm here to help, but she doesn't like physical contact and said no to a rape kit," Jemma went on. "I don't think this is the first time she's been abused. I suspect she's been molested since she was little."

"Sick fucks," he muttered, his hands curling into fists. His mother didn't even chastise his swearing.

"I cleaned her up as best I could." Jemma glanced at Cinnia. "I think we should get Dr. McKauley in here."

"I'll call her first thing in the morning."

Logan slowly rose to his feet, wondering why this was important to him. He didn't know the girl from a bar of soap! "Can I see her?"

"I gave her something for the pain and she was lying down when I left, so she might be asleep. Try not to wake her."

"Thanks." He squeezed his mother's hand and went inside.

The girl was on her side on the narrow bed, her knees drawn up to her chest. She was facing the wall, and he relaxed once he saw the even rise and fall of her breathing. The dirty sheet she'd been wrapped in lay crumpled in the corner of the room. She now wore a light grey Raptors MC shirt and matching bottoms, but they were several sizes too big. She couldn't have seen three meals a day in a very, very long time. She was like a tiny, damaged bird and he wanted nothing more than to assure her safety.

She twitched and glanced up, jolting once she saw him looming over her. She nearly tipped the bed as she scurried into a seated position. Her swollen eye was seeping a clear liquid. Was she crying?

Logan held his hands up. "Sorry, I didn't mean to scare you."

She stared at him, frightened. Her good eye kept drooping, as if she was going to nod off, but she was forcing herself to stay awake.

"I'm not going to hurt you." He backed away, to the opposite wall, and pulled up a chair. "I just want to talk, okay?"

She didn't give any indication that she was comforted by his words.

"You gave us a scare," he murmured conversationally. "I was minding my own business, doing one of my favorite climbs and there you were. I thought you were dead at first." He grimaced. "I'm glad you're not. I've never seen a dead body."

The tension steadily began rolling out of her.

"Have you ever gone rock-climbing? God, what a rush. Granted, I've only been to our local spot, but I'd love to travel the world and climb the highest ones, you know? If you're good enough, you can even do it professionally. Do you think that's worth it? It's one thing to love adrenaline, but quite another to *live* adrenaline." He shook his head with a soft laugh, amused by his own babbling. "I don't know if it's healthy to be on a constant high."

She stared at him, her face beautiful and ugly all at once. He wanted to know what she looked like when she wasn't recovering from injuries, when she was happily living, carefree and young.

"I'm sorry this happened to you. And I know my apology doesn't make it better. What those people did to you is wrong and I want you to know you're safe here. We'll keep you out of danger if you'll allow it."

Almost imperceptibly, her head dipped in acquiescence.

He braced himself, asking the most burning question: "What's your name?"

She hesitated, nibbling on her tender bottom lip. "Luca."

"Luca. How old are you?"

"Fifteen."

"I'm Logan." Taking his time so she could see he wasn't a threat, he rose to his feet and walked over, extending his hand. He kept it outstretched, willing to wait as long as it took for her to respond. "It's good to meet you, although I wish it was under better circumstances."

This close to her, he was fascinated by the color of her iris. It wasn't entirely blue. Dark, with hints of… purple? Then again, he had no clue about the other one: he'll have to see once the swelling has gone down.

Wordlessly, she shook his hand, snapping him out of his thoughts. A shock went through him at the contact and she immediately let go as if she'd felt it, too.

He cleared his throat with a cough. It made her jump. "I, uh…" He was frozen to the spot. The palm of his hand tingled where she'd touched him. He gestured to the door. "Do you want to go get something to eat, or must I bring it here?"

Her eye widened in fear, like the thought of being around other people scared the daylights out of her.

"I'll bring you something. Are you a vegetarian? Allergic to anything?"

She shook her head.

"Ham and cheese sandwich sound good, with a can of soda?"

She gave him a nod of confirmation.

He paused, hoping he wasn't going to push her too far. "Do you want to move to a more comfortable room? We have one down the hallway. Clean sheets, soft pillows, a blanket, your own bathroom…" He trailed off, waiting.

She swallowed thickly, but inclined her head once more.

"Alright, let me show you where it is." He held his hand out to her. He was probably doing the wrong thing by making her used to him, but he wanted to help her through this. Besides, there was a part of him that wanted her to rely on him.

What's the matter with you? She's never going to trust you!

Another spark of electricity traveled up his arm once her small hand slipped into his. When she put her feet on the floor and straightened, she barely made it up to his shoulder. His male hormones loved that he was bigger, like he could be her protector. Was he doing this to feed his ego?

Mind circling around that thought, he wordlessly led her out of the room. His mother and Jemma were chatting outside, but their conversation died down once they saw he wasn't alone. Luca shifted closer to him, using him as a shield.

"Luca, you've met Jemma, our resident doctor. This is my mom, Cinnia." He maintained eye contact with his mother, who had a slight smile on her face. "I'm going to show Luca to her new bedroom."

"I'm glad you're alright, Luca, all things considered," Cinnia murmured. "Let me know if you need anything."

"Actually, she'd like a ham and cheese sandwich. And a soda."

"Coming right up." Cinnia grabbed her friend's arm and the two of them hurried out of the hallway.

Logan tightened his hold on Luca's hand and kept walking. "This is our club. Have you heard of the Raptors?"

Her eyes on the floor, she nodded.

"I hope you heard good things. Different clubs have different opinions." He entered the bedroom and stopped. "Well, here you are." Reluctantly, he let go of her hand. This room was basic compared to the ones back home, but one thing at a time. He doubted she'd want to go to their house just yet. "You can sleep here. I'll guard your door tonight. Is that okay?"

Luca's hair was entrancing as she gave him that small nod of agreement. Those ebony locks went right down to her waist, and he could only imagine how gorgeous she would be when she was well-nourished, healed and washed.

Snap out of it, fool!

"Make yourself at home," he muttered, falling back. "I'll go see what's happening with your food."

"Logan?" She fidgeted with her hands, her toes curling into the carpet. "Thank you."

His heart melted. What was it about this girl? He's hardly known her for an hour and she was already creeping under his skin. It was unnerving.

Exciting.

"You're welcome."

He was desperate to get fresh air and clear his head. He walked outside, the setting sun a welcome sight. The women could take care of Luca for now. He was sure they knew how to be helpful and unobtrusive at the same time.

"Lo, is everything okay?"

His eyes found Sophie's, and he exhaled slowly. He hasn't seen her since the climb. "When did you get here?"

"A few minutes ago." She touched his forearm. "Jeez, you scared us when you dropped that rope."

"I'm sorry."

"I get it, Lo. Just don't do it like that again."

"I hope I never find a body on the side of the road again. Is everyone back from the lake?"

"Some of them stayed behind to pack up. I wanted to make sure you're okay. My mom gave me the low-down."

"I'm fine."

"Bullshit, you're edgy. What's wrong?"

He rubbed the back of his head and sighed. "I don't know. I'm probably going to spend the night here, make sure she's okay."

"You're being overprotective." Sophie bit her bottom lip to hide a smile, crossing her arms over her chest. "You've got white knight syndrome."

"Soph, please."

She laughed at his exasperated facial expression. "Fine, *fine*. Whatever you've got planned, put a delay on it. Like, a few months. She's damaged goods."

"More like a few years."

"Why?"

"She's only fifteen."

"Jesus." Sophie massaged her temples. "What type of people would do this to someone?"

"I hope I don't find out. I don't know what I'll do." He strode to the bar, craving beer. "She's heard of us, but it doesn't seem to be anything good. I have a feeling she's from another MC, or that she's been involved with one."

"Hmm, you'll have to tell Haye and your dad," she commented, accepting a beer from him. "Thanks."

He spotted his mother and Jemma walking towards the hallway, a tray of food—more than a simple sandwich, that's for sure—balanced in the doctor's hands while Cinnia carried a variety of sodas. He smiled to himself. Whatever life Luca knew before would change now that the Raptors were taking care of her.

"I'd like to meet your boyfriend," he said to Sophie, eager to change the subject.

"Now that I've admitted he exists I want you to meet him, too."

"Have you told him about me?"

She lifted a shoulder nonchalantly. "I've mentioned you, but he doesn't know that we... I don't think our relationship's ready for that."

"How long have you been dating?"

"Two weeks."

Logan's eyebrows rose. "You've kept a secret like this for two weeks? You're getting really good at hiding stuff from me."

"Don't make me self-conscious about it." She tucked a stray lock of hair behind her ear. "This is new, okay? I'm not sure how to go about it. I mean, my dad hates cops." She laughed softly. "I'm probably making this more complicated than it is."

"Way," he agreed.

"Max says I think too much, but he understands why I'm unsure." She picked at the label of her beer. "I keep wondering when he's going to grow tired of me. I mean, it's been two weeks and we haven't had sex yet. These days, that's what people do even before they ask each other's names."

"Damn, you do think too much."

"It's just, I…" Chewing on her bottom lip, she lifted her gaze to his. "I think he's *it*, Lo, and that scares me."

"This is what you wanted, remember?"

"There's a reason why they say, 'be careful what you wish for'."

"I guess that's—" He glanced behind him at the sound of Harleys outside. "Must be dad. Give me a sec." Draining his beer, he headed for the exit. Most of the bikers were back. He approached Byron. "What's going on?"

"We'll talk inside," Byron answered, resting his hand on Logan's shoulder.

Logan peered at his brothers, who were following. "Are we voting?"

"Probably."

"Where's Haye?"

"He'll be here in a few." His stepfather gave him a look. "You smell like beer."

Logan blushed. "It was only one, dad."

"I don't mind, Lo, but you've got school tomorrow."

"I know."

Byron dropped his hand as they entered the boardroom. "How's the girl?"

"I think she'll be fine. Mom and Jemma are with her." Logan scratched the back of his neck, sitting at the table. "Her name's Luca."

"How did you get that out of her?"

"I think she trusts me. Somewhat."

"Good." Byron nodded to himself. "You'll have to stay here tonight, then."

"I figured."

The rest of the men took their seats around the table. Only the highest-ranking MC members were attending. The others remained in the bar area, waiting for the verdict. Nixon and Connor—*where the hell has he been?* Logan wondered, not for the first time—arrived with Haye and shut the door behind them.

"Thanks for coming on such short notice," Haye said. He took his place at the head of the table. "This shouldn't take long. Hero?"

"As you all know by now, Logan found a girl during one of his climbs today. She's beaten up and was probably left for—"

"Sorry to interrupt, VP." Logan knew what he was about to say would shift the energy in the room. "Jemma also mentioned that Luca was gang raped."

Everyone's eyes narrowed and a few of them swore under their breaths.

"In that case, what I'm about to say won't sound irrational," Byron growled angrily, with clenched fists. "We have to find these motherfuckers and make them pay."

"We didn't have much luck following that van," Oscar informed them. "It was abandoned a few miles from where they dropped her, and we could make out three other tire tracks. I think this was done deliberately. If we'd had more backup, we would've pursued them."

"That area isn't exactly known for being a dumping ground," Ryan remarked.

"If it's deliberate, then what's the message?" Logan asked. "We don't know Luca, or where she came from."

"I say we keep her close for the next couple of weeks while we dig into her past," Haye suggested. "We have to know what we're dealing with before we retaliate. I don't want to piss on the wrong person's porch. We have to be *sure* we're fucking up the right motherfuckers."

"Aye," the Raptors brothers chorused.

"Logan's appointed himself as her babysitter—"

"Hey," Logan huffed at his stepdad.

Byron grinned broadly. "He'll look after her tonight. We'll get the prospects to guard her tomorrow while he's at school, but he will have to pick this up again every night until we find what we're looking for."

"All in favor?"

"Aye."

Logan stared at them. They weren't even going to ask his opinion?

Haye hit the gavel on the table. "Good, let's find out who the hell did this so we can return her to her family and carry on with our lives. In the meantime, she's our responsibility. Treat her as one of our own."

"Aye."

"Dismissed," Haye declared.

Logan sat there, shocked. "What the hell just happened?"

Byron's smile widened as he slapped Logan on the back. "You just got your first proper Prez duty."

CHAPTER FOUR

"LOGAN!"

Glancing up, Logan kicked the ball to his teammate. He rushed towards the goal post, ready for the ball's return. It bumped against his foot, and he angled his body before launching it in the direction of the goalkeeper's weakest spot: the top-right corner.

The net rippled and the crowd cheered.

Logan accepted the praise from the team with a laugh, nearly getting knocked over in the process. They were already leading by four points, mostly thanks to the hat-trick he's now scored. They were up against one of their toughest competitors, who were clearly having a bad day.

The freedom that playing ball awarded him was unrivaled by anything except riding and climbing; yet his thoughts were dominated by Luca.

She was the most gorgeous girl he's ever known. Her eyes *were* violet and big, like a doll's. Her bronze skin glowed, in contrast to his ivory hue. Now that she was eating regularly, she's gained some much-needed weight, although she hid the changes in her body under baggy clothes. When he'd left the clubhouse this morning, her injuries had finally appeared healed. It's taken three weeks, but she had youth on her side. Jemma was impressed by her progress.

Luca remained mute, for the most part, only speaking to Logan. He took pride in that. She enthralled him and he hated sharing her.

She isn't yours, he reminded himself, attempting to get his head back in the game. *Once we find out where she comes from, you'll never see her again.*

So far, they haven't been able to track her origins. Her name wasn't common in this area, yet that didn't mean much. She wasn't divulging any personal information, giving Logan the impression that she wasn't eager to return to her people. Connor had theorized that she'd been abducted by a human trafficking cartel, which would make it even more difficult to find her parents.

It was all the same to Logan: the longer he could keep her around, the better. He enjoyed seeing her every morning, looking more beautiful than the day before. The cheerleaders on the side of the pitch were pretty and had phenomenal bodies but, since meeting Luca, no one compared.

He was popular, for several reasons. He was a biker, giving him that bad-boy air that appealed to some. He had many of his mother's features, such as her green eyes and black hair, while his dimples, length and build were thanks to Brennan. He had good grades and was a superb athlete, football in particular: he's already been scouted, although he didn't know how to tell his parents.

He therefore wasn't unused to attention from the fairer sex. He used to take advantage of that, and often, though he always tried to keep it safe.

Luca has obliterated thoughts of sex with other women. It disturbed him. She was three years younger *and* someone who's survived physical abuse and rape. The odds were stacked against him. Why couldn't he move on?

"Logan!"

He snapped out of his reverie to refocus on the match. He's tried to physically exhaust himself in the hopes he wouldn't be good company around Luca but, every time he saw her, he was invigorated. It was infuriating.

I don't care.

The game ended twenty minutes later, with a final score of 6-2. Logan, the captain of his team, shook hands with their opponents, trying not to gloat too much. He then led the way off the field, annoyed when he didn't manage to dodge the cheerleaders.

Nina sidled up to him, kinky promises in her blue eyes. "Great game, Lo."

"Thanks."

"Are you coming to Fitz's after party?"

He shook his head. "Can't."

She pouted, leaning in. "You're never around anymore. What's going on?"

"I have other responsibilities at the moment." *Ones that involve protecting a girl who is much too beautiful for her own good.* "Gotta go."

"Lo, wait!"

He was already halfway to the changing rooms, ignoring the jibes from his friends. He hasn't told anyone about Luca in case word got out and her attackers came back to finish what they'd started. At least, that's what he told himself. His reasons had nothing to do with the fact that they'd insist on meeting her, and he had this inexplicable need to prevent that in case she liked them more.

Nope, couldn't be that.

He cleaned up and stuffed his dirty clothes in a bag.

"You heading to the clubhouse?" Dane asked, joining his side.

"Yeah. You did well today."

"Thanks." Dane lifted a shoulder and rubbed his black hair dry. "I'm thinking of quitting again."

"Coach is gonna burst a vein if you tell him that," Logan chuckled. His cousin was an incredible athlete, but he got bored easily. He and his twin his sister, Hallie, had that in common. "That's, what, the second time this year?"

Dane cracked a smile. "He told me I'll be captain next year, when you're gone. A part of me wants to quit just to piss him off."

Logan burst out laughing. "Take a video of his reaction." He high-fived Dane and gathered his things. "See you at the club later."

"Sweet, dude."

Logan caught up with his friends and they emerged from the boys' bathroom together, heading to the parking lot.

"Jeez, your mom's hot," Fitz commented, not for the first time.

"Don't," Logan warned.

Fitz pretended to wipe perspiration from his forehead as he stared at Cinnia, whose ass was firmly pressed to Byron's front. "I bet he bangs her all the time."

Logan punched his friend on the shoulder. "That's my mother you're drooling over."

"It's a good thing they didn't have a girl," Fitz said, grinning, "or you would've had to beat me up for having sex with your sister."

Logan rolled his eyes. "That's it! I'm leaving." He bumped his fist to theirs, one by one. "Great game, guys."

"Cheers, Lo!"

He waved and made his way to his parents. "Will you stop having sex in front of everyone?"

"Did we do the birds-and-bees talk wrong?" Byron wondered aloud, glancing at his fiancée. "I'm pretty sure we told him how intercourse works."

"We did," Cinnia agreed.

"It involves penetration, Lo. That means—"

"Ugh, stop. Can we get to the clubhouse already?"

Cinnia raised an eyebrow. "So *you* can have sex?"

"No." If they asked, he would say his red cheeks were due to the heat. His pale skin was the only thing he wished he could change. "She's been raped before, for fuck's sake."

"Language," his mother said, smacking him on the back of his head.

He glared at her. Maybe his friends wouldn't have constant boners if she'd quit wearing skin-tight leather pants. But hey, it was her trademark. He wasn't going to tell her how to live her life.

"We're headed straight for the barbecue," Byron informed Logan as he unlocked the SUV. "Do you think Luca's ready?"

Logan winced. "I'll have to ask her."

"We really need to know who her parents are, Lo. What if they're looking for her?"

"We haven't seen anything to indicate that."

"Not locally, no, but what if—"

"I'll see what I can find out," Logan snapped. He shut his door once he was seated in the car, impatiently waiting for them to do the same. He wanted to be with *her*, and they were taking their sweet time! "Can we go now?"

Byron whistled. "Damn, punk, you've got it bad."

"It's… not like that."

His mother gave him a look. "You sure about that?"

He put his headphones on, refusing to engage in this conversation. Didn't they see how selfless he was being? Helping someone who was virtually a stranger, without complaining? Being a responsible Raptors President?

Keep telling yourself that. You're addicted to her presence.

Sometimes he indulged in a fantasy of Luca, one where she was older and not averse to physical contact. One where she was incredibly vocal, curving into him as he sucked on her neck, his hands sliding over her smooth skin...

He suppressed a groan at how hard he was getting, shifting on the seat. He increased the volume to distract his train of thought. He was going to burn in hell for having these urges.

The town. The buildings. How could he use that arch in his next design? Maybe he'll bring about a modern take on the Victorian era.

And then you can christen the place with Luca's shapely legs wrapped around your waist.

Leaning his head back, he closed his eyes and gave up. There was no way to stop his teenage hormones. It would be best if he let this play out, see where it took him.

"Hi, Logan."

Luca, standing in front of him, dressed in one of his shirts. Every time she took a step in his direction, the hem drifted up to give him a glimpse of the treasure between her legs.

"I hope you don't mind, but all my clothes are in the wash." She nibbled on the corner of her lush bottom lip. "I didn't think you were going to be home so soon."

"That's okay, sweetheart." He refrained from moving. "Do you want me to leave?"

"No, I want you to come here." She gripped the edge of the shirt and gradually, seductively, lifted it up. Inch by mouth-watering inch. "I want to thank you for everything you've done for me."

He steeled himself. "You don't owe me anything, Luca."

The shirt was pulled over her head, leaving her ebony hair in sexy disarray. She dropped the article of clothing on the floor and stared at him wearing nothing but a suggestive grin. "That doesn't mean you can't fuck my brains out, anyway."

When he lifted her into his arms, her legs twined around his hips and their mouths melted together. She—

The vehicle came to an abrupt halt, bringing Logan's overactive imagination to a grinding stop with it. He was breathing shallowly and sweating. Not to mention his rigid cock... He sucked air into his lungs as he threw his headphones to the side.

"Lo, is everything okay?" his mother asked worryingly.

"Fine." He filled his mind with the most horrifying images to take care of his arousal before he exited the car. There were several Harleys in the parking lot already. "What time is everything starting?"

"In an hour or so. We're going to help set up."

"I'll see if Luca wants to come."

Byron coughed to hide his laugh. "You do that."

"You're disgusting," Logan hissed through his teeth.

"*I'm* not the one that—"

"By," Cinnia interjected firmly. She took her lover's hand in hers. "Come on, let's give him some space."

Logan's gaze followed them to the warehouse and he exhaled, feeling like shit. He'll have to apologize for his snippy behavior, but he hated how close they were cutting to the bone. He didn't want to have feelings for Luca. He knew it wasn't going to get him anywhere.

He strode into the clubhouse, greeting the prospects and thanking them for their shift.

"She didn't come out," one of the men informed him. "I don't think she likes anyone except you."

He was reminded of Luca's emotional scars. He had no right to harbor such intense desires for someone who wouldn't appreciate or reciprocate his advances. Dr. McKauley has been here twice, yet Luca's recovery from trauma wouldn't happen overnight.

He hurried to her bedroom and knocked on the door. "It's me, Luca. Can I come in?" He waited tensely, hearing her move on the other side.

The door opened a crack. Establishing that he was alone, she fell back.

He stepped over the threshold and quietly sealed them inside. Sophie, roughly the same size as Luca, had donated some of her clothes. Luca was wearing loose-fitting faded blue jeans today, paired with a black tank top. There was a sweatshirt on the bed.

Logan's eyes drifted over her exposed collarbones. Apart from that day when she'd had nothing but a sheet to cover her nudity, he's never seen so much of her skin. The tank wrapped around her figure in a way that made him hard again. Her waist was small and her hips round. Her body called to him like a siren. He wondered if her breasts would fill his hands.

You're scaring her.

Luca had crossed her arms over her chest at his perusal, a guarded look in her eyes, as if she expected him to take what he wanted.

"Have you had lunch yet?" he asked, breaking the silence. He rummaged through the chest of drawers to his right, to appear as if he had something to do. When she didn't respond, he eyed her questioningly.

She shook her head, eyes downcast.

"Well, good news," he announced brightly. "There's a barbecue at the warehouse this afternoon. Do you want to go?"

She repeated the motion.

"Okay, I'll bring you something to eat later." He'd expected she would decline. His fingers tapped a box and, frowning, he retrieved it. He became pensive once he recognized the *Scrabble* box set. "Do you want to play?"

She tilted her head to the side.

"You've never played before?" Logan chuckled and brought the board game to her. Granted, he's only ever used the app on his mother's iPad as a kid, but how much different could the physical game be? "I'll teach you."

He sat down on the edge of the bed and began setting up. After a few minutes of keeping an eye on him while he read through the rules, she finally folded her legs under her on the opposite side of the mattress. He handed the booklet over for her to examine, shuffling the letters. At the back of his mind, he knew this would be a great way to determine if she's literate.

"Ready to see who can draw one closest to A? You go first." She nodded and picked a tile up. He copied her action. "I've got F."

She revealed hers: B.

"You get to start, then," he smiled, mixing those two with the rest. They each reached for tiles and packed their racks. He didn't have many options, based on the letters in front of him.

Luca brought her hands together, her elbows resting on her crossed legs. She was completely engrossed.

His breath caught in his throat. Jesus, she was beautiful! How was he supposed to concentrate on anything when they were in the same room? It was hard enough to keep his mind off her when they were apart.

In quick succession, she placed six tiles on the board, from the middle block downwards. *C-O-C-C-Y-X*. She looked at him for approval, a sparkle in her eyes.

"Wow."

Grinning, Luca took the pad and pencil that came with the box, scribbling their names and dividing them into separate columns. Then, lifting the tiles one by one, she counted up her score and jotted it down. She had legible handwriting and a clear handle on Math.

"Okay, let's see what I can do." He still didn't have much to go on. He placed his *V* next to her *O*, followed by *E* and *R*.

She seemed doubtful.

"I swear, it's all I've got."

Shrugging, she calculated his score.

Logan put his thinking cap on. He tried to show off his own intelligence, but he was too distracted by her and kept picking words that didn't count many points. She seemed to be in her element, placing tiles in an order that he was certain didn't exist. Every time he checked the dictionary, he had to swallow his pride and admit that he was wrong for accusing her of cheating.

In no time at all, she cleared the pool of letters.

"No way," he argued theatrically, chucking the rule book over his shoulder. "This is impossible! You've never even played before!"

She giggled like a delighted child while she tallied up their final scores.

"I demand a recount!" He snatched the notepad away from her. He read their scores, pretending to get more outraged by the second. "I knew it, you've been fixing the numbers!"

She leaned forward to grab it, her mouth popping open in surprise when he held it behind his back.

"It's unfair, sweetheart. I do you a favor by playing a game with you, and then you can't even let me win?"

Narrowing her eyes, she tackled him to the carpeted floor, *Scrabble* tiles flying in all directions. She wrenched the notepad away from him and held it up victoriously, violet eyes gleaming.

Even though it had hurt like a son of a bitch to have his spine connect with the floor, he wouldn't turn back the clock for anything in the world. She was straddling him, though she has yet to realize it. The view was better than his imagination, and she wasn't even naked.

Yet.

Nope, no, he couldn't do that to her. He thought of the most awful things on the planet to talk himself down. Devastating fires, the earth being hit by a meteor, and apocalyptic destruction filled his mind's eye.

Luca's facial expression smoothed out while she stared at him. She dropped the paper they'd been squabbling over.

He wanted to take her face in his hands and kiss her; to feel her fingers sliding under his T-shirt; to take her right here, on the carpet of her safe haven. The craving to drive his cock so deep into her that she would feel him for days completely overrode his need to keep his arousal under control.

She glanced at his crotch, no doubt feeling him harden.

The knock on the door was both a blessing and a curse. "Lo?" his mother called. "Are you coming to the party?"

Luca scrambled off him and got back on the bed.

He shut his eyes, trying to calm down. What the fuck was the matter with him? It usually took a girl much more than *this* to get him hot and bothered. Why was he so damn attracted to someone he will never have?

"Lo?" Cinnia asked, opening the door and peering inside.

"Yeah," he sighed, "on my way."

"Luca, are you joining us?"

The girl pulled her knees up to her chin, shaking her head.

Cinnia smiled. "I'll send Logan back with some food, then. Come on, boy, get up."

As he reached the door, he could've sworn he heard Luca say: "Sore loser." He gave her a challenging look. "I beg your pardon?"

She pressed her lips together, trying to hide her grin.

But he saw it. By God, she took his breath away when she smiled. "You're gonna pay for that," he warned, the corners of his mouth tilting upward. He left without waiting for a response.

"Do I want to know why you were on your back?" his mother asked him.

He felt his face heat up. "We, ah... I mean—"

"Lo, if she consents, I don't have a problem with what you two get up to." Cinnia glanced at him. "On the other hand, she's only fifteen. You shouldn't confuse her."

"I'm not. I doubt she wants me that way."

"I doubt she'll want anyone that way after what happened to her, so don't take it personally."

His mother was right, but he didn't want to talk about this. "She's very smart, by the way. We were playing *Scrabble* and she kicked my ass. She can do Math in her head, too. I think we should get a few books in there to keep her company."

"Maybe..." Cinnia trailed off, nibbling on her bottom lip as they entered the warehouse. "I think you should ask her if she wants to live with us until we track her parents down. You haven't slept at home in weeks and I don't like that."

Wrapping an arm around his mother's shoulders, he grinned. "You do realize I'll move out after graduation, right?"

"Don't remind me."

He chuckled and squeezed her. "I won't be skipping town, mom."

"Just ask, okay?"

"I will." He eyed her teasingly. "You'd think with the wedding only three months away, you won't even notice I'm gone."

"Nothing will ever make me forget my son."

He pecked her temple. "I love you too, momma."

"I love it when you call me that." She pinched his cheek, laughing when he groaned. "Go grab dinner before you go back. You should socialize with your friends more often." She grew serious. "She's not the only person in the world, you know."

He silently agreed, nodding before walking to the serving table. Connor and Sophie were there, dishing up and chatting the way siblings did when they no longer hated each other. Logan couldn't relate.

"Hey, guys," he greeted.

"Do my eyes deceive me or is this Logan Bean Drummond?" Sophie exclaimed dramatically.

"Har."

"Can't be," Connor chimed in. "Logan only ever locks himself in that room."

"Guys, come on." Logan rolled his eyes. "I'm not that bad."

"You really are, though," Connor argued, grinning. "It makes me wonder if she's as pretty as everyone says she is."

"She's prettier."

"Man, you've got it bad." Connor slapped his biker brother on the back. "Have you told her yet?"

"She's been through a rough time, and she's surrounded by strangers." Logan stabbed a lamb chop with unnecessary force to get it on his plate. "I'm not going to add to her stress. Besides, she'll be gone soon."

"Bummer."

Logan shook himself and leered at Connor. "How 'bout you and Jesse?"

Glancing at the girl in question, Connor sighed. "It's hard to talk to her when she's always got her nose stuck in a book."

"You should come climbing with us next time. You can be her belay and stare at her ass."

"You make a valid point, but I'm too old for her."

Logan snorted. "Four years? Please. Stop making excuses."

"Why, am I reminding you of someone?" Connor countered.

"Wow, you're worse than girls," Sophie let them know. "Stop gossiping and make space for the rest of us."

Blushing slightly, Logan followed Connor to the dining area, where large tables have been pushed together. The Raptors were vast in numbers and partied loudly, making it nearly impossible for Logan to follow the conversation. A few minutes into it, he no longer cared.

He was with his family. Life couldn't get any better.

It was sometimes difficult to believe how many hardships this club has endured. From Logan's great-grandfather nearly running it into the ground with illegal drug and ammunition trade, to Reade picking up the pieces and making something better of it, to Brennan's death and the retribution that had followed... It had taken a long time for everything to calm down enough for them to enjoy the MC the way it was intended.

And you're inheriting all of this, Logan thought, gazing at the people around him while trying to ignore the doubt churning in his stomach. *You're set to lead them into future generations.*

Connor, who was like an older brother, would be Logan's VP one day and Logan had plenty of respect for him. He was level-headed where Logan was impulsive, and happy-go-lucky where Logan was somber. As long as Connor's violent temper wasn't ignited, he was quite pleasant.

The twins were identical in nearly every way, their genders being the only difference. They had the typical Sloane traits: black hair and pale skin, but with aunt Piper's amber eyes. They were both artistic daydreamers. They hardly ever argued, yet they loved debating politics and religion with everyone else. Logan sometimes forgot that they were a year younger than him, since they were more mature than others their age.

Connor eventually dragged Logan into a debate with them. Logan finished two beers and a second helping of food, laughing at the conversation and relaxing for the first time in weeks. He couldn't wait to move in with Connor next year: the guy was hilarious.

All too soon, though, his thoughts turned to a certain violet-eyed girl.

"Excuse me, guys," Logan said, wiping his mouth with a napkin. "I have to go."

"Duty calls, 'ey?" Connor smirked. "Sucks being you."

"You know it." Logan bumped his fist to Connor's, and then Dane's. "See y'all later."

"No, we won't!" Sophie called after him.

He smiled and shook his head, dumping his dirty dishes before taking a plate for Luca. Having watched her intently since her arrival, he quickly picked out her favorites and grabbed a can of soda along the way to the clubhouse. There were a few men drinking at the bar and he wasn't surprised to find her bedroom door locked. He knocked three times and called out to her, briefly wondering if she was asleep.

The door parted, revealing her face, and he forgot his resolve not to fall for her. He had no valid argument why he shouldn't make her his, not when her aura was so magnetic, pulling him in.

"Sorry I'm late."

She shook her head and moved out of the way, giving him space to walk inside. She shut the door and stared up at him. She'd braided her hair over one shoulder in the meantime, exposing the side of her neck.

Logan felt his loins tighten at the sight, longing to lick his way to her ear. Would she moan if he found the right spot to nibble on? Pull him closer, pressing her body to his in invitation? Help him take her clothes off?

He cleared his throat, holding the plate out to her. "It's cold, but still edible."

"Thank you," she said softly. Food in hand, she went to sit on the bed. She looked up once she noticed he wasn't following and patted the empty spot.

I shouldn't be anywhere near you and a bed.

He pulled a chair closer and sat down, pretending to be interested in his hands.

"Did you have fun?"

Even her voice was a turn-on. What was happening to him?

"The twins were on form, as usual. Sometimes I think they say things just to get a rise out of people, 'cause they were laughing at how angry everyone got. I love their opinions on stuff, though. They really make you think."

Luca listened attentively while she ate. He was her link to the outside world.

"Sophie didn't have her boyfriend here. I'd like to meet him, to see if he's good enough for her. I'm very protective of people I…" He trailed off, steering his eyes away from her. "She's my best friend and deserves the world. Usually, she's open and honest about guys, but lately she's been reserved." He shrugged. "Maybe she's ready to get serious."

Sipping on her soda, Luca gestured for him to continue.

"I don't know if that's in my future, you know?" He ran his fingers through his hair. Damn, he needed to go for a trim. "I mean, 'serious' implies calming down, becoming boring. I like going on adventures and doing crazy shit, and I'd hate to think that'll change just because I've met the person I'm spending the rest of my life with." Was he imagining the blush tinting her cheeks? "I've seen the way my parents are together. They just… *work*. Weird to think they were friends for so long and then, when my dad died, they finally realized they were in love with each other."

"Your dad…" She frowned, confused. "I thought Byron was your dad."

He was pleased that she was paying attention to the names of the people he talked about. "Not biologically."

"Oh, I'm sorry."

"Don't be. My mom was never pregnant with me. Tessa—you met her the other day—was my surrogate. They became really good friends and my mother made Tess my godmother."

Luca's eyes were wide. She finished her meal and said: "Wow."

"Yeah." He watched her put her plate on the bedside table, dread flowing through his veins now that they were talking about families. He flexed his fingers for a moment to ready himself. "Luca, I know you've been through a lot, but we need to know who your folks are so that they can come get you."

If Logan had thought she looked scared before, she was downright petrified now. Her hands trembled and she nervously shifted on the bed.

"I'm sure they're worried sick," he went on, leaning forward. "We have to tell them where you are and—"

"*No!*"

Her exclamation took him by surprise, mostly because she's been so soft-spoken in the past. The way that her voice insisted—no, *commanded*—that he listen up had a strange effect on his hormones. It was quite the turn-on.

"Luca—"

"I know you're only trying to help," she said evenly, her violet eyes boring into his, "but please, don't make me go back there!"

He held his hands up in surrender, giving her a moment to compose herself. "Tell me why not, and I'll find a way to let you stay."

Pure agony dominated her facial expression and she wrapped her arms around herself. "Logan," she pleaded.

"I can't help if I don't know the truth."

She inhaled deeply, a tear slipping off her cheek. She wiped its trail away and linked her fingers together, contemplating her options. Her bottom lip quivered once she realized that there was no way out.

Her eyes locked on his and he instinctively knew that whatever she was about to say would be bad news.

"My father's name is Ian McDermot." She nodded when his eyes widened in recognition. "I'm from the Falcons MC. They beat me up and dumped me close to the lake, because they knew your club was going to be there. They want revenge for what happened when Georgie Warner destroyed their trade." She took a shaky breath and plunged ahead. "They thought by doing something you hate, you'd go after them in a blind rage and they could annihilate you. They had an ambush ready and everything. They wanted me to tell you where I came from once you rescued me."

Logan struggled to keep up. "Why didn't you?"

"I needed a way out. I... It wasn't the first time they've hit me. *Raped* me," she whispered fiercely. "I've tried running away, but they always find me. When they talked about this plan, I pretended to go along with it. Then you found me, and I figured I could use a couple of weeks to get better before I run away for good. They tried to brainwash me about your club, but I'm smart, Logan." She was angry now. "They never believed it, but I *am*! I knew any club that hated violence against women is much better than the one I was in. I *knew* what they were doing to me was wrong. My own father... That's *wrong*. I wanted out. *You*, of all people, should know how impossible that is if you're the child of a Prez."

He took a while to absorb that. She kept referring to "them" and "they", not "us", which confirmed that she hated the Falcons. On the surface, at least.

His family was going to be upset. Sure, they'll want to do their own research to make sure her story checks out, but no one could deny that she'd been abused and taken against her will. That, in and of itself, was enough to drive the MC to murder.

"I'm grateful for everything you've done for me," she murmured, her voice losing its aggressive edge. "I can never repay you for the kindness you've shown me, Logan, but I can't go back. They'll kill me. You can throw me out now that you know the truth. But please, don't send me back!"

He wanted to take her in his arms, to assure her that he'll never let her go. "Sweetheart, you're not going anywhere. I'm not letting you out of my sight."

She burst into tears, covering her face with her hands. "Logan, I'm sorry I—"

"Shh, sweetheart." He sat down next to her and draped an arm over her shoulders. "It's okay. You're safe. I'll keep you safe."

CHAPTER FIVE

"LUCA TOLD ME where she's from."

His brothers were gathered in the social area of the clubhouse, all in different stages of inebriation. They gazed at him in anticipation, openly curious about the girl they'd found abandoned on the side of the road.

After calming her down, Logan had left her in the room and singled out his uncle to do some digging. Logan had needed to know if there was any truth to her claims. Teagan had found some mention of Luca on social media, which suggested that Ian McDermot was her father, although her mother's identity remained a mystery.

The Falcons MC has grown in numbers over the past sixteen years and, like how Ian's previous plan of vengeance had taken ages to develop, he'd once again waited patiently for his next opportunity to strike. The Falcons were a bunch of outlaws now, detested by their local police force and the citizens of their town. Successful drug busts were the norm, and several of the Falcons have been implicated in assault or rape charges over the years.

Similar events repeating in another generation weren't lost on Logan: he often mused on the cycles of his own bloodline.

With every report and article Teagan unearthed, Logan's rage grew. He wanted to torture and kill every single one of those motherfuckers for what they've done, and in that moment he realized what a brilliant strategist Ian was: that Irish fucker *knew* how the Raptors felt about drugs and violence against women and that they'd get worked up to the point of retaliation, which guaranteed they'd fall into his trap along the way.

He couldn't let this happen. In the space of an hour, he's assumed the leadership role of the MC, although he would leave the final decision up to Haye.

"She's a Falcon."

His brothers' facial expressions varied from disgust to shock, and every emotion in-between. They were in for a long night.

"Ian McDermot is her father. She has been molested and abused as far back as she can remember by various members of the MC, including Ian. They left Luca like that to get our attention. She was supposed to tell us about them from the get-go, but she saw it as a chance to escape." He motioned to his uncle. "From what we've learned, the Falcons' morals are completely twisted."

"Those sons of bitches!"

"Good for nothing *cunts*!"

"Fucking sick fucks!"

"We're not going to send her back: they'll kill her." The silence that followed felt appropriate. "I offered that she stays with my parents, and she's agreed. We'll keep her safe while we figure out how to deal with them."

Byron raised an eyebrow, probably curious why Logan had decided to make that call without consulting him and Cinnia first.

"I hate to be that guy, but how do we know she's telling the truth, that she's not playing us to gain more information about us for the Falcons?" Nixon piped up.

"We'll have to monitor her closely."

"I don't know, Lo," Connor hedged, his eyes narrowed. Next to Nixon's equally doubtful facial expression, the resemblance between father and son was uncanny. "Maybe we should rather take her to a women's shelter."

"Fair enough, if your assumption of her being a spy turns out to be true." Logan clenched his fists on his lap under the table, where no one could see. "But what if you're wrong? What if the Falcons find her and finish what they started because she didn't hold up her end of the bargain? Could you live with yourselves?"

No one answered.

"I get that this is dangerous, which is why we'll take the necessary precautions. If there's any hint that she's still in contact with the Falcons, I won't hesitate to kick her out myself." It'll be hard, but he would do it for the club. His family ranked first in his life, always, and he wouldn't endanger them just because someone had pretty eyes. "In the meantime, we'll get her into school so that she can get back to normal. It's the least we can do."

Byron had a slight smile on his face. Haye, seated next to him, gazed at Logan with pride, mirroring many of the other men's faces. This club was in their blood: they would never do anything to jeopardize someone's safety.

"All in favor?" Haye asked.

A broken chorus of "aye" went around the group. Logan breathed easier now that he knew he had their support.

"I'd like to vote on something else." The Prez rose to his feet and went to stand next to Logan. "This was bound to happen sooner or later but, in light of recent events, I'm sure I'm not the only one who feels that Lo is ready for this. All in favor of Logan Bean Drummond getting patched in as Prez?"

Logan felt as if the world was ripped out from under him.

He's always known this would be his future, but in a matter of seconds, his dreams of being a professional athlete and paving his own way died. His stomach churned with fear, with nausea. How had he convinced himself the outcome of his life would be any different?

Because it could be.

No, that was a fantasy. At the end of the day, he was a Drummond. Drummond men founded the Raptors Motorcycle Club. They were meant to rule for as long as their lineage lasted. He was a fool for entertaining other ideas.

He hardly heard the enthusiastic chorus of "Aye!"

Haye clapped Logan on the back, unknowingly jolting him back into his body. "Good, I'd like to officially retire."

"Go get your girl so we can meet her," Byron added.

Mouth dry, Logan briefly dipped his head and walked out of the social area. He felt like he was wading through water: it was steadily rising from his thighs to his neck. There was a ringing in his ears, and he barely made to the hallway without breaking down. Was he having a panic attack?

"Logan? Are you okay?"

He rubbed his forehead, snapping back to reality and wondering how long he's stood in her room. "I spoke to my brothers. You're moving in with us."

Her eyes widened. "With... *them?*"

"No, with my parents and I."

She seemed to relax. She wiped a stray tear from her cheek and stood on tiptoes to wrap her arms around his neck. "Thank you."

He basked in her display of affection, in dire need of something to ground him. "You're welcome."

She angled her head and her lips brushed his neck, making him jerk at the sparks that went off between them. "I can never repay you for this."

Just stay, and I'll be happy.

He gave her a final squeeze and let go. "Come on, the guys want to meet you. I know that you don't like clubs, but you need to learn to trust them at some point."

She looked uncertain.

"You're under my protection." He held out his hand and she linked her fingers with his. It caused his heart to stutter, knowing how much she trusted him. "They'll never do anything to harm you. You have to believe that."

She cracked a wan smile. "I'll try."

He led the way to the social area. His brothers and some of the women were congregating there, excited to meet the girl that's taken up his time and attention. She tightened her grip on his hand and shifted slightly behind him, her eyes downcast.

"Everyone, this is Luca. She's one of us. Treat her accordingly."

Cinnia stepped forward and reached for Luca's free hand. The girl didn't flinch, and the corners of his mother's mouth turned up. "We're happy to take care of you, Luca."

"Thank you," Luca said quietly.

"Would you like to go home now, or would you like to meet some of the others?" Cinnia enquired.

Luca glanced from mother to son, questions in her gaze.

"Whatever you want, sweetheart."

She moved closer to him. "I'll meet the others."

Cinnia nodded proudly. "Alright, then. Let's go."

Leaving behind speculative murmurs, they made their way to the warehouse to join the party. The music was blaring and everyone was either on the dance floor or at the bar. Logan's awareness of Luca broadened. She was overwhelmed, yet intrigued. He smiled, heading for his female friends, as he doubted the guys would set her at ease.

"Hey, ladies."

They glanced up, taken aback at the sight of Luca. Hallie got to her feet first. "Hey, cuz. Who's this?"

"Luca, this is Hallie. Would you mind if she joins you?"

"Of course not!" Hallie gestured to empty seats. "Have you eaten, Luca?"

"Yes, thanks," Luca responded.

"Soda?" Aurora offered.

Luca accepted it silently, sitting down. She gazed up at Logan with guileless eyes, as if to say: "You're not leaving, right?"

The girls were already asking her questions in the gentlest way, so he knew she would be fine, but he couldn't breathe. The pressure of leading the club—not to mention the fact that Luca's moving in—held his mind prisoner. He couldn't take it anymore. He was going to explode!

"Lo, can I talk to you?"

He jumped about a foot in the air, shifting his gaze to his dad. "Sure."

Byron motioned for him to follow and made a beeline for the bar. There was a frown between his dark eyebrows.

"Something wrong, dad?"

"I remembered something. It might not be important, though."

"What is it?"

Byron took a moment to gather his thoughts. "After your father died, we worked on a plan of retaliation. Reade called in a favor with Georgie Warner."

"Mom's mentioned that."

He let out a breath of relief. "Good, so you know the basics. As it turned out, the favor was too big. Warner saw something in me and I agreed that I'll pay off the debt, as long as he kept the rest of the MC out of it. I'm afraid to tell you the rest." He ran his fingers through his hair. "You'll look at me differently."

Logan didn't know how much more he could take, but he motioned for his dad to continue.

"When it was time to pay off the debt, Warner abducted me. I agreed to a couple of months of service, thinking that he wanted me to push drugs since he knew I was in recovery..." He shook his head with a humorless laugh. "Instead, he had me working as an escort. He knew how much I love your mother, had set up cameras in the house without anyone noticing. He wanted to torment me. Break me."

The emotions swirling in Logan was reaching fever pitch. "Dad, what does this have to do with Luca?"

"During my… employment, I became friends with one of the women I lived with. Her name is—or *was*, I have no idea if she's still alive—Jasmine." Byron stared at Luca, lost in a memory. "I can see similarities. I wonder…"

"Wonder what?"

"A few years after I got released from Warner's service, Guilietta Sequera came to see me. She offered me compensation if I took Jasmine in and placed her under the protection of the club. She mentioned a daughter, then. Your grandmother talked me out of it, but I feel like—" He cut himself off. "If Luca is Jasmine's daughter and this all happened because I said no—"

"You can't blame yourself. If she is Jasmine's, which we don't know for sure, it wasn't your fault."

Byron seemed pained.

"Dad." Logan saw that Byron was mentally retreating. He dropped his hands on Byron's shoulders. "Dad, stop it! You'll drive yourself crazy."

"If she's the girl Guilietta told me about, then she can't be Ian's."

For the second time today, Logan's world froze. "What?"

"Jasmine got pregnant before Ian became her client. In fact, I was worried that *I* might've been the father, but Guilietta said it was a random stranger."

"This…" Logan held his hands up. "This is too much."

"I'm sorry, I shouldn't have dumped this on you tonight, but I couldn't…" Byron trailed off, shaking his head. "I had to tell someone."

Logan sank onto a barstool, eyes locked on the man that had raised him. God, the demons Byron must wrestle with! How could anyone survive that kind of torture and go on to be happy? To find a way to put himself first?

"I have no idea how you made it through."

"Sometimes, I don't know myself."

"Is that how you got the scars on your back?"

"Courtesy of Guilietta, who was Warner's wife at the time."

"Did they…?" Logan cleared his throat, not sure he really wanted to know. "Did they give you money after?"

"Yes, Guilietta opened a trust fund for you, which will pay for university.

Your mother and I decided to keep it. At least *one* good thing will come out of all that."

"Dad," Logan whispered. A part of him felt dirty knowing that the money had originated in Byron's suffering.

"It's all for you, Lo. I've only ever wanted to give you the life I never had."

Logan cast his eyes on his hands, fidgeting. "Why did you think this would make me look at you differently?"

"I've done horrible things. Sometimes I wonder how your mother could forgive me."

"I wonder how you could forgive *them*."

"It was hard work, but worth it."

They sat in silence, both coming to terms with Byron's confession. Logan had already respected his dad so much; he couldn't have imagined that it would keep growing.

"Hang on, why did *Guilietta* set up the trust fund?"

"I killed Warner."

The ringing in his ears was back. "I thought he died in a plane crash?"

"Then her plan worked."

Whoa! "She wanted him dead?"

"Everyone wanted him dead. Anyway." Grinning broadly, Byron slapped Logan's knee. "What do you want to drink?"

"A few shots of Jäger?" he asked hopefully.

"A beer it is." Byron placed their order with the prospect manning the bar. "You can have Jäger to your heart's content when you go to Amsterdam."

Logan brightened. "You're letting me go?"

Byron mimed locking his lips and throwing away the key, although the waggle of his eyebrows spoke volumes.

"You actually got her to say yes!" Logan laughed happily, unable to believe his luck. "Jeez, dad, you're a smooth operator!"

"You owe me."

"Name it."

"Be my best man at the wedding."

"Isn't it a bit late to let Ryan know?"

Byron shrugged. "He'll get over it."

"Then you've got a deal." He lifted his bottle to Byron in salute. "It'll be an honor, old man."

Chuckling, Byron swiveled his seat and observed the party. "Luca looks much better now. I think it'll do her good to be exposed to more people and go to school. Look out for her until you graduate. By then, she should have her own friends."

"Yeah." Logan still didn't like the thought of sharing her with anyone. "Should I ask her about her mother?"

"Yes, but maybe not tonight. If I'm right and she's Jasmine's, I'll have to do what I can to get her away from the Falcons. Permanently."

"You can't save everyone, dad."

"Things could've been different, Lo. If I'd taken Guilietta's offer, Luca could have been raised here. We could've spared her all the violence she grew up with. Heck, *you* wouldn't have to walk on eggshells around her. You could've been dating by now."

Logan's heart clenched. "At what cost? Maybe you and mom would've broken up and I'd be calling someone else 'dad'. Maybe you would've *died*."

"Maybe." Byron finished his soda and rose to his feet. "I'm glad we're okay."

"Dad, there isn't anything you can say that'll make me love you less."

Byron's eyes softened and he pulled Logan into a hug. "Thank you, punk."

Savoring the embrace, Logan patted his stepfather on the back. "Go bang mom or something," he quipped, "you're starting to get too sentimental."

Byron stepped back with a laugh. "Have you got a date for the wedding yet?"

Logan's gaze landed on Luca. She was the obvious choice.

"She's invited anyway, now that she's part of the family." Byron peered at Logan, concerned. "It'll be good for you to bring someone else, take your mind off things."

"What are you implying?"

"You can't pretend to be an innocent virgin, four years down the line."

Logan blushed slightly. "I never should've told you."

"I'm serious, Lo. Find someone else."

"Why is this so important to you?"

"Because that girl is fifteen." Byron's facial expression brooked no argument. "I'm not saying it's never going to happen, but I won't stand for it while she's under my roof, especially considering what she's been through. I know we've been teasing you about it, but I want to make sure we understand each other."

Taking a long sip of his beer, Logan nodded. "We do."

"I'm proud of you, punk."

Logan smiled absently, watching Byron saunter through the crowd and join the others. He knew his father was right, but hated it. There had to be a way for him to have a happily ever after with Luca.

Three years won't kill you.

He spotted Connor chatting to Jesse, whose cheeks were red from the attention. Logan wondered when they were going to make it official. Why was she resisting Connor's charms? He could be a dick, yeah, but Logan knew that his friend kept his best side polished for Jesse. Was that part of the problem?

Who am I kidding? I know nothing of love, he thought wistfully, finishing his beer and ordering another.

Sophie's eyes were glued to her phone's screen, a smile tugging at the corners of her mouth. She must be chatting to her new guy. She's never looked like that because of *him*, that's for sure. He was happy for her.

Looking at her reminded him of the day he'd asked her to be his first, the pack of condoms Byron had provided—not to mention his mother's advice—burning a hole in the back pocket of his jeans. He'd been fourteen, curious and horny. And she had been the most incredible introduction to sex.

With the bond of their friendship making him feel comfortable enough to ask and do what he wouldn't have with someone else, he had explored her body at length and allowed her to do the same. His first time had been explosive, and the three times after that better still. He had taken tremendous pride in getting her to unravel, and to do so repeatedly.

That he'd been too young had never crossed his mind.

Although his parents didn't judge his choice to lose his virginity at fourteen—mostly because he's always been careful and responsible about it—he sensed that his mom would've preferred for him to have waited. She'd told him that Brennan had also had many sexual liaisons with women he hadn't loved.

Logan didn't appreciate the comparison since he loved and admired Sophie to this day. They might not be romantically involved, but that didn't mean that he didn't care about her and, from what he's heard, Brennan had hooked up with women simply because he felt it was his right.

"You okay there, Lo?" someone asked in the present.

He jerked and glanced to his left. It was jarring looking at his friend so soon after that particular walk down memory lane. He cleared his throat and replied: "Yeah, fine."

"You've been standing here for over ten minutes, staring into space." Sophie eyed him curiously. "Don't bullshit me."

He raked his fingers through his hair and breathed deeply. "I was remembering my first time."

"Digging in the archives, are we? You must be really sexually frustrated," she laughed. "Maybe you should call one of your regulars."

"My dad said something similar."

"You need to get laid. How long's it been, anyway?"

"Not since Nina, a few months ago."

"Damn." Her blue gaze traveled to Luca, who was attentively listening to Hallie and Aurora hash it out, as they so often did. "Being around someone you can't have isn't helping. The quickest way to get over her is to get with someone else."

"I know."

"And please help my brother with his game, while you're at it," she said, gesturing to Connor. "How long's it been since he said Jesse's his? He's yet to make his big move."

"She makes him shy."

Sophie rolled her eyes. "This generation of men are soft."

"Is *that* why you haven't banged Max yet?" Logan teased.

"No," she mumbled.

"Do you want to talk about it?"

"Nope. You'll tell me I'm being stupid."

"Sounds about right."

She turned to him. "Are you okay now?"

"Yes, thanks."

"Good. I'm glad your boner's settled down, too. I don't think it would've been cool if Luca saw, given her history." Sophie patted him on the shoulder with a mocking smile on her face. "Keep that shit contained, Drummond."

He threw his head back and cackled, feeling tons lighter, and hugged her. "Don't know what I'd do without you. Think I can slip away for a few hours?"

"Not unless you warn your parents. You've been drinking."

"Fine, I'll be responsible. Thanks for the chat, Soph." He walked to Luca, his heart stuttering when she looked up as if she's been aware of him this whole time. "Are you having fun?"

She nodded once.

"I'm going to duck out. I'll be back soon." When her gaze widened in panic, he hurried to set her mind at ease. "You'll be safe here."

"Can't I come with you?"

Not when it's you I'm trying to avoid. "Maybe next time, sweetheart."

Her facial expression fell and she turned her head.

"I won't be long," he assured her as he leaned in and kissed her temple. Horrified that he'd overstepped a boundary, he backed away and coughed. "I'm sorry."

"It's okay," she said, one corner of her mouth rising.

He swiveled on his heels without another word, eager to stick to the plan. He needed to blow off some steam or he'll lose his mind. His life was spinning out of control and, to top it off, she was moving in with them.

He should get a girlfriend.

He felt guilty for interrupting Connor's conversation with Jesse. "Dude, can I use your bike? I'll be back in an hour or two."

"This better be important," Connor muttered as he dug in the pocket of his jeans. He handed his key over. "Let your parents know, or I'll never hear the end of it."

"Thanks, Con."

"Just don't get me in trouble with your mom."

Logan shook his head with a laugh and headed out, typing a text to his mother on the way. He straddled Connor's Harley, which was bigger than his own, and ignited the engine. He clicked the helmet in place and pulled out of the parking spot, ignoring the constant vibration of his mobile against the top of his thigh. He stopped at a convenience store to buy protection and peeked at his messages.

Shit, Cinnia was pissed.

He sent another reassuring text in the hopes of diffusing the situation, but he had a suspicion he was going to be grounded for pulling this stunt.

The sex better be worth it.

Seven minutes later, he easily maneuvered the Harley between the cars parked in Fitz's driveway and cut the engine. From the sound of it, the party was in full swing. Stashing the helmet, he made his way inside, greeting everyone he passed.

"You made it!" some of them called out.

He took a detour to the kitchen to grab a soda. If he was going to have sex, he needed to sober up, pronto. He gulped half of it down and turned, freezing at the sight that met him. "What the fuck are *you* doing here?"

Meghan beamed at him deceptively sweetly. He was reminded of how that smile had pulled him in once, all the way to her bedroom, where he'd discovered the shrine of Byron in one corner. She'd also gate-crashed his seventeenth birthday party and insulted his mother.

"Logan! How's your dad?"

"Shut your fucking mouth, Meghan," he said through clenched teeth. "You're lucky we didn't press charges."

She pouted and threw back a shot of tequila. "He'd never do that. He loves me."

"He doesn't even know you exist."

Her eyes narrowed. "Of course he does! He's just waiting for me to turn eighteen so we can be together."

"You honestly believe…" He didn't know how to finish that sentence. Or why she hasn't been sent for psychiatric evaluation, for that matter: she was completely delusional! He couldn't deal with this shit, not after everything. Coming here was a bad idea. "Stay away from him," he warned as he left the kitchen, dead set on exiting the house.

He bumped into Nina in the entryway. She was holding hands with Vivienne, her best friend. They were swaying slightly, obviously intoxicated.

"Lo!" Nina exclaimed happily. "When did you get here?"

"Doesn't matter, I'm leaving."

"No!" She blocked his passage and exchanged Vivienne's hand for his, mostly to help her balance in those ridiculously high heels. "Stay."

He let out a short breath, undecided. "This was a mistake. I need to go."

Vivienne wordlessly stepped away to give her friend an opportunity to score, and Nina didn't waste it. She pressed her ample bosom to his chest and blinked up at him with faux innocence. Her breath was minty as she leaned in close to whisper: "I know why you came. Why are you still fighting this?" Her hand was warm through the material of his shirt. "We both need this, baby."

Shutting his eyes, his mind immediately conjured a vision of Luca being as brazen as Nina. His cock stirred, effectively making his decision for him. "Bedroom, now."

"That's more like it," she grinned, dragging him deeper into the house. Although those heels looked extremely uncomfortable, they put a hypnotic sway to her hips and he couldn't stop staring at her ass.

She stopped at the first empty room they could find, pushing him inside and locking the door. When she turned to him, she was barely suppressing her delight. Dressed in a low-cut, loose-fitting razer-back shirt and a short skirt, she had her best assets on display. Her blonde hair was piled on top of her head.

She was the total opposite of Luca.

They've messed around on occasion, so much so that she trusted him enough to use bondage and gags. The BDSM lifestyle intrigued him, though he wasn't sure why: it's not like his mother and stepfather had sex swings or other kinky paraphernalia. Maybe it was a Drummond thing: he's overheard conversations between his grandparents that have revealed as much.

"What now, baby?"

He caged her in against the door and bent his head to kiss her. She responded instantly, sliding her tongue over his while she rolled her hips to tease his erection. He wondered if Luca would ever do that to him and, instantly, his lust became incensed.

Nina moaned when he pulled her clothes off and loosened his jeans. She took a condom from him, sheathing his throbbing cock, and led it to her soaked entrance. She exclaimed his name when he thrust inside and wrapped her legs around his waist.

Gripping one of her tits in his hand while the other clutched her ass, he buried his face in her neck and pounded into her like a man possessed. Flashes of black hair, bronze skin and violet eyes filled his vision, no matter how hard he tried to keep them at bay. It wasn't fair to the girl he was currently fucking.

Not that it mattered: they were using each other.

Nina cried out as she reached orgasm and, with a final thrust, he followed her over the edge. Luca was on his mind; he bit down on his lip to stop her name from being vocalized.

"Hmm, that was pretty quick," Nina giggled, nibbling on his neck. "Not like you. Feeling better?"

"No."

He carried her to the bed and started all over again, swallowing her surprised gasp with a searing kiss. They explored each other's bodies slowly this time, making every caress count, and he spent a while devouring her pussy. The second time they fucked, he finished when she was on top of him. After the third, she was passed out under him.

He retreated with a sigh, disposing of the used condom. They've gone through the pack he'd bought, but it was becoming clear that he could fuck someone multiple times a night and still crave Luca. He was screwed.

Careful not to wake Nina, he got dressed and left the room. He shut the door and snuck out of the house, pretending not to hear his friends yelling after him. The Harley was a welcome sight though dread filled the pit of his stomach at the mere thought of his mother's mood.

It was a couple of minutes after nine when he arrived back. The party was reaching its crescendo, the music blaring out of the warehouse. Logan paused at the sight of a familiar silhouette, swallowed past his nerves, and headed right for her.

"Sorry, ma."

Her arms were crossed over her chest, face stern. "I don't even know what to say to you."

"You can think about it and let me know."

"Don't get cute," she said, narrowing her eyes. "First of all, you rode after drinking. And for what, tail? Jesus, Logan!"

He hung his head. He would like to point out that it had been one beer and that Byron had encouraged this behavior, but not only would it cause a bigger argument, he didn't think his stepdad had meant for Logan to pursue sex *tonight*.

"You're grounded for a month."

Ouch. Harsher than I'd thought. "I figured I would be."

"Keep this up and you won't go to Amsterdam anymore."

"Noted."

Losing her mean exterior, she linked their arms together and bumped her hip on his. "You make me so angry."

"I know." He pecked her on the cheek. "I'm sorry."

She sighed deeply and squeezed him tighter. "Were you at least safe?"

"Yeah," he replied, knowing that she was referring to more than just the ride. "Always am. You guys raised me right."

"Sometimes I wonder."

He hugged her. "You shouldn't. So many of my friends can't even talk to their parents about sex, much less get advice. I'm lucky that you two have always been open about it."

"Fine, you're grounded for two weeks."

"Thanks, momma." He knew how much she adored it when he called her that. He fluttered his eyelashes at her. "I love you."

She barked a laugh, shaking her head. "Don't push your luck, boy."

CHAPTER SIX

BEING GROUNDED FOR fourteen days ended up working in his favor: during that time, he'd been able to keep an eye on Luca while she settled in. Cinnia had made a special arrangement with the high school and, by the following Tuesday, Luca was accompanying Logan every morning.

Despite being shy, he could tell how much she enjoyed school. She was the first one in and last one out of every class, and her violet eyes shone brightly by the end of the day: the total opposite of other teenagers' experiences. When he had football practice, she sat in the stands while she waited for him to finish, either reading a book or doing homework.

Unfortunately, he wasn't the only adolescent boy that appreciated her striking physical features. If it wasn't for the fact that he continually blocked other guys from approaching her—*for her protection,* he told himself—the hordes would descend.

Everyone wanted a piece of the new girl, and word of her spread fast.

At one point, a suspicious car frequented the parking lot of the school. When his uncle had run the number plates through a hacked government database, they'd learned the car had been listed as stolen. Haye had tipped off the cops and the vehicle had then been found abandoned at a nearby park. Since then, the surveillance on Luca and, to a lesser extent, Logan doubled.

As long as she was safe, Logan didn't much care what the MC did. He was ready to wipe the Falcons off the face of the planet by any means necessary, although he knew he wouldn't get much support for such a hot-headed plan. Now that he was Prez, he had to take everyone's feelings into consideration before he decided.

The final bell rang, and the seniors heaved a collective sigh of relief. It was Friday, and everyone was excited about yet another party at Fitz's house. His parents went away so often that Fitz practically lived alone: he made up for the loneliness by constantly surrounding himself with people and noise.

Gathering his books, Logan rose from his seat and headed to the hallway. The closer he got to the end of his final year, the more work he had to revise for the upcoming exam block. It also meant that his parents' wedding was around the corner, and so was the trip to Amsterdam.

"Lo!" Fitz joined his side and slapped him on the shoulder. "Please say you're going to be there tonight!"

"Wouldn't miss it," Logan chuckled.

"And Luca?"

Logan shrugged. "I'll ask, but I doubt she'll say yes."

Fitz shook his head sadly. "That's too bad. She's so fine! Would love to see her unwind for a change."

"You are controlled by your hormones."

"Pffft, as if *you* wouldn't tap that."

Don't even go there.

They exited the school building and the rest of his friends joined them, chattering excitedly about Fitz's "small get-together". The girls were quizzing each other on outfits, while the boys spoke about how plastered they were going to get. Logan grinned, allowing himself to be a kid for a few minutes. At school, he didn't have to consider the repercussions of his actions much.

The group fell silent, and Logan glanced up with a frown, which smoothed out when he spotted Luca's approach. He didn't understand why the girls didn't make more of an effort to get to know her. Were they intimidated by her appearance? Or did she refuse to engage with them?

"Hey," he greeted, holding his arm out. Gaze cast to the ground, she took hold of his bicep. Was Logan imagining the venomous glares the girls sent her way? "How was your day?"

"Good, thanks," Luca mumbled in reply, "yours?"

"Long." He bumped his fist against the boys' in farewell, giving some of the girls a sideways hug. "See you tonight!" he called over his shoulder as he strode to his bike with Luca on his arm.

"What's happening tonight?" she asked once they were out of earshot.

"Party at Fitz's house. Do you want to come?"

She chewed on her bottom lip. "Will there be a lot of people?"

"Yes."

"Then no, thanks. I don't think I'm ready for that."

Logan had expected as much. With a curt nod, he watched her get on the bike, shifting back and waiting for him to do the same. He stared at her for a moment, once again mesmerized.

Her thick, wavy dark hair had been trimmed recently, but it went all the way down to her waist. She wore baggy distressed jeans with black ankle boots and a matching long-sleeved shirt. He knew she preferred to wear neutral colors so as not to attract attention, yet she came across as a stylish rebel and garnered awed scrutiny wherever she went. It didn't help that she was one of the prettiest girls at school.

"Logan?"

Snapping out of the spell she'd unknowingly cast on him, he moved forward, only to stop at the feel of his phone vibrating in his pocket. "Hey, mom."

"Oh good, I caught you before you left school!"

Eyes narrowing at her nervous tone, he asked: "What's wrong?"

"Could you...?" She cleared her throat and muttered something away from the microphone, presumably to someone next to her. "Please come to your gran's shop. I need your advice."

"Which one? The one in the mall or—"

"No, the boutique. Bring Luca."

Logan grinned broadly. "Pre-wedding jitters?"

"Just get here!" Cinnia pleaded, hanging up.

He chuckled as he slipped the phone into his pocket and secured his shoulder bag diagonally over his chest. He mounted the bike, glancing at Luca. "Change of plans."

"Why?"

"You'll see."

He ignited the engine and pulled out of the parking lot, aware of the eyes on them. He barely noticed the two other Harleys that trailed behind them, distracted by the feel of Luca's arms around his waist. Would he ever get used to it?

Mid-afternoon traffic was congested around the school and on the way to Mysie's boutique, called *Jolie*. To this day, Logan had no idea why his grandmother had settled on that name when she was the furthest thing from French, but it made a clear distinction between *Drummond's Tailors* and the place she co-owned with aunt Piper. *Jolie* has opened three other branches in nearby towns that were doing well. Due to his aunt's influence, they specialized in women's apparel and undergarments.

Stopping at the curb, Logan waited for Luca to dismount and did the same. They stuffed their helmets in the side panniers. "This is my gran and aunt's place." He led the way inside. "Mom?"

"Here!" came her anxious voice from the back of the shop.

The changing rooms were there, and he hoped he wasn't about to see his mother in lingerie or, worse still, nothing at all. He's lost count of how many times he's walked in on her and Byron and was fine with nudity, but that didn't mean he wanted to scar Luca.

When they rounded the corner, he stopped in his tracks, his jaw hitting the floor.

"See?" Cinnia stressed, glaring at Piper. "I told you it's too much!"

"It's not!" Piper stood with her hands on her hips. Her curls made her look artistically deranged today, like a mad scientist. "Logan, tell your mother this dress is amazing on her!"

He would, once he remembered how to speak.

The dress was form-fitting and, at first glance, didn't look like a dress at all. It was as if someone had painted dark green lace and shiny emeralds all over the upper part of her body. The swirling patterns were incredibly flattering: displaying his mother's toned and tattooed back, while keeping her chest conservatively covered. From mid-thigh, it flared out in a solid shade of green, breaking away from the delicate design of the top part.

"Wow, Mrs. Drummond," Luca murmured. She took a step forward to touch the material. "This is so beautiful."

Cinnia looked hopeful. "Really?"

"Yes. It's exquisite! Will you be wearing your hair up?"

"That's the plan," Cinnia answered. Her demeanor softened and a slight blush tinted her cheeks. "Are you sure it's not too much?"

"Mom, you look incredible," Logan said, finding his voice.

"*I told you!*" Piper sang triumphantly.

"Real question, though: how the heck are you gonna keep the wedding PG13? You know you're only allowed to bang *after* the ceremony, right?"

Cinnia's blush deepened, and his aunt sent him a look of warning.

"All I'm saying is that dad's going to love it," Logan amended.

"That's exactly what I said," Piper agreed, mouthing "thank you" to him. "Damn, Cin, your body hasn't changed since the last time I fitted you for a wedding dress. Bitch."

Cinnia laughed. "Of course it has!"

Piper pointed to her jean-clad thighs, which have filled out over the years. "You don't have this to deal with."

"You women are crazy," Logan sighed, plopping down on a sofa. "You all look beautiful!"

Shaking her head, Piper remarked: "You've raised him well, Cin. All Dane ever tells me is that I should delve into my Self—with a capital S, mind you— and realize that I am not my body. That I am, in fact, everything *except* my body. And that, when I die, none of this will matter, anyway."

"At least he thinks about the bigger picture. All Logan cares about is football, rock-climbing, and Amsterdam."

"Ouch, momma. I'm sitting right here."

Luca seemed to find the exchange mightily entertaining, hiding her grin behind a hand.

"Boys! The reason for my grey hair." Piper let out a long breath and turned to Luca, regarding the girl seriously. "Have you got an outfit for the wedding yet?"

"No," Luca answered softly.

"You should pick something while we're here, Luca," Cinnia urged. "Piper can help."

"Oh my gosh, say no more! This is going to be so much *fun!*" Piper grabbed Luca's hand and dragged her into the main part of the shop.

Logan rubbed the back of his neck with a chuckle. "Where are the rest of your bridesmaids?"

"They'll be here soon."

"Right, let's hope Luca finds something before that. I have plans."

Cinnia rolled her eyes and turned to her reflection in the mirror. The uncertainty that had greeted Logan has dissipated, revealing the modest confidence she usually exuded. "I doubt she will if Piper has her way. You don't have to stay if you've got better things to do."

"I'm good," Logan shrugged. "That dress really looks amazing, by the way."

"Your dad insisted that Piper make something 'green, with lace'."

"Damn, woman, you are whipped."

"Remind me how you're my kid again?"

"Well, see, you and Brennan loved each other very much and wanted a souvenir. So, you called a random woman to get knocked up on your behalf." He waggled his eyebrows theatrically. "Nine months later, *et voila*! Logan Bean Drummond, in the flesh."

She burst out laughing, taking a seat next to him. "That's the shortened, more humorous version. Have you got a tux yet?"

"Unless you want me telling dad what he's missing out on, I'm not breathing another word."

"Fine." She rested her head on his shoulder. "I can't believe it's almost time."

"It's *about* time, if you ask me. Raising a kid out of wedlock... Shame on you."

"I'm scared, Lo."

He frowned, confused. "Why?"

"We've been together so long. What if something changes?"

"I can't believe you're being the cliché, mom. You're doomed to spend the rest of your life with dad, 'cause he doesn't have eyes for anyone else."

"That sounds like something I can live with." Women's voices drew closer and Cinnia rose. "Brace yourself."

Jemma crossed the threshold first, screeching excitedly. "Oh my God, *Cin*!"

"You look *phenomenal*!" Dawn chimed in.

"Piper's totally outdone herself!" Jemma continued.

Jesse, Aurora and Hallie entered last, and Logan plugged his ears at the ensuing sound: most of it coming from Aurora. "Hopefully you've got it out of your system now, 'cause this shit won't fly at the wedding."

"Language!" his mother reprimanded him.

He had no clue how she'd even heard that over the noise of four zealous women. Damn, they acted bizarrely about weddings! He was tolerant to a point but, like many other men, could only handle so much at one time. Luckily, Jesse and Hallie were able to contain themselves. Between Hallie and Dane, he could never pinpoint who was more blasé about life.

He looked up when Luca and Piper returned, the former seeming cautiously optimistic at the choices draped over the latter's arm.

"Why don't you try them on while I sort out these hooligans?" Piper suggested with a friendly smile, gesturing to the first cubicle.

Logan got up. The girl that frequented his fantasies was about to get naked, which meant that he needed to get the hell out of Dodge. "Mom, do you still need me?"

Cinnia pulled him into a quick hug. "Nah, you can go. I'll drive Luca home."

"Great, thanks." He avoided eye contact with Aurora, high-fived his cousin, and gave Jesse a small smile. Then he backed out of the room, suppressing a laugh. "By the way, I'm going to a party tonight. Bye!"

"What party? Logan!" his mother yelled after him. "Get back here!"

"Can't hear you!" he exclaimed as he ran for the safety of his motorcycle. He got on and rode home, glad to get away from the drama. *Or maybe not,* he thought as he neared the house. Connor was in the driveway, leaning against his Harley.

Stopping next to his friend, Logan cut the engine. "What's up, bro?"

"Sorry I didn't let you know I was coming. I've been working for two days straight and needed a break."

That wasn't the whole reason, but Logan would wheedle it out of Connor eventually. He nodded and strode to the front door. "You look like you need a beer."

"I won't say no."

"Coming right up. Wait here," he added, pointing to the living room. He got two ice cold bottles from the fridge and took them to his friend, eyeing the man speculatively.

Connor was a head shorter than Logan, but still a huge hit with the ladies. He had the same build as Nixon: broad shoulders, tapered waist, and muscular legs. He kept his dark blond hair short, military-style, mostly because his entire life consisted of his ongoing studies in medicine and his residency at the hospital and, as such, he didn't have time to keep up with the latest trends.

The scar over his right eye, courtesy of a parkour-trick-gone-wrong when they'd been younger, was paler than usual today, hinting at a lack of sleep.

"Thanks, man." Connor accepted the beer and gulped down half of it. "Fuck, I needed this."

"Wanna talk about it?"

Connor began picking at the label. "I asked Jesse to go to the wedding with me. She said no."

Logan wondered why: he knew for a fact that Jesse was infatuated with Connor. "Did she give you an explanation?"

"No."

"That's rough."

"Yeah." Connor sighed deeply and leaned back on the couch. "Our trip to Amsterdam can't come soon enough, man."

Logan dipped his chin in agreement. A month after his parents' nuptials, Connor and Logan were going to the Netherlands for three months. They were lucky enough to have the flight tickets and visas taken care of, although they've had to line up bartending jobs to fund their accommodation and the wild partying on their agenda.

"What if she doesn't like me?" Connor asked quietly.

"She does, Con. Whatever this is, I don't think it's you."

"You keep saying that, and yet she rejected me." He gazed at Logan, somberly. "What makes you so sure?"

"You just have to believe me."

"Nah-ah, Drummond, spit it out. Did you make this shit up for your own entertainment?"

"She made me promise, dude."

"I don't give a fuck." Connor straightened and leaned forward, fixing Logan with a solid glare. "Is there someone else? I swear to God, if some other motherfucker thinks he can put one filthy finger on her—"

"Jesus, you're dramatic," Logan interrupted with a laugh. "I know she's obsessed with you because of what she writes."

Connor froze. "How the fuck would *you* know? She never lets me read anything!"

"I, uh…" Logan coughed uncomfortably. "I was reading this story online, right, and left a comment for the author. She replied and, I dunno, I noticed a Jesse-nuance or whatever, so I texted to ask if it was her. She said yes, but made me swear not to tell anyone."

"What's the book about?"

"From the sound of things, you."

Scoffing, Connor finished his beer. "You must be joking."

"You don't understand, Con. The way she describes the character in her book... Except for the difference in names—and even *that's* not so different—it's you, down to an art." He gestured to his friend's face. "She even got the scar in there."

"Give me the name. Nope, don't even try that puppy-dog look on me. We both know I'm not gonna quit until you give it to me, so stop wasting our time."

"Will you promise to keep it down when we start living together?"

"I can't promise that." Connor grinned naughtily. "You know why."

"Man-whore." Logan got his phone out and opened the app on which he'd found Jesse's work. He sent Connor the link. "Maybe *that's* why she won't go to the wedding with you."

Connor ignored the jibe, smiling when his phone pinged. "Thanks, man. I'll see if you're right."

"I'm warning you: it gets very steamy. That's actually why I stopped reading." Logan pulled a face. "I didn't want to get hard because of the two of *you*. It's fucking creepy."

"What do you mean?"

"The main character is basically Jesse, although she's got some weird ideas about her looks. She doesn't think she's pretty," Logan explained when Connor made an impatient gesture.

"I'll spank that idea right out of her."

"TMI, dude." He brightened, remembering about the party later. "Hey, do you wanna come to Fitz's with me? There will be hot girls. That should help with your asshole routine."

"The last thing I need is to hook up with someone who's underage. I'm twenty-three, Lo."

"Yeah, old man, I'm not likely to forget that."

"Fuck off."

"Come on, it'll be fun! Are you working tomorrow?" Connor shook his head, and the smile on Logan's face widened. "See? This is meant to be. Maybe you'll get a date to the wedding and make Jesse jealous."

The idea seemed to become more appealing. "Okay, fine. I'll come."

"If you wear your cut, chicks will be all over you."

"This ain't my first time," Connor drawled.

"There might even be a fight."

A delighted glimmer entered Connor's eyes. Logan has uttered the magic words. The only thing the man loved more than fucking was fighting. It's something Nixon has unintentionally passed down to his son.

All these family cycles, Logan mused. *What bad habits am I continuing?*

"Now you're talking. Let's get another beer."

They headed to the kitchen. Logan finished the bottle in his hand and retrieved another two from the fridge. "Maybe you should stop being such a prick and just tell her how you feel," he hedged, removing the caps before giving Connor one.

"Do you think I don't know that?" Connor scrubbed a hand over his head and sighed deeply. "It's hard, okay? I don't want her with anyone else, but I don't think that she should be with me, either. I'm fucked up."

Logan sent his gaze to the ceiling. "Are you kidding me with this tortured shit?"

"Like *you're* one to talk."

"Hey, my situation is entirely different."

"You can have any girl you want, but you're stuck on someone who'll never be one hundred percent okay with physical contact. I mean, she'll have nightmares and flashbacks, like your parents do. I know you aspire to have what they have, but that doesn't mean you should copy them from beginning to end. Why don't you try falling for someone who's not afraid to show her feelings?"

Connor, in that abrasive way of his, was cutting closer to the bone than anyone. Logan chucked the caps in the direction of the sink and took a long drink of beer. "Do you want my fist through your face?"

"Make my day," Connor grinned. "We haven't done that in a while."

Their childhood had been riddled with fights. Connor was the older brother Logan never had and, even though he had preferred Sophie's company, Connor was the only one who could keep up with Logan's daredevil side.

"You can be such a dick."

"I'm the one who keeps shit real." Connor lifted a shoulder. "It's not my fault people aren't ready for the truth."

"Bear *the truth* in mind the next time you talk to Jesse." He motioned for Connor to follow him. "Let's play *Halo*."

When Cinnia and Luca walked in two hours later, Logan and Connor were on the living room floor. They'd removed their shirts at some point and were swearing at each other while they played Xbox. There were eleven empty beer bottles scattered around them. Logan had a thrilling buzz going, and not even the disapproving look his mother gave him could dampen his mood.

"Hello, Connor."

"Hey, soon-to-be Mrs. J!"

Logan tried to keep a straight face. Fuck, he'd missed hanging out with Connor!

"If this is what the people of Amsterdam have to look forward to, I should send my apologies in advance," Cinnia muttered, walking to the kitchen.

Luca's eyes were wide as she took in their current state. Her one hand held a shopping bag, while the other was fisted.

"Did you get something you like, sweetheart?"

She didn't answer. Her violet gaze pinned him to the spot. Then, turning on her heel, she stormed up the stairs.

"What's up with her?" Connor snorted.

"Dunno."

"*I* think Amsterdam is going to love us. We'll fit right in!"

"I'm telling you, dude. Maybe it'll be so good, we'll move there!"

"Only if Jesse comes with."

"Man, do you have it bad or what?"

"Look who's talking."

The front door opened again. Byron paused once he spotted the two in the living room, pushing his hands into the pockets of his formal pants. His jacket, like the top button of his crisp white shirt, was undone. "Hey, boys," he greeted tentatively.

"Mr. Hero, sir."

Logan punched Connor on the shoulder, laughing.

Byron raised his eyebrows. "Having fun?"

"Harmless fun, dad. Please tell mom to stop worrying." Logan waggled his eyebrows, knowing how he could derail the interrogation that was bound to ensue. The last thing they needed was a speech from an ex-addict: Connor got enough of that from Nixon, too. "You're gonna shit yourself when you see her wedding dress! For real, dad, you're marrying one hot mama."

Fighting a smile, Byron loosened his tie. "This isn't over. We'll talk tomorrow."

"Actually, about that…" Logan paused the game, much to Connor's dismay. "Can you drop us off at Fitz's later?"

"I suppose I should be grateful that you have enough sense not to get behind the wheel," Byron replied after a long silence.

"You da man!" Connor cheered.

"Thanks, dad. Mom's in the kitchen."

When they were left alone, Connor sniggered. "Damn, Lo, you know how to play them."

"Don't pretend as if you've never done the same."

"My mother is a fucking drill sergeant." Connor shuddered. "She runs that household like clockwork. Dad lets me get away with shit, although he's strict with Soph. I don't know why he bothers: she's been going to clubs since she was fourteen."

"Speaking of, have you met Max?"

"Yeah, he's a really cool guy. They'll probably get married next year."

"She hasn't mentioned much."

Connor tilted his head to the side, surprised. "Seriously? You guys talk about everything."

"It's weird, right?"

"Maybe, *because* you're so close, she doesn't want you to meet him yet. Maybe you're some kind of rite of passage Max has to work up to."

"That makes me feel better."

"I'm just glad *you're* not her boyfriend." Connor lifted a shoulder. "No offense, Lo. I love you like a brother, but that doesn't mean I want you to be my brother-in-law."

"Soph and I will always be friends, although I'll be lying if I said her latest YouTube video didn't do something for me."

Connor glared daggers at Logan. "Careful."

"Even you have to admit she knows how to move!"

"Sometimes I wish mom never sent her to dance lessons. The number of times I've had to put up with this shit…"

"*I* thank Dr. Tyrell every damn day," Logan joked, mostly to get a rile out of Connor.

"Keep talking smack about Soph. It's not like I've had a rough week or anything."

Logan took note of Connor's fists, the rigid tension in his shoulders, and decided to back down. As much as they loved pissing each other off, he wasn't in the mood for a physical fight. "You're right, I'm sorry. Let's go get ready for the party."

That dangerous glint in Connor's eyes dimmed. "Sweet. I'll need a new shirt."

"Got you covered, bro."

They dumped the empty beer bottles in the kitchen, where Cinnia and Byron were talking in hushed tones, and headed upstairs to Logan's bedroom. Logan was not looking forward to his parents sitting him down the following day to discuss his drunken behavior.

"We should go climbing tomorrow," Connor remarked, shutting the door behind him.

"You're speaking my language." He opened his closet and motioned for Connor to help himself. Whatever the man chose would span very tightly over his upper body. He was ripped. "Best way to get rid of a hangover."

Connor perused his options carefully. "Can it just be us, though? I don't feel like being around the rest of the gang."

"Tess is out of town and uncle Teagan's busy, as far as I know. I haven't spoken to Soph, but she probably has plans with her guy."

"Nah, I think she'll come."

"I'll text her." Logan got his phone out to do that, and connected it to a Bluetooth speaker to play music. "Jeez, Con, pick a shirt already."

"Totally zoned out." Connor grabbed a red one from the large pile. "Remind me why I want to be a doctor?"

"So that you can give your patients sexual healing?" Logan teased.

Connor nodded, pulling Logan's shirt over his head. He seemed amused by their difference in size. "How could I forget? Seriously though, you should see the way some of them look at me, as if I can't possibly be bright enough to accurately diagnose, let alone *fix*, their medical issues. It's like they keep waiting for the lights to dim, music to play and me to start stripping. I have to remind myself that my foot up their asses will only exacerbate the situation."

"Wow, you actually used 'exacerbate' correctly."

Rolling his eyes, Connor sat on the edge of Logan's bed. "Big words impress Jesse."

"Let's hope that's not the only big thing that impresses her," Logan chuckled. He selected a light grey muscle T-shirt. He couldn't wait to add more ink to his body, since the only tattoo his mom has allowed him to get was the customary Raptors MC crest on his left shoulder. "We all know that you can *be* a big dick, but she doesn't know that you also *have* one."

"You'll know when she finds out," Connor grinned.

"Gross." Logan sprayed deodorant under his pits and chucked the can in Connor's direction. Then he got his climbing bag from under the bed, double-checking that everything they'll need tomorrow was packed. It was one less thing to do later. "Do you want to eat before we go?"

"Yeah, let's make a sandwich. We can get something that's bad for us on the way back from Fitz's."

They trudged to the kitchen, chatting about Connor's residency and Logan's applications to various universities while they pulled a quick snack together. Logan could barely wait to move in with Connor next year. They'd already picked out an apartment, which grandpa Reade owned, and arranged to start renting it once they got back from Amsterdam.

Putting their dirty plates and cutlery in the dishwasher afterward, Logan pecked his mother on the cheek. "We're off."

"Please don't do anything stupid," Cinnia said, doing her best to keep the edge out of her tone. "You just got out of being grounded."

"Don't sweat it, Mrs. D, I'll keep him in check," Connor chuckled, draping an arm over Logan's shoulders.

"It's not only him I'm worried about."

Connor lifted a hand to his heart in a dramatic fashion. "You wound me."

"I'm serious, Connor. We know how you get when you're overworked."

"I'll take it easy for once."

No one believed him, which was why no one said anything. Byron met them at the car and Logan slid onto the passenger seat. Now that he had food in his stomach, he felt more grounded. He was certain his stepfather could appreciate the change.

"Are you sleeping over?" Byron asked, reversing out of the driveway.

"Nah, we've got an early day tomorrow. Can you fetch us at, say, eleven?"

"Sure." Byron glanced at Logan. "What do you mean by early day?"

"We're going rock-climbing." The tense silence that followed had Logan shifting in his seat. "Dad, come on."

"I know you're eighteen and legal, Lo, but I'll always worry that you're taking it too far, and your mother will always want you to stay her little boy. That's all I have to say about the alcohol. As for rock-climbing, I don't take issue with it, but you're gonna owe me for distracting your mother about it."

"Name your price."

"I'll think about it and let you know."

Satisfied with that arrangement, Logan turned to chat with Connor for the rest of the ride. Cars were already parked outside Fitz's house by the time they arrived. Byron pulled over at the curb and waved them off.

"He's easily one of the coolest dudes ever," Connor commented.

"Agreed."

Logan's spirits lifted at the familiar sound of loud music and booming voices. In less than three months, high school will be over and, to an extent, so will these parties. Striding to the front door, Logan located his friends in the billiard room. Fitzgerald Mason's parents were obscenely rich and liked showing it off, and yet Logan's friend was one of the most down-to-earth guys he knew. If Fitz couldn't laugh about something, to him it simply wasn't worth doing or pursuing.

"I didn't sign up for a sausage fest," Logan announced.

Fitz glanced up from a game of pool, his grin widening. "Then you've come to the wrong place. What's up, Con? Long time, man."

Connor shrugged, eyeing the bar. "Seriously though, where are the chicks? It's literally the only reason I let Logan talk me into hanging out with you losers."

Jason and Carlisle burst out laughing, while Jordan walked up to Connor to shake his hand. They were used to Connor's mood swings, considering how long they've known him. They, like Logan, always tried to add to that runaway temper.

"You know how girls get about looking perfect," Carlisle reminded him. "Wanna play with sticks and balls in the meantime?"

Rolling his eyes, Connor relieved Fitz of his pool cue. "Let's go, Gordon."

"Ooh, it's on, Tyrell."

Fitz got everyone another round of beers and shooters, while Logan joined a conversation with his teammates, who were some of his closest friends. As the captain, he believed that a team worked together seamlessly when they knew each other's deepest fears.

By eight-thirty, the large house was crowded. It seemed as if the seniors of every high school in town had decided to show up, whether they were invited or not. Logan saw Connor hitting it off with a girl whose dyed hair resembled Jesse's natural mane—and by "hitting it off" he meant "had his tongue down her throat"—and the other guys flirting with those wearing exceptionally short skirts.

"Bored?"

Looking to his right, he gave Nina a slight smile. "On the contrary. I enjoy observing people."

"Want to observe me?"

Oh, it was tempting, but he'd forgotten a vitally important ingredient. "I don't have condoms."

"I've got you covered, babe."

Nina clutched his hand and led the way to Fitz's bedroom. Logan was going to have a lot of explaining to do later, but his cock has taken over as the primary decision-maker. He didn't hesitate when Nina locked the door.

Thinking of Luca while balls-deep in Nina has become the norm. He hasn't made any promises of commitment, yet they both agreed that they would only fuck each other. She didn't push him for an emotional connection: she will be moving overseas once she graduated and becoming romantically entangled was the last thing on her mind.

Sexual liaisons with Nina were always mutually satisfying. Logan was breathing harshly by the end of it, watching her stretch like a satisfied cat before she rolled off him and started putting her clothes back on. There was a pang in his heart: when was the last time he'd cuddled with someone?

Sophie was the only girl you ever held after sex and, even then, it wasn't a regular occurrence.

He felt like he should get a girlfriend, but that was difficult to do when Luca was the only person he was interested in. If they got together, would she prove Connor right by never fully trusting Logan, or would he manage to get through to her eventually?

"Lo, you good?"

Clearing his throat, he turned to put his feet on the carpet and pulled the condom off. "Yeah."

Nina narrowed her eyes. "It looks like you need another round."

"Nah, I'm okay."

"This is about fun, remember?" Topless, she ambled over to him and rested her hands on his shoulders. "Your face says you haven't had fun and that hurts my feelings."

He chuckled. "I had plenty of fun."

"Can I have Dominating Logan for an hour?"

His face hardened. She was tapping into his favorite part about sex and the only thing that ever fully distracted him. He usually wouldn't do this under the influence, but his dick was already hard again, effectively preventing him from thinking about anything except exerting control.

"On your knees."

She bit her bottom lip and obeyed, kneeling between his legs and dropping her gaze from his.

"Suck my cock."

Without hesitation, she took him in her mouth with a soft moan. Her tongue swirled over his shaft to make him wet, and then she applied suction. He clenched his jaw at the resulting sensation, breathing deeply to maintain control.

"Deeper," he urged. Nina whimpered as he gave an experimental thrust to show her how far he wanted to go. There was some resistance as he hit her gag reflex, and his balls tightened at the feel of her tongue flexing around his tip. "Open up and take me deeper." When he hit the back of her throat, he gasped. She trusted him not to hurt her and he gently moved his hips to get more friction.

She accepted his hurried pace, mewling at how he was using her.

"I'm gonna cum, tap my thighs if you don't want to swallow."

She didn't.

With a low growl, he pounded faster and erupted, throwing his head back at the tingle in the base of his spine. "Fuck!"

Obediently, she remained where she was until he told her to get up.

"Look at you." He rose to his feet, cupping her jaw. "Ready for the taking, but that's not going to happen tonight."

For a brief moment, her stunned gaze flicked to his.

"You heard me. Until the next time I see you, you won't make yourself cum." Gripping her hair in his hand, he tilted her head back to make eye contact. "If you slip up and give in, you will receive ten lashings for every orgasm you had without permission. Am I clear?"

Her eyelids fluttered and her mouth was swollen from the blowjob. "Yes, sir."

"Good." Leaning in to lick a thin trail of his orgasm from her chin, he kissed her deeply for a few seconds. "Get dressed." He did the same, his mind already focused on finding Connor so they could go home. "We'll pick this up in a week."

"Logan?" she called out as he unlocked the door.

He stared at her. "Yes?"

"Were you serious? Will you really punish me?"

She was right to ask, since they've only dabbled in bondage before. "Deadly serious. Don't you want that? Did I read it wrong?"

Looking relieved, she shook her head. "I didn't know how to ask, but it's something I want. Can I bring a riding crop?"

He raised an eyebrow. "Are you planning on disobeying?"

"Just in case," she amended, hiding a smile.

"Alright. See you then."

Forty minutes and five rounds of shots later, Connor and Logan were stumbling into the Johannson house, ignoring Byron's knowing chuckles. Logan's vision was blurry, and he had no idea how they remained upright. Connor had been running on empty for too long. Logan wasn't much better off.

"Thanks for being our taxi, dad."

"You da man!" Connor cheered for the second time.

"Get some rest, guys. I'll lock up."

Logan led the way to his room and they passed out without further preamble.

He jerked awake what could've been mere minutes later, feeling as if he's forgotten something. Blinking in the darkness of his room, he heard his friend's soft snores and checked his alarm clock for the time. 5:02 AM. He rubbed his throbbing forehead and grunted: "Con."

Except for becoming quiet, Connor didn't give any other indication that he heard.

"Con," Logan said again, smacking his friend with the back of his hand.

"Get up."

"Why?" Connor croaked miserably.

"Time to go climbing."

"Fuck off."

Logan turned a lamp on and swung his legs off the bed. "Come on."

"Okay." Connor yawned, following suit. "I need a shower."

"Use my bathroom, but hurry, unless you want to share."

"I've seen enough of your ass to last me a lifetime," Connor remarked, exiting the room.

Logan went downstairs to make coffee, surprised to find Luca in the kitchen drinking tea. "Morning."

"Morning."

She wasn't looking at him directly. "Did I scare you yesterday?"

"A little."

"I'm sorry. I didn't mean to."

She finished her drink. "I know. Have fun climbing."

"Do you want to join us?" he asked hopefully.

"No, thank you. I don't think it's my thing."

"Okay," he whispered as his gaze followed her out. He had to remind himself that she's only lived a relatively normal life for about two months. He shouldn't become demotivated.

"I could kiss you," Connor moaned when Logan brought him a cup of coffee. He immediately gulped down half its contents. "Fuck, it's the good stuff."

"Thank my mom," Logan chuckled. "Help yourself to clothes. I'll be quick."

They were out the door ten minutes later, each admiring the lightening sky. They got on their respective Harleys and headed to the lake, which was a twenty-five-minute ride from Logan's place. Logan thought how lucky he was to have grown up here. People could say what they want about city life, but he preferred these rolling mountains over skyscrapers.

That's funny. Don't you want to be an architect? Oh no, wait, a footballer! Do you even know who you are?

He hoped whichever climb they chose today would kick his ass and snap him out of that mental spiral.

There was a gathering at the lake already, much to Logan's surprise. He counted six cars as he came to a stop. It's not often that these climbs garnered attention from a big group. Lifting his helmet off, he saw Connor do the same.

"Weird, huh?"

"Fuck if I know," Connor shrugged.

"There you are!"

Logan smiled once he recognized Sophie, who was rushing towards them. "Hey!" he greeted, pulling her into a tight hug. "You made it!"

"I tried to get a hold of you after you texted me," she informed him.

"Ah." He stepped back sheepishly. "Party."

She rolled her eyes. "That figures. Well, I brought friends!"

"Jesus, Soph," Connor muttered, "how many people do you actually know?"

"A few. Come on, let me introduce you."

"I hope you told them to bring their own ropes," Logan said, trailing behind her less enthusiastically. This was his and Connor's least desirable scenario.

"Don't worry, they've all done this before."

Logan's eyes were immediately drawn to a woman with bright pink hair, cut short. She had an easy smile on her heart-shaped face and a dimple on her right cheek. Her left ear had at least six piercings along the top curve, and three in the lobe. Her body was athletic, and her behind was the perfect combination of full and toned. She wore dark grey yoga pants, lime green trainers, and a neon yellow sports bra, putting the athletic definition of her stomach and lower back on display. She didn't seem to mind the cool, early morning breeze.

He couldn't look away. Something about her pulled him in, like a moth to a flame. His shameless ogling must've tipped her off, since she glanced his way with soulful brown eyes. One corner of her mouth tilted up.

Logan did his best to give Sophie his full attention, succeeding only when she gestured to the woman he'd been staring at and declared with flourish: "And this is Alyssa. She's the fucking bee's knees."

Alyssa rolled her eyes and held her hand out. "I wouldn't trust her on that, if I were you. She thinks she has a flat ass. Call me Lys."

At the touch of her hand, he became addicted.

CHAPTER SEVEN

LOGAN COULD BARELY contain his excitement and ended up pacing next to his Harley while he waited. He did his best to clear his mind, but he could only think about the pink-haired beauty that has captured his heart.

That's a bit dramatic.

Sadly, he didn't really care.

It's been a week since he met Alyssa Edgar. They exchanged numbers that day at the lake and haven't stopped talking. Whenever he thought that they were going to run out of subjects to discuss, they somehow kept going.

Alyssa was a bit of a smarty-pants, although she would be the first to deny it. Her mind had an unbelievable capacity for retaining information and she wasn't at all shy to rope him into the most bizarre and cool conversations, like UFOs, astral projection and metaphysics. Thankfully, he was able to keep up with her ideas and she seemed to enjoy his company, too.

She loved physical activity and it hadn't taken much persuasion to get her to exercise with him. Logan was in awe of her stamina and enjoyed being able to work out with someone he liked: it gave him a glimpse into the type of relationship he wanted.

She's been to his house once—it would've been three times if Cinnia hadn't insisted that he focus on his studies—and got along with his parents. She wasn't shy, which stemmed from her personal philosophy: life was meant to be enjoyed to the fullest. She didn't allow people to walk all over her.

She was three years older than him and halfway through her degree in physiotherapy. Being as obsessed as she was with various sports, it hadn't come as a surprise that she'd recognized him from the few times he's featured in local athletic articles. She wrote a travel blog in her spare time that got her plenty of attention and many offers to stay at luxury resorts across the country.

Logan was smitten. He stopped moving at the sight of her pink hair, wondering if he was able to keep the stupid, goofy grin off his face.

She was walking towards him with a skinny guy that had a blond mohawk. She made eye contact, those brown orbs drawing him in, and answered his smile with one of her own. It felt like an eternity had passed before she halted in front of him. "Hey, Beanie."

Alyssa had learned that his middle name was Bean and tried using it in the most embarrassing ways possible. Well, two could play at that game: Bethany was hers, and he'd derived his own nickname for her.

"Hey, Betty."

The guy gave Logan an obvious and thorough once-over. "I take it you're Logan," he sing-songed.

"Mee-Lee, I'm warning you," Alyssa sighed.

"What? I haven't done anything. Yet."

Logan held his hand out to the guy. "I'm—"

"Absolutely, every bit as gorgeous as Lyssie said you were," the guy interrupted while shaking Logan's hand. "The pleasure's all mine."

Alyssa rolled her eyes. "This is Emile, my annoying best friend."

"In other words, the only person who can put up with her crap," Emile insisted, wagging his eyebrows.

"It's good to meet you, Emile," Logan chuckled.

"Even his laugh is sexy!" Emile stage whispered as he leaned towards Alyssa.

She barely suppressed her growl. "Okay, I let you come along against my better judg—"

"Yes, I admit that I overstepped." He huffed a theatrical breath, kissed her cheek and winked at Logan. "Can't say I'm sorry. Cheerio, lovebirds!"

Logan and Alyssa's gazes were locked on each other as Emile left their side. Logan didn't know why every moment with her felt so profound, as if he could learn the answers to the universe just by standing next to her.

You know what this means.

This was a new voice, one Logan wasn't accustomed to, which was the reason why he didn't take it seriously. He rubbed the back of his neck, slightly self-conscious at the silence that has grown.

"Charming guy."

"He means well, but he has absolutely no filter."

"I gathered." He stepped closer to hug her. "Hi."

"Hi," she murmured, her hands sliding up his back to stop on his shoulders.

Logan breathed in her citrusy scent and briefly closed his eyes. Whenever he was around her, he felt so light. Buoyant, even.

Clearing her throat, she stepped back and stared at his bike. "Can't believe I'm about to get on that thing."

He raised an eyebrow. "And here I thought I was taking a fellow daredevil for a ride."

"I think there's a difference between daredevil and suicidal."

"No way," he reasoned as he handed her a helmet. "Of all things, you're actually terrified of motorcycles?"

"No, motorcycles are fine." She secured the helmet and waited for him to get on before she mounted. "Harleys are a different story."

He snorted. "Why?"

"Because in this town they're not just Harleys."

"Fair enough," he said, igniting the engine.

Her thighs pressed against the outside of his and she wrapped her arms around his waist. "Where are you taking me?"

"One of my favorite places."

She gave him a squeeze. "Can't wait."

Logan pulled away with another silly smile. He was forced to go slow at first, seeing as her estate had a speed limit, but once they hit the road, he opened the throttle. Traffic was sparse the further they got from town.

There was a little-known waterfall in the area that he'd discovered while hiking the nearby mountains with friends. Not many people went there, because it was hidden in a forked-off, nearly overgrown section of a mountain trail.

This is where I feel free, he mused at the changing scenery.

He had no idea how to reconcile the part of him that loved his home with the part that wanted to explore, expand. He felt simultaneously tied to this town and had the urge to leave as soon as possible, especially now that he was nearing the end of his high school career.

Would it be those scouts knocking on your door that make you leave? the new voice queried. *Or will you stay to lead the community?*

He turned into the parking lot of the reserve and killed the engine, waiting for Alyssa to get off before he did. They were the only ones here, by the look of it.

She had a glimmer in her eyes that fascinated him. "What?"

"Are you taking me to the waterfall?"

Of course she knows all about it, he thought, laughing. "Damn it, I was hoping to be like Aladdin."

"Might've worked if I was a princess raised on castle grounds," she teased.

Lifting a shoulder in a nonchalant shrug, he reached for the backpacks he'd stowed in the side panniers. "Your parents are quite rich."

"So are yours," she reminded him.

"Fair." He helped her with the backpack and shook his head with a laugh. "I'm glad you remembered to wear comfortable shoes."

"I had a feeling you weren't joking around when you said we'll walk a while."

Gesturing for her to follow him, he headed for the trail. "Remind me how a spoiled rich girl started getting her hands dirty?"

She burst out laughing. "I used to run away from home."

"Really?" he asked, glancing over his shoulder.

"Really," she confirmed. "I would pack my clothes into a duffle bag—"

"Louis Vutton, I bet."

"Of course," she giggled good-naturedly. "Anyway, I'd plan it weeks in advance because I had to sneak past my nanny first. My parents' place borders a small forest, so I always tried to go out that way. I thought I could live with the wolves or something." She sighed. "Imagine my disappointment when I found out that everyone pretended to look the other way. They made my nanny follow me at a distance to make sure I was safe."

"I think that's sweet. They obviously care about you."

"In their own way, sure. I'm their only child."

"We have that in common."

Their conversation was interrupted while they had to duck below low-hanging branches. He held them aside for her and she gazed at him as she straightened up, their bodies close in the narrow pathway. The air crackled with chemistry.

"Did you ever get lonely?"

"All the time."

She half-smiled. "We have that in common, too."

He longed to say so many things, declare his feelings for her, but they hardly made sense to him as it stood and, besides, it was too soon. He carefully let go of the branches and looked away in the hopes that it would clear his head. She was a magnetic force.

"It's about to get quite loud, but you'll get used to it."

"You forget, I've been here." She pushed past him with a daring grin, shrugging the backpack off her shoulders. "Race you."

Wow.

He could only stare in amazement as she gracefully bounded up the trail. He went after her at a slower pace, making the moment last, and his heartrate accelerated once he spotted her clothes and shoes in a small clearing. The thunder of the waterfall drowned out his excited gasp.

He looked up, finding her on a rock at the waterfall's edge. She had this air around her that reminded him of a warrior angel. In her light-yellow bathing suit and her skin glowing in the sunlight, she faced the six-meter drop with courage.

"What are you waiting for?" she yelled.

Indeed, what?

He kicked his shoes off, quickly followed by his jeans. His backpack and shirt were next. He quickly joined her on the rock. "You first!"

"Here I go!" She swan-dived into the pool below and he wasn't aware he was holding his breath until she surfaced, unharmed. She swept her short pink hair back and gazed up at him. "It's not so bad!"

He leaped off the rock, feet first, crossing his arms over his chest. The water was colder than he'd estimated but refreshing, nonetheless. He floated on his back, staring at the midday sky. With his ears submerged, the noise in his brain quietened.

The light brush of her fingers on his arm indicated that she was mimicking him. For some reason, it was such a relief to know that even though they could spend time talking and getting to know each other better, this tranquil peace was more effective at solidifying their connection. It was intimate in a way he'd never imagined he would experience.

He turned to her, tugging her closer by her wrist.

She righted herself, staring at him in that way that was uniquely Alyssa.

Cupping the side of her face in his hand, he traced her bottom lip with his thumb. Silently asking if this was okay. Wordlessly saying he was going to kiss her.

She nodded, understanding.

He bent his head with the intention of capturing her mouth. A movement to the left caught his attention and he went cold once he saw a leather-clad man hurriedly climbing towards their things. He recognized the emblem on the back of the man's cut.

Falcons MC.

"Motherfucker," he breathed, pushing Alyssa behind him. He saw the man drop a package by their backpacks. "Hey!"

The man made eye contact, his facial expression menacing. "Tell Luca we won't forget what she promised us!" he shouted, reaching behind his back.

He's got a gun, Logan realized, fight-or-flight kicking in. He began shoving Alyssa towards a nearby rock. "Lys, take cover!"

To her credit, she did exactly as he asked. They got closer to the shallow end of the pool, and she took shelter. Logan spread his arms, once again positioning himself between her and the Falcons scum.

He's a dead man.

The thought was as natural as any other. Logan would kill him if he ever harmed Alyssa. Or Luca. Or anyone else he cared about, for that matter.

The man confidently aimed his gun at Logan from the other side of the pool. "It's satisfying watching a Drummond squirm," he sneered. He had a terrifying scar running from the corner of his right eye, down to his jaw; hair and eyes the color of coal. "Just know that my loyalty to Ian is sparing your life. He wants to kill you himself."

Logan had to steel himself to make sure he didn't collapse once the man ran away. He took a moment to make sure it wasn't a bluff before he dropped to his knees next to Alyssa, who was shaking violently.

"Are you okay?" he asked, taking her in his arms and rubbing her icy skin.

"W-what *was* that?" she stuttered.

"Unfinished business." He closed his eyes. It was good to know that she was unhurt; it was infuriating to know that he's put her in danger. These conflicting emotions tore at him. "I'm so sorry."

She clung to him, whimpering from adrenaline.

"Come on, we need to get back."

He slowly helped her to her feet and, keeping his body angled in such a way that no one would be able to harm her without getting to him first, he maneuvered them back to their belongings. The only indications that their peaceful moment had been ruined were a few boot prints and that box.

Logan shuddered to think what could be in it, but he'll only open it once he's with the rest of his club. He swiftly dried her and told her to get dressed. She was in shock, which meant that instructions were helping her cope. He couldn't yet allow himself the luxury of being affected by what's happened, because he had to take care of her first. He would fall apart later.

What does Luca have to do with this?

Instinctively, it felt much greater than the plan they'd hatched when they had dropped her at the side of the road. There must be another level to her presence in the Raptors' lives and he could only hope that he hadn't led a spy into their midst, as Nixon and Connor had suspected.

Logan was overly aware of every sound and movement on the way to the Harley, which was still the only vehicle in the parking lot. He wracked his brain trying to remember if anyone had followed them and, while there had been others on the road behind them, none had sent his inner alarm bells ringing at the time.

They must've tailed you from town. They're experts at keeping a distance.

He hated giving a club like the Falcons any credit, but this wasn't their first time playing a long game. They were patient. Their strikes weren't obvious. Perhaps the Raptors have grown too used to always winning.

"Everything's going to be fine, I promise," he heard himself say when they were on the Blackline. "Hold on tight, because I'm gonna go fast."

"Okay," she said, her voice sounding more certain.

He touched her knee, thinking: *Atta girl.* Then, gravel flying, he sped to the road. He's ridden recklessly before, of course, but never with someone else on board. While he didn't want to stress her out more than she already was, he had to take risky chances now.

Get the club together.

He tapped the side of his helmet to activate the hands-free calling function. "Phone Haye." The dial tone sounded, and he had to grit his teeth while he waited for the current VP to pick up.

"Logan?"

"Get Nixon, Connor and my dad and meet me at our house. I'm ten minutes out of town."

"What's happened?" Haye asked, his tone firm.

"Falcons."

"Where? Are you riding?"

"I'm coming back from the waterfall. Alyssa and I were ambushed by one of them."

"Fuck. I'm sending other bikers to you."

"I don't think they're going to try anything else. They've made their point."

"Regardless," Haye insisted, "get your ass home safely, Logan."

Logan hung up and overtook another truck. Alyssa hasn't eased her grip once and leaned into every twist and turn as if she had been born on the back of a Harley. He allowed himself a moment to acknowledge how lucky they were to be alive and unscathed. Who knew he would be grateful for Ian's vendetta?

The convoy Haye had assembled fell into formation five minutes away from home. Logan breathed a bit easier, feeling less alone. By the time he pulled into his parents' driveway, the men he'd asked for were ready and waiting.

Byron lurched forward, a worried expression on his face, and grabbed Logan's shoulders as soon as his helmet was off. "Are you okay?"

Logan gave a curt nod and reached into the side pannier for the box. "Ask Luca to meet us in the dining room. Is mom here?"

"On her way."

"I'm staying with Lys until she gets here."

Byron opened his mouth to say something, glanced at Alyssa, and then nodded. "See you in the dining room."

Logan turned to her, lightly touching her hair. She had a dazed expression on her face, although there was an element of alertness that made him incredibly proud of her. He'd never been in this type of situation before but, if their relationship was to progress further, her reaction was a good sign.

No one should have to get used to this.

He swallowed. "You with me?"

"Yeah, just confused. I… don't understand what happened, or why."

"It's a long story and I promise I'll fill you in later." His mother's SUV rounded the corner of the street, and the last bit of tension left his body at the sight. He shifted his gaze back to Alyssa's dark brown eyes. "Do you mind staying with my mom while I sort a few things out? I think that guy saw you and I want to make sure you're completely safe before I take you to your place."

"Okay." She gave him a half-hearted smile. "I trust you, Beanie."

He kissed her forehead and held her tight, not knowing how else to convey how much that meant to him. A day that had started with such promise was quickly turning to shit. He would do and give anything to go back to the moment they'd felt closer than he's ever been to anyone.

Cinnia rushed up to them and cupped the back of their heads as she joined their hug. "I'm so glad you're both okay," she whispered fiercely.

"Will you take care of Lys?"

"Of course, my boy." Cinnia pressed her lips to his temple and took Alyssa's hand. "Irish coffee?"

"As long as it's got more whiskey than coffee," Alyssa quipped.

Cinnia grinned broadly. "My kind of girl. Come on."

Logan followed behind them, apprehensive about what came next. He found the guys and Luca in the dining room. They looked at him expectantly. The box was still unopened on the table.

He cleared his throat and met Luca's terrified eyes. He could only imagine how she must've felt when Byron called her down. At the same time, he couldn't care less.

Easy does it.

"Who is the guy with a scar from here to here?" he asked, using his forefinger to illustrate on his own face.

Her fear visibly doubled. "Kane."

"What's his role in the MC?"

"Sergeant at Arms."

Nixon, Connor, Haye and Byron's heads were whipping back and forth as if they were watching a tennis match, but they didn't interrupt his interrogation.

Logan dipped his chin. He'd suspected as much, given the way that man had carried himself, how he'd moved: stealthily, like someone who knew how to use his body and weapon to do the most damage.

"What did you promise them?"

"I already told you," she answered slowly, her eyebrows coming together. "They wanted me to tip you off, to say who beat me up, so you would go after them."

"What else?"

The sudden silence was nearly deafening and caused the dread in the pit of his stomach to start churning. He'd been so enamored by her, so set on assuring her safety, that he'd never imagined she could have had additional instructions.

"What else, Luca?"

"Logan," she whispered, pained.

"Answer the question," Connor all but growled.

Her back flattened against the wall behind her, as if she was worried they'll attack her. "They thought I might not go through with it, because of what they did to me, so they asked me to…" She bit her lip. "To get close to you and eventually… seduce you. To do what I could to 'get you alone'."

He felt like such a fool. "Why?"

"You're a Drummond. They want to kill you."

There it is.

Finally, everything made sense. He'd like to believe that she wasn't that good of an actress. She'd been gang-raped and beaten to a pulp: Jemma, a qualified doctor, had confirmed that after her physical examination. But since then, while in recovery, had Luca contrived ways to always isolate Logan from the rest of the club, to endear him to her?

Later.

He stepped forward and reached for the box to open it. He gagged the moment he realized he was staring at a severed, tattooed hand. He pushed it across the table to Luca.

"Whose is that?"

She peeked inside and let out a strangled noise. "No!"

"Whose fucking hand is that?" he asked again, his voice unrecognizable to his own ears. Wounded, authoritative, enraged.

"Kristen," she mumbled while her eyes filled with tears, "my best friend."

He looked away, disgusted by this whole situation. "How were you going to do it, huh? How were you planning on 'getting me alone' for them to kill me? Because it looks like you'll have to, or Kristen's going to be chopped into more pieces."

"Logan, I didn't—"

"Surely the choice isn't that hard?" he exploded. "I'm cannon fodder, just a silly obstacle between you and Kristen's life!"

"But I—"

"One bat of your eyelashes and I'm putty in your hands, is that it?!"

"Logan, enough." Byron stepped in front of him with a clenched jaw. The former VP was ready to diffuse the situation and he proved that by barking out orders. "Connor, take Luca to Jesse's. Haye, get guys to guard your house and then come back. I'll fill you in on what we decide."

Quietly, those two men left to do Byron's bidding.

Logan turned his back on Luca so that he wouldn't have to see her lying, deceiving face, but he did hear her whisper an apology on her way out. In his current state, he didn't believe it: the betrayal was too recent, went too deep.

"Sit down," Byron demanded, pointing.

Logan dropped into the chair next to Nixon, watching his stepdad close the box and take a seat at the head of the table. Byron was such a natural leader that Logan didn't know how he was ever meant to live up to that standard. Or Brennan's, for that matter.

I'm not a Prez.

"Okay, that was unfortunate to hear, but I don't think we should just automatically assume that she was going to do it," Byron reasoned.

"Until she saw Kristen's hand," Logan pointed out.

"We're failing at the most basic surveillance of those fuckers." Byron glared at the box. "Logan, you are not to move anywhere without at least two guys watching your back. The fact that you were riding alone today is unacceptable. Never do it again." He waited for Logan to incline his head. "Nix, we'll have to call for church to decide how we retaliate. The timeline has jumped forward. We have people like Kristen to consider now."

"Aye, I'll get on that," Nixon nodded, rising to his feet again. He was talking on the phone by the time he left the room.

"Logan—"

"I want her out of this house."

Byron sighed. "I'll agree to that, but I don't necessarily think that we should send her back, either. She can stay with Jesse for the time being. Haye will keep an eye."

Logan nodded distractedly, his mind whirring.

"I know this hurts, Lo. It's not what any of us expected. For her to have been in that state and still play this angle... It doesn't seem possible to me. We couldn't possibly have anticipated that—"

"I don't want this life."

The shock on Byron's face made Logan realize that, for once, he's spoken his thoughts aloud. He's always imagined that this conversation would make him anxious and apologetic, but all he felt was peace and relief that he was finally letting it out.

"Okay, we'll have to talk about that later," Byron murmured, looking like he was choosing his words very carefully. "Thank you for telling me."

The calm compassion that Byron was known for drove Logan over the edge. He burst into tears and covered his face with his hands to hide his shame. Byron jumped up to comfort him, whispering that everything would be alright.

Logan wanted to believe him, but he wasn't so sure anymore.

CHAPTER EIGHT

"*I CAN'T BELIEVE you're making me wear a dress.*"

Logan grinned at the text from Alyssa, his fingers moving rapidly to type his response: "*I'm guessing all the pantsuits were sold out?*"

"*Thin ice, Beanie. I don't wear a dress for just any guy.*"

"*I am both honored and on my way, Betty.*"

He fixed his dark green bowtie, smoothed the white waistcoat, and buttoned the black formal jacket he had on. His dark hair has been trimmed recently and he was freshly shaven. His green eyes critically analyzed his posture and appearance.

He's changed so much over the last three weeks that he couldn't fathom why his looks have stayed the same. Whenever he caught his reflection in the mirror, it felt like he was staring at a stranger.

After he'd confronted Luca, she had moved in with Haye and Dawn. His parents, especially Cinnia, frequently visited Luca to make sure she's okay. For the most part, everyone refused to believe that Luca would betray Logan, which was proven when more bits of Kristen arrived in boxes and she didn't try to get him alone to stop it. The Raptors had done what they could to find and rescue her best friend, but the Falcons kept evading them somehow. Not even uncle Teagan could get a trace of their activities anywhere on the web.

They didn't make Luca look at the last delivery, Kristen's head, but they did still have to break the news to her. Logan empathized with Luca's loss, but not enough to agree that she move back to the Johannson household.

Cinnia has also become closer to Alyssa, after giving her the rundown on the violence associated with motorcycle clubs. While Logan was happy that Alyssa hasn't retreated from his life, he could tell she wrestled with what it would mean to know him. It made him wish for a different direction that much more.

No one spoke about his rejection of his Raptors legacy. It's like his outburst had never happened, and he was too wracked with guilt to bring it up again.

You'll have to talk about it eventually.

And he would, once the wedding was out of the way.

Satisfied that he looked the part of a best man, he rushed downstairs where he found the groom and his men congregating in the living room. "Dad, it's almost go-time."

"Yeah." Byron seemed completely calm, as if this was a regular day and not the one on which Cinnia took his name. "Where are you off to?"

"To pick up my date. I'll meet you there?"

"Sure thing. Can't wait to see Lys again."

Logan's jaw clenched. This wasn't the first time his stepfather has hinted at something more to their relationship than what existed. Alyssa has put more walls up after the run-in with the Falcons, like she was more determined than ever to remain "just friends".

"It's not like that, dad."

Byron grinned. "Put her in line of the bouquet, and that might change."

A mental flash of Alyssa in a wedding dress, walking down the aisle towards him, momentarily distracted Logan. It was so strikingly clear, it nearly passed for reality. Her hair was much longer and dyed golden blonde; her makeup accentuating her dark, brown eyes behind a thin veil. The gown was strapless, cream-colored and form-fitting, and—

"Lo?"

Logan blinked and the vision disappeared. He cleared his throat at the worried look Byron gave him. "Uhm, right, I'm going. Don't skip out on the wedding, old man." He pretended not to hear the many jibes following him outside. He straddled his bike and read Alyssa's latest message.

"Careful. Being too suave could make the ice break."

Laughing, he ignited the engine. He rode slowly to Alyssa's apartment, hardly noticing the guys that trailed behind. His mood was quickly shifting from melancholy to celebratory: his parents were finally tying the knot!

And then there's Luca...

She was at grandma Loraine's house with the rest of the bridal party. As if she'd wanted to make up for the damage she'd nearly brought to the club, she had earned herself a stellar report card. If Dr. McKauley was to be believed, Luca was opening up more than ever, thanks to the club's support. The suspicious activity that used to surround her has dwindled to nearly nothing now that Kristen was dead, yet the Raptors weren't letting up on their plan to exterminate the Falcons.

A part of him was immensely proud of her. It's the same part that still carried a torch for her. He wasn't sure how to handle it, which was why he generally avoided her, and suppressed his thoughts and emotions.

Healthy, as always.

Logan stopped at Alyssa's parking spot, smirking at her 1970's Mini Cooper while he sent a text telling her he's arrived. It was amazing that she didn't die from lack of air-conditioning in that thing, or that her father hasn't convinced her to accept his offer of buying the latest model.

She appeared around the corner with Emile in tow, seemingly nervous.

Logan's smile widened, both because of Emile's blatant teasing and Alyssa's outfit. She'd dyed her hair yellow, orange and red recently, although she'd styled it back. Silver earrings dangled from the front of her lobes. Her makeup was simple and elegant, a scarlet color tinting her plump lips. The sleeveless black dress she wore wrapped around her curves and had a high slit on the one side. Silver heels and matching clutch rounded off the picture.

Not quite the natural, glowing look from the vision he'd seen earlier, but exceptional in its own right.

She came to an abrupt halt once she saw Logan on his Harley. "You expect me to get on *that* wearing *this*?"

"Hey, sexy!" Emile greeted with a wave. "Damn, boy, you're looking mighty fine."

"Emile, don't!" she whined.

Logan was riveted by her. He held out his hand, inwardly cheering when she took him in from head to toe and, with open appreciation in her gaze, slid her fingers over his palm. It's not the first time her touch caused sparks to go off between them and he was certain it wouldn't be the last.

"The church isn't far from here. Hike your dress up," he suggested.

"Fine." She grabbed the hem of the skirt with her free hand, revealing her strong, shapely legs. Swinging one over the bike, she settled on the passenger seat.

Logan followed suit, feeling his cheeks warm at the press of her body against his back.

Emile stepped forward to adjust the dress, making sure it wouldn't get caught on the bike chain or exhaust. "Perfect. You two make a great couple."

"We're not a couple!"

"Shame on you. Have you seen how gorgeous he is?"

"He is also *right here*."

"He knows his effect on both sexes, don't you, Lo?"

Logan coughed to hide a laugh. "I will neither confirm nor deny. Ready to go, Lys?"

"Yes please. Bye, Mee-Lee."

"Love you, Lyssie!"

Logan slowly accelerated. When she locked her arms around his waist, he basked in how good it felt. Was he a romantic sap, or did she still share his feelings?

The fleet of motorcycles in the church's parking lot tugged at Logan's guilt. To the outside person, it wouldn't make any sense to want to abandon such a thriving community. Could he actually go through with it?

Cinnia had scaled the wedding to epic proportions, insisting that the former VP of the MC deserved nothing less. Byron had reluctantly given in, as long as she complied with a list of terms and conditions. Logan had luckily received the omitted version. He loved his parents, but that didn't mean he cared to know the details of their sex life.

"Wow," Alyssa murmured when he cut the engine. "How many people are going to be here?"

"As many as the church can fit." Logan dismounted, stood to the side and lifted her off in one, smooth motion. He adored her answering yelp of surprise. "Around five hundred."

"Jeez." She straightened her dress and turned to him. "Do I still look okay?"

His gaze took an unhurried journey down her frame, pausing on the bodice. Not for the first time, he admired her fit silhouette. Like most, she was shorter than him, but her personality was so massive that he didn't always notice until they were standing face-to-face.

"You look beautiful, Betty."

Smiling, she fixed his bowtie. "You look pretty fabulous yourself, Beanie."

"Let's go see if my mom's freaking out." He offered his arm. "Whatever you see today, don't judge."

"Damn, I was hoping to make a list and give you shit for it later."

"Why are we friends again?"

"Are we friends?"

The underlying sexual tension was the main reason they had kept in touch after his presence in her life proved dangerous. They haven't come close to kissing again, mostly because Alyssa was trying to wrap her head around everything he represented. He respected her too much to push.

They were in limbo, neither moving forwards nor backwards, and with no promises of forever.

"We could be."

"I have enough friends."

"Do you have room for one more?"

"We're just Beanie and Betty for now."

"That's something I can live with." He opened the door to the changing room, unsurprised to find a flurry of activity on the other side.

Aunt Piper, Dawn and Jemma were clucking around his mother, who seemed to be hyperventilating. Jesse and Luca were in a friendly debate with Hallie, while Aurora sat on her own with a glass of bubbly in hand. The latter looked absolutely miserable.

"Those dresses are beautiful," Alyssa murmured next to him.

The bridesmaids wore tailored golden dresses that stopped mid-calf and had cap sleeves, with matching high heels. Aurora's pink dress was puffy and girly, as expected, while Jesse's light blue one was elegant. Logan could only imagine how Connor was going to react. Hallie wore a black dress and had accessorized it with layers of gold and silver necklaces of varying lengths.

His lungs ceased functioning when he took in Luca's outfit. Despite their complicated relationship, he couldn't deny that she was breathtaking. She'd donned a light grey long-sleeved dress that had a small cut-out between her shoulder blades. She was self-conscious about her scars and usually preferred to cover up. It was refreshing to see some of her bronze skin.

"You're here! And you brought Lys!"

Blinking out of his stupor, Logan saw Alyssa greeting his mother. "Mom, you look amazing." He was acutely aware of Luca's gaze on his back. He hated that it thrilled him.

Cinnia wasn't paying attention. Like aunt Piper, she was captivated by Alyssa. "You have such good style!" Cinnia gushed, touching Alyssa's colored tresses fondly. "I never know what to expect when I see you, but this… Stunning!"

"Thanks, Mrs. Drummond," Alyssa mumbled, blushing. "But have you looked in the mirror recently? I'm pretty sure you don't know the definition of 'stunning'."

"Thank you, Lys. I'm glad you could make it." Something dawned on her. "Wow, today's the last day I'll be known as a Drummond."

"I, for one, am glad you haven't decided to double-barrel your surname," Jemma piped up.

Dawn nodded. "It would've been such a mouthful. Eight syllables total? Yikes!"

"I should get to dad." Logan turned to Alyssa. "Are you okay hanging out here?"

"You can sit with us," Hallie suggested.

"Thanks, Hal." Alyssa winked at Logan. "I'll be fine."

"Cool." Fixing Cinnia with a firm glare, he instructed: "Breathe. Be on time. It's going to be okay."

She embraced him tightly and pressed a kiss to his temple. "I love you, Logan."

"Love you, too, momma," he whispered as he let go. Great, she was getting *him* emotional! He strode to the door, frowning when he realized that Aurora was right behind him. He hoped she was going to the bathroom or getting fresh air, because he had no time for—

"Can I talk to you?"

Dammit!

"Rory, I—"

"It's important." She grabbed his elbow and led him to a secluded corner.

He's heard that people become sentimental at weddings, confessing things that would remain better unsaid. Was she going to admit her infatuation? "Rory, are you sure this is the best time?"

"Just listen to me! Listen!" she sobbed. How many glasses of champagne has she had? Had she started drinking at home already? "Logan, I'm—"

"I don't—"

"For fuck's sake, *I'm gay!*"

What?!

Logan stood in shocked silence, certain that he'd misheard. "But I thought—"

"I know what you thought." She wiped her tears with the back of her hand. "I only acted that way around you so my parents wouldn't know I bat for the other team. They want me to be this perfect girly girl." She tugged at her gown, seeming disgusted. "I mean, look at this! Who wants to look like a Barbie doll?"

His mind was reeling. He held his hands up and ogled her, as if seeing her for the first time. It wasn't infatuation in her light eyes: only companionship. How had he misread it for this long?

"Why did you always hang out with me?"

Aurora lifted a nonchalant shoulder. "You attract the hottest girls."

"Wow, Rory. Have you told your parents?"

"Are you crazy? They keep talking about me getting married to a 'nice boy' and giving them loads of grandkids, like I'm some sort of broodmare. I'm not about to crush that dream."

"Jesse?"

She nodded, linking her fingers together. "I just had to tell you, too. You've been avoiding me lately and I know it's because you're under the impression that I'm into you. Maybe if you were female and curvy." She burst into giggles, as if the idea was preposterous. "Nope, not even then."

He pulled her into a tight hug. "Oh my God, I am so sorry for being a dick. You should've told me sooner!"

"If I'd known you would be this cool about it, I would've."

"Your parents deserve to know, too."

"I'll get to that eventually." She stepped back, crossing her arms over her chest. "Are we okay now?"

"We're cool."

"That's a relief." She pinned him to the spot with those light eyes. "Your new girl is really special. I wouldn't mess it up if I were you." She shrugged. "Or do. I can comfort her after."

He guffawed loudly, startling a few latecomers who were hurrying into the church. "Damn, remind me not to get on your bad side."

"I will."

"And tell your parents." He draped his arm over her shoulders and walked her to the room they'd escaped from. "Stop lying to everyone. If you don't want to wear a dress, don't."

"Thanks, Lo. I appreciate that."

The door shut between them, and Logan's gaze shifted to the ceiling for a moment. He didn't know if he could take any more surprises. He just wanted to see the arse-end of this wedding and spend the rest of the day with Alyssa.

One step at a time.

He sauntered further inside, ducking past people who were chatting in the aisle. His stepfather was leaning against the podium with Nixon and Ryan.

"I was about to send a search party," Byron commented when Logan joined them.

"Sorry, I had to deal with something." Logan spotted Haye in the second row. Surely he wouldn't mind that his eldest was a lesbian? "How're you feeling?"

"Ready to get this over with." Byron tugged at his collar. "I don't even enjoy wearing suits for work. I can't wait to take this off."

"Oh, I'm sure," Ryan chuckled suggestively.

Byron rolled his eyes. "How's your mom, punk?"

"Hanging in there. Distracted by Lys."

"I really like that girl."

"I think you've mentioned it a few times."

"Thought I'd say it again."

Nixon snorted. "He won't listen to you about girls. Connor's just as hopeless."

"I've never been a nagging parent. Maybe I should start today."

"Hard pass," Logan muttered.

"By the way, the puppies arrive on Monday."

Logan groaned theatrically. His stepfather had thought up the most torturous payback plan for Logan's transgression a few months ago. Cinnia wanted dogs to fill the void Logan will leave once he moves out and whatever his mother wanted, Byron gave her. Unfortunately, Byron had made it Logan's responsibility to house-train them while the newlyweds flew into a Hawaiian sunset for their honeymoon.

He wouldn't admit this out loud, but Logan's biggest concern was getting attached to the dogs and then cancelling his plans to live with Connor.

"I left the shelter's contact details on the kitchen table," Byron added.

There was a commotion at the entrance and Logan's heart skipped a beat at the sight of Hallie, Jesse, Aurora, Luca and Alyssa hurrying to the front row. Alyssa was hitching her dress up to move more freely, and was inadvertently showing off those amazing legs. Logan swallowed past the lump in his throat and sent his gaze over the rest of the attendees.

A thought occurred to him then, one that caused a bead of ice-cold sweat to roll down his spine: if the Falcons wanted to do anything stupid, today would be the perfect opportunity to obliterate the Raptors once and for all. They were all sitting ducks. He whispered his concerns to Byron, surprised when his stepfather merely smiled.

"Punk, what Haye and I have forgotten about running this MC, you'll still learn. There are prospects parked at every corner of the block and reception venue, and a couple of charter members outside. If something goes down, there are guns stashed under the tables with flowers on them, all within easy reach."

Logan relaxed, although Byron's confidence in him taking over the MC made it feel like a weight was settling on his shoulders again. "Thank fuck."

"Language. We're in a church."

"Sure, dad. You're prepared to kill today, but me swearing will push the Big Guy over the edge."

"Smartass."

A hush descended over the crowd and they rose as one when music began playing: an acoustic version of Metallica's *Nothing Else Matters*. He never imagined it could be used as a wedding march but, listening to the lyrics, he understood why his mother had selected it. He glanced at the groom and felt tears burn at the content smile on Byron's face.

Jemma was first, appearing in time for the first chorus. Her platinum-dyed hair was tied at the nape of her neck, her bangs framing khol-rimmed blue eyes. Even in her early fifties, she was an attractive woman. She locked eyes with Nixon and winked as she came to a standstill.

The burly biker mimicked the motion, making Logan wonder if there was pepper spray in the air from the way he was getting choked up.

The second verse came around, revealing aunt Piper. She had opted to grow her greying hair out naturally, although she had added a few blonde and red highlights. She blew Teagan, who was sitting with their kids, a kiss and took her place next to Jemma.

Dawn, Cinnia's maid of honor, followed shortly after. She was the shortest of the three, yet made up for it in spunk as she sashayed to the front of the church. Haye smacked her butt when she passed. She flipped him the bird, igniting chuckles from those around them.

A collective gasp sounded at the sight of Cinnia. Byron's response was immediate: his jaw dropped and gaze widened, locked on her every move.

Logan discreetly wiped a tear away. He happened to meet Alyssa's eyes, who smiled at him. His face mirrored hers until he saw the borderline irritated set to Luca's mouth. It immediately got his guard up: why did she look like a villain whose plan has been foiled?

Cinnia arrived at Byron's side, already emotional. They held hands and Byron mouthed: "I love you so much."

Here we go again, Logan thought, his vision becoming blurry.

"Please be seated," grandpa Reade announced. He'd completed an online course to marry them, as per Cinnia's request. "We are gathered here today tae witness the union between Byron an' Cinnia. Ah've had the pleasure of knowin' both of 'em, together an' apart. Never thought Ah'd have tae see her get married tae someone other 'an Bren, but Ah know tha' Bren is watchin' from above an' gives his blessin'."

Logan's stomach clenched as some reached for tissues. Most of the people here remembered Brennan. Fifteen years later and they were still affected by mention of his name.

"Hero, ye were there for Cin whenever she needed ye, an' ye raised ma grandson tae be a great man." Reade placed his hand on Byron's shoulder. "Of all the people Ah've known, *ye* deserve all the happiness in the world. Ye're the only other man good enough for this lass an' it is ma honour tae marry ye."

Byron accepted the praise with a nod. "Thank you, Reade."

"Cin, Ah've known ye since ye were a wee lass. Yer strength an' tenacity amazes me. Ye've survived so much pain an' heartache, an' Hero is yer reward.

Ah believe ye were made for each other."

Sniffing, Cinnia grabbed a tissue from the podium. Logan wondered who'd had the foresight to put it there.

"Hero, is there anythin' ye'd like tae add?"

Byron cleared his throat. "Cin, when I look back on my life, meeting you was when it started getting better. I've loved you since the second I saw you. You were kind when I had myself convinced I was worthless. You made it impossible not to care about you. To this day, I'll do anything to see you smile and keep you safe. Thank you for the many memories we've made so far, and for those to come. I'll continue to love you for as long as I'm alive."

When Byron had slipped the wedding band on Cinnia's finger, Reade turned to her. "Cin?"

She gazed at her partner. "You've never liked having eyes on you."

"You don't say."

Everyone laughed.

"And yet, you're so intriguing to us all." She smiled tenderly. "You are my best friend. I've always felt safe with you, like I could trust you with my life, and you've never let me down. You were there for me through thick and thin. It wasn't difficult to fall in love with you, even when I was so sure I could never love anyone again." She added the band to his ring finger and tenderly kissed his knuckles. "You're a wonderful father, an exceptional leader and the gentlest soul I know. I love you. You're my favorite person."

"Ah now pronounce ye husband an' wife. Kiss yer bride, Hero."

Logan had no idea how any of them made it through those vows, but he needed several tissues by the time his parents locked lips. He reached for a handful and passed the box to Nixon and Ryan, who weren't much better off.

"Ladies an' gentlemen, Ah present tae ye: Mr. an' Mrs. Johannson!"

The crowd cheered loudly. Byron and Cinnia parted on a mutual laugh, holding hands while they hurried to the exit under a shower of small flowers. That had been a quick ceremony, which meant the Raptors intended to party until the early hours.

Logan slowly followed, stopping once he reached Alyssa. "Photo time."

"That was so beautiful." She took his scrunched-up tissue and pressed it to the corners of her eyes. "Do I look like a panda?"

"The cutest panda."

She smacked his chest. "Charming."

"Lo!" Sophie called out, dragging an attractive black man towards them. Her dancer's body was tucked into a knee-length velvet dress the color of red wine, and her hair was pinned back. She hugged Alyssa and shifted to Logan. "I want you to officially meet Max, my boyfriend. Max, this is Logan."

Max extended his hand. "I've heard so much about you, I feel like I already know you."

"Is that so?" Logan said dryly, giving his best friend a knowing glance and shaking the man's hand. She stubbornly lifted her chin. "Good to meet you, Max. I'm trying to remember if I've seen you at the station before."

"Probably not. I transferred here six months ago."

"Do you think we can skip photos?" Sophie asked, clearly eager to change the subject.

Logan was curious as to why she didn't want him and Max talking, but he'd confront her later. "Don't ruin my mother's day, Soph," he whined, glad he got one of her exasperated eye-rolls in response.

"Let's get on with it, then."

If not for Alyssa's dry remarks, Logan didn't know how he would have survived an hour of posing. Most of the attendees had moved on to the reception venue but, seeing as Logan was family—not to mention best man— he had to tough it out.

"Here we go again," Alyssa muttered when they were standing at his motorcycle, clutching the hem of her dress in preparation.

He stared at her, coming to terms with the fact that he didn't want to wait anymore. She reminded him of flowers and butterflies; the sun's warm rays on a meadow in springtime. She was the embodiment of light.

He pulled her into his arms, tilted her chin up and pressed his mouth to hers, effectively swallowing her surprised gasp. His action was for one, simple reason: she was beautiful, and he wanted her. Why did they keep complicating it?

Her lips quickly became pliant. She rested her arms on his shoulders and returned the kiss eagerly, stepping closer to him. Her fingers rubbed the back of his neck while she tested his mouth.

Logan toyed with her lips, his hands sliding from her waist to her perfect ass. Her breath was minty and her mouth melted on his, as if they've been doing this for years. Taking her reaction as an invitation for more, he added his tongue.

Alyssa moaned softly, and he instinctively knew it was a sound he would enjoy hearing for the rest of his life. She returned his passion with her own, nearly knocking him on his ass with the intensity. The whole world faded to the background, leaving them fused together in every way except one.

"Logan, have you... Whoa, sorry, bro!"

He reluctantly pulled back, briefly resting his forehead on hers. "This isn't over."

She nodded dazedly. "Okay."

Logan shifted his attention to Connor. "What's up?"

"Have you seen Jesse?"

"She's probably at the reception already. Where's your date?"

"Ditched her."

Logan shook his head. "Come on, let's get going."

"Sweet, I'll follow you."

He and Alyssa mounted his Harley. As has become habit, he savored the feel of her behind him all the way to the swanky hotel where his mother had booked a large conference room for the reception.

Logan parked, sitting undecided for a moment. He wanted to be alone with Alyssa, to discuss where they could go from here. When Connor stopped next to them, though, their decision was made for them.

"We should go," Alyssa whispered.

"Yeah," he sighed.

The three of them walked inside. Logan tried his best to keep his thoughts clean, but his imagination was running wild with what he could get up to with Alyssa in one of the rooms upstairs.

"You're officially the youngest boy I've ever kissed."

"Whoa, you guys finally kissed?!" Connor exclaimed drily. At Logan's answering glare, Connor became contrite. "I'll, uh, go find Jesse."

Once they were alone, Logan turned back to Alyssa. "Does it bother you?"

"Not as much as I thought it would."

"I don't think it's weird. My mom's seven years older than my dad."

"She doesn't look it!" She glanced around. "Where are they, anyway?"

"It's probably better that we don't know the answer to that." He steered her to the table that they'll be sharing with his parents and their friends. "Something to drink?"

"Vodka on ice with a splash of lime. Or a beer."

"I'll see what I can do. Before I go…" Tugging her closer, he claimed her lips again. Now that he knew what she felt and tasted like, how was he ever going to stop craving a repeat?

She gasped as he pulled away. "Hurry back."

Striding to the bar, he nodded at Ryan and Oscar and placed his order. It was cool seeing father and son do this together, considering their volatile history. These days, Oscar's dedication to the club and his father's empire could not be overstated.

"Who's the girl?" Oscar asked.

"Alyssa." He liked the way her name sounded. Everything about her was likeable, from her smile, to her citrusy scent, to her mind… to those kissable lips. "Met her through Soph."

"Ah." Oscar poured Alyssa's drink and slid a bottle of beer onto the counter. "Here you go, Prez."

Usually it was strange for men twice his age to call him that, but Logan was on cloud nine and took it in stride for once. He carried the drinks back to the table. Nixon, Jemma, Haye, Dawn, Piper and Teagan had taken their seats in the meantime and were keeping Alyssa company. He handed her drink over and shifted his mouth to her ear. "Are you okay?"

"Just thinking about that kiss," she whispered.

"Should I not have done it?"

"That's not it."

"Want to do it again?"

"Hell yes."

He grinned, catching the unpierced part of her left lobe between his teeth. "I can make that happen. Give me—"

"Ladies and gentlemen, the bride and groom!" the MC interrupted, his voice booming through the speakers. "Let's give 'em a cheer while they go straight to opening the floor!"

Logan clapped jovially as Byron and Cinnia entered the room. His mother had a suspicious red tint to her cheeks and his stepfather's bowtie has disappeared. Everyone could guess what they'd got up to. They moved to the center of the dance floor and began swaying to the music.

"They look good together. How are you feeling about your dad being part of the vows?"

Trust Alyssa to remember his conflicting feelings about his biological father. "I think I'm okay."

She smiled. "That's progress! Not at all bitter and filled with regrets, like bikers are supposed to be."

"I could still act tortured, if that's what turns you on."

She let out a startled laugh. "The more damaged, the better."

"I've got a lot more to be bitter about."

"Oh really?"

"Yup, like the fact that I'm about to ask you to dance with me, only to hear you say no." He took her hand and got up. "Let's skip to the part where you accept your fate, shall we?"

"I'm gonna get you for this," she grumbled.

He laughed softly as they went to the dance floor. Both sets of his grandparents have joined the newlywed couple in the meantime. "I figured you might say that. I guess I know you better than you thought."

Alyssa went into his arms. "Your funeral. I suck at this."

"I'd much rather be hanging from a cliff somewhere, myself."

"Agreed. Can we go now?"

"Nice try."

The tempo of the playlisted songs increased and, before he knew it, he was dancing his heart out with her. The DJ's set included the latest hits, which prompted the younger crowd to join in. Logan smiled at the sight of Jesse and Connor moving together. Sophie and Max were clearly deeply in love. He couldn't wait to see what cute babies they'll have.

His heart stopped when he spotted Luca sitting alone.

As conflicted as he currently was, he couldn't stand to see how out of place she felt. He excused himself and walked to the girl with the violet eyes. She looked up as he approached, her beauty almost unbearable. How was it possible that he could still feel drawn to her, after everything?

"Are you okay?"

"Fine," Luca answered curtly, "you should go back to Lys."

"I'm worried about you."

"Don't." She closed her eyes and shuddered. "I'm fine."

"Luca, look at me."

"Why? You hate me now."

"I don't..." He sighed, raking his fingers through his hair. "How was I supposed to react?"

Those interesting orbs reconnected with his. "I lost my best friend because of your reaction."

"That's not fair. We tried to help."

She stared at him in silence, as if deciding his fate, before she let out a long breath. "You're right. That wasn't your fault: it was mine. I didn't do what they wanted. Doesn't that tell you everything that you need to know about me, Logan?"

His heart stuttered in his ribcage. "I don't know."

"Then you're blind."

For a second, he longed for the days when she'd been less verbose. "I don't want to fight," he said quietly.

"I don't, either."

"Okay, good. What did you think of the wedding?"

"It was beautiful." Her shoulders relaxed slightly. "Your parents really love each other. I never saw that between mine."

Since she'd brought the topic up, he decided to press. "Who's your mom?"

"Her name was Jasmine."

If it's the same one dad mentioned, then Ian McDermot isn't her father. Why does she think he is?

"What do you mean, *was?*"

Her hands clenched. "I've never seen her in person, only pictures. I think she's dead."

"Do you know what happened to her? Maybe we can…" He trailed off, noticing two prospects striding to Byron with purpose. Whatever they told him made Byron whisper something to Cinnia and leave the dance floor. "Hold that thought, I'll be back." He dashed after Byron, who was already in the hotel's reception area by the time Logan caught up. "Dad!"

"Go back inside."

"What's going on?" He grabbed Byron's shoulder when the man kept walking. "I'm the fucking Prez, dad. Start treating me like one."

Byron didn't say anything for a couple of moments and Logan half-wished he could take the words back. "Five Falcons were trying to start shit with the prospects. I'm going to the clubhouse to sort this out."

"I'm coming with you."

Byron rested his hands on Logan's shoulders. "Regardless of whether or not you're in the MC, I'm always going to stop you from getting blood on your hands. You don't deserve that kind of weight on your shoulders."

"Killing someone on your wedding day isn't better," Logan protested.

"Haye, Nixon and I will take care of this. *Let us.*"

Logan realized that he wasn't going to change Byron's mind. "What's the plan, then? Don't shake your head at me, dad. If you're not going to let me help, at least tell me what you're putting the club's name on."

There was a hint of pride in Byron's smile. "We'll question them. If we don't like what we hear, some of them will die. We'll keep one or two alive to take a message back to Ian. If all goes well, that buys enough time for me to get back from Hawaii before shit goes down. Until then, you'll have to liaise with Haye and Nix and keep everyone safe, especially Luca."

"Okay, how long will this take?"

"An hour, at most. Can you keep your mom distracted?"

"I'll do my best."

"Thanks, punk." He turned on his heel, halting when Logan called out his name. He gazed over his shoulder.

"Luca just told me that Jasmine's her mother, but she thinks she's dead."

Byron's dark eyebrows pulled together. "Where does Ian fit in, then? Jasmine couldn't have fallen pregnant with his kid. He happened after."

"I don't know, but I'll see what else I can find out. Be back in an hour."

Logan's heart pounded fast once his father slipped outside, wishing he could go with him. It felt as if the world had dropped out from underneath his feet and—

"Do you love Luca?"

Logan jumped, finding Alyssa behind him. "How long have you been standing there?"

"Does it matter?"

She'd been told the basics after the incident at the waterfall, but he knew that she wouldn't approve of the violence he'd discussed with his stepdad. He wondered how much she heard. At the same time, he couldn't get himself to ask.

"I needed to... get fresh air."

"Right."

He couldn't tell her more because he didn't want to scare her away. What if she thought that this was the norm, and decided to leave him?

Alyssa inhaled deeply. "Logan, I'm not a jealous girl. We're not together and you don't owe me anything. But I need to know if you're in love with Luca."

His mouth opened to refute that, but no sound came out. His emotions were all over the place. Why couldn't she have asked an easier question, like how he felt about *her?* She was an amazing woman; one he didn't want to lose, but one he was beginning to see he would.

Alyssa inclined her head, breaking eye contact. "That's what I thought."

He clasped her elbow when she tried to get past him. "Alyssa, wait."

"I can't be your consolation prize, Logan. What happened today won't change that you're in love with someone who isn't me."

"I'm also—"

"That's not better." She smiled at him, although it didn't reach her eyes. "We shouldn't see each other again. Meeting each other was… We can tick it off the list as the reason part of 'reason, season, lifetime'." She pecked his cheek. "Good luck with everything."

"Lys, don't do this." But he didn't know how to save this, so had no right to ask her to stay simply because he couldn't stand the thought of life without her.

"I'll ask Emile to pick me up. Thanks for an amazing couple of weeks."

He watched as she headed for the exit, unable to move his feet. He liked Alyssa so damn much, but by being her observant self he had no way to get her back. Running his hand through his hair, he tried to think what his next move should be. He couldn't leave it like this.

The Falcons are still out there!

He ran after Alyssa, finding her in the parking lot. He held his hands up in surrender when she glared at his arrival. "I just want to make sure you're safe."

"I've got a Taser in my clutch."

"Was it meant for me?" he tried to joke.

"Doesn't matter now."

Why was he fucking this up? Why couldn't he say what she wanted to hear?

The thing you love about her—that she doesn't take shit from anyone—is the very thing that's taking her away from you.

"Does she know?" She frowned when he shook his head. "Why not?"

"It's complicated. It would overwhelm her."

Her Mini showed up in the parking lot, coming to a halt in front of them. Emile laid on the hooter, eyes narrowed at Logan through the windshield: not an expression Logan was used to seeing.

"Why don't you let *her* decide if she can handle it or not?"

"It's not that simple."

"Life is very simple, Beanie. It's a shame you don't believe that yet."

She slammed the door shut before he could respond, and he did nothing but stare as they drove off. He already missed her; missed Emile's incessant teasing. Taking a seat on the steps, he gazed straight ahead. How had everything spun out of control so fast?

He was in the same position when three Harleys arrived an hour later. He barely took note of the men striding his way. "Is it done?" His voice sounded dead.

"Yes," Byron replied. "What's happened?"

"Nothing."

Logan stormed inside, ignoring his father calling out to him. He hadn't kept his promise about making sure his mother was distracted, but none of that mattered. The light has been drained from his life. What was the point of anything anymore?

He ended up at the bar to drown his sorrows.

INTERLUDE—1—CINNIA

HER EYELIDS SLOWLY parted and she blinked in the early morning sunlight, the crash of waves a welcome yet unfamiliar sound. It took her a moment to remember why she was at a beach. She rolled around to reach for Byron.

He wasn't in bed.

Cinnia sat up, alarmed. A mouth-watering scent reached her nose and she glanced at her bedside table. The corners of her mouth tilted upwards when she spotted the fresh cup of coffee. Wherever her husband was, he couldn't have gone far.

Husband.

Byron has been her partner for years and now they've moved into a new chapter of their life together. She liked that her surname has changed: her identity has been tethered to the Sloane and Drummond traditions until recently, and becoming Byron Johannson's wife had a liberating effect.

She took a sip of coffee, taking in the incredible view. Byron didn't often splurge, even though he made an obscene amount of money as a lawyer. This honeymoon bungalow was secluded from the rest of the resort, situated a mere fifty-odd yards from the ocean, and contained an open-plan lounge area, a massive bedroom and an ensuite bathroom with an outdoor shower. The foldaway glass walls made her feel like she was at one with the environment.

Cinnia spotted his silhouette at the water's edge. His legs were crossed, his hands resting on his knees with palms turned upwards. Meditating.

She recalled the night before, when he had made love to her for the first time since they'd said, "I do". It shouldn't have been different from the countless times they've been together before, but it had been so much *more*. Just thinking about it had her crossing one leg over the other, eager for a repeat performance.

His phone vibrated, drawing her attention to the other nightstand. She grinned once she saw her son's name and swiped her finger across the screen. "Hey, Lo."

"Uh, you're not dad."

"Nope, but I couldn't resist when I saw your name. How are you?"

"A little hung over. You and dad know how to throw a wedding, that's for sure. How about you? How is Hawaii?"

"So beautiful," she answered dreamily. "If it wasn't for you, I'd definitely move here."

"Honestly, I'm surprised someone answered my call," Logan teased. "I thought for sure that you would be busy with… whatever married couples get up to."

"I could tell you?"

He made gagging noises. "No, thank you. I'm an innocent little lamb."

She rolled her eyes. Her son hasn't been innocent in years. She still wasn't certain how she felt about that: he reminded her so much of Brennan. "Is everything okay? Why are you calling?"

"No reason."

"What are you up to?"

"Nothing!"

"Right." She narrowed her gaze, though he couldn't see her threatening facial expression. "Spit it out."

"Mom, I can't."

"Logan Bean Drummond, if you don't own up, Amsterdam is off the table."

"You wouldn't!"

"Try me."

He sighed deeply. "I wanted to talk to dad about the puppies."

Cinnia's heart skipped a beat. Byron had promised that they would start an animal family back when he proposed. She hadn't been sure whether he was on board, but this news settled it. "Really?" she asked excitedly.

"Give dad the phone. It's bad enough that I've ruined the surprise."

That must mean they're already there!

"Turn the camera on, I want to see!" She activated the video call function.

Logan's face appeared. He hadn't been lying: he was looking worse for wear. His dark hair was ruffled and there were shadows under his eyes. The lopsided grin on his face spoke volumes, though. "Prepare yourself! They are the cutest."

Her hand covered her mouth when he tilted the phone to the two brown, spotted German Shorthaired Pointers on his lap. The sight of their floppy ears made her fingers itch to touch them. Byron knew her better than she'd ever imagined: he's chosen dogs that were easy to train, would fit into their active lifestyle and, as a bonus, were hypoallergenic.

"Oh my gosh, how adorable!"

"They came a day earlier than dad said they would. Dad told me I'll get a certain amount per day for training them, so I wanted to find out if he's gonna cough up an extra day's wages."

"Did I raise you to be this greedy?"

"Hey, verbal agreements are binding."

Laughing softly, she said: "I'll pay you the difference."

"Thanks, momma."

"Nice try. You're not getting more than that."

"Dammit." He lifted the phone back to his face. "Where is dad, anyway?"

"Meditating on the beach."

"Why can't kids come along on honeymoons again?" he pouted.

"Many reasons. What happened with Alyssa?"

The way Logan's facial expression changed confirmed her suspicions. She knew that he idolized her relationship with Byron and, while that was flattering, she often worried that he would go to extreme lengths to get it. That's why she really liked Alyssa as a romantic partner for her son: he got to share his passions with someone he has chemistry with.

She had noticed Alyssa's abrupt departure from the reception; somehow, Luca had something to do with it. It had been a huge knock to his ego when he found out Luca had been tasked with seducing him and, essentially, leading him to his death. Cinnia wasn't quite ready to forgive Luca, either, although she knew the girl wouldn't have gone through with it.

"I don't want to talk about it."

Dipping her head in acknowledgment, Cinnia said: "Luca wants to come over today to get the rest of her things. Will you be there to let her in?"

"Sure."

"I know you're still hurt—"

"Mom, please."

"—but I think we should give her another chance."

His jaw was clenched and, for a moment, he resembled Brennan so clearly that Cinnia caught her breath. "Do we have to do this now?"

"No, you're right." She forced a smile. "Thanks for taking care of the pups while we're away."

"Pleasure," he said, relaxing. "Enjoy the rest of your honeymoon."

She ended the call and gazed at the new wedding band on her finger, allowing her thoughts to wander to Brennan. She still loved him, deeply: he'd helped shape the person she was today. More than that, he lived on in their son.

Logan is so lost, yet so ready to become his own man. Will it take him away from me?

Leaving the bed and, to a lesser extent, that depressing thought behind, she ventured outside to join her new husband. She enjoyed the feel of the early morning sun on her naked skin, the ocean scent in the air, and the crashing sound of the waves.

Byron was leaning back on his elbows, splendidly nude.

"Morning, husband."

His chocolate-colored eyes met hers; then took a leisurely stroll down her body. "Morning, wife."

Not for the first time, she wondered what he thought when he looked at her. She dropped to her knees and straddled his thighs. "Thanks for the coffee. It made up for you not being in bed."

"Thought it might." He stroked her thighs with his fingers. "How'd you sleep?"

"Like I'd been fucked gently. How was your meditation?"

"Needed." He sat up to rest his chin on her shoulder. "I can't believe we're here."

Curling her fingers into his hair, she held him tightly. She knew what he meant: not only that they were literally in paradise, but that they were finally committed in every sense of the word. She couldn't remember the exact time when she'd got over her fear of marrying him, but it had everything to do with Byron never letting her down. She was so happy she'd taken the leap.

"I'm the luckiest man alive," he murmured, caressing her collarbones with his lips. "When you were walking down the aisle... I've never seen you look so beautiful."

Her breathing hitched. Every year, she felt as if their age gap was becoming more noticeable and, every year, she was proven wrong. There was no longer any doubt in her mind that this man will love her more with each passing day.

"I once dreamt about that dress."

"Oh yeah?"

"It was a dirty dream."

His chuckles vibrated on her skin, sending shivers down her spine. "How dirty?"

"You and Bren taking turns kind of dirty."

He sucked in a breath. "Damn, that's hot."

She became aware of his hardening member and her core clenched in anticipation. Electric sparks followed his lips over her chest. She leaned back to give him better access, whimpering when he latched onto a breast. His hands massaged the globes of her ass while he sucked on a nipple.

"I don't want you to worry, but we killed some people yesterday."

She froze at the change in subject and shifted back. "*What?*"

"The Falcons tried to cause shit. We had to send Ian a message."

"Jesus, the charters... We were *all* there! Why didn't you tell me?"

"It was your special day. I wasn't going to stress you out."

"I'm pretty sure you were getting married, too."

"Even more reason to keep you safe."

She traced his eyebrows with her fingertips. "Is that why you were out here so early?"

"I needed to clear my head." He shut his eyes, savoring her touch. "Logan wanted to get involved, but I can't have him carry this kind of burden. Once he pulls the trigger, there's no turning back. Look at how easy it was for *me* to make that call after so many years of walking on the straight and narrow."

She didn't judge him. How could she? She grew up with the motorcycle club lifestyle and knew that, inevitably, shady shit happened. Her only consolation was that they were a tight-knit family that would stop at nothing to ensure everyone's safety. The fact that Byron had done this so that Logan wouldn't have to…

Hero.

"I want the violence to end."

"Maybe now it finally will." She gazed into his dark eyes, smiling. "I heard about the puppies."

Byron swore under his breath. "When?"

"Lo called you, and I answered because it's him. He couldn't keep it a secret. You know how I get."

"Poor kid."

"They were dropped off early. He was negotiating getting paid an extra day."

"I've taught him well," Byron chuckled. "Did you see them?"

"Yeah, they are the cutest!" She brought their lips together for a moment. "You're the best, honestly."

"I was hoping you'll show your gratitude in other ways."

"Hmm, now that we're married, I think we should be like other old married couples and restrict sex to anniversaries only."

He rolled them around, anchoring her to the sand. "We'll see what you say about that after I eat you out."

"By, I was only—Fuck!" She cried out as his mouth closed over her core, her fingers grabbing hold of his head.

He lazily ran his tongue over her folds and spread her open to suck on her clit. She's lost count how many times he's gone down on her, but every time was better than the last. Even yesterday, after the ceremony, he'd feasted on her on the way to the reception. Her legs came up to keep him where he was, and she gasped when he pushed them back down.

He was in control.

His tongue alternated between laving her throbbing clit to spearing her entrance, making her sopping wet within seconds. One of his fingers slid inside and he groaned once he felt how ready she was. He added another, moving them in a way that caused her to crave his cock. He shifted up, scraping his teeth over her stomach towards a breast, where he bit her nipple.

"Ah!" she exclaimed, loving the pain.

The palm of his hand pressed on her clit while his fingers fucked her. He sucked every inch of her tits, no doubt leaving marks. "If you only want this once a year, I guess we should make it count."

To argue that she'd been joking would be pointless. His tone indicated he was going to fuck her until she couldn't walk and even after that, and she was going to love every second. She rocked against his hand, chasing her release.

Byron nuzzled the side of her neck. "Tell me when you cum, babe, I want it all over my face."

Her eyes crossed at the mental picture and she jerked under him. "Fuck, *now*. I'm coming!"

His head was between her legs again, moaning as he slurped up her orgasm. It was too soon after her release and she writhed beneath him, hoping for a reprieve. He massaged and kissed and licked and nibbled and *squeezed...* And she shuddered with a cry, flying over the edge once more.

"Ah, Jesus, Cin, you squirted!" He rested his forehead on her thigh, panting. "I love Hawaii."

"Me too." Leaning on her elbows, she stared at the man she loved more than life itself. "Are you going to fuck me?"

He raised his head. His mouth, chin and cheeks were glistening, like he'd wanted. "Did you pack the toys?"

She nodded.

"Good," he murmured, sitting back on his haunches and lifting her hips up. He positioned his hard, thick cock at her entrance. He pivoted forward, impaling her on his length. "I'm going to fuck every orifice before the end of the day."

"Byron!"

His pace was fast and hard, rattling her teeth. He held her hips in the air, leaving her at his mercy. The wet noise of their groins joining over and over was as titillating as the waves breaking within reach.

Last night had been gentle, sensual and sweet, like a first time. Now they were frenzied, animalistic and driven by lust, as if they were having an affair. The underlying love, that bond that tied them together, was what catapulted her into a third orgasm, screaming his name.

He was right behind her, his muscles tensing as his release claimed him. Once he came down from the high, he leaned forward to take her in his arms. He picked her up and shakily walked into the ocean.

The temperature of the water was soothing. She kissed his neck as he dipped them lower. "I think I'm going to love being your wife. I'm going to be clingy and needy and insist that we spend every available moment together."

"Nothing out of the ordinary, then?"

They both laughed, holding each other tightly. There was some activity farther down the beach, yet Cinnia couldn't be bothered. This trip was about her and Byron.

He caressed her mouth with his while they drifted in the ocean. "How many times do you think we've had sex?"

"We've had our fair share, babe. I've compared notes with the girls, and some of them think we're not normal."

"I could've told you that."

Reluctantly, he let go of her to dunk his head under the water. When he surfaced, he swiped those dark brown locks back with his hands, his arms flexing deliciously. The way the droplets glistened in the early morning sun made her feel like she was watching a *Dolce & Gabbana* model doing a photo shoot for their latest underwear collection.

Byron tilted his head to the side, curious by her sudden silence. "Cin, you okay?"

She dipped below, trying to clear her head. How could she be eager for more sex when he's already given it to her so good? "You distracted me with how handsome you are."

A smile twitching at the corners of his mouth, he straightened until the water barely covered his lower body. Water trickled down his sculpted chest, slipping into the indentations of his six pack. Her gaze travelled down to the dark, vertical trail from his belly button to his trimmed pubic hair.

"I'll never get tired of the way you look at me. I don't know what I did right to get you, but I'm never letting you go."

She stood up, pleased when he returned the favor by ogling *her* physique. She took pride in her appearance: she's adapted her exercise routine to stay in the shape he knew and loved. *Then again,* she thought as she traced his pectoral muscles with her fingers, *he would still be attracted to me if I let myself go.*

"Breakfast should be ready," he commented lightly. "I'm starving."

She cocked an eyebrow. "I thought you've already eaten?"

Those chocolatey eyes twinkled. "And I will again, later today." He took her hand and led her out of the ocean, across the beach and to their bungalow.

Cinnia counted her lucky stars at the sight of a delicious spread. Someone must have delivered it while they'd made love, within earshot. Her skin heated up at the thought and she quickly donned a bathrobe before taking a seat.

"I love this place," Byron murmured, wrapping a towel around his waist as he joined her.

Loading her plate with fruit, bread and cheese, she asked: "What's the plan for the rest of the day?"

"That depends. Are you jetlagged?"

She poured herself a glass of orange juice. "Not really. I feel like taking a hike."

"Great, 'cause I've got a surprise for you."

"Another one? Damn, By, I feel like I'm living in a constant state of surprise. First this honeymoon, then the puppies…" She trailed off, thinking. "Hey, what about Charlie and Bobby? Because they're brown? Charlie and Bobby Brown?"

"Sounds good to me, babe," he said, laughing.

She went to their bedroom to pick up her phone, texting Logan the dogs' names on the way back, before sitting down to eat. She frequently found herself staring at the waves, enamored. She's always loved her hometown with its winding roads and mountain passes, but there was something about the ocean that called to and soothed a deeper part of her soul.

"I thought about your other wedding this morning."

"Me too."

"Brennan loved you so much."

She smiled, reaching for his hand. "I loved him. I still do."

He raised her hand to his mouth and caressed it with his lips. "I've been in love with you for so long. I tried to convince myself that it only happened after Brennan passed away, but that's a lie. I had fantasies about you, Cin."

"I had fantasies about you, too. And both of you, together."

He seemed intrigued. "Right, the dream. Hold that thought."

She barely had a moment to wonder what he's up to when he returned with the sex toys box. She crossed one leg over the other at that gleam in his eyes.

"Tell me about the dream, Cin."

"I had it the day you moved out."

"You mean the morning you were screaming with pleasure, as usual?"

Closing her eyes, she nodded. "I woke up so horny that I basically... took what I wanted from him." She heard the box open: it was an absolutely thrilling sound.

"What happened in the dream?"

"I was dancing with you at first. Then Brennan joined and I was between the two of you. My clothes eventually disappeared and..."

The silence between them was thick with sexual tension. Cinnia kept her eyes firmly shut, half-embarrassed she was admitting this aloud, which somehow heightened her arousal.

"Holy hell, Cin. I had no idea you were so filthy." Her heartbeat kicked up a notch when his lips touched the base of her neck, his teeth and tongue teasing her skin. "Brennan wasn't bisexual, so it's not like we could've put on a show for you. But we could've taken you, one after the other... Maybe even at the same time."

Cinnia's core clenched greedily. "Oh God."

He parted her robe, pulling the one side off her shoulder to gain access to her upper arm. "He could've watched as I ate you out." One of his big hands cupped her breasts, thumb stroking a nipple while his lips caressed the base of her throat.

She barely noticed that he turned her chair. She arched her back in the hope that he would suck that nipple. Her breath came out in pants and her fingers gripped his hair.

"I would've made you scream my name," he went on as he positioned himself between her legs, on his knees. "You would have ground your pussy on my face, soaking me, and cum with a loud scream. And then I would've flipped you around, raised your hips and fucked you from behind."

She gasped as she felt the cool tip of a vibrator push into her.

"I wonder if he would've let me cum in you without a condom," he mused once the toy was firmly inside. "I would've fought for it. That way, a part of me could be inside of you while he took his turn. His dominant side would've come out then, to show us both who you truly belonged to. He wouldn't know what a huge turn-on that would be for me... I would've jerked off to the two of you. Maybe he would've let you watch."

Her body twitched as he switched to the lowest setting, and she moved her hips in the hopes that he would pick up the pace. Bend her over the table.

Something. Anything!

"I saw you that day, at your house, when I came back from rehab and you were fucking in the kitchen. I stood at the door with the biggest erection, watching him take you. Christ, porn wasn't a match for the two of you. You looked so good together."

"By," she moaned, "By, please."

"You want my cock, baby?"

"Oh my God, *yes*."

"Here."

Her eyelids parted and she licked her lips when she saw that he'd stood up in the meantime, dropped the towel and aligned his dick with her face. Carefully, yet eagerly, she grabbed the base and leaned forward to swallow him down; all the while, squeezing her thighs together to get the most out of the vibrations.

"Fuck yes," he grunted, tangling his fingers in her hair while he thrust into her mouth. "You're so fucking good at sucking my cock, Cin."

The praise made her tingle, as it so often did. She worked her mouth down his shaft, as far as it could go, and repeatedly made herself gag. She gave zero shits about how sloppy and wet this blowjob became. It was filthy and animalistic and perfect.

She whimpered in protest when he pulled back. "By—"

"Bend over the table," he ordered, reaching for the bottle of lube.

Scrambling to do his bidding, she hardly noticed that she bumped a plate off the table. She shivered at the feel of her robe lifting to expose her ass. Her anticipation increased at the first drop of lube on her crack.

"Just imagining Bren and I fucking you together has me hard as a rock," Byron murmured as he pumped one finger, then two, into her puckered hole. His free hand switched the vibrator to the second, slightly faster setting. "That's his cock." The thick head that she knew so intimately by now pressed against her back door. "This is mine."

Her eyes rolled to the back of her head as he slowly thrust into her, slightly deeper every time. She's taken Byron like this many times before, but it always felt like the first. She clutched the edge of the table, unaware that she was making noise.

"You like that, Cin?" he bit out, gripping her hips as he picked up the pace. "Do you like feeling both our cocks?"

"Oh God, yes! By, please!"

He retreated and pitched forward, again and again, until she accepted all of him. The vibrations intensified once more, and her erect nipples were being stimulated against the smooth wood of the table. She loved the way he was using her and fulfilling his promise of fucking every orifice.

The spank he gave her ass jolted and thrilled her.

"You're so fucking sexy, baby. You're gonna make me cum so hard."

"*Ah!*" she exclaimed when he flipped the highest setting of the vibrator. "By, oh my God, yes!"

He squeezed the globes of her ass when the first contraction started. "Cin, fuck!" he shouted, unravelling right after her.

He didn't immediately switch the vibrator off, which meant that the device wrung orgasm after orgasm out of her while he softened in her ass. When her legs started shaking, he finally pulled out and gently turned her around to perch on the edge of the table.

"You okay?" She nodded, dazed, which made him smile. He pulled the robe down to her waist to cup her heavy breasts in his hands, stroking his thumbs over the sensitive peaks. "Ready for your next surprise?"

"Gosh, I don't know."

"Okay, let's take a nap first."

They went to the main room and stumbled onto the bed, spooning in the nude with the fan circling above them. Cinnia had a dreamless slumber and awoke at the feel of her husband's lips planting wet kisses on her shoulder. "Hmm, that feels so good," she whispered as she arched her butt against his erection. "Again?"

"Again."

He took her hand and led the way to the outdoor shower. There, they washed each other's bodies, hands lingering on sensitive areas, while kissing deeply. Cinnia wasn't at all surprised when she ended up pressed against the wall with his cock lodged all the way inside of her, or that they were both satisfied at the end of it: this is how it's always been for them. She was a lucky woman.

At his recommendation, she dressed in shorts and a tank top, with comfortable trainers. They walked to the front entrance of the resort, where a shuttle was waiting. She absorbed the scenery to their destination, loving the lush Hawaiian vegetation.

Byron got a call from Nixon, who gave him an update on the Falcons situation. It didn't seem as if Ian McDermot had planned any blowback as yet, meaning the Raptors had everything under control.

Cinnia could barely contain herself once the bus halted at a sign that read *ARV Adventures*. Hand-in-hand, they got their keys from reception and met with their tour guide. The trip took two hours in total and, while not the Harley experience she was used to, it was exhilarating. She didn't fail to notice the tension dissolving from Byron's shoulders and how his smile transformed his whole face. By God, he was a gorgeous man!

Afterwards, they headed to a nearby restaurant for lunch, talking about an article Byron had read on the flight here. Like her, he was interested in psychology and the writer of this particular piece had argued that certain events were inherited via genetics, unless children decided on a different route.

"I want Logan to follow his dreams," she admitted. "I want him to have more happy memories than sad, and no trauma. And loads of kids! Bren was an only child. *You* are an only child."

"From what he's told me, he wants at least three."

"Yeah, but *wanting* that and *getting* it are two very different things. I wanted two at some point."

"It'll happen as it should, Cin." He cleared his throat. "About his dreams... What if he doesn't want to be part of the club?"

"What do you mean?"

"I get the feeling his heart isn't really in it."

She blinked. "What makes you say that?"

"He mentioned something along those lines once. But I see it when he plays ball: something comes over him that I've never seen in the club. Or architecture, for that matter. I know you'd like to keep him close," he added, sensing her retort, "but if him living his dreams is really what you want, you should at least prepare for that possibility that he won't choose to stay."

Her argument dried up. She has witnessed this, too, but largely ignored the signs of Logan's need to explore the world. He was more like her than she gave him credit: she'd wanted to leave town and make a life for herself elsewhere, although she'd done it for the wrong reasons and hadn't fully appreciated the freedom away from the club. It was different for Logan because he was a Drummond. He represented the continuation of the

Raptors MC.

Then again, Logan also had a complicated relationship with Brennan. Did he even see himself as a Drummond?

Does it really matter who wears the Prez patch?

"I want him to do whatever makes him happy. Final answer."

Byron smiled. "Good."

"Let's talk about something else. How's that new case going?"

She listened intently while he explained the complexities, occasionally interrupted by their waiter taking and serving their orders. She admired Byron for being dedicated to his work. He'd been made a named partner at the firm this year and wanted them both to be retired five years from now. He was putting in a lot of extra hours to make it happen.

Filled to the brim with local cuisine, they meandered through a marketplace. She loved everything about these islands and could see why people braved the threat of a volcanic eruption to share in the magic.

With jetlag setting in, they went back to their bungalow for another nap. This time, it didn't lead to anything sexy because the resort had scheduled an evening of entertainment that Byron insisted they attend. They were shown to their seats at a large dinner table with other happy couples, most of whom were also on honeymoon. Cinnia had a few glasses of champagne, while Byron stuck to sparkling water.

Byron easily laughed at the corny jokes Joshua and Mary, their bungalow neighbors, were telling. She was too tired to do the same. Mary continuously called her Cynthia, like so many people who've come before her, and Cinnia didn't have the energy to correct her.

When desert was out of the way the show began. Cinnia was hypnotized by the movements of the dancers: there was something about the tribal drum beat that contributed to the romantic setting and she accepted shyly when one of the women pulled her towards the front to teach her a few steps. She quickly learned how to roll her hips the way the dancers did and, finding her husband's eyes in the crowd of men left at the tables, she showed off for him.

Byron was casually leaning back in his chair. To anyone watching, he was paying attention to Joshua's incessant chatter, but she could tell he was captivated by her. It wasn't long before he excused himself to join her, tugging her into his arms and holding her close.

"I'm in love with you, always."

Her heart melted and she leaned her head against his neck. "Always."

They swayed to the beat of the music. So many memories of being with Byron filled her head, flowing in and out of one another. Their level of devotion was incredibly rare.

He kissed her cheek. "Ready for bed?"

"Definitely."

They strolled back to the bungalow and, once inside, helped each other undress. He got into bed first, opening his arms to her, and she crawled in to cuddle into his chest. She lay listening to his heartbeat, feeling at peace. So much has transpired for them to get to this moment: she was grateful that she hadn't lost him along the way. Whatever happened with the Falcons—and whoever else decided to disturb the Raptors' peace—she was happy to be by his side.

"Thank you for an awesome day."

"The first of many, Mrs. Johannson. If every day isn't awesome, then I'm failing as a husband."

"I don't see how. Life is beautiful with you, Byron."

He tightened his grip, likely recalling when she'd said it before. "So beautiful."

CHAPTER NINE

LOGAN WOKE WITH a killer headache, although it came as no surprise. He'd continued drinking long after his parents left for their honeymoon, so much so that Connor had abandoned his attempts at wooing someone that looked like Jesse in favor of driving Logan home.

"You're such an idiot," Connor had muttered as he hauled his friend into bed.

"Where's my phone?" Logan had slurred, patting his empty pockets.

"You can have it back tomorrow."

"No!" Logan had frowned fiercely. "I need to phone Alyssa!"

Connor had sighed deeply while he pulled Logan's shoes off. "You've done that already. Fifteen times. What did—No, wait, I don't want to get sucked into this."

"Con!" Logan had exclaimed, sitting upright. The world had spun, momentarily disorienting him. "Where is Alyssa?"

"She went home."

Logan pouted. "Oh yeah."

"Look, if she really was that important to—" Connor had cut himself off again. "Nope, not doing this! You'll forget this conversation in the morning." He'd fixed Logan with a somber expression. "Sleep it off. I'll see you tomorrow."

Logan groaned in the present, pressing his palms against his temples. Connor was wrong: Logan remembered everything. He rolled over and his stomach heaved. "Shit," he muttered, rushing to the bathroom to hurl into the toilet bowl. What the fuck had he been thinking?

He remained in that position for a while. Flushing the toilet, he shakily rose and rummaged in the bathroom cabinet for painkillers. He swallowed two, brushed his teeth and took a quick shower. Dressing in sweatpants and a baggy shirt, he stumbled his way to the kitchen. It was nine-thirty, and he needed a big breakfast if he was going to survive the day. He took eggs from the fridge, bacon from the freezer, and got to work.

His phone rang somewhere nearby.

"Fuck," he muttered as he began the search. He found it on the dining room table and frowned at Connor's name on the screen. "What?"

"Good morning, sunshine!" Connor was being unusually bright, probably to piss Logan off. "How are you feeling on this beautiful Sunday?"

"Fuck off." Logan shuffled back to the stove.

"If you're answering, that must mean you're making breakfast," Connor sang. "Wanna go for a climb?"

"Stop talking or I'll shove my foot up your ass."

He burst out laughing. "How serious are you about that? I'm outside."

"You better take it down several notches when you come in." Logan hung up and carelessly chucked his phone on the counter. He heard the front door open and shut. Taking another trip to the fridge, he got out three eggs for Connor.

"Damn, you look worse than you sounded," Connor announced as he crossed the threshold.

"If you want this, you better be nice to me."

Contemplating his options, Connor let out a breath. "Fine. Have you taken something for your headache? I wrote you a prescription for schedule five drugs, just in case."

"Jesus, I'm not *that* much of a baby."

"I don't know, hey. You were bumbling like one last night." When Logan shot him a deathly glare, Connor held his hands up. "Sorry."

"What do you want, Con?"

"I've got the day off and wanted to go climbing, okay? But seeing as you're not up for that and it's way too late to head out there, I'll stick around and nurse you back to health." He grinned. "Dr. Tyrell, to the rescue."

Logan added bacon to a hot pan, his stomach grumbling at the sizzle. "Where were you last night? Why didn't you make me stop?"

"I thought you were drinking like you always do, not that you were trying to forget something. What happened with Alyssa?"

"She's way too smart for her own good. Put bread in the toaster, will you?"

"She figured out you have feelings for Luca, then?" At Logan's curt nod, Connor whistled. "Damn, that sucks. You two looked good together. For a second there, I really thought you were going to surprise me by going for the less obvious choice."

"Is it shit-on-Logan day?"

"You're way overdue."

"Fuck. *Off.*"

Chuckling, Connor turned the kettle on and prepared two cups of coffee. "Are Jesse and Luca here yet?"

"No." Logan frowned as he plated up, handing Connor one and sitting at the breakfast nook. "Why would they be?"

"Your mom told me Luca has a few more things she needs to take to Jesse's."

This was news to Logan. Mercifully, he was left alone while they ate, which gave him time to come to terms with everything that happened. Part of him wanted to wallow in self-pity. He should've known the Universe wouldn't allow that.

A knock on the door had Connor on high alert, reminding Logan of the day before when the Falcons had attempted to gate-crash the wedding. "Maybe it's Luca and Jesse."

Logan headed to the front. He opened it slightly, narrowing his gaze at the woman on the other side. "Can I help you?"

"I'm really sorry to bother," she said, wringing her hands in front of her. "I was meant to deliver the puppies tomorrow, but my mom fell ill and I urgently need to get to her. Can I give them to you now?"

It took him a moment to make the connection. "Oh, right, sure." He swung the door open and followed her to the van that was parked in the driveway. "Sorry about your mom."

"Thanks." She opened the rear door. "Hey, babies!" she cooed, pulling a big box closer. "Guess what? You're at your new home!"

"Here, let me get that for you," Logan suggested, picking it up. His heart melted at the two sleepy dogs huddled together. Yup, he was definitely already in love with them. "What's up, dawgs?"

Giggling, the woman grabbed another box. "You did not just say that."

"I know, I'm pretty lame. What's in there?"

"Uhm, your dad...?" She inclined her head when he did. "He asked me to put a few things together, like bowls, toys and food. Usually we leave that to the owners to buy, but he made a very generous donation to the shelter. He's such a nice man."

Logan smiled. "That sounds like him. You can leave that here, I'll get my friend to bring it in."

"Thank you. I'm really sorry for the inconvenience."

"It's no inconvenience. Good luck with your mom."

With a grateful wave, she ducked into the van and reversed out of the driveway.

"Let's get you guys inside," Logan said to the puppies. Connor was in the living room, watching highlights of the game they'd missed the night before. "Make yourself useful and grab the box outside."

"Sure, what've you got—" Connor broke off as he caught sight of the dogs, his hands diving inside to pick one of them up. "Oh my fuck, look at those ears! Hey, little guy! Who's a good boy?" His eyes briefly flicked to Logan. "What are they?"

"German shorthaired pointers, if I remember correctly. Give me that and get the other box!"

Reluctantly, Connor handed the puppy over. "I am cuddling these dogs today."

"Get in line." He placed the male with his sister and rushed to the kitchen to get his phone. Back in the living room, he dumped them onto his lap, petting them happily. They must be around nine weeks old and seemed to consist of gangly limbs and stretchy skin.

"So fucking cute," Connor said. "What're you doing?"

"Calling my dad."

When his mother answered, Logan had to backtrack fast. He did his best to evade her pointed questions but, once she threatened his trip to Amsterdam, he caved and told her about the puppies.

She looked blissful. Half of it had to do with the tropical honeymoon destination, yet he could tell that being married was attributing to the glow in her cheeks. Logan wished he could share in her exceptionally good mood, but after what happened with Alyssa, his own life seemed bleak in comparison. Her mention of Luca had his guard up again. In his current mood, he wasn't sure how he felt about the girl he'd rescued from the side of the road.

They said their goodbyes, and Logan stared at the device in his hand. He texted Alyssa: *"I'm sorry about yesterday. Can we talk?"*

"For fuck's sake," Connor muttered from behind him, grabbing the phone. "I leave you unsupervised for one second and you go back to digging your own grave."

"Give that back!"

"No way." He gestured to the dogs. "I think they need to pee. Off you go."

Growling "this isn't over" under his breath, Logan picked the puppies up and carried them to the backyard. His sour mood evaporated as he watched them clamber down the patio's steps and onto the grass. Damn, they were cute! They did their business and hurried back to him, yelping excitedly.

"Hey, guys," he murmured while he stroked their smooth fur. He quickly learned that they enjoyed being scratched behind their long ears and under their jaws. Why hadn't he grown up with pets? He's missed out on a ton of love.

"…a cup of coffee."

Logan's interest was roused at the sound of Connor's voice. Who was he talking to?

"I'll have tea, thanks."

Jesse.

Logan was interested to know if Connor would ever make his move. The man talked a big game that worked wonders on other women, but he turned into a meek little lamb whenever he was in Jesse's presence.

"Right, you don't drink coffee."

"Only if I'm having biscuits." There was a short silence and Logan had to strain to hear them over the sound of the kettle starting up. "So, uhm, what happened to your date? Trade her for that girl at the wedding?"

Connor coughed. "Yeah. She's from Garrett's charter."

"Have you… seen her before? You looked cozy."

"We met last night."

"Oh."

Any fool could hear that Jesse didn't enjoy hearing about his conquests. Why wasn't Connor picking up on that? Surely he wasn't *that* worried about his anger management issue that he would deny them both the relationship they wanted?

"You're probably looking forward to Amsterdam."

Ah, that's *the reason why Connor isn't telling Jesse how he feels.*

"It's gonna be fun to get away for a while. Work is killing me. How's your writing coming along?"

"Great. I had to pull myself away from the screen to bring Luca here." Jesse laughed to herself.

"I'd like to read what you're working on."

Logan frowned. He'd given Connor the link! Had he not read it yet, or was this his way of letting her know that he might in future?

"Oh no!" came Jesse's rushed response. "I mean, uh, I don't think you'll like it."

"And you know what I like?"

Logan suddenly felt guilty for eavesdropping. He turned his attention to the puppies, who were tugging on his sweatpants. "Are you guys hungry, hmm?" They followed him to the kitchen, sniffing their new surroundings along the way. He came to an abrupt halt, immediately sensing the thick sexual tension in the room.

Jesse's freckled cheeks were pink and her arms folded over her ample bosom, while Connor stared at her from the counter with hooded eyelids.

"Hi, Jess."

"Hey, Logan. How's the hangover?"

"Better." He gestured to the puppies. "Look what we got."

"Oh my gosh!" Jesse dropped to her knees and called them over, giggling when they began licking her outstretched hands. "They are so cute! What're their names?"

"I don't know yet."

Jesse grinned at him. "While your folks are away, you can use these two as chick magnets."

"They're just about the only game I've got," Logan said, playing along.

Connor snorted. "Oh, please."

"I don't know how you're going to focus on finals with them around." She hugged them lightly, laughing as they attacked her unruly copper hair. A brief glance at Connor confirmed that he wished he could be a puppy right about now.

"Here's your tea, Jess."

She let go of the dogs and accepted it from Connor. "Thanks."

Logan heard his phone beeping with a message and made a beeline for the living room while Connor was distracted. His heart was beating fast at the mere thought of hearing from Alyssa. He was crushed when he saw his mother's name.

"They're Charlie and Bobby Brown. Love you. Xx."

He answered with a thumbs-up. The dogs had followed him and were scratching at the box, as if they longed to go inside again. He tilted it on its side and adjusted the blanket. His heart swelled with love, momentarily forgetting that Alyssa wasn't talking to him.

He began unpacking the additional box, wondering where he could store the food and toys. Movement from the staircase caught his attention and he held his breath at the sight of Luca. She was wearing a long-sleeved shirt with abraded jeans, which has become her signature look. Her silky black hair was in a ponytail, leaving her pretty face bare.

"Hi, Logan," she greeted with a wary tone to her voice. She was carrying a small duffel bag. "Your mom said it's okay that I come here."

He nodded. They stared at each other in awkward silence for a moment; then Logan cleared his throat, causing her to twitch. "She said she invited you back."

She winced. "Don't worry, she's just being nice."

"I think you should, if… if you want."

"Why? You hate me."

God damn, those violet eyes were unnerving. He couldn't focus when she gazed at him this way: earnestly, not at all the femme fatale he's made ger out to be. "I don't, Luca," he said truthfully.

"Well, you don't trust me. That's worse."

He raised an eyebrow. "You didn't trust me, once upon a time."

She turned away, hiding her facial expression. "It hurts, Logan. To trust people, I mean. I never could before. And now that I do, you can just…

decide you're done with me and that hurts even more."

Is this an act?

He hated that his mind went there but, until that moment when the truth about her instructions from the Falcons came out, he never would've considered that she could be anything except a downtrodden young girl who needed his help.

The way you like her, right? Helpless little victim.

He shook his head and stepped closer to gently touch her shoulder. She visibly squirmed but didn't step away. Instead, she turned back to him with tears in her eyes, biting her full bottom lip.

"I'm sorry," he whispered. "I didn't want to believe that you could go through with it, but it would've been so easy for you."

"Why?"

Because I was falling in love with you. I might still be.

He couldn't tell her any of that: not because he thought she'd use it against him, but because he would be broken if she didn't feel the same. Alyssa's words echoed in his mind and even though he hated that she'd left, he now understood that there was unfinished business between him and Luca.

He was saved from having to answer when the puppies showed their cute faces.

Luca jumped, looking terrified. "When did you get dogs?"

"Dad got mom these, for when I move out. Don't you like dogs?"

"Not really. I was bitten once."

"You'll change your mind when you see how adorable they are." He motioned for her to walk closer. "They're still young. We can teach them not to bite."

She stood next to him and gazed at the sleeping puppies with an imperceptible facial expression. "Okay, they're adorable," she confessed.

"Told you."

"What happened to Alyssa last night?"

His heart clenched. "She had somewhere else she needed to be."

"Oh." Luca tugged at her ponytail, probably not realizing how flirtatious that came across. "I like her. She's so... *open.*"

Me too, he thought numbly. "Do you have plans for today?"

"I'm writing my final essay for English. Jesse said she'll help."

"I've got to study, too." Bowls and dog food in hand, he led the way to the kitchen, where the sexual tension between Connor and Jesse had tripled. How was that possible? "Con, are you gonna stick around today?"

"Nah, you've got work to do."

"How about you, Jess? Are you going to hang out here?"

Jesse and Luca exchanged a glance that only they could possibly understand. "We could, if that's okay. It's quieter here than at my place."

"Sure, it would be cool not to be alone today."

"I'll just go get our laptops," Jesse said, tucking a thick red curl behind her ear.

Connor smirked. "Let me give you a ride."

Her facial expression read: "I wish you would". She abruptly turned on her heel and marched out of the kitchen.

"It's fun riling her up," Connor chuckled.

"One day, she's going to have fun at *your* expense."

"I can't wait."

"Gross."

"I have a question." Luca squirmed when their gazes landed on her. "Uhm, why don't you just take her, Connor? Isn't that what men do?"

"She has to want me, too."

Luca's dark eyebrows bunched together. "Want... you?"

He rubbed his shaved head. "Unless she tells me that she wants me to have sex with her, I won't do it. It's not right."

"Oh."

It was clear that Luca didn't really understand. Despite knowing that rape was wrong and that she'd been a victim of sexual abuse, she had no way of knowing what role desire played between consenting people. Her trauma was too recent.

"You'll know what it's like one day, if you choose," Logan murmured. The idea seemed appalling to her and he coughed, shifting his attention to filling the puppies' food bowls.

"Connor!" Jesse yelled from the front.

"Let me go help my girl," Connor muttered as he headed out.

Logan rolled his eyes. "Hopeless."

"He's very protective of her."

"That's 'cause he loves her." Logan watched the puppies eat, smiling. "I'll set up in the dining room. Are you going to be okay working in... your room?"

"Yes." She caught his eye. "Thank you, Logan."

He dipped his head and walked to the dining room. Once his textbooks and study notes were on the table, he went to fetch the puppies and moved them to the covered patio, leaving their toys and bowls within reach. Then he checked his phone.

There were no messages from Alyssa.

Sighing, he hunched over the mock exam, trying to focus on the multiple theories and equations he needed to know. In his current state of mental fog, it was easier said than done. His latest conversations with both Alyssa and Luca kept swirling in his mind, making it difficult to concentrate.

Fifteen minutes later, he'd read one page and completed zero questions.

With another deep sigh, he rubbed his closed eyes. He couldn't afford to be distracted. Damn Alyssa and her silent treatment! Maybe he should show up at her apartment—

Don't be pathetic. Who's to say she'll let you in? Besides, what are you going to tell her: that you've miraculously been cured of your attraction to Luca? Especially now that Luca might be moving in again?

The whole situation was too complicated. He had never expected to meet someone like Alyssa mere months after rescuing Luca, or to go through anything that's happened since. He couldn't deny that he wanted them both, in very different ways.

You're so messed up.

He shut his book and pushed the chair back, staring out of the window. His parents must be having the time of their lives and here he was, overthinking life. He had to pull his shit together.

He decided to text Nina. The only way to rein in his scattered thoughts was to wear the Dominant hat for a couple of hours.

"I'll be there in twenty," came Nina's reply.

Relieved, he went upstairs to prepare his bedroom. He checked his nightstand for condoms, righted the covers and plumped up his pillows; then chucked his discarded suit from the night before in the laundry hamper in the bathroom. He paused in front of Luca's door, knocking twice.

"Come in."

She and Jesse looked cozy around Luca's small desk. Logan hadn't realized until this moment how much he's missed seeing Luca in this house.

"What's up, Lo?" Jesse asked.

"Uh, Nina's coming over."

Jesse cocked an eyebrow. "Is she helping you study?"

"Something like that."

"Cool."

Logan couldn't decipher the expression on Luca's face. The doorbell interrupted before he could ask her about it. "See you later," he muttered, shutting the door. By the time he stood facing Nina, he was ready to get down and dirty.

"Hey," she greeted with a slight smile. "You seem… tense."

"Go to my room, strip down to your underwear and kneel in front of the bed."

She bit her bottom lip, her blue eyes sparkling as they dropped to the base of his neck. "Yes, sir."

He watched her take the stairs two at a time, rolling his shoulders to get rid of excess tension. He got a couple of bottles of water from the fridge. He checked on the puppies, happily noting that they were keeping themselves entertained, and grabbed his phone from the dining room.

He slowly walked to his room, placing his mind under strict control. His eyes landed on Nina's half-dressed form, placing the bottles on a nightstand and shedding his T-shirt. He put two condoms next to the water.

"When's the last time you came?"

Her brief hesitation was revealing. "This morning, sir."

"Was that the only time?"

"No, sir."

He tilted his head to the side and crossed his arms over his bare chest. "How many times have you made yourself cum since the last time we were together?"

Nina's blonde locks covered her facial expression, since she was gazing at the floor, but he got the feeling that she was excited. "Three times?"

"Is that the truth?"

"Hard to tell. It's been a while since we saw each other."

"Don't give me lip."

"Sorry, sir."

He strode to his closet to take out a leather belt. "What did I say would happen if you made yourself cum without permission?"

"You would give me ten lashings for every orgasm."

Kneeling to get his climbing bag from under his bed, he took out one of the shorter ropes. "Bend over the edge of the mattress. Cup your elbows behind your back." He used the rope to weave an intricate pattern from shoulders to waist and secure her arms against her spine. "Too tight?"

"No, sir."

His feet pushed hers apart and he pressed his crotch on her toned ass, grinding against her. "Did you pretend I was fucking you like this while you got yourself off?"

"Yes."

"Excuse me?"

"Yes, sir!"

"Better." He reached between them and tugged her lace panties to her knees, securing them there. Then he trailed his fingers up and down the back of her thighs, watching her pussy intently. "Did you think you deserve to be fucked?"

"Y-yes, sir."

"Did you beg for it?"

She moaned softly, arching up as if she wanted to be closer to his breath. "Yes, sir!"

"Let's hear it, then. Beg."

"Please fuck me, sir!"

He couldn't ignore the desire in her tone. He licked his forefinger and slipped it between her folds, finding her sopping wet. Suppressing a knowing chuckle, he pushed his appendage inside and murmured: "Like this?"

"Faster!"

"Anything else?"

"More!" She rocked her hips when he added another finger. "Harder!"

He allowed her to believe that she could tell him what to do. He nibbled on the round globes of her ass, whispering dirty words of encouragement as she set the pace, her body's needs trumping her usual control.

"Oh fuck, I'm gonna—"

Logan withdrew and straightened.

"No, please!" she begged, her undulating hips seeking friction. "Please don't stop, sir!"

He picked the belt up, letting its tip slide over one of her butt cheeks. "I want you to think carefully: how many times did you make yourself cum without me?"

She whimpered as her orgasm subsided. "Please, sir!"

"How many times, Nina?"

Her heavy breathing belied her sexual frustration. "Six," she admitted finally.

"So, you lied to me earlier?"

"Yes, sir," she whispered.

"That's going to cost you." Without further ado, his belt landed on her skin with an audible *thwack*! He grinned when she remained quiet. "Why aren't you counting?"

"I'm sorry, sir! That was two!"

"Start again," he ordered as the leather connected for a third time.

"One!"

He watched the red streaks blossoming on her behind and added another. "Two!"

Logan started slowly, softly, and increased the power of the lashings incrementally. She counted each one eagerly. He stopped and dropped the belt, biting his lip at the sight of her crimson ass. It reminded him of the hue of Alyssa's mouth the day before, and how her kisses had made an imprint on his soul.

Stop it!

"Twenty," she panted.

"Does it hurt?"

"A little, sir."

"We're not even halfway." He got a condom, dropped his pants, and sheathed his aching dick. "Should I take the pain away?"

"Please, sir!"

Positioning his tip at her entrance, he thrust inside and grunted. He gripped her long, blonde tresses in one hand, remembering how much she loved that, and held her hips with the other. He pounded into her, fast and hard, while he tried to forget about the girl with the colorful hair.

"Oh yes," Nina mumbled, "oh God, oh fuck, oh *yes*!"

Logan pulled out at the last second, before they both unraveled. It couldn't be over this soon! He swiped a hand over his face, hoping to get his head back in the game. *Fuck Alyssa*, he thought angrily. *She didn't want me enough!*

"Please don't stop!" the girl in front of him pleaded.

His hand took hold of his belt once more. "Count," he said curtly, bringing it down on her ass repeatedly. His body was rigid with tension as he pushed his own insecurities aside. The last thing he wanted was to injure Nina in a fit of rage.

"Sixteen!" she screamed, nearly sobbing as her body continuously tipped between pleasure and pain. "Logan, *please!*"

He didn't hear the knock at first, which was why he nearly jumped out of his skin when he heard someone other than Nina cry out: "Logan, *no!*"

Glancing over his shoulder, he went cold once he spotted Luca and Jesse. He could only imagine how this had to appear to someone who's been physically and sexually abused. That clichéd saying, "this isn't what it looks like", threatened to spill from his lips. He chucked the belt aside and pulled his pants up.

"Stop it! Don't hurt her!"

"Luca, I'm not."

"Yes, you *are!* You're one of them! I can't believe you're one of *them!*"

God, it hurt being compared to the fuckers that had done such unspeakable things to her! Logan leaned over to place one end of the rope in Nina's hand. With a simple tug, she would be free. "I'll be right back," he murmured, steering the hysterical girl—and an obviously curious one—into the hallway. "Luca, calm down."

She fought against his hold. "Let go of me!"

"Look at me, sweetheart." He cupped her face. Her fingers scratched his wrists, and he clenched his jaw at the sting. "Breathe, Luca. Nina is okay. I wasn't hurting her."

"I saw you!"

"I know what it looked like, but I promise you that I didn't do anything Nina didn't want me to."

Luca didn't understand. "You *hit* her with a *belt!* How can—"

"The thing is, sometimes that's what women want," Jesse interrupted quietly.

"What?! Why would someone—"

"It feels good!" Nina shouted, appearing in the hallway. She had a sheet wrapped around her body and her mascara was smudged from frustrated tears. "I wanted him to punish me for getting off without his permission! *Urgh!*"

Logan had to fight an amused smile as the blonde stormed into the bathroom. He made eye contact with Jesse, who would no doubt use this interaction as material for one of her books.

"I thought you said she's helping you study," she winked.

"I couldn't concentrate." He turned to Luca. "We help each other. We're what's called 'friends with benefits'. We dabble in bondage and spanking. It's consensual."

She was shaking her head, refusing to believe him. "But she was hurting, and you didn't stop!"

"I couldn't stop unless she asked me to."

"That doesn't make any sense!"

He sighed. "I realize how it looks and I'm sorry you had to see it. Just know that I'll *never* hurt a woman. Nina and I were playing."

"Come on, I'll try explain it," Jesse murmured, steering Luca back into her room. "Keep it down, Lo."

"Sorry." Logan raked his fingers through his hair once the door was shut between them and turned to the bathroom. "Nina? Are you okay?"

"No, I need a fucking orgasm!"

"Were you trying to get off in here?"

"It's not working." She pushed past him and headed for his bedroom.

He caught her elbow and swung her around, pressing her against the door. "I haven't finished with you."

"Wow, that's hot." One corner of her mouth lifted. "What're you going to do, force yourself on me?"

"Is that what you want?" He was unable to deny how intriguing the idea was, especially considering that it went against everything he'd been told, growing up.

"Yes," she answered simply. "The safe word is 'red'."

A thrill went down his spine. Grabbing her aggressively, he shoved her towards the bed. His fingers curled around her ankles and he forced her legs apart, grinning when she began kicking.

"Do you really think you can fight me off?" he challenged, stepping between her thrashing limbs. He hooked his thumbs into the waistband of his sweatpants to push them down, and then realized he'll have to replace the limp condom on his cock.

Nina's strong nudge against his chest nearly sent him sprawling, and she took the opportunity to climb further onto the bed. Damn cheerleader strength!

Logan flipped her onto her stomach and pulled off the pesky condom. He raised her hips while using his other hand to keep her upper body flattened on the rumpled covers. He reached for the spare condom on his nightstand and lifted it to his mouth to rip the foil packaging.

When his hand's pressure against her back eased, she wriggled away and bolted for the door. He darted after her, stopping her from escaping just in time by crushing her body between his and the solid wood.

"No!"

He hurriedly rolled the condom on and once again parted her legs. "Yes."

"Get off me!" she moaned.

He had to bend his knees to get a good angle. His cock's tip went in and he struggled to go further: her constant squirming made it difficult. He clasped her hips and righted his posture, slipping fully inside her tight pussy and preventing her feet from finding traction on the floor.

She gasped in surprise and slammed her hands on the door to keep from falling over. "Oh *God,* stop!"

He rammed into her almost brutally, amazed that her fantasy was this good. They both grunted whenever he hit home, and he cupped her tits as he retreated all the way, intent on driving inside harder than before.

Nina used his new position and angle to turn around and push him away, eyes widening with appreciation when he didn't budge this time.

He smirked. In one smooth transition, he had her sandwiched against the wall with her calves hooked over his shoulders. His cock entered her again while he pinned her arms above her head, successfully rendering her immobile.

Her eyelids fluttered and her lips parted. "You got me."

"Always get what I want."

Their soft cries and the sound of their bodies joining together filled the room. Logan buried his face in the crook of her neck to suck on her skin, and she exclaimed another profanity as she tipped over, finally getting that orgasm she'd longed for.

He followed shortly after, breathing harshly.

"Wow. That was… amazing!"

His body was weak, but he helped her to her feet before he stepped away. He stumbled onto the bed. "Fucking hell."

"I should thank Luca," Nina mused, using the discarded sheet to dry herself off. "She went from interrupting what could've been the best punishment, to causing the best sex of my life. That was exactly the way I wanted to end this."

Logan's afterglow was shot to shit. "What?"

"My flight's leaving Friday night, after our last exam, and I'm starting my period tomorrow."

"Damn, wish I'd known that sooner. I would've got roses petals or something."

She burst out laughing. "I'm not a rose petals kind of girl, Lo." She tied her hair into a bun and sashayed over to kiss him on the cheek. "Thanks for these last couple of months. It's been fun."

"Likewise."

"I'll let myself out. See you Friday!"

He watched her leave the room and breathed out harshly. Damn, was he wrecked after that round of Hurricane Nina! How had she been so energetic?

Five minutes later, he felt recovered enough to clean up his bedroom. He donned a shirt and sweatpants again and sauntered to the dining room. This time, his mind was as clear as he needed it.

Before the sun dipped below the horizon, he fed the puppies again and prepared food while they played at his feet. He wondered how the talk between Jesse and Luca had gone. He called them downstairs when dinner was ready, but didn't receive a response. Had they left?

Maybe that's for the best.

He took his plate to the living room and fluffed up the dogs' blanket. He smiled as they curled up together, his heart warming at their cuteness.

Luca joined him for the eight o'clock movie, a steaming plate on her lap. "Thanks for cooking."

"You're welcome. Where's Jesse?"

"She went home." She gave him a sideways look. "I'd like to spend the night."

"Sure."

For a while, they sat in silence: watching the movie while she finished her meal. He could already feel the distrust between them fading, which was a relief. He had no idea what the future had in store, but he was glad they were on the mend.

"Jesse Googled what you told me, to show me how… I'm sorry I jumped to conclusions, or if I made things weird between you and Nina."

"Don't worry about it. I know it's confusing."

"Yeah, I still don't understand how it can feel good, but I wanted you to know that I don't judge you. I'm sorry that I said you're like the others. I know you're not."

"Thank you, Luca."

She seemed relieved that he wasn't making a big deal of her reaction. With a smile, she took her plate to the kitchen.

Logan stared after her, thinking: *maybe one day, you'll ask me to do what I've done with Nina.* Apart from playing for Everton or Alyssa texting him back, he couldn't imagine something more exciting.

CHAPTER TEN

AMSTERDAM WAS EVERYTHING Logan had hoped it would be, and more. He and Connor were making every moment an adventure. The two-bedroom apartment they rented had an easy commute to the bar where they worked. For the most part, they had the same shifts, which left them with loads of time to explore together.

Naturally, one of their first stops had been the red-light district. They'd smoked weed and partied with other tourists, and they weren't shy about taking girls home. It took his mind off Alyssa, who still wasn't answering any of his calls or texts. He missed her.

A month in, he'd fallen into a comfortable rhythm. Connor joined him whenever he went to a field to practice football. The guy was as hung up on Jesse as Logan was on Alyssa and, to an extent, Luca, so they tended to look for as many physically exhausting activities as they could. By the time they got home, they barely had enough energy to make dinner before they passed out.

His parents kept him up to date with news via frequent video calls and he did his best to omit the boys-gone-wild scenario he was living overseas. Every once in a while, Luca sat with Cinnia and Byron. She'd moved back in with them a few days before Logan left and, as far as anyone could tell, she wasn't selling the Raptors out.

It was now his first day off in nearly a week and he's decided to go sightseeing alone, since Connor was working: he's wanted to visit a string of museums that Connor would find boring.

There wasn't a cloud in the sky. He had a smile on his face as he took a tram, only half paying attention to the chatter around him. He consulted a *Good Food* list on his phone and settled on going for brunch at a cozy restaurant that had rave reviews for their ice cream. He needed to get something in his stomach before he could brave the long queues at museums.

He alighted at a busy street and followed the directions on the restaurant's website, easily meandering through the crowd. A spot of turquoise caught his eye as he approached the entrance and he looked up, coming to an astonished halt.

Alyssa sat alone, typing on a tablet device. Her hair was the color of the Mediterranean, styled in a messy mohawk. She wasn't wearing makeup, and her loose-fitting blouse and denim hot pants suggested that she'd hit the ground running this morning. A neon pink bikini was visible underneath the translucent material of her top.

His feet were moving before he'd made a conscious decision to go to her. This couldn't be coincidence: it had to be fate that the girl he couldn't quit thinking about was sitting here, at the very restaurant he'd picked on a whim, in Amsterdam. He stopped in front of her.

"Hi."

She gasped as she made eye contact. "Logan?"

"May I join you?"

"S-sure." Her dark eyes were glued to him as he took a seat. "What're you doing here?"

"I told you about my Amsterdam trip. I'm here for three months before I start studying."

"Right, I forgot about that."

"What about you?"

"My last blog post went viral, so a travelling agency offered me a one-year contract to write articles for them. They want me to visit every country in Europe, all expenses paid, as long as I produce a daily post."

He was impressed. "Wow, that's huge! Congratulations."

"Thanks." She shifted her gaze to the waiter, who'd placed her order on the table and turned to Logan expectantly. "Uhm, do you want anything?"

So many things. For one, I want to take you right here, right now, and make you scream.

"Sure." He gestured to her order, a silent request for the waiter to get him the same. He absorbed her appearance, struck by that light that's been missing in his life: it was like her every pore exuded it. "It's good to see you, Betty."

She bit down on the inside of her cheeks, fighting a smile. "You too, Beanie. I've missed you."

"You have no idea." He raked his fingers through his hair. "You could've texted me back."

"And say what?"

"I don't know, just… *something*. I shouldn't have let you get in the car. We were on our way to something really great and—"

"Are you with Luca yet?"

Sighing, he shook his head and answered: "She's fifteen and a victim of physical and sexual abuse, and was dumped in our territory a few months ago. I'm protective of her, I'm not going to apologize for that. *That's* what I should've told you."

"There's more to it than that."

"Lys—"

"Logan, hear me out." She motioned at the space between them. "This would be intense. We could be incredible together. I felt it the first time I saw you. But you'll always wonder about *her*. I won't be in a relationship with someone who's holding out for another woman. I'm not a placeholder."

She was right about everything. He was pining for Luca, but Alyssa deserved to be a leading lady in someone's life.

The waiter brought Logan's smoothie and meal, breaking the tension.

"I respect you for not settling for less than what you want."

She picked her cutlery up and dug in. "I know."

"What's your itinerary?"

"I don't really have one. The agency doesn't necessarily want me to tread on the beaten path, you know? They already have people who plan the conventional trips. They want to cater for people like me."

"Can I join you today?"

She nearly choked on her food. "Why?"

"I have the day off. Let me experience the kind of holidays you'll be suggesting to people reading your blog."

"Lo—"

"Please, Alyssa. I'd like to spend time with you."

She gazed at him for a while. "Okay."

His spirit lifted, buoyant with giddiness. "Do you like travelling alone?"

"For the most part, yeah. I can go where I want, when I want... But I sometimes miss having company. Then again, I haven't really been able to travel with anyone for extended periods of time. They all start irritating me after a while."

"Do you at least, you know, get wild in each place you visit?"

She raised an eyebrow, reading between the lines. "What if I do?"

Yeah, Lo, what if she does? What if she has incredible sex with every suave European that comes her way?

"I'm glad you're putting yourself out there."

"Don't pout. You're probably messing around, too."

"It doesn't mean anything."

"What, are you using them to forget about me?" she teased.

He became somber. "Yes, actually."

The energy between them shifted. Alyssa sat back, pushing her plate aside as if she's lost her appetite. She winked the waiter nearer and asked for two glasses of still water. Logan added ice cream to their order and finished his delicious brunch.

"You don't have to say anything, Betty. It's not your fault I can't stop thinking about you."

She toyed with the cutlery on her plate. "I think about you, too."

Thank the gods!

The large bowl of ice cream arrived and he handed her a spoon. "How's Emile?"

"Good. He's got a boyfriend now, which means I don't get to see him often. This trip happened at the perfect time. How about you? Is Amsterdam everything you wanted it to be?"

"It's better, actually. It feels good to be away from home for a while, to not worry about the club."

"That's right, you're like their king. Is your head getting heavy, Beanie?"

He rolled his eyes. "You try being eighteen and running an MC."

"I haven't been eighteen in three years." She gazed at him seriously.

"What's the MC about, anyway? With everything that happened, I never got around to asking why it started in the first place. From what I experienced, it's... dangerous."

"It's not supposed to be. Any motorcycle club starts because a bunch of people have a shared love and interest in a certain type of bike, or because people enjoy travelling on one, or both. For us, it's Harleys. We love doing breakfast runs and weekend trips away."

"But it's not that simple, is it?"

"No, my great-grandfather immigrated from Scotland and banded together with a couple of families. They got into Harleys because there was a craze in the area and formed a gang, which later became the Raptors. They took the law into their own hands and, because of that, got approached by drug cartels and gun traders to move product. They also had loads of run-ins with other clubs in the area, like the Falcons." He swallowed thickly. "The guy who ambushed us at the waterfall was a Falcon."

"Right, I remember. How come the Falcons still have it out for you?"

"Grandpa Reade tried to stop it, way back when, because a club is meant to be enjoyed by its members, not put them in danger. But Ramsay had set up too many dodgy deals and it took years before the blowback stopped, and it only did because my grandpa made a deal with..." He trailed off and rubbed his forehead, suddenly exhausted. There has been so much violence in his family line: he wanted no part of it. "We had to fight for our territory."

She pointed the spoon at him, thoughtful. "But it's not *your* territory, is it? It's owned by people, and the government."

"Sure, on paper."

"And these days, does the club, you know, kill people?"

He sat back, clenching his jaw. "Not if we can help it, but other clubs don't agree with our ethos. So, if we do... It's more like self-defense."

"Sure," she nodded, only half-skeptically. "What happened to that guy from the waterfall?"

Logan remembered Luca's confession; the long nights uncle Teagan wasted in an effort to track down the Falcons. His shoulders were tense, like the weight of the world resided there. Maybe his head *was* heavy.

"Don't know. They disappeared."

She gazed at him for a long, silent moment. "So, it's like being in an old Western movie?"

"Basically. The complete opposite of your life, which is old Hollywood glamour."

Alyssa snorted. "Sure."

"You can't deny that your family is filthy rich."

"Neither can you."

"But yours *acts* rich."

"One of the many reasons why I try to see them as little as possible." She sighed deeply, putting the spoon down. "Nothing is *real* with them. It's all about superficial connections to further your own agenda. Maybe it was different in the beginning, but I'm from old money and by now they've accepted their lives as is. They don't question anything. Relatives insist on relationships because of blood, not because they actually like each other. It's not real."

"And you want real?"

Her eyes locked on his. "Don't you?"

Yeah, Logan, don't you?

He couldn't look away. Something was altering in his heart. "Of course."

"Be careful what you wish for: breaking generational curses can be a lonely road." A hint of a smile was on her lips as she tucked her tablet into her backpack. "I guess it's time we get out of here. Ready for a day full of fun and adventure?"

"Bring it on."

Logan insisted on paying the bill. She only gave in because he promised he'll let her buy magic mushrooms later. Excited to see the city through her eyes, he walked alongside her.

"Where's Connor today?"

"Working. He'll be pissed when he finds out I saw you. Everyone likes you and they all blame me that you're not around anymore."

"It was your fault," she grinned, bumping her hip against his. "Why did your parents never have another kid?"

"My dad didn't want any, apparently."

"How about you? Do you see yourself as a father?"

"Definitely. I'd love a big family, like three or four kids."

"Ugh, I feel sorry for the woman who ends up bearing your kids, 'cause you are huge."

Leering at her, he said: "But you've never seen my dick, Betty."

"Oh my God!" She burst out laughing and smacked his shoulder. "You know what I meant!"

"How about you? Will you be a mom?"

"I don't know. With the right guy, sure."

"How will you know he's the right guy?"

Her eyes darted to his for a second. "I'll just know."

"For what it's worth, I think you'll be a great mom."

"Thanks, Beanie. You're gonna be a pretty cool dad, too."

They arrived at the beach. Alyssa was adamant about going kitesurfing, not that he was complaining. He liked being able to share his love of extreme activities. She wasn't afraid to throw herself into dangerous situations, which matched his own temperament: she didn't have a fear of death, and he could relate.

They zipped up each other's wetsuits, grabbed their surfboards and headed for the water.

"Not really a windy day," she commented.

"Guess we'll have to make lemonade. Race you!"

They waded deeper into the water and straddled their boards while they waited for a breeze to pick up. Logan gazed at her, smiling at her enthusiasm. It was addicting.

"Oh, yes!" she exclaimed suddenly. "Here I go!"

He followed her lead, jumping to his feet as the wind tugged at his sails. He generally had good balance, mostly thanks to yoga, but he could feel his core working at stabilizing the rest of his body while the board moved over the water. Alyssa was ahead of him, giggling in delight.

They were in the ocean for over an hour, and yet it felt like five minutes. Laughing on the way out, they returned their boards to the rental hut and strode to the outside showers.

"Help me out, will you?" she asked, struggling to grab hold of her zip.

Logan pulled it down from her neck to the small of her back. She had an incredible body: it took all his willpower not to sexualize the moment. He remembered how kissing her had changed his perspective on desire and—

Friends! You can't be anything more than friends.

"Thanks." She turned around as she peeled the top part off. "Do you need a hand?"

"Please." He swallowed thickly at the feel of his wetsuit loosening. If he didn't calm the hell down, he was going to show everyone in their vicinity the effect she had on him.

"When did you get that tattoo?" she asked, touching the geometric lion design on his ribs.

It felt like she'd electrocuted him. "A week ago."

"It's healing nicely." She carefully tugged her wetsuit off her legs, seeming relieved when it didn't pull her bikini bottom down. "Wasn't your real dad tattooed all over?"

Logan frowned at the mention of Brennan. "He was a tattoo artist."

"Interesting how you never knew him, but are a lot like him. It makes me wonder about the whole nature versus nurture thing."

Like I haven't thought about that enough.

She opened the taps of the shower, and he watched the water splash on the places he longed to feel. She ran her fingers through her hair when she was done and reached for a towel, only then becoming aware of his ogling. Her gaze met his.

He could definitely not get out of this wetsuit here. "I'm, uh, gonna go to the bathroom."

"I'll meet you at the entrance?"

"Deal." He grabbed his belongings and hurried into the male restroom. *Pull it together, man!* He took an ice-cold shower and, although it took care of his erection, it did absolutely nothing to his general state of arousal. "Fucking hell."

His underwear was soaked through from sweat, leaving him with no other option but to go commando. He shoved his briefs into his back pocket, inhaled deeply and sauntered out. Alyssa was fully dressed.

"Where are we going next?" he asked.

"I don't know about you, but I'm hungry."

"We could head to the district for a bite to eat, and then grab those shrooms?"

She wrinkled her nose. "I can't believe I suggested that."

"You said you've done it before."

"Sure, but…" She trailed off and shook her head. "Let's go."

The streets were busy on the way to the city center. Loud music played in every other shop, announcing the impending arrival of another night of wild partying. If Connor had been here, they would've ended up at a bar until the early hours of the morning.

With a crowd this thick, Alyssa looped her arm around his to prevent them from being separated. He's craved close contact with her the entire day, but he played it cool. The last time he'd enjoyed himself this much was at the wedding, but that was when she'd left him. He didn't want that to happen again.

They purchased a small bag of potent shrooms from a vender who was gazing at them with unabashed interest. Logan absently took note of the instructions as Alyssa paid. They thanked the man for his assistance and went to the closest food stall for a bite to eat.

Logan used every excuse he could think of to touch her, from wiping imaginary sauce from her chin to smoothing her shirt because it was "riding up". He was addicted to the feel of her skin and felt a bit high already.

"Where are we going to take this?" she asked, waving the bag in the air.

He considered that. "I've got a great view from my apartment building's rooftop. We should wait for our food to digest first, though. We can't take shrooms on a full stomach."

"Okay, let's stop at a few museums." She shrugged when he raised an eyebrow. "I feel bad that you're not getting something you want out of today."

Oh, you don't know that for sure, Logan thought wickedly. "Cool, follow me."

He's seen plenty of different expressions on Alyssa's face, but has never witnessed true wonderment until they were at a contemporary art exhibition. In fact, he was glad she got distracted, since it gave him an opportunity to stare. He adored the curve of her neck and how her short hair drew attention to her big, brown eyes. Those plump lips that had once been pliant against his parted as she saw a piece she liked more than the others, making him wish he had the guts to kiss her again.

Why don't you?

He didn't want to ruin her moment, so he kept staring until she eventually noticed.

"What? Do I have something stuck in my teeth?"

"It's nothing."

"Weirdo." She clapped her hands, startling the people around them. "I think I'm ready for that view you were bragging about."

They walked to a nearby tram and found an open seat at the front. He listened intently while she talked about her blog and how she was going to omit their upcoming high from her new entry.

"It's Amsterdam," he argued, "everyone knows you can legally get high here."

"You think I should write about it?"

"Definitely."

"Let's see how it goes." She leaned her head on his shoulder. "If I have a bad trip, I might not want to share."

"Unless you want your readers to be scared of fungi." He loved the sound of her trilling laugh. "When are you leaving?"

"Tomorrow afternoon. I'm off to Belgium next."

He'd hoped for more time. "That's awesome."

"Say it like you mean it, Beanie," she joked, poking him in the ribs.

How could he lie? He didn't want her to go: he's never wanted that. He was saved from having to respond when the tram came to a halt. "This is our stop."

"Looks to me like bartenders make way too much money," she remarked when he gestured to the building.

"Connor pays a bit more rent from his savings. Life of a doctor, hey?" He held the door for her and trailed inside, heading for the elevator. "Do you want anything to drink? I'll grab a few things from the flat."

"Aren't you going to invite me in?"

"I—" He broke off and raked his fingers through his hair. "I figured you'd think I'm trying to seduce you if I did that."

"And you're not?"

"Not actively. Should I?"

She fell silent, watching the numbers on the display. "I don't know. I'll meet you on the roof. I'd like water, thanks."

The doors opened on his floor. "Great. See you in a bit." He fought the urge to turn around, push her against the wall of the elevator and fuck her brains out. His breathing was ragged once he was in the apartment, as if he's run a mile. His thoughts consisted of Alyssa: taking her on the couch, the kitchen counter, in the shower, on his bed…

He thanked the heavens that Connor was still on shift. The last thing he needed was an interruption or, worse, his friend's incessant teasing. Mentally talking his boner down, he retrieved the underwear from his pocket and dumped it on his bed before grabbing two pillows. He snatched three bottles of water from the fridge, two blankets from the closet in the entryway, and headed up.

Alyssa stood at the edge, watching the sunset. He slowed as his eyes roamed on her body, his erection returning with a vengeance.

"You weren't lying," she murmured, "the view is amazing."

Especially my view.

"I come here to think sometimes." He spread a blanket on the rough surface and placed the pillows on top, leaving the spare blanket for later in case the temperature dropped. "Water, as promised."

"Definitely not a seduction."

"I don't think you'd be able to handle it if I seduced you."

"Is that so?" Alyssa eyed him, looking like she was tempted to ask him to try, if only to prove him wrong. She dug in her backpack for the bag of mushrooms. "How long did that guy say it's going to take before this kicks in?"

"Half an hour or so. Did you see the way he looked at us?"

"How?"

"I don't know, almost as if he thought we were a couple."

She chuckled nervously. "He couldn't be more wrong about that, hey?"

Logan made eye contact, thinking: *If we were a couple, I could touch you whenever I want. We could build a life together, make love and, afterwards, cuddle...*

Clearing her throat, she opened the bag. "Right, so if we take this now, we'll drop by the time night falls."

Logan took the bigger dosage, since he was taller and heavier. He chugged down half of his water bottle to get rid of the aftertaste, unsurprised that Alyssa quickly followed suit. They stood gazing at the busy streets below.

"What did you want to say earlier, by the way? About the shrooms?"

"I've never been high with a guy I like before."

"You still like me?" he asked, only half-teasing.

"It's hard not to." She glanced at him. "You're a great guy, Logan."

"I feel the same about you. You know, except that you're a girl." He smiled at her laugh, delighting in the sound. His hands itched to touch her but, somehow, he kept them to himself. "I've always wondered, why do you keep changing your hair color?"

"I don't want to be boring."

"Betty, you are anything but that."

"Thanks." The sun had dipped below the horizon and she went to the blanket, making herself comfortable. "I don't want to be like my parents."

"I wouldn't mind ending up like mine."

Her eyes stayed glued to his movements as he took his place next to her. "They're good people, though."

"They're amazing together. I've always wanted that for myself."

"Is that what you see with Luca?"

He was far from home and it was often difficult to remember why he liked Luca so much, especially compared to what he felt when he was with Alyssa. Her rejection had hit him hard. "I don't know."

They were each consumed by their own thoughts. The light faded from the sky, revealing some of the brighter stars as night descended. Logan began noticing the odd optical illusion, as if patterns were appearing above him. His hands tingled and his sense of smell heightened. Alyssa's scent was an intoxicating mix of the ocean, citrus-infused perfume, and something *more*.

Okay, you've dropped, he realized. "Do you feel it yet?"

"No."

Wow, her voice was the most alluring sound he's ever heard! He rolled his head to the side, taking note of the content look on her face. A layer of white light, as wide as his hand, was projecting from her skin, causing the many silver rings in her left ear to shimmer.

Beautiful.

"What?"

"Did I say that out loud?"

"You said something."

"You're beautiful."

She looked at him and her eyes widened. "Lo, you… You look like you're made of light."

"If you think about it, all of life is a frequency and, the higher the frequency—"

"Shh, you're ruining it."

He obediently shut his mouth. It would be much better if she kept talking.

"Do I look like that, too?"

"Yes."

"No wonder you think I'm beautiful."

"I don't have to be high to recognize your beauty, Lys."

"Sweet talker."

He became aware of a pink glow between them, linking the left side of his chest with hers. It made him think of her parting words. "So much for reason."

"Huh?"

"You said we're the reason part of 'reason, season, lifetime'." He turned on his side, reaching out to trace her jaw line with his finger. It felt like thousands of electric sparks were dancing on his skin from that simple contact. "That we'll never see each other again."

"Maybe this is more of a 'season' thing, then," she whispered.

"There has to be more to it." The light turned crimson wherever he touched her, pulsing along her cheek, neck and collarbone. *Wait, how did my hand get there?* he mused as it made a beeline for her cleavage. But did it really matter, when she didn't seem to mind? "Alyssa."

"Yes?"

"I'm going to kiss you."

Her gaze settled on his mouth and she swallowed thickly. "Okay."

He shifted closer. Her breath fluttered along his face; his heart pumped blood to his cock in response. "You're magic."

She let out a moan, her fingers gripping his hair. "Logan."

His hand went under her shirt and traced circles on her stomach. He was overly aware of where their mouths touched and, although he longed for the stroke of her tongue on his, he was enjoying this, too. He sucked her bottom lip, her gasp sending a shiver down his spine.

"Should we be doing this?" Her pupils were dilated. "I mean, when we're high as fuck?"

"I've wanted you the whole day, Lys. At the restaurant, the beach, the museum." He flicked his thumb over a covered nipple, his eyebrows drawing together when he couldn't recall how his hand had arrived on her breast. "Do you want me to stop?"

Brown eyes locking on green ones, she didn't answer.

His hand gave her nipple a break, sliding down the dip of her waist to her hip. "Should I stop?" Her fingers massaged his scalp and her hips undulated against him, yet she never broke eye contact. "Alyssa, answer me."

"Don't ever stop." She tilted her mouth up to claim his.

Logan got on top of her, using one of his knees to push hers apart. Their tongues got reacquainted: carefully at first, but soon growing in intensity. Sensation consumed him, as if this was the first time he's ever made out with a woman.

"Too many..."

He pulled back at her muffled cry. Her body was glowing like she was made of silver. "Huh?"

"We're wearing too many clothes," she declared, his shirt bunching in her hands. "Off, off, take it *off*, Lo!"

His shirt was thrown over his shoulder. His shoes and shorts followed. "You're so beautiful," he murmured as he took his time with her shirt, revealing an inch of her radiant skin at a time.

"Logan, don't tease me!"

The fabric was easy to get off. He unbuttoned her shorts carefully, savoring the process of getting her naked. When he yanked them down, her bikini bottom came along. Logan's brain had trouble functioning at the sight of her shaved pussy. "Sure you weren't expecting to see me?"

"I don't know anymore." She pulled the strings of her top, chucking it to the side, and parted her thighs in invitation.

He sat back on his hunches. He could feel the warmth radiating from her body, smell her musky scent, from where he was. His green gaze raked over each curve, his loins tightening when he spotted the rings in her nipples and the stud glittering between her legs.

"Alyssa."

Her eyes were doing the same, taking stock of his assets and settling on his erection. "Logan."

Curious about her pierced clit, he cupped her core with the intention of rubbing his thumb over that bundle of nerves. He quickly became distracted. "Jesus, Betty, you're drenched."

"I know," she whimpered. She squeezed her breasts while she rocked against his hand. "I'm always wet around you."

He spread that liquid to her clit, loving the hiss she gave when he bumped the piercing. "Always, huh?"

"Oh!" Her back bowed. "Yes, always!"

Logan lifted his fingers to his mouth and licked them clean. Her flavor burst on his tongue. "Fuck." He bent forward to swipe his tongue where his hand had been, catching the piercing between his teeth and plucking it softly.

"Logan!" she exclaimed, her tits turning white from the grip she had on them.

He thrust his tongue into her opening, slithered it up to that sensitive part of her, sucked her clit into his mouth and tugged the piercing. He repeated those motions several times, basking in her tortured moans. Not only was she the most beautiful woman to look at while he ate her out, but her noises were pleasing him to no end.

She came powerfully, her shriek echoing in the night. *"Logan!"*

His head moved to her stomach, where he scraped his teeth over her delicious skin. Why has it taken him this long to get her naked? It felt like satisfying her was his sole purpose in life.

Alyssa was the light, and he was drawn to her like a moth.

"You're pulsing," she mumbled as she grabbed onto his shoulders. "Beanie, you're *vibrating!*"

Whatever that man had sold them was more potent than anything Logan has tried before. Either that, or Alyssa was like no woman he's been with.

"So are you. Jesus Christ, you feel good!"

He pinched her nipple rings and pulled, fusing his lips to hers. Their tongues dueled frantically, hungrily, while he teased those peaks. He shuddered once she caught his cock in her hand. She rubbed it against her slick folds and his balls drew tight.

"Need you," he grunted.

"Yes."

He pitched his hips forward, sinking an inch inside. When she scratched her nails down his back, it felt like she had six hands; her assault was overwhelming. "Oh my God, Alyssa!"

"Keep going!" Logan complied, and those sharp talons dug into his shoulders. "Yes, yes, *yes!*"

Another inch. His awareness broadened to include her heartbeat and breathing, which were just as frenzied as his own. Her pussy was so goddamn tight!

"Logan," she pleaded. "Logan!"

He knew what she wanted because he did, too. Framing her face with his hands, he made eye contact as he rammed inside, right to the hilt. Her jaw went slack and her eyes rolled back, while his toes curled at the feel of her throbbing core. Could she have been made for this, for him?

"Alyssa," he murmured, plunging in and out of her.

Her legs wrapped around his waist as she returned his thrusts. They repeated each other's names like a mantra, moving luxuriously. Logan bit her bottom lip, loving this. It was meant to be, destined, that they become one. It was so fucking clear: how couldn't he have seen it before?

"Logan, I'm gonna cum!"

"Give it to me," he growled. "I want it."

She clung to him, meeting his pace. "Cum with me! Now!"

Her command tackled him over the edge. "Alyssa!" His cock erupted, welcomed by her flexing inner muscles. Her answering cry seeped into his skin. He collapsed on top of her as they came down from the mini-high.

"What did he give us?" she laughed softly. "All I want to do is keep fucking you, forever."

He raised his head and gave her a cheeky grin. "I'm down with that."

"Then let me be on top."

He rolled them around. Fuck, she was even more gorgeous from this angle! That luminous tone to her skin, against the pitch-black sky, made her seem both angelic and like a fierce warrior. Her short hair was ruffled; her piercings sparkled like the stars.

"You're beautiful," he murmured as he held her in place. He was still inside her, and already hard again. What was she doing to him?

She threw her head back with a soft "oh!" Her hips rose and fell rhythmically, as if she was listening to a sensual song and mimicking its beat. A few seconds later he heard it, too, and followed her lead. She leaned against his chest, her fingertips gripping his pectorals.

"Alyssa, look at me."

Their eyes stayed fixed on each other. He relished in the way her face changed as she got closer to orgasm. Her pace increased, taking him to the pinnacle with her. Their screams were loud, victorious, as they released.

"Logan." *I love you.* "I want to do it again." *I love you.*

He read the message in her eyes. "I'm not done," he vowed, while mentally transmitting, *I love you, too.* "Stay with me."

"Okay." *Because I love you.* "Fuck, I'm high."

High on you. You're everything. Logan moved onto his side, careful not to slip out as he took her along with him. He stroked her skin, kissed her. *I'll always want you. I'll always love you.*

"I didn't think this would ever happen."

"After the way you left things, neither did I."

"When you showed up today…" She trailed off, pressing her fingers to his lips. "What were the odds?"

"It doesn't matter. You're here now, where you belong."

"Belong?"

"Don't you feel it, Alyssa?" With his hand on her left breast, he could sense her heartbeat quickening. Fuck, she was turning him on so damn easily, as if he hasn't had two orgasms already. "You belong with me."

She didn't say anything for a long while, simply stared at him until he began to grow inside of her again. She rolled her hips. "You're so big."

He gripped her round ass roughly and pounded into her. "Alyssa."

"Logan." She hooked her leg over his hip to bring their bodies closer together. She returned his thrusts with renewed vigor. Her hand slipped between their bodies to fondle her clit. Her soft cries rose in volume, even though they were absorbed by his mouth.

He pressed a finger to her puckered hole. Their joint lubricants had collected there, making it easy for him to slip inside. She mewled and moved faster. He sensed her orgasm was right around the corner, as if it was communicating with him directly. His balls tightened and, as one, they unraveled.

"You're ruining me," she wheezed.

He leaned his forehead on hers. They were in their own bubble, removed from the rest of the world. Nothing mattered but her. He could stay here, in this moment, forever.

I love you.

"I wish you could come with me."

He nodded. "When will you be home?"

"Ten months."

"I'll wait."

"Beanie, no, don't say that."

"I'm serious."

She sighed deeply, pecking the tip of his nose. "I know, that's what scares me."

"The Alyssa I know isn't afraid of anything."

"Except you." She pulled away, wincing as his cock slipped out, and turned around. "You're this big question mark. I don't know what to do about you."

His hand trailed up her spine. "What do you want to do?"

"I'm sure you can guess."

Alyssa's tone had his dick hard in an instant. He spooned behind her, holding her tightly. "Your wish is my command."

He fucked her from that angle, until she called out his name in pleasure, her pussy rippling around his hard cock. As much as he loved being inside her, he preferred to see her eyes while he was. She turned to face him, and he made love to her once more. Then he pushed her onto her back and chased his own orgasm, thinking that would be enough.

It wasn't.

They were both raw, yet unable to stop. Their highs wore off, but not their desire. He lost count of the number of times they joined. When the sky began to lighten, they tore apart, gasping for air. She cuddled into his side and he pulled the spare blanket over them.

"I'm glad I saw you," she whispered.

"Me too."

"At least now I know what it's like to have you for a night."

"It doesn't have to be just for one night."

"I'm leaving tomorrow, Beanie."

"That doesn't mean it's the last time we'll see each other."

"We don't know that for sure. Anything can happen in ten months."

He tried his best not to be overly optimistic about their chances. Long-distance relationships weren't ideal, even with the assistance of technology, and once he was home he'll be back in reality, which included the MC, his studies, and Luca. What would that mean for him and Alyssa?

You're getting ahead of yourself.

"I don't think we'll change, no matter how much time or distance is between us."

She was silent, her breathing deep and even.

He glanced to his left, a soft smile on his face. She was completely knocked out. He brushed her turquoise bangs from her forehead and stroked her cheek with his thumb. Her lips were swollen, inviting, and he couldn't resist their siren call. He pressed a tender kiss to her mouth.

"I love you, Alyssa."

Eyelids growing heavy, he drifted off. He dreamt of a warm, bright light wrapping around him like a cocoon, merging with his bloodstream and elevating his soul. Then it disappeared entirely, leaving him in a darkness that was riddled with confusion.

When he woke up, Alyssa was gone.

CHAPTER ELEVEN

CONNOR WAS MAKING breakfast, which made Logan feel like he was doing the walk of shame into the apartment. "Rough night?"

Logan sighed as he dropped the items from the roof in the living room. His dick ached from overuse: he could only imagine how Alyssa must be feeling. How had she been able to walk, let alone walk away?

"You can say that."

"You look like you were attacked by a cat." When he raised an eyebrow, Connor gestured to his body. "You've got scratches all over you, bro. Who's the lucky girl?"

Combing his fingers through his hair, Logan strode to the full-length mirror in the hallway. Damn, Alyssa hadn't held back! He had two huge hickeys on the right side of his neck and several long, red lines marring his skin. He spotted the same marks on his back.

Drugs or not, that had hands down been the best sex of his life.

"Alyssa," he replied finally, going to the kettle. He needed caffeine.

Connor's eyes stretched wide. "What? How?"

"Surely I don't have to explain how sex works to you of all people."

"You know what I meant, dickhead!"

Logan extracted cups for them both. "I bumped into her yesterday. Her blog's doing well, and a travel agency is paying for her to explore Europe for a year. We hung out, got high and… well, you can see the rest."

"Damn," Connor muttered. "I guess I'll have to make extra eggs."

"Don't bother." Logan's heart gave a few painful beats and he rubbed his chest. "She left."

"Oh."

Pouring hot water into the cups, Logan stirred the contents and handed Connor his morning dose. "It's the first and last time that I'll have sex like that."

"That intense, huh?"

"She really fucked me up."

"You should call her."

"Like she'll answer." Logan shook his head, ignoring the pang in his gut. He's walked down this road with her before. He'd poured everything into their time together and she hadn't even stuck around for an awkward morning after. He should hate her.

You can't hate someone you love.

"Of all the places…" Connor chuckled to himself as he scraped eggs from the pan onto buttered toast.

"What?"

"I'm just thinking about you and Alyssa. I mean, what are the odds of you seeing her *here?* It must be a sign."

"It was a coincidence."

"Like when you met her, sure."

"If she'd wanted us to be something more, then she wouldn't have left me twice," Logan said through gritted teeth.

Connor had a smug know-it-all look on his face that Logan wouldn't mind wiping off with his fists. "Poor Logan, thinking that life should always go his way. As if life doesn't have unexpected twists and turns, or women don't need more than a night of furious fucking to be convinced that you want more than nights of furious fucking."

"It's weird that you're still single when you give such good advice, Dr. Tyrell."

"The difference is that I haven't taken my shot yet." Connor lifted his fork in the air, as if to emphasize his point. "When I make my move on Jesse, I won't blow it. It'll take *one shot* for her to be mine."

Logan stuffed his face with food before he said something he'll regret. Although his time with Alyssa had been spectacular, it would be so easy for her to argue it was only due to the shrooms. She was hesitant to confess the depth of her feelings for him, given the fact that she didn't know where he stood with Luca. Heck, *he* didn't even know.

"I thought you were going to put up a fight," Connor grinned.

"Fuck off."

"There it is."

Wolfing down the remainder of his breakfast, Logan drained his coffee and took his dishes to the sink. "Seriously, Con, shut the fuck up about Alyssa."

Connor sighed theatrically. "I guess you'll be fucking your way through town now to forget about her?"

"If only Jesse knew what you get up to unsupervised."

"You know, Drummond, maybe we *should* hash this out. Man to man."

"I wouldn't give you the satisfaction. Why don't you wrestle your own demons? They've been winning so far."

They glared at each other. Logan was ready to throw down and, from the look on Connor's face, so was he. Heart hammering in his ribcage, Logan hoped that Connor would make the first move. That way, Logan could get rid of the frustration Alyssa had left him with.

Connor inhaled deeply and broke eye contact. "I'm sorry."

"Yeah, bro, me too." Why was he taking his shit out on Connor? "I'm gonna take a shower and go to bed. Thanks for breakfast."

"You're welcome. Are you on shift tonight?"

"Yeah. See you tomorrow?"

"Sweet."

Once in the bathroom, Logan stripped and stepped into the shower. It took a while to warm up. He closed his eyes and leaned his forehead against the tiles. An ache was developing in his temples, mimicking the one in his heart. He thought of Alyssa's laugh and his cock became hard.

"Jeez, dude, give it a rest."

Unsurprisingly, his genitalia didn't listen. It was throbbing painfully, reminding him of being inside her multiple times. Until recently, Sophie had been his record at four times in one day. He tried to remember how many times he'd joined with Alyssa and lost count after nine.

He finished up and, as he reached for a towel, a cold chill ran down his spine. In the heat of the moment, they hadn't stopped to consider the consequences of their actions. Rushing to the living room to get his phone, his thumbs moved over the screen's keypad. *"We didn't use condoms. Are you okay?"*

Her reply was instant, as if she's been waiting for him to contact her: *"I'm on the Pill. Took the morning after, just in case. I'm clean."*

"Me too." He stared at the screen, craving to say so much more, but he didn't know where to start.

"I'm sorry I left."

"Why did you?"

"Last night was amazing, but too much, you know?"

Logan nodded to himself. *"Fair enough. Can we keep talking?"*

"Yes, I'd like that."

"Great!" Deciding to keep the conversation going, he video called her.

Her face appeared on the screen, taking his breath away. Her turquoise hair was damp and ruffled, her lips swollen. There was a bruise on the corner of her mouth.

"I don't usually have sex without a condom. No wonder you wrecked me."

"I've got an ice pack on my crotch. Who wrecked whom?"

He chuckled and got more comfortable on the couch. "I really like you, Betty."

"I like you, too."

"What do we do about it?"

She sighed. "The romantic part of me says go for it, fly high. But I'm scared we'll crash and burn, or end up hating each other after. I don't want to hate you."

It was interesting that they've both come to that conclusion. No matter how it had hurt to wake up alone, he couldn't hate her. He loved her too damn much. "Don't know which part of you I like more."

"Oh, that's easy! The part with the ice pack on it."

He guffawed loudly.

"Shut the fuck up, Lo!" Connor yelled from his bedroom. "I'm trying to sleep!"

"Sorry!" He lowered his voice. "I'm curious about the piercing."

"I used to struggle to get off, even by myself. Almost like a touch or a tongue wasn't enough. Emile suggested I pierce my clit, 'cause that'll make it more sensitive. I already had pierced nipples so I figured, why not? Now, you can look at my clit and I'll get off."

He raised an eyebrow. "I'm not sure if I should feel better or worse."

"As if anyone's ever complained about your performance, Beanie," she mumbled, rolling her eyes.

"They didn't have pierced clits."

"Oh, you're fishing for compliments! Do you want me to tell you you're the best I've ever had?"

"That's exactly what I want to hear." He couldn't stop himself from rubbing his cock under the towel. It was still sensitive, but he could bear it. "Considering you broke my dick."

She gave him a sassy smile. "That's too bad, then. You'll have to wonder if destroying your dick was worth it or not."

"I'm not afraid to say you're the best sex *I've* ever had."

"You think I'm afraid?"

"You leaving without saying goodbye is all the proof I need."

Alyssa contemplated that with a serious facial expression. "That's fair. Then again, it could've been the shrooms."

"What if it's *us*, Betty?"

"Maybe one day we'll know for sure."

"I look forward to that day."

They gazed at each other in comfortable silence. Logan's heart was full of love for her, and he saw it reflected in her eyes. He had no idea where they were headed or how it was going to work out, but a calm settled over him whenever he thought of their future together.

"I wish you could come with me. You know, for the first week or so. After that I'll probably get annoyed with you."

"Sounds about right. Most people can't stand being in my company for longer than that."

"That's 'cause you're just a pretty face."

"One you enjoy sitting on," he quipped.

Her cheeks turned red. "Your face was made for that."

He licked his lips, remembering her intoxicating taste. "Unless you want me to come over there and finish what you're starting, change the subject."

"I've always wondered if you can get bossy."

"Alyssa."

She smiled sweetly. "Sorry, Beanie."

"Are you taking the train to Belgium?"

"Yeah, it's leaving at four-thirty. I should probably get some sleep."

"I feel like I'm about to pass out, too. I hope I survive my shift tonight. Let me know when your post is up?"

"I'll text you." She blew him a kiss. "Bye, Logan."

"Bye, Alyssa." He hung up, feeling tons better than when he'd woken up this morning. He set an alarm, placed his phone on the coffee table, and shut his eyes. He lost consciousness almost immediately.

His dream could've passed for reality.

He was in a house that looked familiar, but it was set in a different era. He recognized his grandmother, years younger than she was today, storming down the hallway. He followed.

"Bren, what the hell?"

The young man with the auburn hair ignored her, patting his bleeding knuckles with a tissue.

Mysie turned to the hole in his closet door, her hands curling into fists. "Do you want to tell me what this is about?"

"There was a fly," he muttered.

She seemed on the verge of an explosion, but somehow reeled her temper in. "What happened?"

Brennan sank onto the bed and let out a loud sigh. "It's Cin."

"Of course it is."

Blazing ice-blue eyes met hers. "I don't have the patience today, ma."

She crossed her arms over her chest. "Talk to me."

"She found out about Dawn."

"You sound surprised."

"Ma—"

"No, don't even. How many times did I tell you to keep it in your pants?"

"The difference is you want me to mess up 'cause you don't want her in my life!"

Mysie's gaze narrowed. "I might not like her, but that doesn't mean I want you to be unhappy!"

"Ye dinnae even know her!"

"I know her well enough. I raised you to be a better man. How can you cheat on someone you claim to love?"

Brennan jumped to his feet. "Ah can do whatever Ah want."

"It doesn't mean you should." She pointed to the hole. "Fix that. When you're done, fix this attitude of yours. There are many ways that you can deal with Cinnia Sloane, but you always choose the hardest route, and it will nail you in the end."

That berserker rage slowly calmed. "Sorry, ma."

She shook her head. "Apology not accepted. You—"

The shrill sound of Logan's alarm interrupted the scene and he sat up, panting heavily. He rubbed the sleep from his eyes, wishing he could skip work. He shut the alarm up and eyed his phone. What time was it back home? He had the inexplicable urge to talk to his gran.

Fuck it.

He tapped the video call option on Mysie Drummond's profile.

She was smiling as she answered: "Hello, Logan."

"Hey, gran. Did I wake you?"

"No, I was up. I had a feeling you were going to call."

"You and your feelings."

"Don't even get me started." She tilted her head to the side. "What's going on?"

"I had a dream about you and… my father. He punched a hole in a closet door because of mom."

Mysie laughed softly. "Those were the days. It took him a long time to become the man she deserved."

"Wait, it really happened?"

"Yes."

That blew his mind. How on earth had he dreamt a memory that wasn't his?

"Does that mean you hated mom?"

She sighed deeply. "At first. I had a vision of her standing at Brennan's grave and wanted to protect him. I didn't want to lose him. In the end, she made him so happy that I loved her for it. And then, of course, there's you. I could never hate the mother of my grandchild. You're an extension of Brennan."

Logan didn't know what to say to that. "So, what, you predicted mom and dad ending up together, too?"

"A sick, twisted part of me hoped that they would be together *before* Bren died, thinking that he would survive that way… But he would've been angrier and more reckless. I settled for seeing him happy. That's all a mother wants for her child."

"Mom's mentioned your visions are reliable, but I didn't know they were this prophetic."

"And now you're having dreams of the past." She ran her fingers through her wild, grey hair. "I was wondering when you'll be activated."

"You must be joking."

"It all depends on what you choose, my boy. Now, not that I'm complaining, but what made you want to talk to me about the dream?"

"Could you... tell me about him?"

The shock on her face made him feel guilty. Everyone was under the impression that he didn't care about his biological father and, up until this very moment, maybe he hadn't.

"I'm not really sure where to start. He was everything to me, but I'm biased because he was my son. Other people will tell you that he was intimidating and a man of few words. Intense. Controlling. Even entitled."

"But you didn't see him that way?"

"I saw him for what he was. He had those qualities, but he also had the biggest heart. Once you earned his loyalty, he would move mountains for you. He was a great leader and people easily trusted that he had their best interests at heart. He had a wicked sense of humor, although he didn't always let it show." She paused, wiping a stray tear from her eyes. "He was obsessed with your mother."

Logan frowned at her choice of word. "Obsessed?"

"From the second he first saw her. He loved her more than anything. Except you, naturally. The way he focused on her, purposefully overlooking other potential love interests... I often wondered if that was healthy." She shrugged. "At the end of the day, it doesn't matter. The choices he made set his life on a different path."

He absorbed that in silence. "Do you think I'm like him?"

"In some ways."

"But I never knew him."

She smiled kindly. "Half of who you are exists because he gave it to you."

"I don't believe in that."

"I'm not trying to convince you. If you hope to understand yourself better, though, consider all angles: the conventional and unconventional. It'll make it a smoother transition, since you won't be flying blind."

His gran always gave the kookiest, best advice. "That makes sense."

"Are you sure you're okay?" she asked, peering at him. "Is there a reason this is coming up now?"

"I, uhm, ran into Alyssa yesterday." Frustratingly, he couldn't say anything more. He hoped Mysie would read between the lines.

"Ah, you're in love." She had a knowing, if somewhat distant, expression on her face. "I really like that girl. You're a fantastic match. What's the plan?"

"There isn't one. Our paths won't cross again for a while."

Mysie nodded to herself, her gaze sliding to the top of his head. "And Luca?"

He sighed deeply, raking his fingers through his hair. "I don't know. When I'm with her, nothing else matters. When I'm not, I remember that she was told to seduce me. I don't know if I can trust her."

"Hmm, you have some growing up to do."

"Ouch, gran. Can't you just tell me what's going to happen? Tell me what to do, who to choose."

She cackled mischievously. "Oh, my boy. I could tell you anything and you'll believe me because you're that desperate for guidance. But I learned my lesson with Bren. You need to experience things for yourself and come to your own conclusions. It'll be more worthwhile, in the long run. Plus, we won't be at each other's throats."

"It was a long shot." He checked the time, his stomach dropping. He had less than an hour to get to work, and he'll be traveling in peak traffic. "Gran, I've got to go. Thank you for the chat."

"Anytime, Logan. I love you."

"Love you, too. Say hi to grandpa for me."

"Will do." She waved and ended the call.

"That was cool."

Logan jumped in fright, gazing over his shoulder.

Connor was leaning against a wall, a small smile on his face. "I like the effect Alyssa has on you. You're starting to ask the right questions."

"Do you make a habit of eavesdropping?"

"Hey, you woke me up with your babbling. I was on my way to smack you."

He tied the towel around his waist and got up. "Sorry, bro. I'll be out of here in half an hour."

"I'm up anyway," Connor shrugged. "There's this BDSM club I heard great things about. I was thinking of going tonight."

Logan halted. "Since when are *you* into that kind of thing?"

"Try everything once, right?"

"Well, let me know how it is. If I ever recover…" He motioned to his bruised body. "Who knows? I might be up for it." He patted Connor's shoulder on the way to his room. "Have fun!"

He got dressed, brushed his teeth, ran a brush through his unruly hair before hurrying out of the apartment. His stomach growled and he decided to grab a bite to eat on the way to work. Jogging towards the closest tram stop, he was amazed to see that two were heading his way.

One would take him to work. The other, the train station.

What will you choose?

Logan hopped onto the latter mere moments before the doors shut. The excitement thrumming in his veins trumped the worry of being late. Miraculously, they made it to the busy station five minutes ahead of time. Logan checked the clock as he alighted. 4:07PM.

He sprinted inside, his gaze sweeping over the crowd to find her. He didn't have to search for long: her vibrant hair color stood out from the masses. She was dragging a large, red suitcase to the security checkpoint, her backpack leaning against the handle.

"Alyssa!" he called out as he ran after her.

She gaped at him. "Logan?"

"I had to say goodbye in person," he murmured, stopping in front of her and cupping her face in his hands. "I can't let you go without this."

She inhaled to respond and he pressed his mouth to hers to silence whatever she'd been about to say. Her lips trembled under his. The kiss started gently, as if they were high school sweethearts and hadn't spent the previous night exploring each other's bodies. It was innocent, sweet.

His eyelids shut, and he savored the feel of her soft skin, citrusy scent, and subtle whimpers that echoed his own. He toyed with her lips, sucking one after the other and allowing her to return the favor.

Images of what their future would be like flashed through his mind. There would be plenty of adventures like rock-climbing, surfing, four-wheel driving, bungee-jumping, and exotic holiday destinations. They would be supportive of their dreams, both individually and as a unit. The word *fun* has been the best way to describe their times together so far, and he had no doubt it would continue to be applicable.

She gripped his hair, deepening the kiss. Her tongue nudged and stroked his, emphasizing her hunger for more.

The vision morphed, influenced by their passion, to show him the countless nights they'd spend finding new ways of pleasuring one another. Their attraction would set the sheets alight and result in a big family, just like he wanted. He could see her pregnant with his children; how it would do nothing to extinguish his desire for her.

His arms locked around her waist, pulling her closer. His dick ached for a whole new reason: what he wouldn't do to make love to her one more time! He had no idea how the future he envisioned would turn into reality, but perhaps abandoning control was the first step. He could do it for Alyssa.

As if hearing his thoughts, she tilted her head back to stare into his eyes. "Logan, I love you," Alyssa whispered tearfully. "I'm not afraid to say it anymore."

"Thank the gods, 'cause I love you, too."

"I don't know what that means for us." One corner of her puffy mouth tilted up. "I kinda want to leave it up to fate."

"Right there with you."

She stroked his stubble, nose and forehead. "If I see you again and we're both single, I won't hold back."

"Neither will I."

"So, let's not be sad about today."

He smiled and touched his forehead to hers. "Okay."

She hugged him tightly. "Thank you for seeing me off."

"I'm glad I did." He released her and stepped away. "Have a safe trip."

She nodded, checking her bags and taking hold of the handle, but she remained rooted to the spot. "My blog post is up. Let me know what you think."

"I will."

Logan didn't care that they were standing in the way of other tourists, or that his manager would be upset with him for being late. All that mattered, in that moment, was being with her.

They both jumped when her train's imminent departure was announced.

"Bye, Beanie."

"Bye, Betty."

His eyes stayed glued to her until she disappeared from sight. Letting out a breath, he headed outside while navigating to her blog on his phone. He tapped the latest entry as he waited for a bus.

With my time in the Netherlands coming to an end, I decided to visit the capital and see what the fuss was about. After all, I've done plenty of gallivanting in some of the smaller towns and villages, enjoying the scenery, the food, and the friendliness of the locals. What could Amsterdam possibly have on offer that's better than that?

Turns out, it deserves the praise: not only because of the indulging attitude towards mind-altering substances and sexual freedom, but because of what I experienced there. I realize that you, dear reader, will probably not have the same 'a-ha!' moment I did, so bear that disclaimer in mind while I tell my story.

I don't believe in The One. Sure, I've often witnessed couples who have such a deep connection that it's impossible to imagine them apart, but never have I applied that notion to my own life. People say Paris is the City of Love (note: I can't argue until I've visited it myself), but I'd say Amsterdam is a strong contender!

I was sitting at the lovely Rosery Restaurant, enjoying their dish of the day (which, if you ask me, should be their dish every day), when a 'friend' showed up at my table. I use the quotation marks because he is smokin' hot and I've never been interested in being his friend. He joined me and I can confirm, thanks to his suggestion, that the Rosery offers the most incredible ice cream you'll ever taste.

He accompanied me to Wijk aan Zee's Noordpier Beach for kitesurfing. If you are an adrenaline junkie and you've dabbled in extreme sports before, then this is for you, but I would caution less adventurous readers to book a lesson with the experienced staff before braving the choppy waves.

After that, we were off to the red-light district to buy hallucinogens, settling on 'magic mushrooms' at a place called Kom Opnieuw. (Roughly translated to 'come again', which should include a nudge and a wink, if you ask me.) The man that worked there seems to take in your 'vibe' before suggesting a certain potency or strand, almost like he's tailoring the drug to your desires...

Another disclaimer: enjoy responsibly! It's legal in Amsterdam, but that doesn't mean you should feel obligated to partake, or that you should ingest every available drug in one go.

...He sold us a pack and sent us on our way. We made a stop at a fabulous food truck for a late-afternoon snack and then visited museums in the area. There is something to be

said for the art and architecture that adorns this city but, seeing as I'm more articulate in sports, I'll leave you to find suggestions on the most captivating pieces in a post from a blogger more qualified.

I won't tell you how my 'trip' went, as I don't want to give you any expectations. Everyone has a different kind of high. But since you probably have questions about the hottie I hung out with, I will admit that it was a happy ending, for us both.

All in all, Amsterdam lived up to its reputation. I advise everyone reading this to spend at least three days exploring everything the capital has to offer.

PS: to the guy who sold us the shrooms… You were right.

Logan was grinning goofily by the time he finished reading. He wondered why she'd decided to study physiotherapy when her writing was so compelling. The post had sucked him in completely, and not only because he was a part of the events.

The bus came to a halt and he exited, typing a simple reply to Alyssa: *"I love it, but not as much as I love you."* He greeted the waiters and manager, taking his place behind the bar to relieve the day shift. The bar was popular, and he wasn't surprised that he had to jump in immediately. There was a music festival later tonight. It would all be downhill from here.

Alyssa's reply came ten minutes later. *"Don't be cheesy, Beanie. Glad you love it/me, though. Xx."*

He couldn't answer, but he knew she would understand. He'd never stopped for food and his stomach rumbled as he served people their drinks. Most women tried to strike up a conversation and, although he was polite, he was too busy to flirt back. Besides, his heart belonged to the woman that was moving further away with each breath.

It took him way too long to recognize Fitz was next in line. Logan nearly dropped the bottle of whiskey he was holding. "What the hell are you doing here?" he hollered to be heard over the noise.

Fitz shrugged with a happy smile, leaning over the counter to give Logan a handshake. "I was bored out of my mind! My parents aren't home, our friends are on holiday, and you keep posting these amazing photos of Amsterdam! So I booked a ticket to crash your fun!"

Logan laughed. "First class?"

"Isn't that the only section on the plane?" Fitz joked. "I have a penthouse suite nearby!"

"It's so good to see you! What can I get you?"

"For now, a beer! Later, a tour!"

Logan bowed his head. "I am at your disposal." He grabbed a glass and poured a local craft beer, sliding it to Fitz.

"What time do you knock off?"

"Around two!"

"Sweet! I'll see you then!"

Logan bumped his fist to Fitz's and smiled as the guy headed to the closest group of girls. Logan was in for a long night: there was no way Fitz would let him go to bed once he's done with work.

He was ravenous when he clocked out, hours later. Fitz was waiting outside and they happily hugged each other.

"So, where are we off to?" Fitz asked.

"I need food if you want me to be decent to you."

"Fair enough." Fitz gazed at their surroundings, the crowded streets, while they walked to a nearby food truck. "You know, we've travelled to most of Europe, but I've never been here. I get why you like it."

"It's been amazing."

"Where's Con tonight?"

Logan chuckled. "He's at a BDSM club, probably getting the shit spanked out of him."

Fitz guffawed loudly. "Great mental image." He ordered four burgers and two large packs of fries. "Are you working tomorrow? Don't worry about this, I'll pay."

"Thanks, man." Logan sighed deeply. "I've got another night shift."

Fitz's grin spoke volumes. "We're getting high as fuck."

"Bro, I already—"

"Nah-ah, Lo, the only decision you need to make is: shrooms, weed or acid? MDMA? Coke?"

"Jesus," Logan muttered, horrified by some of those choices. He rubbed his forehead, which was throbbing from hunger, dehydration, exhaustion and the previous night's activities. "I'll go with weed."

"Great! Take me to the place that sells the best. We'll drop acid next time."

"Until when are you staying?"

"However long I want, I guess."

"Must be nice, being so spoiled."

"You'd know."

They ate, caught up and walked further into the city. Fitz wasn't looking forward to university, since he knew he would be expected to take over his father's business. If he'd had his way, he would wait until he got money from his trust fund and retire in the Bahamas at age twenty-five.

In contrast, Logan was keen to start his career, whatever that may be. He was still secretly hoping to become a professional athlete, although he wondered if he was deluding himself. He should stick to studying architecture on a part-time basis while he worked at the firm. It kept him closer to the club, too. He would be there for Luca, make sure she's protected.

Thoughts of the girl he'd found at the side of the road inevitably led to his current feelings for Alyssa. They've parted on good terms, and he was excited to see what fate had in store for them; at the same time, he didn't know if he would ever resolve his feelings for Luca.

Fitz insisted on paying when they ordered a couple of joints, and they sat in the corner of the shop to light up.

"Wow," Logan said after the first drag. "It's almost sweet."

"Maybe I should move here, instead of the Bahamas."

"You mean, in your imagination where you're allowed to retire early?"

"Yes," Fitz sighed.

"What did you do while you waited for me to finish work?"

"Invited a couple of girls to my room," Fitz answered, shrugging. "It's amazing what the word 'penthouse' does to some women."

"Not that you're complaining."

"I've had plenty of foursomes before. Frankly, I enjoyed the others more. Maybe it's because I was friends with the other girls." Fitz inhaled another lungful. "Speaking of, have you heard from Nina since she moved?"

"No, why?"

"I miss her." Fitz paused. "I've always had a thing for her."

"Dude, if I'd known that, I wouldn't have—"

"It doesn't matter, Lo." Fitz waved that comment away. "I was firmly placed in the friend zone."

"Still, I broke the bro-code," Logan insisted. "I could find out where she is now. Maybe you could go visit her."

"What kind of fantasy world are you living in? Shit like that doesn't fly in real life."

Logan thought of Alyssa, unable to stop the content facial expression that followed. "You never know, man."

"Okay, what the hell happened to you? Last time I saw you, you were hung up on two chicks."

"I'm letting go and trusting that everything will work out."

Fitz seemed befuddled. "I think you're just high."

"Maybe," Logan hedged. "Humor me. Let me text Nina."

"I know I can't stop you."

Fitz couldn't hide the twinkle in his eyes, though. Logan sent a friendly message to the girl he used to mess around with, informing her that Fitz would like to hear from her. Five minutes later, when Logan's world became super chilled, Fitz's phone beeped.

"How the hell did you do that?"

"I have no idea what you're talking about."

Fitz shifted his focus to his phone, rendered speechless.

Happy to have helped a brother out, Logan closed his eyes and enjoyed the high. Whatever happened, he would do his best not to control the outcome. He's had a major breakthrough, courtesy of that dream and the conversation with his grandmother, and didn't want to ruin his momentum. Brennan might have been unable to let go, but that didn't mean Logan had to follow in his footsteps.

He could choose his own future.

CHAPTER TWELVE

LOGAN COULD SEE sounds.

He leaned his head back as he watched the geometric patterns oscillate in front of him, in sync with the song currently blaring from the speakers. He lifted an apple to his mouth, eyes widening at the ear-splitting crunch and burst of flavor that followed. Was this one superior to all others?

There was a presence in his periphery, one he refused to acknowledge.

"Guys, I'm melting," Fitz declared dryly.

Connor, who was blowing spit bubbles, chuckled his agreement.

It's been this way for nearly seven hours. As enjoyable as the experience was, Logan never wanted to drop acid again. Every time he felt like he was finally coming down it kicked in again, as if he was glued to the seat of a never-ending rollercoaster.

"Have you ever seen Jesse's freckles?"

Logan glanced at Connor. "What?"

"They're like—" Connor made wavy motions with his hands. "*Camouflage!* It's like she can move between dimensions or something. That's why I feel her." His covered the left side of his chest. "She's right here."

"If I wasn't high as fuck, none of that would've made sense," Fitz laughed. "But man, that's exactly how I feel about Nina! She's only arriving tomorrow, but it's like she's already *here*."

"You both sound crazy," Logan concluded.

"You need to get laid."

Logan closed his eyes. As far as he was concerned, his dick has yet to recover from that marathon session with Alyssa, nearly three weeks ago. Keeping Fitz entertained without getting girls involved was currently his only plan of action. Fitz and Nina have been chatting non-stop and the guy didn't want to mess up his chances of scoring the woman of his dreams by having sex with strangers.

They uttered a combined "woah!" when the bass dropped.

"Sound is the fundamental basis of reality," Connor mused.

Logan arched an eyebrow. He was consciously aware of that entity moving closer. "Is that your professional opinion, doctor?"

"Connor, the doctor. Ha! Imagine he walks up to you after you've been in an accident," Fitz sniggered.

"Most women probably think they've died and gone to heaven," Logan added.

Connor was too high to care that they were making fun of him. "I knew it: you have a major crush on me. You're lucky I'm not into guys, or you would've needed diapers for the rest of your lives."

"Yeah, you've got a monster schlong. Poor Jesse is going to be bedridden when you two finally hook up."

Fitz's eyes widened. "Is it that big?"

"Big enough to make you question the grace of the gods, and Con being a doctor. He could've been a millionaire by now if he'd gone into porn."

"Yours could've made some money, too," Connor told Logan.

"The difference is that mine's in proportion with the rest of me," Logan countered. "Yours doesn't make any fucking logical sense. How do women not run away screaming?"

"I tie them down."

Fitz, who'd been sipping on a glass of soda, choked on a loud guffaw.

The corners of Connor's mouth twitched in response. His dark blond hair was longer than usual, and he'd picked up the habit of tugging at the ends, like he was doing now. "There were two girls who left me with blue balls, actually. Bruised my fragile little ego."

Logan snorted. "Your ego isn't little. It's the size of your dick."

"For the record, my dick is the main reason why I even have a fragile little ego." Connor lifted a finger in the air and swiped it across, as if he was underlining that sentence. "That *and* my average height. It's no wonder why I have a fragile little ego."

"Stop calling it your 'fragile little ego'. It almost makes me feel sorry for you."

"Yeah, you can give me some of your inches if you don't want them." Fitz went red when the other two cackled in response. "I didn't mean it like that!"

"Sure you didn't," Logan giggled, wiping tears from his eyes.

"Your major crush on me doesn't bode well for your interest in Nina."

Logan eyed Connor. "Bro, what's with your impeccable English tonight?"

"Do I have to remind you that I'm a doctor and, therefore, incredibly smart?"

"Uh, *yes?*"

Connor picked up a pillow and threw it at Logan's face, seeming glad that it made contact. "Fuck off."

They dissolved into a fit of chuckles, their bodies convulsing in amusement. Logan ignored that somewhat familiar aura less than a foot away. Ever since that conversation with his grandmother, he's become aware of inexplicable phenomena, and wondered just what the hell she'd meant when she had said that he was "activated".

Don't fight this.

Logan coughed, shaken to his core, and reached for his drink.

"Jeez, we had a whole conversation about our dicks," Fitz said. "Do you think girls talk about their clits?"

"Why wouldn't they? Clits are amazing," was Connor's input.

The sound of a video call interrupted. Logan lowered the music's volume and searched for his phone. A glance at the screen had him panicking: Byron Johannson.

He rushed to his room. He'd promised that he would always answer, but his parents usually phoned when he wasn't this… high. He sat on the edge of his bed, slapped his cheeks and breathed deeply before accepting the call. "Hey, guys."

A nearly imperceptible look crossed Byron's face.

"Hey, Lo," his mother smiled. "I hope we're not interrupting?"

Logan shook his head. He was getting distracted by the patterns pulsing between them, weaving a delicate and beautiful web that connected their auras. *What the fuck?*

"Con and Fitz are here, but we're having a lazy day. What's up?"

"We're going to an early viewing at the cinema, so we wanted to check in now, 'cause we won't get the chance later," Cinnia explained.

"Cool. Is Luca going with you?"

"She suggested it!"

"Wow, that's a big deal." Logan was unnerved by his stepdad's silence. It didn't help that the presence from before had followed him into the room. "Where is she?"

"Jesse's taken her to school today."

He wished he could will Byron to speak. "Any Falcons news?"

"No, it's still quiet on that front." Cinnia glanced at her husband, noticing that something's wrong.

An uncomfortable silence descended.

"Uhm, I get the feeling my boys want to have a private chat," Cinnia mumbled as she tucked her hair behind her ears. "I love you, Lo. Chat tomorrow!"

"Bye, momma."

Logan watched as Byron cupped her jaw and gave her an adoring kiss on the lips, a total juxtaposition to the cold vibes he's been sending Logan's way. Those patterns swirled around them, melted together, and fascinated Logan to no end.

With a final wave, Cinnia moved out of view.

"You two belong together, you know?" Logan blurted out.

Byron's dark eyebrows rose.

"I can see it, it's like…" Logan interlaced his fingers. "Meant to be."

"You're high."

Logan gulped. The knowledge in Byron's gaze caused his stomach to drop. "Weed?"

"Acid."

Byron nodded thoughtfully. "Have you snorted or injected?"

"No, of course not!"

"Good."

Byron's clipped tone made Logan feel like he was five inches tall. "Dad, I've got it completely under control. It's Amsterdam, you know?"

"You're an adult and I respect whatever you choose to do with your free time, Lo. That being said, this stays there, do you hear me?"

"I hear you."

Rubbing his eyes, Byron let out a long sigh. "I don't want to be an overbearing parent, Lo, but I remember what it's like to lose myself in drugs and alcohol. I'd hate for you to go through that. Don't ever use to run away from your problems."

"I don't have problems. You made sure of that," Logan teased lightly.

"You're the reason I'm going grey, punk," Byron laughed.

Logan absorbed the sound, which loosened the knot in his gut. "I only want to make you proud, dad."

"Oh, Logan." Byron leaned forward; his features soft now that he was smiling. "You make me proud. I'm sorry if projecting my fears on you makes you doubt that, because that's not my intention."

"I'm sorry if what I do makes you worry."

"I don't think it's possible for a parent not to worry. As long as we keep talking things out like this, the worry won't consume me. I love you, punk."

Moisture accumulating in his eyes, Logan whispered: "I love you, too."

"I've got to get to work. Enjoy the rest of your…" Byron trailed off and shook his head with a grin. "You know."

"Thanks."

"And talk to your dad."

Ice pumped through Logan's veins but, before he could ask Byron how he knew, his stepfather ended the call. That left Logan alone with… whatever's been hanging around lately.

Logan.

"Nope, I can't do this," he muttered, jumping to his feet. Annoyingly, his body refused to move back to his friends, to safety, to sanity. He stood there and tried not to acknowledge the dark cloud that's hung over his head ever since he asked his mother why there were no pictures of her pregnant with him. The same cloud he's pretended away for years.

Amsterdam was supposed to be an escape, but instead it was making him confront the very thing he'd been running away from.

Calm, Logan. Breathe.

"What do you want?" Logan lowered his voice in case Connor or Fitz overheard and dialed the nearest psychiatric ward. "Who are you?"

You know.

"This isn't real."

Isn't it?

Raking his fingers through his black hair, he mentally counted backwards from five. "What do you want?"

To give you a choice.

"Does it have to be now?"

How much longer do you want to put it off?

He sighed in defeat and dropped onto the bed. Lying on his back, he succumbed to his body's need for rest. Every spare minute of the last couple of weeks has been spent with Connor or Fitz; he hasn't even exercised lately. He was burnt out.

Logan drifted into a dream.

"Bren, stop showing off!"

Grinning, he quit bouncing the ball on his knees and kicked it in his best friend's direction. "Can't help I'm awesome."

Haye passed it to Ike with an eyeroll. "That's debatable."

They continued their makeshift match and Brennan did his best to suppress his competitive streak. With the raging teenage hormones in his body, it was tricky at best.

There were boys of all ages in this section of Drummond's Customs & Repairs, *either playing football or watching. The rest of the MC was in the warehouse, although he'd overheard his father calling for church earlier. Unfortunately, Brennan wasn't old enough to attend those meetings yet. He wished he was.*

"Can I play?"

Brennan froze once his gaze landed on the thin girl who'd asked. She looked about eight, although she was much taller than other girls her age. Her long, ebony locks were styled in a French braid, with a few strands framing her pale face. Those big, green eyes of hers made him wonder how he was ever going to look away.

She visibly squirmed under his scrutiny, toeing the gravel under her bare feet.

He was consumed by something he's never felt before: fierce protectiveness. He knew that he would do anything to keep this girl safe. "Sure, lass," he replied gently. "What's your name?"

"Cinnia."

The Sloane girl, *he remembered. "I'm Brennan."*

The other guys introduced themselves and, after passing the ball to her a few times and explaining the most important rules, resumed the game. They played less aggressively to accommodate the only girl on the team. His gut clenched when she tripped and fell fifteen minutes in.

"Are you okay?"

"I'm fine," she said stubbornly. She touched the scrape on her knee and hissed softly.

"Here, let me help you up." She placed her small hand in his, causing tingles to dance along his skin, and he hauled her to her feet. "Do you want to keep going, lass?"

She nodded with flushed cheeks. "Yes."

The dream morphed into another scene.

He wanted her to like him, to be his. He wouldn't accept a different outcome, no matter what his mother said.

"Who're you waiting for?" Haye asked, interrupting Brennan's thoughts. Purposefully, too, seeing as Haye had the knack for sensing when he was mentally trapping himself.

"Cin."

Haye cocked an eyebrow. "Are you two together now?"

"She's ten. I'm sixteen." Brennan sighed when Haye simply shrugged. "Don't you think it's weird?"

"You've always been weird." Haye burst out laughing at Brennan's irritated facial expression. "Of course it's weird, brother, but since when do you care what I think?"

Since I'm in love with a girl six years younger than me.

Brennan shook his head. He hasn't been in love before, and he doubted that's what he felt for Cinnia. He simply wanted to be around her all the time, to make sure she's okay. That didn't mean... love, did it?

His brain shut down as she exited the warehouse, chatting to a petite blonde.

"Who's her friend?"

"Dawn."

"She's cute," Haye commented.

"Hmm," Brennan hummed in agreement, thinking Haye was referring to Cinnia.

She glanced up and her cheeks went red as they made eye contact. Slowing her walk, it took a couple of seconds before she was in front of them. "Hi, Bren."

"Hey, Cin."

Haye chimed in: "Good to see you again, Cin. And you're Dawn, right?"

"Yeah," Dawn giggled, shaking hands with him.

"I'm Haye."

The conversation that followed was lost on Brennan. His attention was trained on the skinny girl with emeralds for eyes. He's never met anyone with a gaze that green.

"Do you want to go to the movies with me?" he heard himself ask.

Cinnia seemed taken aback. "Uh, sure?"

"Great, let's go."

"Right now?"

"Aye." He's already purchased the tickets. When he had planned this earlier, he'd done so with the intention of hearing "yes". He's been unable to get this black-haired beauty out of his mind. Perhaps now that they were going to spend time together, he'll get enough of her and—

"Lo?"

Logan bolted upright with a racing heart.

"Jeez, sorry bro." Connor held his hands up. "I would've left you to sleep, but you should get ready for your shift."

Logan glanced at the window. "What?"

"You slept for fourteen hours. Fitz has gone to pick Nina up from the airport."

"Thanks for waking me up." He rubbed his forehead, the remnants of those dreams looping in his mind. "Do we have pain tablets left?"

"In the bathroom. Are you hungry? I'm making grilled cheese." Logan's stomach rumbled loud enough for Connor to hear. "Coming right up," he chuckled as he headed out.

Bits and pieces of his trip came back, prompting him to pick up his phone and select a number he knew by heart. He continued to massage his temples while he listened to the dial tone.

"Lo?" his mother asked sleepily.

"Hey, momma."

"Are you okay?"

"I think so. Sorry for waking you. I just have a few questions."

She paused. "Okay?"

"Did you scrape your knee the night you met… Brennan?"

Her sharp inhale was all the answer he needed. "Who told you that?"

"I kinda dreamt it."

She was silent for a moment, coming to terms with what he was saying. "What else?"

"When you were ten, did he ask you to the movies after Dawn and Haye met each other for the first time?"

"My boy, how could you know something like that?"

His stepfather's voice interjected: "Cin, what's wrong? Is Logan okay?"

"I shouldn't have called," Logan mumbled, gaze fixed to the floor.

"No, you can call me whenever you want. I'm putting you on speaker."

"What happened?" Byron persisted.

"He dreamt of Bren, but they were actual memories. Lo, was this the only time?"

"No, I called gran the first time, 'cause it had her in it."

"How do you feel about them, punk?"

Logan contemplated that. "It feels like it's a lesson, like I'm supposed to learn something, but I don't know what." He remembered his biological father's emotions, how they'd seemed so real and relatable. "Brennan really loved you, mom."

There was a smile in Cinnia's tone when she said: "I know, baby, I know."

"He wanted you to love him."

"I did. I still do."

"No, this isn't coming out right." Logan closed his eyes. "He planned things. I mean, he bought the movie tickets before you said yes."

"That's Bren," Byron said. "Always in control."

"Yeah, he was always surprising me by making all the necessary arrangements for lunch at the lake, or a holiday."

"Arranging Tessa as your surrogate," Byron added.

Cinnia laughed softly. "Getting you patched in behind your back."

Logan listened to their retelling of the times Brennan had acted the same way as in the dream. "Am I like that?"

"Hmm, interesting question," Cinnia responded slowly. "I think you have those tendencies and you like being in control, but it's not on the same level."

"I agree."

"Gran said some people thought he was entitled."

"I mean, he cheated on me a horrifying number of times because he'd seen it as his right as VP, and because he wanted me to stay a virgin until I was old enough to marry. So yeah, he had an entitlement problem. It's probably got to do with him growing up as an only child."

I can't believe he would do that to someone he loved! Maybe he didn't really care about her?

"How many times did he cheat?"

Cinnia let out a short breath. He imagined that she was twisting a lock of hair around a finger and giving Byron worried glances. "I don't know exactly.

He slept with Dawn. She told me about it, and I broke up with him then. I only found out about the others years later, after he got me back."

Logan couldn't believe his ears. "How could you forgive him?"

"Gosh, I'm not sure how to explain that in a way that you'll understand. The short answer is that life didn't make sense without him, without the club, and that I believed he could change. I'll save the long answer for when you're back home."

"I don't know how to feel about him."

"I know, my boy," Cinnia sighed.

"He's…" Logan swallowed past the lump in his throat. "I'm hearing so many conflicting stories about him, but sometimes, I feel like he's with me."

"Use that connection, Lo," Byron suggested. "This is coming up for a reason."

"How did you know, dad?"

Byron laughed softly. "I had a feeling that he was around. Maybe it's the dream *I* had two days ago."

"By's always had dreams about him, ever since he passed," she explained. "Your gran, too."

"I don't want to be weird."

His parents burst out laughing. "Oh, my boy," Cinnia breathed, "that ship sailed a long time ago, but it doesn't make me love you any less."

"You're definitely one of a kind, punk."

"Thanks a lot, guys," Logan muttered dryly.

"I wish I could give you a hug right now."

Logan chuckled at the familiar undertone in his mother's voice. "Do you miss me, momma?"

"Every damn day, boy. I'm counting down the seconds until you're back."

"With your strange capacity for math, I'm not surprised to hear that." He looked at the time, getting anxious once he realized he was running late. "Sorry, guys, but I have to get my butt to work. I can't get fired now."

"If that means you'll be home sooner, why not?"

"You're acting clingy again, mom."

"Who's acting?" Byron laughed.

"Shut up, both of you," Cinnia joked. "I love you, Lo. Call me anytime, okay?"

"Gotcha. Love you!"

He hung up, feeling tons lighter. He hurried into the shower, brushed his teeth and swallowed two pain tablets to combat his headache. Connor was watching TV, motioning Logan to the cold grilled cheese sandwiches on the coffee table.

"You heard all of that, didn't you?"

Connor's eyes were glued to the screen. "I have no idea what you're talking about."

"Asshole."

"I would offer a hug, but you'll probably say no."

"Damn straight." Logan finished wolfing down the sandwiches. "Thanks for the snack, Con."

"I bill by the minute."

Sending his gaze heavenward, Logan gathered his things and walked to the front door. "Later!"

It was a mad rush to the bar, but he managed to arrive on time. The dream and subsequent conversation with his parents remained at the forefront of his mind and, whenever he had a moment to consider what had been said, he sensed Brennan's presence.

I need to play ball or climb. Run.

After work, Logan headed to the football field he's been frequenting. It was safe and open all hours. He took his phone out of his pocket as he checked in, intent on texting Connor his location, and sighed deeply when he saw the battery had died. He was going to get into shit for that.

He grabbed a couple of balls and did stretches to warm up. If he'd known he was going to end up here, he would've packed better clothes, but he didn't have the patience to swing by the apartment first. He ran five laps, satisfied that his thoughts withered more with every pounding beat of his heart.

Sufficiently out of breath, Logan lined the balls up at various spots in front of the goalpost. He started by aiming for the center, the sound of the net like music to his ears. He tried the top-left corner next, slipping further into the zone as he went. From there, he targeted the top-right corner.

This is when I feel most alive.

How was that supposed to work? Sure, he's always had the attention of scouts, but he was the President of the Raptors Motorcycle Club. There wasn't any space in that identity for something that would take up as much of his time as professional football would.

But wouldn't it be an absolute joy to play ball for a living?

He missed the post and swore under his breath as he went around collecting the balls. He wiped the sweat from his brow and started again.

Alyssa makes me feel alive, too.

They've kept in touch. Every day apart made him miss her more. He had no clue how he was meant to last another ten months without her.

Join her?

Well, then he'd definitely have to put the dream of furthering his athletic career on hold. He was still young enough to make something of himself, but he'll have to get his arse into gear if he—

Oh, so you've made up your mind, then? You're going to put your personal desires ahead of the club's?

"Fuck," he muttered, once again missing. He stared at the goal box with his hands on his hips.

How was he ever going to reconcile the part of him that wanted to explore, succeed and exceed his own expectations of being the leader he was born to be? How could he stay true to himself *and* make his family proud?

A life of Harleys and designing houses won't be so bad.

He bit down on the inside of his cheeks. That sounded so... boring.

What about Luca? She won't follow you to athletic stardom: she doesn't like crowds.

He didn't even know if she desired him, anyway.

You can't woo her if you're going to be halfway across the world.

Logan let out a frustrated cry and kicked the balls, one after the other, into the box. He dropped to his knees and held his head in his hands, feeling tears mingling with the sweat on his cheeks. He was nowhere closer to finding answers to his innermost questions. Brennan's cryptic insights only succeeded in further muddling Logan's ambitions.

"Are you alright?"

Logan jumped in surprise and glanced up. He should have better situational awareness: Amsterdam was safe, but that didn't mean he should let his guard down.

The man had a friendly smile on his face. "That was pretty impressive," he remarked in accented English. "Which school did you go to?"

"Oh, I'm not from the Netherlands."

"That's too bad." The man stuck his hand out. "I'm Marcus Du Randt. I'm a scout for premier football clubs. What's your name?"

"Logan," he replied, rising to his feet.

"How long have you been playing, Logan?"

"Since I can remember."

"You've been approached before, I take it?"

Logan swallowed thickly. "Yeah, but I don't think it's in my future."

"You're wrong." Marcus dug in his pocket and produced a business card. "I'm sure my clients will make serious offers."

Logan stared at the piece of paper, unable to believe what was happening.

"Don't take too long to decide. In your case, you should strike while the iron's hot."

Before he could figure out what to say, Marcus strode off the field. Was this all a crazy coincidence, or an answer to his internal dilemma?

Logan put the balls away and took a tram home. The card felt like it weighed a ton. He flipped it over and read the few words printed on it repeatedly. He was so tempted to accept Marcus' offer.

The tram arrived and he hurried up the stairs instead of taking the elevator. The keys rattled in his hand as he turned the lock, and he pushed the door open to find Connor pacing in the kitchen.

"Where the fuck have you been?" Connor snapped as soon as Logan stepped over the threshold.

Raising his eyebrows, Logan turned the kettle on. "I played some ball, darling."

"Don't." Connor pointed at Logan's chest, his eyes spitting pure rage. "Why the fuck is your phone off?"

"I forgot to charge it."

Connor fumed in silence for a full minute. Logan hasn't often been graced with Connor's rage, especially lately. It was terrifying.

"The next time you disappear without a word, I'll punch you in the fucking face. Do you understand me?"

Connor had joined Logan on this trip to set the rest of the MC's minds at ease, even though it had also served as a chance to get away from the hospital. The deal was that Logan would always keep Connor informed of his whereabouts.

"It won't happen again."

"Fitz phoned." Connor marched to his bedroom and slammed the door shut.

With a sigh, Logan went in search of a charger. His phone switched on and he winced as Connor's string of messages and missed calls filled the screen. He hoped that Connor hadn't contacted his parents about this: Logan wouldn't survive the ensuing argument with his mother.

"You rang?" he texted Fitz. He heard the kettle boil in the kitchen and made a beeline for it, eager to get caffeine in his body. There were three messages waiting for him when he got back.

"Yes. I have a MASSIVE favor to ask. HUGE."

"What's up?"

"Nina's here. We talked. We're together now."

"Damn, bro, you moved fast! Congrats!"

"Thanks," came Fitz's reply. *"She says she's always liked me, but didn't make a move because I don't look like the kind of guy that can 'take charge'."*

Logan had no clue where this was going. *"OK?"*

"You do."

"What?"

"You know how to take charge. Nina told me."

Had he wandered into an alternate universe? One where Connor hated his guts and Fitz was about to ask what no friend should ever ask? *"What's your point?"*

"She said the whole BDSM scene is her thing. I want to make her happy."

"Connor knows a place."

"Hold up, I'll phone you."

This was the absolute last conversation Logan wanted to have, but the device was already vibrating in his hand. Letting out a long breath, he swiped his finger across the screen, accepting the video call.

Fitz had a glow about him that Logan hasn't seen before. "You know what I'm going to ask, right?"

"I hope I'm wrong."

"But why? It's not that weird."

"Are you kidding me?"

"I only ask for one session. Show me the ropes." Fitz quirked a smile at the pun. "Nina said this happens all the time: that this is how one Dom trains another."

"Yeah, but—"

"You're a Dom. Teach me how to be one."

"Fitz, doesn't it bother you knowing why Nina knows I'm a Dom?"

"You'll never do that to her again. You're just going to show *me* how to do that to her."

"What makes you think I'm agreeing?"

"Help a brother out, man! I promise you'll get to be the best man at the wedding. Besides, you owe me for breaking the bro code."

"Jesus." Logan rubbed his eyes. "How are we friends again?"

Fitz grinned broadly. "I buy the best weed and I always share."

"You're impossible."

It wasn't every day that friends asked him to help them dominate in the bedroom—in fact, this was the *only* time that's ever happened—but there was a part of him that wanted to. He shuddered to think what would happen if two people he cared about fell into the wrong hands. There were sick predators out there and, judging by the glint in Fitz's eyes, they would go to someone else if Logan refused.

"Fine, but we do this my way. I'm not touching her *or* you."

"Has anyone ever told you that you're the shit?"

"Not nearly enough."

"I'll tell Nina you're on board." Fitz smiled self-consciously. "Thank you. You're the only person I trust with this."

"And then you had to go and say *that*," Logan mumbled.

"You love me."

"Goodbye, Fitz."

The guy burst out laughing. "Bye!"

He was beginning to look forward to going home.

Well, that's one way to end your Amsterdam trip. One final hoorah! It's not like you haven't done weird shit here…

He dug into his pocket to retrieve the business card. Perhaps it was time to seriously consider the kind of life he wanted to create, instead of accepting the one that he'd inherited.

CHAPTER THIRTEEN

"YOU DON'T HAVE to do this, you know?"

He gazed at his mother. She had her arms crossed over her chest and was nibbling on a full bottom lip while her eyes darted between the open suitcases on his bed. Her dark grey hair was piled on top of her head in a messy bun and, for once, she wore jeans and a T-shirt instead of leather.

"We've talked about this."

"I know," she sighed, "but it's so soon after you came back."

"A month is soon?"

She glared at him. "Why do I want you to stay when you're always giving me lip?"

"Because I make it okay when I call you 'momma' and tell you I love you," he soothed as he embraced her.

"Promise you'll still come around?"

"Whenever I can." He squeezed tighter. "You can visit me, too. Make a trip out of it."

"Hmm, we'll see. I get the feeling you're going to have constant orgies."

Logan burst out laughing as he stepped back. "Nah, I'm not into that anymore."

"Anymore?" she prompted, raising a dark eyebrow.

Logan's cheeks flushed and he busied himself with packing. He did his best not to remember his last couple of days in Amsterdam, but the memories quickly pulled him in. He was back in that BDSM club, about to meet Fitz and Nina.

"I can't believe you agreed to this," Connor had chuckled as they entered.

"I made a promise to a friend."

"I've made plenty of promises to you, but that doesn't mean I want you to show me how to fuck my girlfriend."

Logan had rolled his eyes. "You don't have a girlfriend."

"*Yet*," Connor had insisted, grinning. "And even when Jesse's mine, I still won't come to you for tips or advice."

"There must be a God, because you're the last two people I'll help."

"Weirdly, that offends me."

Logan had punched Connor's shoulder. "Go tell some dominatrix you've been a bad boy and get out of my hair, or I'll take you over my knee."

Connor had cackled loudly, his blue eyes sparking with humor. "Damn, Lo, be careful or you'll make me hard."

"Fuck. *Off.*"

"Fine, fine. Go get 'em, tiger."

Logan had headed to the private rooms upstairs, as per Fitz's instructions. *I can't believe I'm doing this*, he'd thought as he knocked on the designated door. He had given Fitz suggestions on how to set the scene and therefore hadn't been surprised when Nina opened. She had been dressed in a white corset, matching G-string and thigh-high stockings, the picture of innocence. Her gaze had been fixed on her toes, already embodying the submissive role.

"Hi, Logan."

"Nina." His vocal cords had felt strained. He had stepped over the threshold and made eye contact with Fitz, gesturing to Nina and his own ears.

"Pet," Fitz had called out from the mini bar. "Time to put on those headphones and kneel in front of the wall."

Nina had obeyed immediately, eager to get started.

"How am I doing?" Fitz had asked.

"Hard to tell," Logan had answered dryly, "I just got here."

"I'm so nervous. I keep thinking that I'm going too far. The things you sent me are so controlling and—"

"That's the whole point, Fitz. Relax." Logan's heart had softened at the panicked expression on his childhood friend's face. "This is consensual. You're not doing anything against her will unless she tells you so. She holds the power in the scene."

"What if I go too far?"

"You won't. I'm here to guide you. You'll find it becomes instinctual after a while, like you can sense her needs."

Fitz had breathed deeply for a moment and inclined his head. "Who taught you?"

"Uh, no one," Logan had muttered, embarrassed. He had no clue why he'd been drawn to BDSM to begin with, although he's overheard some rumors about the Drummond appetite. Perhaps it was another thing he's got Brennan to thank for. "Have you established safe words?"

"Yes, they're the usual red, yellow and green."

"Good. It's important to remind her that you're here with her. You never want her to feel like you're not engaged, that you don't have your eyes on her, even if you're not touching her." Logan had glanced at Nina. "So, what do you want to start with?"

Logan shook out of his reverie, aware of his mother's worried gaze on his back. "Doesn't matter now."

"Should I look into that?"

"I'm fine."

"You've been different since you came back."

"That was kinda the purpose of the trip."

"I'm not used to you being so withdrawn, that's all."

"I've grown up, mom. It was exciting to chase tail. For a while, at least. That's over now."

A look of relief passed over her face, but he didn't know if it was because she was happy he'd confided in her or because he wasn't a player anymore. "You know, I was concerned."

"Why?"

"You remind me so much of your father sometimes." He knew she was referring to Brennan by the wistful tinge to her tone. She stood at the edge of the bed, touching one of his shirts. "I told you, he was very sexually active as a teenager and, even while we were together the first time, he didn't stop chasing skirts. I didn't want you to become numb to emotionally connecting with your partner the way he did. It took him a long time to realize sex didn't have to be a power play."

He thought about Alyssa, about the love he'd witnessed between Fitz and Nina, and silently agreed. "I'm not going to fall into that trap, mom. I want it to mean something."

"I'm proud of you, Logan." She blinked her tears away and cupped his face in her hands. "You're turning into an incredible young man. I'm lucky to be your mom."

He soaked up the praise. "You get to take all the credit for who I am."

She shook her head and pecked him on the cheek. "My boy, I gave you some guidelines and a safe environment to grow up in. The rest is all you."

A soft knock pulled their attention to Byron hovering in the doorway. "Am I interrupting?"

"Mom's getting mushy, as usual."

Cinnia laughed tearfully and smacked his chest. "Come downstairs when you're ready to leave."

"Thanks for the chat, mom." He watched her disappear into the hallway and shifted his gaze to Byron. "Do I have more crying to look forward to?"

"Not today," Byron chuckled, shutting the door.

"Okay, shit just got serious." Logan crossed his arms over his chest. "Hit me."

"Teagan found evidence that Ian isn't Luca's father."

Logan held his breath.

"Like I've told you before, Guilietta mentioned Jasmine had a lover before Ian. From the photos Teagan found, they were getting serious." Byron inhaled deeply. "When Ian found out, he flew into a jealous rage and kidnapped her."

"Jeez."

"It's not a happy story," Byron muttered. "He kept her hostage for the rest of the pregnancy, convinced the baby was his. When Luca was born, he used her as leverage to make Jasmine stay. After two years, Jasmine couldn't take it anymore. She killed herself."

Logan struggled to absorb that horrible piece of information. *So much pain and violence. Does Luca know her own history? Has she suppressed it to cope?*

He remembered arriving home after his Amsterdam trip and how one glance in Luca's direction had made him lust after her all over again. Her bronze skin had been glowing; her ebony hair pulled back in a sleek ponytail.

His exhaustion and jetlag had lifted at the sight.

And then, to his surprise, she'd smiled.

In the three months he'd been away, Luca had learned to be more open to those in her inner circle, expressing herself more freely. Cinnia had brought Logan up to speed, proudly stating how well Luca was doing in school. It had given Logan hope that she was fully a part of the Raptors now and that, one day, she might return his feelings.

"I could have stopped all of this."

Logan shook his head in the present, forcing himself to focus on the here and now. "You don't know that."

"When Guilietta came to me—"

"We've been over this." He fixed his stepfather with a firm stare. "Maybe you would've gone to Jasmine and protected her against Ian. Maybe that would've driven a wedge between you and mom, and you would've ended up with Jasmine. Maybe you would've been happy and Luca wouldn't have had to face all the horrors she's seen. But in that reality, you're not with the love of your life and you're not *my* dad."

"I'll always choose your mother. *You.*"

"Her mushy moods are rubbing off on you, old man," Logan quipped, turning away so that Byron couldn't see the tears in his eyes. "Are you going to tell Luca?"

"I don't know. She never really knew Jasmine, but it could be rough for her to learn why. I don't want to mess with the progress she's made."

"Not telling her could be worse."

"Luckily that's not your problem anymore. Finish up: it's almost time to go."

"Hey dad?" Logan called, stopping Byron from leaving. "Things won't change because I'm doing this, right?"

"What do you mean?"

"We're still cool? Even though I won't be around as much anymore? Even though I won't be Prez?"

Byron stepped forward and placed his hands on Logan's shoulders. "There isn't a thing in this world that will ever pull us apart, do you hear me? You're my son. Why don't you tell me why you even had to ask?"

"I don't know." Logan's emotions were irrational lately. "Amsterdam was great, but it made me think about so many things and I don't know if I've made the right decision."

Byron shifted to the bed and sat down, patting the spot next to him. "Come on, let's talk about it. Are you having second thoughts, or is this the nerves talking?"

Rubbing his forehead, Logan sensed a full-on panic attack forming. "I feel like this is a dream. What makes me think I'm good enough to pull this off? What if I don't, and then I've wasted time that could've been spent studying?" He raked his fingers through his hair. "But what if I *am* good enough? What if I'm so good that I make the team and can't ever move back?"

"Is that why you think things between us will change?"

"Won't everyone change towards me?"

"Logan, you're a phenomenal athlete. I'm not just saying that because I'm your dad." He eyed the many trophies on the shelves that lined the bedroom walls. "If anyone can make it big, it's you. You have our full support."

"Why do I feel like there's a 'but' coming?"

Byron laughed softly. "If you're worried about somehow losing out on another career, then enroll at an online university. Have a backup plan."

"What about the club?"

"The club will be fine. Connor has stepped up."

"But what if people start digging into the club's past because I—"

"Logan, breathe," Byron interrupted. "I'm not going to tell you how to live your life. Whatever you choose, you'll be successful, I've always known that. Give this opportunity everything you've got. Leave the rest to us."

"Dad," Logan whispered, dabbing at the corners of his eyes, "you've done so much for me. I don't know if I can ever thank you enough."

"I thought you didn't want more crying?" He pulled Logan into a sideways hug. "You don't have to thank me. Besides, I've got to deal with your mother now that you're leaving the nest. You owe me."

Logan threw his arms around Byron. He savored the sound of the man's pleasantly surprised laugh and shut his eyes in contentment. "I love you, old man."

"I love you too, punk."

"I'll make you proud."

"You already have. I'm happy you realized you should be your own man and that you don't have to be what you think we want you to be." Byron pulled back, smiling gently. "No one expects you to be the second Brennan,

Cinnia, or even me."

Nodding in understanding, Logan dried his tears.

"Finish packing. You don't want to miss your flight."

"No pressure, huh?"

"I know you're placing enough on yourself already," Byron commented as he left the room.

Logan shook his head with a dry laugh.

Ever since meeting Marcus Du Randt, his whole life has changed. He'd returned with a renewed sense of purpose and had immediately spoken to his parents about the opportunity. To his surprise, they'd been nothing but supportive. Even though his mom was reluctant to wave him off, she'd said she would never stop him from giving it his all.

He didn't know what had changed during their honeymoon, but she's grown in leaps and bounds. It had seemed inevitable that he would become the Raptors Prez and find a job somewhere local: not quite breaking away from the life of the generations that came before him, but not necessarily repeating the cycle, either.

Now, he was free to follow his own path. It was liberating and terrifying. It must be how Fitz had felt that night in Amsterdam… Logan had quickly realized that his role wouldn't be as involved as he had anticipated. Fitz had merely needed the reassurance that his desires weren't taboo; that he was allowed to express himself with his partner. Logan had observed, transfixed, as Fitz manipulated Nina's body. He'd watched Fitz's confidence grow until his dominance had appeared natural, like it's always been there. The peculiarity of the evening had faded, and Logan had felt proud that his friend had become more comfortable in his sexuality.

"What's up, Drummond? Ready to go?"

Zipping up his last bag, Logan nodded. He was done being nostalgic for the day. "Hell yes. Think you can carry this?"

Connor snorted as he lifted the two heaviest suitcases, his biceps bulging. "I bench press more than this."

"That's in a controlled environment."

"Everywhere I go is a controlled environment, then."

"Alright, Tyrell, time to check that ego."

"Like that's ever gonna fucking happen," Connor muttered, leading the way downstairs.

Logan met his parents and Luca in the foyer. He hesitated, aware that his mother was eyeing him with interest, before stopping in front of Luca.

"Are you okay?"

She nodded silently, not meeting his gaze.

"You can visit me anytime, if you want," he reminded her.

She embraced him firmly and whispered: "I'll miss you." Then she stormed upstairs, her bedroom door shutting a few seconds later.

Logan's heart was beating wildly from her unexpected display of affection. Why did she have to be so damn beautiful? He often fantasized about tying *her* up and replacing her memories of pain with ones of pleasure. What he wouldn't do to make that a reality… She haunted his dreams.

Alyssa Edgar was the other itch he couldn't scratch. He didn't know how to stop thinking about her. They haven't spoken since he got back from Amsterdam, and perhaps that's for the best. If he was ever going to take his career seriously, he couldn't afford to become distracted.

Clearing his throat, he led the way outside. He came to an abrupt halt at the sight that greeted him: every single member of the local Raptors MC charter was lined up on the lawn, breaking into celebratory cheers once they spotted him.

"There he is!" Haye exclaimed with a big grin, striding towards Logan. "The man of the hour!"

"You guys," Logan breathed, awestruck. He was vaguely aware that he'd dropped his suitcase. He gladly returned Haye's embrace. Dawn, Aurora and Jesse quickly joined in, and then Logan was handed from person to person as they wished him luck.

"Crying isn't a good look on you, cuz," Dane teased.

"Fuck you," Logan sobbed, holding him tightly. "You're gonna be the new team captain."

"Only if coach asks nicely."

Hallie, uncle Teagan and aunt Piper were next. Sophie, Max, Nixon and Jemma. His grandparents. His friends. His extended family. The only people who could've set his mind at ease regarding his decision were all here to show their support.

He was going to miss each and every one of them.

"Come on, Lo," Cinnia murmured once he was done. "Time to go."

Logan waved as he got on the backseat of the SUV. "You should've warned me," he accused without much heat.

"And miss the expression on your face?" Connor quipped, sliding in next to Logan. He was swiping on his phone. "So glad I hit record."

Byron backed out of the driveway, and they were off.

Logan had phoned Marcus Du Randt after the discussion with his parents, who had advised that he keep his options open for the time being. Marcus had let slip that Ajax were already interested in seeing Logan in action, which had made Logan's ears ring.

Is this my life now?

Following that conversation, Logan had got in touch with previous scouts to find out if they're still interested. At first, they hadn't seemed overly thrilled seeing as he'd always blown them off but, once he'd dropped Marcus' name, they had conjured further offers for him to consider. One of them was from his third favorite team, Tottenham Hotspurs.

In the end, Logan had chosen Ajax: he would be of more value to any team once he's proven himself. There was also something about Marcus that he inherently trusted and, besides, he would love to live in Amsterdam.

The trip to the airport went by too quickly. Before he knew it, he was in line at the security checkpoint, gazing at his parents and Connor. He had no idea what the future had in store and was terrified of doing this alone, so far away from home.

In the same breath, he would never forgive himself if he didn't take the chance.

"Love you, my boy," Cinnia mouthed tearfully.

His heart lurched and he smiled, giving them one final wave before turning away. He went through the metal detectors, put his headphones on and listened to music while he meandered towards his boarding gate.

A flash of magenta caught his eye at a concession stand and his jaw dropped as he approached. "Alyssa?"

She seemed equally surprised. "Logan!"

They were in each other's arms in the blink of an eye, both laughing in astonishment. Her citrusy scent reminded him of the amazing time they'd had in Amsterdam: how she'd felt, sounded, tasted…

He didn't blame his dick for hardening, although the timing wasn't great. "What are you doing here?" he asked, reluctantly stepping away. "I thought you were still in Europe."

"I came back for a funeral."

His smile faded as he took in the differences in her appearance. Apart from her hair being longer and another color, she was also thinner. There were dark circles under her brown eyes. She wasn't okay, which made his stomach churn. "Whose?"

"Emile."

"What?! *How?*"

She swallowed with difficulty, her eyes filling with tears. "Car accident."

Speechless, he hugged her tightly. Her body convulsed as she began crying while she clung to his shirt. His heart broke on her behalf. "I'm so sorry. I didn't know."

"It's okay, I didn't tell you," she sniffed. "Why are you here, anyway?"

"I got signed to a football team in Amsterdam. I start training in a week."

She gasped and tilted her head back. "No way! Which one?"

"Ajax." The boarding of his flight being announced made him pause. "In fact, that's me."

"Beanie, that's amazing! Look at you, chasing your dreams!"

He cupped her jaw in his hands. "You didn't return my texts."

She sighed. "I know, and I'm sorry. I got busy with the blogs and then Emile…" She gave him a watery smile. "I'll do better. I missed you."

They gazed at each other in longing. Logan found it incredible that, no matter how much time passed, they always picked up where they'd left off. No hard feelings.

Some hard feelings, he thought wickedly.

He bent his head to kiss her. Her lips felt amazing, molding perfectly to his. She tasted of spearmint and his tongue dueled hers to steal that flavor. He had the fervent urge to take her on the closest available surface and—

She pulled away, grabbed his hand, and dragged him through the crowd.

There were bathrooms up ahead and a surge of adrenaline went through him once he realized they were on the same page. He ignored the startled looks from other women as Alyssa pushed him into the closest cubicle, as well as the harsh whispers that followed. As soon as the door locked, he was on her.

"Logan," she whispered desperately, unbuttoning his jeans.

He sealed his mouth over hers and dipped his hand under her gypsy skirt, sliding his fingers up the inside of her thigh to cup her panty-covered crotch.

He quickly pushed the fabric aside to find her drenched, moaning softly as he slipped a finger inside. They didn't even flinch at the knock on the door.

"Miss, is everything alright in there?" someone called.

"I'm fine!" Alyssa exclaimed, gripping Logan's cock. "Just a minute!"

His scalp prickled and he hoisted her up. Her legs wrapped around his hips and he let out a satisfied breath as his tip sank into her tight, warm heat. "Alyssa."

"Logan."

He gently pushed inside, thrusting slowly at first, while his lips toyed with hers. She raked her fingers through his hair and whimpered once he was fully sheathed, immediately rolling her hips in tandem with his.

"Yes," she hissed, "oh *yes*."

They weren't under the influence, which made it a million times better. He felt more connected to her than ever.

The fingers of one hand gripped her ass, encouraged her to go faster, while the other journeyed to her pierced clit. She was soaking wet, and he leisurely rubbed that bundle of nerves with his thumb. Her squeezing grip around his cock was enough to get him to the edge in mere seconds.

"Oh fuck, I'm coming," she breathed.

He increased the pace, chasing that orgasm with her and only half-aware of the resulting thumping sound on the cubicle door. "Alyssa," he grunted as he fucked her in earnest.

"Logan!"

They released as one.

Logan leaned against her, trying to catch his breath and stay conscious. Her mouth was pressed to the side of his neck and he held her closer, wishing they were skin-to-skin. Amsterdam had changed his life, but Alyssa had been the catalyst long before that. She'd made him believe he was in control of his own destiny. She inspired him.

"I've missed you so much," he confessed.

She looked him in the eyes. "Me too."

"I don't like not being with you."

Her thumb traced the edge of his bottom lip. "That's how it has to be for now."

Heart skipping a beat, he kissed her tenderly. As much as he wanted to run away with her and simply feel this every moment of his life, he couldn't withhold her from chasing her dreams and he had no doubt she felt the same. They loved each other in the way he'd often fantasized about, but the timing was off and there was no guarantee that it would ever change.

The second boarding call cut through the intimate moment. With a sigh, he pulled out and helped her to her feet. "I should go."

They straightened their clothes, gazes glued to each other, and walked out of the cubicle. Logan washed his hands, aware of several sets of eyes on him. He smiled sweetly. "Sorry for the disturbance."

Alyssa burst into a fit of giggles and held his hand while they hurried out of there. "That could've ended in a disaster."

"Good thing we've got luck on our side." He halted once his boarding gate came into view, turning to her. "We'll keep in touch this time?"

She nodded, smiling. "Promise."

Her brown eyes were so captivating, drawing him in even when he knew he should leave. He let out another breath and pecked her on the forehead. "Until next time."

"Until next time," she echoed in a murmur.

He walked away with a lump in his throat, feeling like he's making the wrong decision. Thankfully, the queue wasn't long. His phone vibrated in his hand as he stepped up to scan his pass.

"Your butt looks mighty fine in them jeans, Beanie."

He glanced over his shoulder and laughed at Alyssa shamelessly ogling his behind. Her next message had him in absolute stitches.

"I hate seeing you go, but I love watching you walk away."

His thumbs typed a quick, to-the-point response: *"I just love you."*

"Sir? You need to get going."

Jolting out of their prolonged goodbye, he hurried to the airbridge to get on the plane, frequently checking his screen for further messages from Alyssa. It came as he was busy getting comfortable on his seat, and it made his heart lurch in his chest.

"Everything is going to change. You're going to be a massive success. Girls will be throwing panties at you. Panties, Beanie! And you're gonna enjoy every moment, okay? Don't hold back. Experience it all."

He wiped the tear trickling down his cheek, not knowing how to respond to that. His phone pinged again.

"I'm your cheerleader. I'll watch every game I can. And I'll always love you. Xx"

He didn't realize he was in a trance, staring at a black screen, until the plane was pushed out of its parking bay and one of the flight attendants asked him to switch his phone to in-flight mode. He rubbed his eyes while he wondered what he could possibly say to Alyssa to convey his feelings. He wanted to set her mind at ease, but he had no idea what playing for Ajax would do to his life. He didn't know if it would change the way he felt about her.

"You are somehow the best and worst thing that's ever happened to me. The best, because you're supportive, kind, generous, loving, intelligent, funny, sexy as hell and incredible in bed. The worst, because our timing is always off."

"Ditto," she answered, *"but we've never done it in a bed."*

He chuckled. *"Something to look forward to."*

"One day. Enjoy your flight."

"Bye, Betty. Xoxo"

Before the glaring attendant could give him a what for, he turned his phone off and settled in.

The flight was long and uneventful. Logan resorted to writing in his journal, a suggestion from Byron, and eventually drifted off while watching a movie. His dream started in an abnormally bright parking lot, where a man with auburn hair was straddling a Harley Davidson Blackline. The man's icy gaze landed on Logan, and he smiled warmly.

Brennan.

"Hey, Lo." He held a helmet out. *"Let's go for a ride."*

The dream shifted and then they were speeding on a highway. Logan felt giddy and free, like nothing could catch them, and he was somehow able to hear Brennan's amused chuckle over the rumble of the Blackline's engine. The scenery changed once again, until they were standing on the ledge where Logan had saved Luca.

Brennan had his thumbs hooked in the belt loops of his leather pants. He gazed at the dam in the valley, a content smile on his face. *"You've chosen a different path."*

"Is that bad?" Logan asked self-consciously.

"No." Brennan glanced at his son. "You're braver than I ever was."

"Did you want to leave?"

"I considered it, once, but I was too invested in the club. It was in my blood." Brennan laughed softly, shaking his head. "You've got too much Sloane in you to stay."

Logan didn't know what to say to that. He stared at Brennan as if spellbound, wondering if this was real.

"It's as a real as you want it to be," Brennan murmured. "You don't remember me,

but I get to see you grow up. I'm proud of you, Logan."

The wheels hitting the runway jolted Logan awake.

He wiped away the dampness on his cheeks, the dream—and Brennan's addictive presence—already fading. The conversation had settled him and, somehow, he felt calmer than before. Byron and Cinnia have done what they could to get him to trust his inner drives and ambitions, but for some reason that didn't hold nearly as much weight as Brennan's support.

Seeking the approval of a dead guy? Classic, Logan.

Once the plane came to a halt, he got his things together and waited to disembark. He went through customs to have his passport stamped and meandered to the carousel to grab his luggage. From there, he kept an eye out for his name: Marcus had told him a team representative would fetch him from the airport. He came to an abrupt halt the second he recognized the captain of Ajax.

Andries de Wet waved as he stepped closer. "Hello, Logan. Welcome back to Amsterdam."

"Th-thank you, Andries," Logan stuttered, shaking the man's proffered hand. They fell into step. "I didn't know you were going to be here."

"I try to personally welcome all new players," Andries explained in only slightly accented English. "How was your flight?"

"Honestly? Emotional."

Andries nodded to himself. "This is a big change for you. Are you excited to get started?"

Logan considered that while he slowly became accustomed to his new surroundings. "Yes, I am."

"Good," Andries smiled, "then your time with us will be well spent."

PART II

THE CLUB

CHAPTER FOURTEEN

'CONRAD WAS TAKING a shower.

Jazz licked her lips, wondering if she should be so brave as to walk into the bathroom and watch him wash his muscular body. Her panties dampened at the mere thought of acting that brazenly, and she lifted her dress to run a fingertip over her covered slit. She shivered at the sensation, imagining it was Conrad feeling her up.

Why did she agree to this trip? She should've known it was a bad idea to watch him hit it off with so many beautiful women while she—'

"We followed the last suspicious car that hung around the school," Nixon was saying, dragging Connor from the recollection of the chapter he'd been reading a few minutes ago.

He ran his fingers over his short hair and did his best to focus on the matters at hand. The late nights at the hospital were finally catching up with him. He needed to get some sleep or get laid. It felt like the last time he'd been truly relaxed was in Amsterdam, and even then he'd been pining for Jesse. Nothing helped to take his mind off her, which was why he hasn't done the dance-with-no-pants in the six weeks since he's been back.

If she wasn't his soon, he was going to lose his goddamn mind. Then again, should someone argue that's already happened, he couldn't offer much of a defense. Connor was *not* fine, especially not after coming across the autobiographical novel she'd written, posing as romantic fiction.

He sniggered in amusement. It had taken plenty of courage to finally open the link Logan had sent, causing a whole other world to unfurl: one filled with sex, sex, and more sex. No wonder she's always tried to prevent him from reading it! Who could've known his vixen had such a kinky side?

"Something funny?" Haye questioned.

Blinking, he returned to the present and coughed uncomfortably. Jesse's father wouldn't like Connor's train of thought. "No, carry on," he muttered. Nixon shot him a worried glance, unsatisfied with the nonchalant shrug Connor gave in response. Shit, he was going to be interrogated after this.

"As I was saying," Teagan went on, "I couldn't find any suspicious activity on their message boards or internet searches."

Nathan Poole sighed. "Sounds like they've moved underground. She must be important if they're going through all this trouble to get her back."

"Ian's convinced she's his daughter," Byron reminded him.

"I think it has more to do with the fact that she promised them Logan," Ryan argued.

Byron's jaw clenched. "No one can get their hands on him now."

The silence that followed made Connor realize he and Byron weren't the only ones happy that Logan was living his dream in Amsterdam. It was one less thing to worry about. "How do they get messages to and from each other when they go underground, anyway?" he asked Nathan.

"Ian used to leave a note at the clubhouse with details on the location of the next meeting." Nathan spread his hands apologetically. "I haven't spoken to any of them in thirteen years. They probably changed their protocols since I became a Raptor."

"She didn't do what she was told. If Ian gets a hold of her, he'll kill her: they killed her friend for less. We can't allow that to happen," Byron insisted.

"Aye," Nixon and Haye chorused.

"How can we know what they're planning?" Teagan wondered aloud.

Byron let out a short breath. "I could ask Guilietta."

"Fuck no," Ryan piped up. "We're not going that route again."

"I agree," Connor said firmly. "We'll have to find another way. In the meantime, we continue taking turns watching Luca. Business as usual."

The men around the table nodded solemnly. It's been over a year of the same routine and they were all tired of it, but until they had a breakthrough, they will have to continue as is.

"If you come up with any ideas, let me know and we'll call for church. If there's nothing else, you're dismissed."

Connor slammed the gavel and, one by one, the men rose and left the boardroom. He was hoping to do the same, but his father's glare forced his ass to remain glued to his seat. He didn't want to get a Tyrell lecture: he'll most likely snap and do something stupid, like pick a fistfight with a renowned underground boxer.

"Want to tell me what's going on with you?" Nixon queried once they were alone, resting his feet on the table.

"Tired," Connor answered honestly.

"The hospital?" Nixon's eyes narrowed when Connor nodded. "Do you need time off from the club?"

Connor was shocked at the suggestion. "No, the club's keeping me sane."

"You forget that I raised you and can tell when you're lying." Nixon got up. "Do your mother and I a favor and ask Jesse out already. It's been years and if I have to go one more day with you moping around because you don't have her... So help me, I will beat the shit out of you." He crossed his arms over his chest. "Or are you going to lose her to that guy that's been sniffing around?"

Connor's head snapped up at that. "What guy?"

"I don't blame her. Rumors of your supposed feelings don't mean shit when you haven't acted on them. If a new guy comes along and sweeps her off her feet, why should she show him the door?"

He lurched to his feet and clenched his fists. "Message received, dad."

"Good," his father said, his facial expression softening. "She's in the warehouse."

Connor swiveled on his heel and marched out of the clubhouse, wondering if there really was another man interested in Jesse. He wouldn't be surprised: it's like she didn't know how fucking appealing she was. All wide-eyed innocence and a fiery temper fitting of her red curls... And that ass!

If there is someone else, he'll be at the receiving end of my fists soon enough, Connor thought murderously. His strides lengthened at the sight of the warehouse. Why has he waited this long, anyway? He was so annoyed at the prospect of someone stealing Jesse from under his nose, he couldn't remember. His steps slowed once he spotted her, and he was thrown back into that chapter:

'She leaned her forehead against the door separating them, her fingers spreading her arousal all over her throbbing clit. Blood was rushing through her ears and she moaned, wishing it was him touching her, making her ready for him. Her nipples stood to attention, begging to be sucked.

She didn't hear the shower shut off. She nearly lost her footing when the door swung open, her jaw going slack once she made eye contact with Conrad, which mirrored his aghast facial expression.

"Jazz?" he asked, his eyes drinking her in. The scar above his right eyebrow reminded her of their childhood, the stunt he'd pulled... He's always done dangerous things and she's tried joining him, but she simply didn't have the guts most of the time.

"C-Conrad!" she stuttered as she removed her hand from her panties. "I d-didn't—"

He grabbed the back of her head and smashed their lips together, cutting off what she'd been about to say. She melted in his arms, rubbing herself against him like a cat in heat while he—'

"Snap out of it," he muttered as Jesse went inside. He was rock hard. Fuck! He massaged the top of his head for a few moments, thinking about everyday things to get himself under control. *I need a haircut, and I need to shave.*

There. That's better. His cock has softened: not by much, but it'll have to do.

He briefly traced a fingertip over his scar, amused by how similar Conrad was to *him*, Connor Tyrell. She's even incorporated some of their real-life experiences into her storyline, like the fact that he'd got into parkour and fractured his skull from doing a trick he hadn't been fully prepared for.

Go get your girl, Conrad, he thought with a smirk, heading inside.

Jesse wore a short denim skirt, a dark grey baggy sleeveless shirt, and cowboy boots. Her copper hair was piled on top of her head in a messy bun. No doubt she'd been more eager to jot down a few more pages of her steamy novel than to bother with her appearance. Her pale skin was littered with freckles and he had the familiar yet inexplicable urge to run his tongue over every single one of them. He wondered if she knew how sexy she looked.

Great, he was back to being fully erect!

Adjusting himself, Connor walked to her side. There was a huge birthday party tonight, one he wouldn't be attending due to his need to catch up on some Z's. Most of the old ladies were here to help with the setup, although

Jesse stayed solo off to the one side. Unsurprising, since there was no sign of Luca. That girl, broken as she was, was one of Jesse's only friends and Connor loved her for it.

"Hi, Jess."

She glanced at him over her shoulder, startled by his presence. She pushed her black-rimmed glasses up her nose and cleared her throat. She was the cutest fucking thing he's ever seen, like those nerdy girls in anime series he used to salivate over as a kid.

"Hey, Con. What's up?"

"That's what you've got for me? 'What's up'?"

"I…" She trailed off, eyes wide. "What should I say?"

"Oh, I dunno," he replied sarcastically, "how about, 'wow, Con, I haven't seen you in a while. How've you been'?"

"You're right, I'm sorry. Are you well?"

"Yeah." Only, he felt like a dick for saying what he'd said. If he'd been female, he would've been certain that he was PMS-ing. The hospital—and med school—was turning him into an asshole. *You sure you wanna be a doctor, Con? It's not too late to get into fighting, or porn. Or both.* "How about you?"

"Can't complain. I mean, I can… Work's a drag at the moment. But what's the point?" She let out a short breath, turning to the table she'd been arranging. "How're your studies going?"

"Shit, but it'll be worth it." He joined her side, taking the other end of tablecloth and helping her spread it. "I don't like always complaining about how tired I am, but damn, I can't remember the last time I had a decent night's sleep."

Peeking at him, her pale cheeks went red once she saw that his gaze was locked on her. "And the club's keeping you busy now that Logan's gone. Dealing with Luca's stuff must be tough."

"It's worth it if it means she's safe."

She quirked a smile. "Good. She's nice."

That look on her face nearly brought him to his knees. Did she ever think of him with such fondness? "So, uh, the grapevine tells me you're seeing someone."

"Someone's having a laugh."

Thank God! "Are you interested in anyone?"

"I mean…" She abandoned her efforts in straightening the tablecloth.

He knew she struggled with perfection, and that it had to do with Aurora. He silently applauded her every time she decided against being what everyone wanted her to be. "I don't think that's in the cards for me."

He frowned. "Any guy would be lucky to have you." *Nope, I'm lying. Any guy that isn't this guy would be the unluckiest motherfucker, 'cause I'll fuck his shit up if he so much as looks at you.*

"You have to say that because you're my… friend." That brief hesitation deepened his frown. She didn't notice, since she's moved on to stacking plates. "What about you? Are you done whoring around now that you're back from Amsterdam?"

Whoring? Was her opinion of him that low?

"So done," he growled. "I'm basically a virgin again."

"Shit, Connor, I'm sorry." She touched his arm, misunderstanding his anger. "I didn't mean to sound like a bitch. I was only teasing."

Her skin burned his. He wanted to feel that sensation all over his body, sink into her and go so deep that he'll always be a part of her. Jesus, he wanted to knock her up a few times, too. Would her D-cup tits get even bigger during pregnancy? What would their kids look like?

What the actual fuck, Connor??? Reel it in!

He briefly shut his eyes, remembering another scene in her book, this one less sexy, yet more revealing:

'She wished she could admit the way she felt about him; the way his mere presence caused her heart to gallop and her hands to get clammy. She longed to be the type of woman who could seduce him, satisfy him, but she could never be that. She was too plain.'

Connor wouldn't call Jesse "plain" and will snap the neck of the person who'd put that ridiculous notion in her head. She was the most beautiful woman in the world. He adored the freckles that covered her skin, the amber hue of her eyes. The fact that she had such luscious curves added to her appeal.

"W-why are you looking at me like that?" she stammered, pulling him back to the present.

He steeled his nerves and stepped into her space, smirking when her eyes went wide and she bumped into the table behind her. It was time for him to take his shot. "Because I read your work, Cherise O'Hare."

Her mouth popped open while the red tint to her skin deepened a shade.

"How long have you been pretending to fuck me?" And there went his mouth, fucking things up again.

"What is this?" she hissed between clenched teeth. "Are you making fun of me?"

"No, Jesse, I'm trying to figure out how long you've wanted to fuck me, and why you haven't made your move."

She squirmed at his close proximity and direct inquisition. "Are you kidding? Have you seen me?"

"I've looked at you more than you know. Cut the crap."

"I'm... *me*. Bookish. Clumsy." She chewed on her bottom lip. "Ugly."

"So help me..." He caged her in, intent on setting the record straight. Their faces were inches apart. He caught a whiff of her strawberry-scented lip gloss and promptly became distracted. How was he supposed to think when he was this close to her? If he leaned forward, they could be kissing!

They both jumped at the sound of women wolf-whistling close-by.

"Ooh, get it, girl!"

"And then tell us all about it!"

Connor shot a pissed off glare in their direction, which only served to increase their teasing. Jesse took that moment to wriggle out of his reach. She looked like she was going to sever her bottom lip from her face, the way she was gnawing at it. She made a beeline for the back exit.

"Oh no, you don't." He caught up with her as she burst outside, and slammed the door shut. No one else needed to witness this conversation. He grabbed her elbow and swung her around. "You need to answer me, Jesse."

"They're just fantasies!"

"Why haven't you made them real, then? I guarantee I can do better than your imagination."

She twisted out of his grip. "Stop playing with me, Connor."

"You think I'm playing?" He pushed her against the wall, noting her fluttering eyelashes with satisfaction, and he realized he was behaving like Conrad, the literary hero to her protagonist. How had she known that he could be like this? Until this moment, he's saved his best side for her. "Don't pretend as if you haven't heard that I've got a massive crush on you."

"Yeah, right. You can do so much better."

"Dammit, Jess, stop talking yourself down." He cupped her jaw in his hands. "How long? How long have you wanted to fuck me?"

A soft sigh escaped her lips. When she licked them, he thought he would come undone. "Five years."

Jesus!

"Why haven't you?"

"Because I… I don't know what I'm doing. I've never kissed a boy, much less…" She swallowed, embarrassed. "*Fucked* one."

He found it amusing that she struggled saying the word out loud, seeing as she had no shame using it in her book. Why was she pretending to be innocent when they both knew she was a hot-blooded woman underneath it all, one that very much turned him on?

Then the ramifications of what she'd confessed dawned on him. His stance became less predatory, and he slid his hand down to clutch one of hers. "Come with me."

"Con—"

"We're leaving," he cut in, heading for his Harley. He mounted and gave her a stern look. "Get on."

She hesitated. "Why are you being such an asshole?"

"We need to have a serious conversation in private." He handed her the spare helmet. "Don't you agree?"

Giving in, she donned the helmet and swung her leg over the bike. Her hands were trembling when they rested on his midriff and he covered them with one of his, closing his eyes in bliss. Having her this close… His dreams were coming true. Why wasn't he saying that to her? She needed to know the extent of his feelings.

Soon.

He ignited the engine, revved a few times, and accelerated out of the parking lot, which caused her grip to tighten and her tits to press against his back. He weaved through traffic, disregarding road rules in his hurry to get to the apartment he would've shared with Logan.

He didn't often admit how much he missed that kid, but a whole possible timeline got obliterated when Logan left. The ramifications were still being felt.

Connor parked and waited for Jesse to get off first. He took her hand again and headed for his block. They rode the elevator in silence, while he fought the urge to press her against the wall and have his filthy way with her.

She deserves more than a quick fuck for her first time and, besides, that can't happen today. She's a virgin.

With a loud ping, they arrived on his floor. He led the way to the front door, unlocked it and ushered her inside. She hovered at the back of the couch, looking nervous as hell. Connor couldn't believe that she was here. The caveman in him wanted to keep her forever.

He breathed deeply to calm down, the aggression and urgency fading. "Come sit with me. We need to talk."

"So far, we haven't been good at that," she informed him, although she did as she was told.

"That's my fault." He angled his body to hers. "It's no excuse, but I do and say stupid shit when I'm this tired."

"I've noticed. You should manage your time better, Con."

"Maybe you can help me with that. I mean, how the hell do you write so much and still have a normal life?"

"I don't have as many friends and… girlfriends as you."

"I hope you don't have *any* girlfriends."

She narrowed her eyes at him. "Where are you going with this?"

"Jess, I want to be with you. I've *always* wanted to be with you."

"Really." Sarcasm was dripping off her tone. "How could I not have seen it before? Silly me."

"I deserve that. I should've told you a long time ago."

"Wait, are you only saying this to get in my pants?"

"What? No!"

"I find the timing awfully suspicious. Sure, you chatted to me and drove me home every once in a while, but you never made me feel like you wanted something more than a platonic friendship. You haven't even tried to kiss me, Connor! And now I admit I'm a virgin, and you suddenly want… What do you want, a relationship?"

"I never claimed not to be an idiot." Connor sighed. "I have an anger management problem. I'm aggressive and domineering and I like doing stupid shit. I didn't think I was good enough for you and, honestly, a part of me still doesn't."

She opened her mouth to say something, and then shut it again. She glared at him for several seconds. "Why today?"

"My dad made it sound like there's another guy who's interested in you. I lost my shit. You can't be with someone else, because you belong with me." He tucked a wayward curl behind her ear. "You know it, too. Why haven't you made a move?"

"Because I'm not meant for you," she shrugged. "I can't do any of the stupid shit you like, 'cause I'm afraid of heights and spiders. And dying."

He burst out laughing. "What makes you think we have to do everything together? Do you really believe I have any desire to sit glued to my laptop for eighteen hours a day?"

"Well, no."

"Do you know what I *do* have a desire for?" When she shook her head, he smiled naughtily. "I'd like to show you that all those sex scenes you write are better in real life, and that I *can* fuck you until you can't walk." She swallowed with wide eyes. "Who knows, maybe I can inspire some new ones along the way 'cause, all jokes aside, you are an epic writer, and I can see Conrad and Jazz's story spanning over an entire series."

"Really?"

"Of course. They're getting into so much shit with that mob boss that I won't be surprised if the guy has a kidnapping in store."

"That's actually exactly where I want to go with the plot! At first, I thought it was just going to be a short story, but these characters have such depth and complicated lives that, before I knew it, I was a hundred pages in and going strong. And with Conrad's ties to the Secret Service—" She broke off, embarrassed. "Sorry, I got a bit carried away."

"Don't ever apologize for that to me." Watching her talk about something she was passionate about did something to calm the fury inside of him. "Can we agree that you based them on us?"

Falling silent, she nodded once.

"And can we agree that you're in love with me?"

Her cheeks went red, but she repeated the motion.

"Good," he said, sighing with relief. "I love you, Jesse Fields, and I want you to be my girlfriend."

She pretended to be somber, although her semi-suppressed smile spoke volumes. "Do you even know how to be monogamous, Connor?"

"It can't be that hard, right?"

"I'm serious! What if it's weeks, months, *years* before I sleep with you? What if I want to get married first?"

He pulled a face, mostly to hear her giggle. "I guess I could wait, but my balls will be extremely blue and I might forget how to be a decent lover, which means being married to me will pretty much suck at first."

"So, you really want to do this? Be with me?"

"Only if it means you'll be my girl?"

"I must be crazy." She touched his face with a shy smile. "Yes."

"Great!" His gaze shifted to her lips. "Can I kiss you?"

"Have you always asked girls so many questions, Con?"

"No, but you're pure and I'm about to taint you. I have to make sure you're down with that."

She flashed him with a grin that she probably didn't know was seductive and straddled his lap, leaning in close. "I think you'll be surprised to hear all the things I'm down with."

Her mouth covered his and he was happy to be off the hook where conversation was concerned, since he had no clever response. He held her face in his hands while their lips got acquainted. He loved how her plump mouth molded to his, as if they were cut from the same cloth. He was so excited that this was finally happening, he could've stayed at this pace for the rest of the afternoon.

Jesse had other plans. She slipped her tongue into his mouth. He groaned; she giggled and kept sliding that wicked tongue against his. Her hands rested on his chest while she attacked his mouth as if she's been kissing boys for years.

His fingers trailed up her thighs, under the short skirt and around her hips to clutch her ass. With a gasp, she tilted her head back, leaving his mouth to latch onto her neck. "Starting to think you're not so innocent," he murmured.

"Good, 'cause I'm no damsel," she moaned, holding his head in place.

The feel of her firm ass was incredible to him, like no girl that's come before. It took him way too long to notice that she was wearing a thong. He froze. "What the hell is this?"

"Hmm?" She sounded too aroused to give a shit about talking.

He pushed her to her feet, swinging her around and lifting the skirt. His jaw hit the ground. "What the fuck, Jess? What if you bent over something and someone saw your ass?"

"I don't bend over things. You're overreacting." She turned slightly to look at him. "I'm not wearing a bra, either."

Oh no, the caveman was back. He got up and went to stand on the other side of the living room. They were moving too fast: he had to put a brake on things before they did something she'll regret.

"Con?"

He held his hand up, at war with his urges. He craved nothing more than to go further, but she was untouched. He would never forgive himself if he pushed her too far, simply because *he* wanted it. She should be at the steer.

She tugged the skirt down. "Did I do something wrong?"

"No." His voice was hoarse. He coughed and held his head in his hands. Maybe he should ask her where the line was. *That's a great idea,* his penis agreed. "Do you still want to be a virgin?"

She stood paralyzed to the spot. "Are you for real?"

"Jesse, I'm crazy about you. You kissing me the way you do and wearing a thong and then saying you're braless is making me forget about important things, like that you haven't had a first time yet and I... I want to mess around 'cause I'm so fucking sexually frustrated, but you're my girl and I'm not gonna fuck this up. I need to know how far I can go."

"Well..." Her gaze dropped to the base of his neck. "I hate being a virgin."

God help me!

His dick rejoiced at the news, threatening to head-butt its way right through his jeans. "Okay, then." Pulling his shirt over his head, he dropped it to the floor.

"What the hell are you doing?"

"Taking my clothes off. Unless you want to do that?"

She looked like a deer caught in the headlights.

"That's what I thought." He proceeded to remove his shoes, socks, jeans and underwear, until he stood in front of her in all his naked glory. He had a raging erection, but hoped that it wasn't intimidating. Girls' reactions to his anatomy were split between eager to know if he'll fit, and terrified that he won't. He hoped she was part of the former group. "What should I do now?"

"Excuse me?" she countered, eyes dipping below his waist and fixating on the part of him that so badly wanted to break through her barrier.

"This is your first time." He spread his arms wide. "You should be in control. I'm curious to see how much of what you've written is something *you* want to try, and how much is made up."

She licked her lips and unzipped her skirt, stepping out of it. Her glasses ended up on the coffee table. She sauntered to him, took his hand and placed it between her legs. "You sure you're okay with giving me control?"

Jesus, she's soaked!

The silky thong did nothing to conceal the wet patch, and he couldn't stop his fingers from curling and rubbing against her mound.

"Did I ask you to do that?"

His eyes locked with hers. He stopped, mesmerized by her inner vixen coming out to play.

"On your knees."

He dropped down and waited for her next instruction.

"Take my boots off, Connor."

He lifted each leg as he discarded a boot, unable to prevent his lips from caressing the spot above her knees.

"You really suck at taking orders."

"Want to know what else I can suck at?"

She regarded him curiously. "What?"

He hooked his thumb under the band of her thong, bunched the material in his hand and yanked it off. Her carpet matched the drapes, although she kept her pussy trimmed. He salivated at her musky scent. He parted her lower lips and latched onto her clit.

"Ah!" she exclaimed as she grabbed his head. "Connor!"

It felt like the whole reason his name even existed was so that *she* could moan it like that. He continued licking her clit, savoring her taste. The fingers of his other hand found her entrance and slid inside; one at first, to test how ready she was, but a second quickly joined.

First time, first time, it's her first time, he chanted mentally, restraining himself from getting too rough.

Holding his fingers where they were, he rose up to kiss her, removing her shirt along the way. Her breast was heavy in his hand. He stepped back, his breathing harsh. "Jesus Christ, you're perfect."

Everything that he's ever wanted in a woman was currently in front of him. She never wore skin-tight clothing; he hadn't known how tiny her waist was. Her tits were perky, round, and huge; her hips wide; her stomach flat. Above all, she had tattoos spanning from the tops of her legs to below her armpits: layer upon layer of intricate filigree patterns, roses, hummingbirds and a peacock. The designs emphasized the curves of her body.

"So fucking perfect," he mumbled, lifting her into his arms.

Her legs wrapped around his hips and she returned his kiss passionately. His fingers dug into the flesh of her round ass at the feel of his cock sliding along her slick pussy. She began rocking against him, causing his balls to tighten. Was he going to spill too early, like *his* first time?

Common sense fled from his mind when he stumbled onto the couch, leading to his cock pushing halfway inside. They both cried out: she was in pain, and he was in heaven. Her pussy fluttered, drawing soft grunts from him. He thrust into her once, experimentally, and loved how her nails pinched the skin on his back. He did it again, knowing that she'll soon get used to him.

"Con, stop!" Her legs were surprisingly strong as they held his hips in place, preventing him from sinking in further. "I don't want to get pregnant!"

He rested his forehead on hers, attempting to pull out. Every time he tried, her inner muscles rippled around his cock, which made his hips twitch with the need to *own*. He groaned. "Would it really be such a bad thing?"

"Connor, be serious!"

"Fine." He reluctantly got off her and headed for his room. "Come on, then."

She had a baffled frown on her forehead as she stepped over the threshold. "You can be a royal dick sometimes."

"Baby, you don't know the half of it." He rummaged in his bedside table for protection, ripping the foil and sheathing his slightly bloodied cock. "How are you feeling?"

"Really sore." She bit the corner of her lip. "Is it always going to hurt? Are you normal size?"

"'No' to the first, and 'I hope you never find out' to the second."

She burst out laughing when he tackled her onto the bed. "What if I want to?"

He spread her legs and positioned his tip at her entrance. "Not funny."

"Sorry."

He rolled his eyes, eliciting another giggle out of her. "If you want to tap out, now's the time. Once I'm in you, I'm gonna keep going until you scream my name. Then we're gonna cuddle and pass out."

"Wow, you know just what to say to make a girl all wet and tingly."

"Oh, baby, if it's wet and tingly you want…"

He bent to capture a nipple between his teeth. Within seconds, he had her head back in the game, using his mouth to kiss, lick and bite every delicious inch of her. Her sopping pussy had the metallic tang that confirmed *he* got to her first, not some other cunt who wouldn't have appreciated her the way she deserved. He would eat her out come rain, hell or sunshine, whether it was *that* time of the month or not. He did crazy shit and soon he'll show her that even she could take a walk on the wild side.

"Connor, please!" she begged.

"Have I made you wet and tingly, baby?" His mouth stayed on her clit. "Want me to fuck you now?"

"Yes!"

"Hallelujah." He hooked her legs over his shoulders and drove into her, right to the hilt. The condom greatly affected his sensitivity and yet he was on the edge of an orgasm, anyway. "Fuck, not gonna last long."

"Okay," she gasped, meeting him thrust for thrust.

"If anyone asks, I was romantic as fuck and we were at it for hours."

Her laugh turned into a moan, into a squeal of delight, and into his name. He watched her facial expression change with every jab, captivated by his spirited redhead. If this was what he had to look forward to for the rest of his life, then he was glad he had finally got off his ass and claimed her.

"Connor!" She became frenzied, her tight pussy squeezing his cock, wringing it, *milking* it. "Connor, I'm—oh fuck, I'm coming!"

He groaned as he buried his face in her neck. He came violently, his muscles cramping and body shuddering. "Jesse!" He collapsed on top of her. "What have you done to me?"

"You say that," she wheezed, "as if… I'm *your* first!"

"Feels that way." He rolled to the side and scrubbed a hand over his face. "Wow."

Her hand found his and gave it a squeeze. "Yeah, wow."

"As much as I want to go for round two, I'm fading fast."

"Go to sleep, then," she murmured, kissing his temple. "You've done some hard work today." He laughed at the pun in her words, and she smacked his shoulder. "I'll clean up the living room."

"You don't—"

"Shut up, Connor. Get some rest."

As if she'd flipped a switch, he did exactly that. When he eventually emerged from a deep slumber, he still had the condom on. He pulled it off, chucked it in the direction of the bin and turned on his side to gaze at the warm body next to him.

"Hey."

She was on her phone, her thumbs tapping on the screen. "Welcome back."

Spooning behind her, he rested his chin on her shoulder. "What're Conrad and Jazz up to?"

"She wore him out," she answered tartly.

"Poor guy."

"He's passed out on the couch, and she's taking a look around his house." He clicked his tongue. "What a snoop!"

"She's going to find out that he used to be an MMA fighter, and it's going to open a whole can of worms. Will fall in nicely with those five years he can't account for."

"My alter ego is much cooler than I'll ever be."

Jesse was quiet as she finished up and placed her phone on the nightstand. Then she turned to face him. "I did research, by the way, and you're not normal size." She giggled at his raised eyebrows. "You are also what they consider a 'shower', not a 'grower'. A lot of sites suggested that I purchase lube if I'm going to sleep with you 'on the regular'."

"I dunno," he teased, clamping his teeth on the bottom lip she frequently abused, "I got a lot of lube for free earlier."

She blushed. "Thanks for being sweet about that."

"You're my girl, Jess. I'll always be sweet on you."

"I hope this isn't too soon and that you're not going to run away screaming, but I love you."

"Yeah, this was nice and all, but don't go naming our non-existent children yet."

"Says the man who gave zero shits about wearing a condom."

"What can I say? I want to put plenty of babies in you."

Her eyes widened. "Kids are expensive."

"So? I'm going to be a surgeon and you're on your way to becoming a celebrated author. If they could make a *Fifty Shades* movie, then they can find some space for Conrad and Jazz on the silver screen."

She sighed dramatically. "I never knew you were going to make me regret giving up my virginity so soon."

"I'm an overachiever," he grinned.

"More like a cute puppy."

"Babe, if you never want to see my penis again, you'll keep that shit up."

She blinked at him oh-so-innocently. "Am I getting pillow talk wrong?"

"So, *so* wrong. Not surprising, seeing as you were a virgin until an hour ago. But I'll teach you some lines. Like 'oh Connor, your cock is humungous' and 'I want to feel it inside me again right now'."

"Yeah, this was nice and all, but don't go picking out your wedding dress just yet."

He cackled loudly, loving that she gave it as good as she got. "Damn, my girl."

"I like that you call me that," she confessed softly. "I love that I'm your girl."

"Forever and ever, baby. Speaking of babies…"

She sniggered when he pulled her on top of him, and straddled his thighs. "If I'd known it would take sex to turn you from Mr. Hyde into Dr. Jekyll, I would've done it ages ago."

The mirth faded from his features as he cupped her face in his hands. "I'm doing my best to be a good man, one that isn't angry all the time." He touched her thick, red locks. "I feel free with you."

"I'm glad I have that effect on you, but I won't let you off the hook when you're being a douchebag."

He smiled. "Deal. Also, I'm buying you a French maid outfit."

"Classic Connor, covering an intimate moment with a joke." She fought against a smile and lost. "What time do you have to be at the hospital?"

Glancing at the clock, he sighed deeply. "Five hours from now, and I've got to get some studying done before that. Then again, I'd rather take you for another ride."

"You can't do that!"

He made them switch positions and trailed his lips to her succulent tits. "Fuck it, I'll rewrite if I fail."

"Connor—"

"Shh," he hushed her, smiling. Damn, he was a lucky son of a bitch. If he ever escaped from Jesse's presence for longer than five minutes, he'll be sure to thank his old man for nudging him in the right direction.

CHAPTER FIFTEEN

ADJUSTING TO LIFE without Logan was tough. Cinnia never truly realized what a clingy mother she was until he left to play for Ajax.

The first couple of days were absolute torture. The following weeks, even more so. She moved around in a daze, suffering from empty-nest syndrome. Not even Luca and the puppies could make up for his absence.

Her libido took a nosedive, which was unusual given her appetite. Byron was mindful, as always, leaving her to figure out how to adapt to this new rhythm.

There were many other contributing factors to her disposition. For one, she had to admit that she was getting old. Her child was officially building his own life, following his dream halfway across the globe. Her identity had revolved around being a doting and supportive parent for eighteen years. In the space of a second that had shifted.

For another, the Raptors MC was no longer headed by a Drummond. When Brennan had still been alive, Cinnia had enjoyed a certain station within the club that was addicting. Even after he passed, she'd been holding space for the day Logan was patched in as Prez, as if she were a queen regent. She's spoken to Reade and Mysie about it and therefore knew she wasn't the only one fighting to emotionally detach from these traditional notions, but it didn't make it any easier.

The club has been the very foundation of her life, even the reason why Logan existed: if not for it, she didn't know where she'd be. With Logan gone, Cinnia was questioning everything she knew.

To feel needed, she narrowed her focus to making sure Luca didn't want for anything. Cinnia couldn't explain why, but she'd never doubted Luca's intentions: not even when pieces of her former best friend started arriving in boxes. Cinnia had understood why everyone was on their guard, and why Logan had been hurt, but she had secretly longed for the day when Luca would move back in.

Cinnia felt responsible for her. Dr. McKauley seemed to think it was because Cinnia had survived a similar attack to Luca's. Or maybe it's because, deep down, she's always wondered what having a daughter would be like.

The girl was slowly gaining confidence and becoming more comfortable living with her and Byron, yet it was steady going. She hasn't made many friends at school, other than fellow MC kids like Hallie and Dean, and she didn't seem interested in any extracurricular activities. Cinnia had seen it as a personal victory when Luca agreed to join self-defense classes.

Bobby tugged at his leash, jolting her back to the present. She glanced at Luca, who was expertly steering Charlie, and smiled. "Seems like you're getting the hang of it."

"I never thought I'd like dogs."

"Me neither, actually."

Luca gazed at Cinnia, a quizzical look on her face. "Have you never had pets before?"

"No, not really. We had a dog when I was little, but after that one passed, my parents never got another one."

"Jesse's thinking of adopting a cat."

"I'm sure Connor would love that," Cinnia laughed.

"He wants her to be happy."

Cinnia nodded to herself, falling silent. Talking about new love made her feel bad for sexually neglecting Byron. At the same time, she knew that guilt wasn't a great reason to take him to bed.

It won't always be this way.

Only, what if this was the new normal for them? What if her age was finally catching up with her and menopause changed her forever? What if she never wanted his hands on her again? What if he got bored?

You're getting ahead of yourself, Cin.

She sighed deeply, shaking her head.

"Did I say something wrong?"

"No, Luca. I'm just… going through a tough time."

"You miss Logan," Luca realized.

Cinnia's heart skipped a beat. "Every day."

The girl didn't speak for a long moment, peering at their surroundings while they walked. "Do I need to find somewhere else to live?"

Cinnia came to an abrupt halt, stopping herself from grabbing Luca's elbow at the last moment. Luca didn't like physical contact, which was understandable, but Cinnia wished she could comfort the girl. Treat her like her own.

It's the least I can do after—

She winced, remembering when Byron had first shared his suspicion that Luca was Jasmine's daughter: the same one Guillietta had wanted him to take in to protect from Ian McDermot. What would Luca do if she ever found out?

Luca halted, glancing over her shoulder with those interesting violet-colored eyes. "Cin?"

Cinnia cleared her throat, softening her stance. "You can stay with us as long as you want, Luca. I would never kick you out."

Their gazes held for the longest moment and then, finally, Luca smiled and nodded. "Thank you, Cin. I like it here."

"Good, I'm glad." Cinnia began walking again, tugging Bobby along. "Are you ready for class today?"

"I think so. I don't like when they touch me."

"Those memories can be painful, I know, but they have to show you how to defend yourself."

"I'm… learning. Dr. McKauley helps."

Cinnia grinned, although Luca didn't see it. That woman has been a part of Cinnia's own healing journey for over two decades and her advice was as relevant as ever. Cinnia was glad Luca found value in sitting down with Dr. McKauley.

"Well, we better get going," Cinnia remarked as they walked up their driveway. "Class starts in ten minutes."

"Okay."

They hurriedly took the dogs to the backyard and Luca filled their bowls with water, which they happily lapped up. Cinnia led the way to the SUV and, together, they drove to their self-defense lesson. She kept a close eye on Luca's progress, proud that the girl was visibly fighting her aversion to having someone else's hands on her in order to fend off a potential attacker.

Cinnia hoped that Luca would one day stop living in fear altogether.

Once they were finished, Cinnia checked her phone. She was delighted to see a message from Byron.

"Asked Jesse to visit Luca tonight. She's on her way over. I have a surprise for you. 5PM. Don't be late. Xx"

Accompanying his text was a location pin. Cinnia tapped on it, her eyebrows raising when it redirected her to the website of her favorite spa. What on earth was he up to?

"Cin?"

She blinked out of her stupor. "Let's get home: Jesse's hanging out with you tonight. Sounds like she wants a girls' night."

Luca beamed at Cinnia. "Oh, I like those."

"Do you want to invite Hallie, too?"

"Yes, that sounds cool." Luca typed a message while they walked to the exit. "Are you going somewhere?"

"I think Byron booked a massage for me."

"Sounds nice. Is he joining you?"

"I don't think so. He's working late."

They chatted as they got in the car and drove home. Cinnia felt warm inside, knowing how much Luca trusted her. Luca has had a tough life—partly due to Cinnia's insistence that Byron refuse Guillietta's request, way back when—and Cinnia wanted nothing more than to make it better, going forward. She'd hate it if Luca defined her future existence by the trauma of the past.

Jesse was waiting in the driveway when they arrived home. Cinnia noted the glow in the young woman's cheeks and smiled. *Probably Connor's doing.* Thinking of other people having amazing sexual experiences reminded her of her own inability to become aroused lately.

All in good time.

She hoped so!

"Hello, ma'am," Jesse greeted politely.

Cinnia rolled her eyes and unlocked the house, leading the way inside. "You know better, Jess."

"Sorry, habit." Jesse hugged Luca. "Ready for girls' night?"

"Yes!" Luca said excitedly. "I added a few movies to my list that we could watch. Is it okay that I invited Hallie?"

"Of course, it'll be so much fun."

Cinnia grabbed a bottle of water from the fridge. "I'll leave money for you to order in, if you'd like?"

"Thanks, Cinnia," Jesse smiled, adding a wink at the use of her first name.

"I'm glad Connor is rocking your world. I'll high-five him the next time I see him," Cinnia teased. When Jesse's cheeks went red, Cinnia bowed dramatically. "That's my cue! Have fun, girls."

"Bye!" they greeted, before their voices dropped to a whisper.

Cinnia had a spring in her step as she meandered upstairs to take a quick shower. She was grateful that Luca's hit it off with someone like Jesse: she was smart, sassy and saucy, but gentle. Jesse's views on sex would no doubt contribute greatly to soothing Luca's fears regarding the subject and helping her overcome them altogether.

Dressing in comfortable clothes, Cinnia went back downstairs just as Hallie arrived, looking like a younger version of herself. Cinnia smiled broadly as she embraced her niece, stroking her long, silky black hair.

"Hey, auntie," Hallie greeted.

"Missed your face, Hal." Cinnia pulled back, cupping Hallie's cheeks. She noted the dark circles under her niece's eyes and frowned. "You okay?"

Hallie let out a short, sharp breath. "Mom and dad had a big fight again."

"Oh, boy." Cinnia has noticed that Teagan and Piper's relationship has become strained in the last couple of years, and it seemed like their arguments were worsening over time. She was torn, because she wanted her brother to be happy, but Piper was also one of her best friends... She's decided to stay out of it, for the most part. "Maybe I need a girls' night, too."

Hallie held her hands up in mock surrender. "As long as you didn't hear about their problems from me."

"Don't worry, Hal. I've got my ways." She kissed Hallie's forehead. "Have fun with Luca and Jesse. See you later."

"You too."

Cinnia decided to take a ride, needing to feel the wind rush through her hair. The spa was on the other side of town and she opted for the scenic route to clear her head. This meant that she arrived five minutes after the prescribed time.

Wonder what By will do to reprimand me…

A brief tingle of awareness went through her body, giving her hope that her libido was returning.

She gave her name at reception and was promptly led down the hallway to a private room. She had no idea which package Byron had arranged, yet excitement zinged through her as she disrobed and got comfortable on the table, lying face-down. The aromas in the room, coupled with the relaxing music, had her in a drowsy state in no time.

The masseuse didn't speak as she began the tender massage on Cinnia's shoulders with warm, lubricated hands. The touch felt oddly familiar and easily identified the tight parts where she carried her stress. Cinnia moaned softly, loving the pressure that was added to those muscles: it was just the right amount to make her go limp.

The woman's surprisingly large hands slowly moved down Cinnia's back, fingers expertly rounding over each hip with meticulous care. Cinnia felt like putty, totally pliable to the ministrations. She wasn't even ashamed of the tingle settling in her groin. In fact, she imagined that her husband was exploring her body, instead. She couldn't wait for those hands to settle on her—

Oh God! Cinnia thought excitedly as fingers massaged her ass. *Yes, right there!*

She tried not to clench her pelvic floor, but the temptation was great. She gasped when she heard the uncapping of an oil bottle, jolting slightly once the contents drizzle down her crack. Her upper body raised slightly, ready to roll her off this bed, but a hand gently pressing between her shoulder blades had her reluctantly settling back on her stomach.

Knowing Byron, this could be part of the surprise.

That thought made her relax completely. The hand between her shoulders joined the one rubbing oil into her ass' skin. Together, they parted her cheeks and teased the areas around her puckered hole, making her almost beg to feel fingers breach her. She barely stopped herself from grinding her hips to find friction for her throbbing clit, her mind conjuring a vision of Byron doing this to her.

When a fingertip paused over her anus, exerting the slightest pressure, she held her breath. Her nails bit into the inside of her palms. She didn't know what she was waiting for, she only knew that she was ready.

So ready!

The lubricated finger slowly pushed forward and she opened up, needing this so badly she could cry. It pumped in and out, going deeper each time, until it was joined by another. The squeeze of a bottle added more lubrication, making it easier for the fingers to stretch her ass; fuck it good.

"Ah!" she exclaimed breathily once a third finger was added. Her hips were rocking of their own volition now, the soft towel beneath adding beautiful friction to her clit. She clutched the edge of the bed, prepared to push against those fingers. She whimpered when they retreated. "Wait…"

There was a rustle of fabric and she felt the bed move as the masseuse knelt between her parted legs. Those large hands kept her cheeks apart, while also anchoring her hips and making it nearly impossible to move. Not that she wanted to…

She instantly recognized the broad head of a dick pressing on her asshole. "Oh my God, *Byron*!"

"Yes, Cin." The confirmation heightened her arousal, sending electric sparks running up and down her spine. "I'm gonna fuck your ass now."

She let out a guttural breath as he inched his way inside, feeling helpless and sexy and naughty. "By, *please*!"

"Shh, I've got you. Breathe."

She exhaled slowly and he took his cue to breach her further; when she inhaled, he stopped to let her get used to him. They both grunted when he was fully sheathed, relishing in being connected for the first time in weeks.

"Ready?" he murmured.

"Yes!"

He started at a leisurely pace, thrusting into her carefully and allowing her to feel every inch of his cock. "Fuck, Cin, I've missed you."

"Me too," she mumbled drunkenly. "By, faster!"

"No."

If she thought she'd already reached the pinnacle of arousal, that word proved her wrong. She clutched the sides of the table as he took his time grinding into her. The noises she made were guttural and primal, stemming from deep within her. She wasn't at all surprised when she toppled over the edge.

"That's so hot," Byron said breathlessly, gently easing out of her ass.

"Oh God." She shut her eyes, relishing in the fading ripples of her orgasm. She felt him shift off the bed moments before he grabbed her hips and pulled her back so that she was bent over the end of the massage table. Biting her lip, she heard him cleaning and lubing his cock. "By, please."

"You want me in your pussy, Cin?"

"Fuck, *yes.*"

"Good, so do I." He stepped closer, moving her feet wider apart with his own, and pressed against her entrance. This time, he went right to the hilt in one, hard thrust.

"*Ah!*" she exclaimed, the pain pleasurable to her over-stimulated brain.

He grasped a fistful of her hair with one hand, smacked her ass with the other and pounded into her roughly. "Is that what you want?"

Her eyes rolled to the back of her skull. Byron used his aggressive side sparingly: whenever he unleashed it, it drove her wild. She could barely remember her own name, much less form a coherent reply, so she hoped he would take her cries of passion as an affirmative.

"Such a dirty slut," he groaned, slapping her ass again. "My dirty slut."

He targeted her G-spot, plunging into her at a fast, hard pace. Her toes curled and, just as he pulled her up by her hair, she exploded around his cock.

"That's it," he breathed appreciatively. He slid his hands to cup her bare breasts, tugging at her nipples. His thrusts became gentler, slower. "Are you gonna give me one more, babe?"

"Hmm," she moaned.

He pulled out and flipped her over, lifting her onto the edge of the massage bed. He gazed into her eyes with a lazy grin as he spread her legs and pushed inside her swollen core.

"Love you, Cin."

She held onto his shoulders and rocked against him. "Love you, too."

They fell into their familiar rhythm, each excited by the prospect of getting the other off. They were racing to the finish line, murmuring words of dirty sex, of love. Byron released first, crying her name into the side of her neck. His pulsing cock set her off, leaving her clenching around him.

They collapsed onto the table as they recovered. He placed sloppy kisses on her neck and trailed his mouth down to her nipples to suck on them in turn. He bit and licked his way to her pussy, where he made himself at home.

Cinnia rested her feet on his broad shoulders and arched her back, loving the attention of his tongue and lips. After all these years, he knew exactly how to wring another orgasm out of her, and she gripped his hair as the waves crashed over her. Their breathing filled the silence as they came down from the high.

She made eye contact with a tired smile. "Libido reactivated."

"Thank God," he chuckled. He moved to get towels, handing one over. "It was torture falling asleep next to you, knowing you didn't want me."

She sat up, letting her eyes travel the length of his body. So tall, lean, gorgeous... *And all mine.* "It was never about you, babe," she murmured once her gaze lifted to his.

"I know." He leaned forward to kiss her. "I was also going through stuff because Logan's left. I just wanted to feel close to you. You wanted the opposite."

She touched his cheek, her heart aching. "I'm sorry. We're not always out of sync, which makes it tough when we are." She pressed her lips to his for a moment. "Thank you for this. It's exactly what I didn't know I needed."

"You're welcome."

They embraced for several minutes, enjoying the power of reconnection. The spell was broken by the ringtone she'd assigned to Logan's profile. Byron stepped away and she scrambled to her phone.

"Hey, Lo," she said by way of greeting.

"Hey, momma. How are you?"

"Great, now that I'm talking to you. I'm with your dad, so I'm putting you on speaker."

Byron flashed her with a grateful smile. "Hey, punk."

"Hey, dad. What's crackin'?"

Byron laughed softly, eyeing Cinnia. "You don't want to know. How's everything going there?"

"Good. I feel part of the team now. They're really cool guys. And my Dutch is improving."

"Well done, you," Cinnia praised.

"Coach says I'm ready." Logan's excitement was palpable. "I make my debut on Saturday."

Cinnia's heart skipped a beat. "Really?!"

"That's great!" Byron cheered.

"I know, right? I have no idea how I'm going to be able to sleep until then."

"You'll have make a plan," Byron said.

"You don't want to miss it for the world," Cinnia added.

Logan laughed. "I won't, don't worry. I just can't believe this is happening! It's so surreal. All of it."

"You deserve it, baby. We're so proud of you."

"Thanks, mom. How's everyone doing over there?"

Cinnia spent the next couple of minutes bringing Logan up to speed, while watching Byron get dressed. Even though Logan wasn't physically present, this phone call made it feel like the good ol' days: when the three of them had been a family.

You're still a family, her conscience reminded her, *just a different kind.*

All too soon, Logan had to go. She ended up staring at the phone, a bittersweet feeling in her chest.

"Come on, babe," Byron said, "date night isn't over."

She smiled and accepted his outstretched hand. "Sex usually goes after dinner, By."

"Who says it won't?" he winked.

She burst out laughing as she cleaned up. She might never stop missing her son, but that didn't mean she should stop living. She was grateful that Byron kept reminding her of that. "Fine, you're on."

"You could be my sushi plate again."

She flushed, remembering. "Is that your way of saying you don't want me to talk?"

"Uh, yes?"

"You should be so lucky."

They entered the parking lot and Cinnia smiled at the sight of his V-Rod next to her Harley. He must've waited around a corner so she wouldn't see him when she'd arrived earlier. They straddled their respective bikes and exchanged a glance.

"Oh, I am lucky," he winked.

Joy made her buoyant. *So am I.*

CHAPTER SIXTEEN

"OKAY, LADIES!" SHE clapped her hands to get their attention, before signaling her assistant to cue the music. "Five, six, seven, eight!"

They flawlessly executed the moves that Sophie had choreographed, their arms and legs extending to form long, beautiful lines. She gazed at them with pride: that this was her life, and that her routines garnered such commitment from the girls. She'd worked hard to open this studio and she was utterly grateful to live her dream. The endless ballroom, hip-hop, contemporary and tap-dancing lessons she'd taken as a child have paid off, big time.

The fact that she was a bit of a YouTube sensation didn't hurt, either. It gave her the opportunity to create routines for music videos of amazing artists.

Although she personally preferred hip-hop and pole dancing, she offered all the styles she'd grown up with, too. Jules, her assistant, was an incredible ballroom dancer and gave some of those lessons, mostly because they were evening sessions. They posted a new video every week, either of Sophie or Jules dancing.

Today was Sophie's turn, and she was excited to share her latest creation.

"Good job," she cheered when the song ended. The young girls beamed at her with red cheeks. "Let's finish with stretches!"

For the final ten minutes of the lesson, Sophie joined them to warm up her own muscles. They left with happy waves and chatter, which made Sophie smile. She's always wanted to bring people together through her dancing.

"Are you ready for this?" Jules grinned once they were alone.

"I think so." Sophie went into a side split, relieved that there were no aches today. When she tried the other side, though, she silently admonished herself for being too optimistic. She leaned forward to increase the pain, squaring her hips to get the most out of the stretch. "I'm a bit nervous. I don't exactly have a booty associated with twerking."

Jules rolled her eyes. "Not this again."

"My mom's genetics are too strong. If it weren't for the implants and million squats she does every day, she'd look like a stick. Like *me*."

"You have a butt! It's... cute."

"Yeah, 'cause *that's* what every woman aims for," Sophie sighed as she got up.

She headed for the counter at the entrance to change her clothes. She'd recently purchased neon tights for this specific occasion, since the patterns made her ass appear bigger than it was. The bright pink sports bra had funky straps over the back and matched her trainers. She piled her light blond hair in a messy bun on top of her head, walking to the mirror to see the final product.

Ever since she'd started dating Max, she has wished for a curvier body with even more fervor than before. She was four years away from thirty and yet no closer to looking like a woman. What she wouldn't do to have the tits and asses of the bombshells she directed in music videos!

She cupped her small breasts and inhaled deeply to rein in her insecurities. "This is the best I'm gonna get," she muttered, glancing at Jules. "Are you ready for me?"

"Yes, ma'am."

Sophie counted herself lucky to have someone like Jules. The woman has done several courses in camera work, photography and video editing, which she'd based her own business on. To top it off, she was more than willing to fulfil the role of assistant without making any unnecessary demands, such as co-ownership of Sophie's studio. It was one of the many reasons why they've become close.

"Hit it."

Jules raised the camera and counted Sophie down.

As soon as the music started, Sophie was transported to another world. She was a warrior that lulled her enemies into a false sense of security. By distracting them with hypnotic moves, her Amazonian sisters could go in for the kill.

The song she'd selected was from a lesser-known local artist. It revolved around a strong feminine entity that enraptures her audience. The bass undertones of the melody brought something primal and animalistic to mind. The tempo slowly rose and the rapper's adoration of his muse caused him to catch his breath; his tone becoming more consumed and anxious as the song drew to a close.

When she had contacted him for permission and explained the concept of her routine, he'd granted it gladly, with the condition that she would direct his music video. In a week, her studio will be transformed into a jungle, with bamboo and small trees everywhere.

Sophie ended on the floor with an arched back while gazing into the camera, which was close to her face. Then, instead of her well-rehearsed last move, she flipped onto her knees, sliding them outwards and fixing the lens with a stare that clearly communicated who was in charge.

"And cut!" Jules squealed. "Dammit, girlie, you've been holding out on me!"

Sophie laughed breathlessly. "Not too much?"

"Hell no!" Jules replied. "Why did we ever think ending on your back would fit the song? It needed a strong finish. The character is an alpha female, for heaven's sake."

"I don't know why I didn't think of that before."

"It was perfect. We don't need another take."

"Great." Sophie got to her feet and headed to the front to get a towel, only to stop short before she could.

Max stood at the entrance, watching her intently.

She was transported to the first time they'd met, when she had thought: *By God, I've never seen such perfect skin!* Nearly a year later, she still couldn't get over it. His hue brought to mind her favorite coffee. Dark, lush and mouth-watering... Rejuvenating.

"Hi."

He cleared his throat. "Hi."

"I guess I should go." Jules packed the equipment away and winked at her. "Great job, Soph." She sauntered to the door, where Max graciously stepped out of the way. "Nice to see you, handsome."

He chuckled. "Bye, Jules."

Sophie walked to him. He picked the towel up and handed it to her. "Thanks." She couldn't care less about her sweaty appearance, not while he looked so fucking hot in his police uniform. "I wasn't expecting you."

"Jules told me to come over." On top of all his other attractive physical qualities, he also had the sexiest, deepest baritone. She often joked that he should've been a late-night radio DJ. "She said I wouldn't want to miss it. This is what you've been working on the last week?"

Translation: *this is why I haven't seen you in a week?*

She swallowed thickly. "I'm really sorry. I got a bit carried away, but I wanted it to be perfect, especially because I'm directing the music video."

"He's going to love it." Max cupped her face in his hands. "You're so sexy, Soph."

Shivering, she stood on tiptoes to kiss him. Her eyelids slid shut at the feel of his thick lips. He was like every fantasy she had, come to life. How on earth did she get this lucky?

"I need to ask you something," he said as he pulled away.

"Okay?" she asked uncertainly.

"I don't really know how to say it without sounding like a dick."

Oh God, she thought, panicking. *If this is going where I think it's going...* "Nothing's off-limits, right?" she reminded him. They had promised that to each other about a month into dating. "Just tell me."

He took a deep breath. "Is there a reason why we haven't had sex yet?"

There it is.

She stared at him, wondering how she could explain. She knew she wasn't being fair. He was a man and has made it abundantly clear that he found her very attractive. Why the hell couldn't she get on board already?

"I'm not that superficial," he added, perturbed by her sullen silence. "I love every moment I get to spend with you, Sophie. Fuck, I'm so in love with you that I don't really care about the sex. But it's been months, and it's beginning to feel like you don't want me the same."

"I do." She stepped away, her throat clogging up with emotion. Of all the things she'd planned for today, *this* hadn't even made the top five. "It's got nothing to do with you. I'm... I mean, I—"

"Can't see yourself having sex with a black man?" he supplied.

"No, of course not! I definitely can see myself having sex with you." Distracted by the notion, she got lost in regular fantasy. "God, it's all I think about."

"Then what's going on?"

She sighed. "Look at me."

"I am."

"No, *look* at me." She gestured to her slight frame. "I don't look like the kind of woman you should want."

His frown deepened. "Sophie, you're not this insecure."

"Only with you," she whispered.

"That's..." He trailed off, rubbing the back of his neck. "That doesn't sound healthy."

"I'm not saying this right." She took his big hand in hers, smiling at the difference in their skin tones. "You're so perfect, Max. Smart, funny, brave, tall, fit... We get along so great and if you asked me to marry you, I'd say yes in an instant. But I can't help feeling like I don't compare."

"Soph, I want you. *All* of you." He tugged her into his arms, lowering his hands to grip her behind. "I love your body. I've wanted to see you naked since you talked me out of issuing you a traffic fine." He grinned, his teeth dazzlingly white. "You know that getting married to me means that we'll fuck all the time, right?"

She was trembling in his arms. "I was hoping."

"So, will you get all this nonsense about your body out of your head?"

"Are you serious about us getting married?"

"Aren't you?"

Why did he always make her feel shy? Her mother had raised her to be ballsy and brash, and Sophie's always had that attitude in relationships, but Max... He had the ability to bring out her softer, vulnerable side. It both scared and fascinated her.

"I am."

"Good." He lifted her up and she automatically wrapped her legs around his hips. "What do you say we go to my place? I'll show you how badly I want your body."

"We have that dinner tonight."

"Our parents can meet each other without us."

She groaned. "God, can you imagine?"

"Soph, quit stalling. We're going to my place." He nuzzled the side of her neck. "How did you get here, your bike?"

She nodded, biting her lip while she stared at his mouth. "Yeah."

"Fuck," he mumbled, kissing her. "You're distracting me on purpose."

"Maybe." She pressed their mouths together, positively *aching* to get naked already. Now that they were on the same page, she was ready to unleash her sexual frustration. They've spent so many awesome months together, but it had felt hellishly long at the same time. She couldn't wait to have him inside of her.

When their tongues made contact, they both moaned. He tasted like her favorite coffee, too: she'd introduced him to the brand. She clutched the back of his head, terrified that he'll stop this, and rolled her crotch over his significant bulge.

"Officer," she moaned, "is that a gun in your pants or are you just happy to see me?"

"Armed and ready. Let's go, Soph. I don't want our first time to be here."

Letting out a harsh breath, she glanced at the large, mirrored wall and remembered when she and Logan had used each other to appease their loneliness. Although she'd never tell Max every detail of her friendship with Logan, he knew that they'd been together like that.

She inclined her head. "You're right. Race you there?"

"I'd hate to pull you over for speeding again."

"I'm sure I can find a way to make you forget I was speeding in the first place," she teased.

"Yes, you can." Their lips locked for another couple of seconds, and then he let her go completely. "Grab your things. I'll meet you outside."

She double-checked that she had her phone, keys and wallet. Zipping up a hoodie, she added her cut last and slung her bag over a shoulder. She turned the lights off, locked the studio, and hurried to the exit of the building. Her step faltered at the sight of her boyfriend and she recalled the first time she'd introduced him to her parents.

Jemma had taken it in stride, as expected, but Nixon had not looked impressed. Max was in the police force and, seeing as her father had spent two stints in prison, it hadn't been surprising that Nixon had his reservations.

Connor and Max got on like a house on fire and Sophie had joked that she was worried her boyfriend would be leaving her for her brother.

"Be safe, please," Max requested, cutting through the noise in her brain.

She pecked him on the cheek and mounted her Harley. She put her helmet on and pulled away from the curb. Her heart galloped excitedly once his car appeared in her rear-view mirrors.

The day Max had met her parents had been less disastrous than when he'd introduced her to *his*. His mother hated Sophie's guts and wasn't shy about admitting it. If it hadn't been for the fact that Ronny, Max's father, had been so welcoming, Sophie might have reconsidered their relationship altogether. The last thing she wanted to do was cause ructions for Max.

She'd hit it off with his sister. "He's always bringing white girls home," Rowena had confessed to Sophie after dinner, while they were cleaning up. "It drives mama nuts. She wants him to settle down with a 'nice, black woman', and give her 'nice, black grandchildren'. She feels like she did something wrong, raising him."

"And how do you feel about it?" Sophie had asked quietly.

"It's none of my business." Rowena had rinsed out a cloth and eyed Sophie. "I'm not really surprised. He's always wanted a blonde one, like you. His wall used to be covered in posters of Scarlett Johannson."

Sophie had laughed dryly. "Well, clearly, I'm not her."

"Don't worry, he quite liked Cameron Diaz, too," Rowena had winked.

As Sophie parked in front of Max's apartment building, she smiled. The man loved her. It was time that she laid her own insecurities to rest and committed to him fully, with the same fierceness she's tackled previous relationships with.

She scanned the key card he'd given her at the entrance and sashayed into an open elevator, pressing the number eleven button. He would have to park in the basement, which gave her some time to freshen up. She unlocked his apartment and shut the door behind her.

He had the typical bachelor pad: big screen TV and surround sound in the living room, which included an Xbox, and his kitchen had a bunch of trendy appliances. Japanese-style wooden sliding doors separated his bedroom from the rest of the well-decorated area. He'd confessed to saving money while working as a teenager to pay for most of what he owned now.

She headed to his bathroom to take a shower, careful to keep her hair dry.

Grinning when she heard the front door shut, she closed the taps and reached for a towel.

"Soph?" he called.

"I'll be right out!" She let her hair down. The humidity in the room had added a kink to her otherwise straight locks. Satisfied with her appearance, she walked out of the bathroom, finding him at the foot of his bed. "Sit down."

Surprised at her tone, he obeyed. "What now?"

"Now I'm going to show you all of me," she purred in response, letting the towel drop to the floor.

Max's Adam's apple bobbed up and down, his dark eyes slithering from her perky, albeit small breasts to her toned stomach, and further… to the landing strip between her thighs. He licked his lips, shifting his gaze to hers. "I should probably do the same."

He kicked his shoes and socks off first. He unbuttoned his shirt, revealing the white vest he wore underneath, which was then tugged over his head. Her knees weakened at every piece of clothing that came off his tall frame. The sound of his belt unbuckling caused her skin to break out in goose bumps and, when his pants joined the growing pile on the carpet, she found that she was breathing shallowly. His erection was straining against his white briefs; it was understandable that he should alleviate that tension by dragging them down.

Once he stood in front of her in his naked glory, her eyes zoned in on his package, the part of him she'd been most curious about. She knelt in front of him, gripping it by the base. He was thicker than Logan, her last sexual partner, although they were about the same length. She leaned forward and flicked her tongue against the tip.

Max groaned and held her hair. "Soph."

Emboldened by his tone, she sucked him into her mouth. His pre-cum coated her tongue, and she instantly knew that it was a flavor she could spend the rest of her life extracting from him. While one hand moved in tandem with her lips and tongue, the other drifted up his muscled stomach.

He caught her wrist, pulling her to a stand and kissing her hungrily. He swiveled and pushed her onto the bed, covering the length of her body with his. His fingers parted her lower lips to find her drenched and ready, and one of them slipped inside.

She whimpered and rocked against his hand.

He added another digit while his mouth moved to her neck. He nibbled on the sensitive skin close to her collarbone. "You're so fucking wet, Soph."

"That's 'cause I want you," she gasped, arching her back when his lips got to an erect nipple. "Oh God!"

"Max," he corrected.

"Max." She switched their positions, much like the ending of her dance routine. By his clenched jaw, she could tell he loved her renewed confidence. "Max," she said again, staring at him while she caressed his skin. Fuck, he was gorgeous! She reached for his cock, rubbing the tip against her slick folds. "Max."

He inhaled sharply as she tested her readiness by taking an inch of him. "Fuck!"

She lifted her hips, only to repeat the motion. She shivered. "You feel so good."

"Do it," he urged, the veins in his neck showing his restraint.

Driven by the desire to put them both out of their misery, she took him all the way. She tilted her head back once she'd sheathed his cock, her body coming alive at how much he was stretching her. The sensation was life-changing, as if she was experiencing sex anew.

She gave an experimental thrust, awed by the blood that rushed to her clit. His thumb pressed on that bundle of nerves, as if drawn to the part of her that was highly sensitized. "Max!"

He grabbed her ass with his free hand, urging her into a faster pace. "Soph."

She pinched her nipples while she rode Max, amazed by how perfectly they fitted together. The slide of his lubricated cock in and out of her pussy, the feel of his thumb caressing her swollen clit, the sound of his labored breaths… It all catapulted her into an orgasm.

"Beautiful," Max murmured while he caressed her cheek. "I love you, Sophie."

She pressed a kiss to the palm of his hand. "I love you, too, bear."

"Bear, huh?" He grinned as he sat up. "Are you already tired, goldie?"

Giggling, she brought their mouths together for a sensuous dance. "You did *not* just compare me to Goldie Locks!"

"You bet I did." He rested his forehead against hers for a moment. "Get on your knees, Soph."

"But I want to see your face."

"Trust me."

She winced as she got off his lap, missing his cock already. She looked at him over her shoulder.

"Hold onto the bars."

A shiver went down her spine as she complied. He trailed a finger from vertebrae to vertebrae, eliciting a shaky whimper from her mouth. The tip of his engorged member pressed on her opening, and she braced herself for what was to come. She's never been a fan of doggy style, but was willing to give it a go with Max.

"Fuck, your body is something else," he praised, holding her hips. His tip slipped inside. "I love your ass."

Her scalp prickled once he nudged her cervix. Whatever she'd been expecting, it wasn't *this*. He was thrusting in and out as if he had all the time in the world. Languidly, luxuriously. Maybe the men she'd slept with before simply hadn't known that it could be so much better for both parties if aggressive pounding was taken out of the equation.

She shut her eyes, her hands tightening around the bars of the headboard. Max shifted her knees further apart with his own, restricting her movements. And then he fucked her gently, giving her the sense that she was going to start drooling from pleasure.

With whispered dirty promises, he brought her to the edge of her first G-spot orgasm. The hair on her arms stood upright and she uttered sheer nonsense. When he reached forward to cup her breasts, she held her breath and tipped over.

Wow, she thought dumbly, savoring the ripples in her core.

He withdrew and helped her onto her back, looking like the cat that got all the cream. "Seriously, Soph, are you going to pass out? I'm having so much fun."

"I was sure *I* was in control," she mumbled.

"You took me off guard." He spread her legs and speared into her again. "But I recovered."

She twined her limbs around him and held on for dear life, her toes curling at what a phenomenal lover he was. Has sex always been this good, or was this what having sex with the love of one's life felt like? Would it always be like this?

Max moved faster, chasing his own release. She was eager to hear him come undone. She kissed him passionately, amazed that her body was nearing the precipice again. Sure, she's always enjoyed doing the dirty and was no stranger to multiple orgasms, but this was on a whole different level. What if she lost consciousness?

"Oh God!" she exclaimed as another wave crashed over her. "Max!"

He shuddered and pressed his face into her hair, his moans like music to her ears. "Soph."

They both went limp, trying to catch their breaths, and she stroked his skin while she recovered. "For the record, I think I put this off so long because you're clearly going to kill me."

Laughing, he dropped a kiss on her jaw. "Death by sex with you sounds like a good way to go. You ride my cock like you dance."

"And how's that?"

"Like you own me."

She pressed her lips to his. A part of her felt foolish for being this far gone. The bigger part was relieved they were in the same boat. Whatever happened, she knew that she could trust him with her heart.

Max pulled out, laying on his side and touching her cheek. "We need to have a serious conversation."

"Right now, when we're both learning how to use our bodies again?"

He chuckled. "Yes. How many kids do you want?"

"Are we really doing this?"

"We've already agreed that we'll get married, but I'd like to know that we've got similar goals. How many?"

"Three."

His smile broadened. "Two for two."

"I can't believe we're talking about this so casually."

"Life doesn't have to be complicated."

"Says the cop who wants to marry into a motorcycle club."

He laughed again, pressing his lips to hers. "Maybe I haven't thought this through, after all."

She sucked on his bottom lip while one hand slid to his waist. "I mean, we're not the worst sort, but there are things that happen that... well, we have our own way of dealing with. We have an understanding with local law."

"My boss spoke to me when he found out about us."

"How do you feel about it?" she asked, her hand curving around his ass.

"If you keep doing that…" He trailed off suggestively. "Soph, I can play by the MC's rules. I'll do it for you."

"My ass must be pretty spectacular, then."

He playfully spanked said ass. "And about to get ravished again."

She eagerly responded to his kissing, stroking and touching. They explored each other's bodies at length, admiring and celebrating their differences. She'd suspected that he was going to be sensual, but being at the receiving end of his lovemaking took their attraction to new heights.

She was a hopeless romantic, although she hardly ever confessed that to anyone. For a long time, she had hoped that her friendship with Logan would grow into something more, thinking: *why else would we be so close if we're not meant to be?* And yet, she'd never looked at him the way she did Max. Logan will always be a friend, and nothing more.

"How fast can you get ready?"

She snuggled closer to him. "Ten minutes, tops? I'll have to take a shower again."

"That gives us another half an hour." He turned his head to her. "What do you wanna do?"

"Hmm," she mumbled, fighting to keep her eyes open. After four hours of dancing lessons, her routine, and three rolls in the hay with Max, she was beat. "I really want to take a power nap, but talk to you at the same time."

"What do you want to talk about, goldie?"

She smiled at the nickname. "What kind of wedding do you want?"

"Small and intimate," he replied, his fingertips trailing over her skin. "I mean, Byron and Cinnia's wedding was beautiful, but that's not how I see myself promising to love you for the rest of my life."

"That's three for three."

"We'll have to get a place together. What kind of house do you want?"

"Single story, but with a pool. And a cottage in the back that I can convert into a home studio."

"Tell me there's space for a gym in there, and you've got a deal."

Shifting, she propped her head up and gazed at him. "How did I not know you before? We could've been on the way to baby number two by now."

"We don't exactly move in the same circles," he reminded her. "It took you being late for a shoot for me to notice you."

"I was driving pretty fast that day," she admitted.

"I thought I'd have a chase on my hands."

"I considered it, but figured I could sweet-talk myself out of a fine better than I could sweet-talk a judge out of a prison sentence." They both laughed at that. "Then you stepped up to the bike and I thought, 'damn girl, if you don't leave with his number, you'll have to start stalking him'."

"And I thought, 'I can't believe that was a woman driving'." When she rolled her eyes, he chuckled. "What can I say, you handled that bike well. My next thought was the most important one, though." He tucked her hair behind her ears. "'I think I just met the woman of my dreams'." Tracing her lips with his thumb, he added: "I wanted to keep you. Soph, I'm serious about getting married."

"I know."

"You don't get it." He leaned back to open the drawer of his nightstand, retrieving a black square box. He held it out to her with a soft smile on his face. "I've had this for two weeks."

Her heart skipped a beat. She took the box from him and flipped it open, gasping at the ring inside. Its design was delicate: three thin golden bands joined by different gemstones, all circling a diamond in the middle.

"I had a plan for the perfect proposal," he murmured. "Dinner at that Italian restaurant you love so much, followed by a walk in the park. I'd get down on one knee and ask you to make me the happiest man in the world by agreeing to be my wife."

She blinked to fight a few tears, with no success. She smiled and slipped the ring on its designated finger. "Yes, I'll marry you."

"Dinner with our parents just got a whole lot more interesting."

"They can all suck it." She kissed him with a sudden burst of energy, straddling his lap. She loved the way his arms locked around her, and how he met her passion equally. "They'll be too confused about me arriving in a wheelchair, anyway."

He burst out laughing, that deep rumble vibrating against her chest. "Sophie Tyrell, I love you."

"Hey, stop making me mushy. Are you going to give me one for the road or not?"

"I'd like to state, for the record, that you're giving yourself a wheelchair sentence." He moved out from under her and got off the bed. Throwing her over his shoulder, he marched to the bathroom. "Might as well kill two birds with one stone, then. We're definitely going to be late."

She smacked his butt. "Counting on it."

He got the shower going and placed her under the spray. While they waited for the water to warm, he hoisted her up, sandwiching her between his body and the tiled wall. She cried out when he impaled her on his length.

"I'll never get tired of that," she gasped, rolling her hips.

He bit her shoulder. "Fuck, me neither."

She loved how, earlier, they'd made gentle love over and over again; and now, in complete contrast, they fucked like animals. Her nails dug into his shoulders, and she was sure she would be bruised later. None of that mattered when it felt so good, so *right*, to have his cock in her.

Hooking her legs over his arms, he changed his angle and went deeper. Their moans echoed in the bathroom, growing louder by the second. She screwed her eyes shut, sensing the beginning of a toe-curling release.

"Fuck!" he groaned, his dick pulsing in her tight grip.

His release fed her own, and they remained against the wall as they recovered. He let her legs down, his erection slipping out in the process, and reached for his shower gel to wash her. She grabbed a sponge and got to work on his glorious body.

The shower lasted much longer than expected, so they hurried to get ready for dinner. Sophie got distracted by her ring every once in a while. It glowed against her skin, as if it had a life of its own.

Donning a purple long-sleeved mini dress, she watched him put on a suit. She pushed her feet into black heels and braided her damp hair over one shoulder. She swiped her lashes with mascara and added a bit of color to her lips. Then she walked to him to help with his tie.

"You look so handsome, bear," she smiled.

"And you look elegant. I love that you don't wear a ton of makeup."

She smoothed out his collar and turned to the mirror. Their reflection matched how she felt about their relationship: despite their differences, they *fit*. "I hope they're not going to make a big deal tonight."

"Only one way to find out."

They spent the drive to the restaurant in companionable silence. Now that they've connected on a sexual level, Sophie relaxed completely. She was so happy he'd cornered her about her reluctance to consummate their relationship. She had no reason to be insecure.

They held hands as they walked inside. She spotted her mother's platinum hair and smiled excitedly as they headed for their table.

"Mom!"

Jemma got to her feet. "Hey, Soph," she greeted warmly, kissing her daughter. She shifted her kohl-rimmed gaze to Max. "You look great, Max."

"I see my parents aren't here yet," he commented as he pulled her into a hug. He held his hand out to Nixon. "I'm sorry we're late."

"Good to see you, Max," Nixon said, his face not quite losing its hard edge.

"Don't worry, sir, I left my cuffs at home."

Sophie smacked her fiancé's arm. "Behave."

Max moved on to Connor, and the two embraced like brothers. "I'm glad you could make it."

"Wouldn't miss it for the world," Connor chuckled, pecking Sophie on the cheek. "Hey, sis."

"Hey, bro. Where's Jesse?"

"Family dinner of her own," Connor pouted.

Gasping, Jemma grabbed Sophie's hand. "I can't help but notice this sparkling ring on your finger. Does this mean…?"

Sophie glanced at Max, who gave her an encouraging nod. "Yup, we got engaged tonight."

"Oh my God!" her mother shrieked happily, looking like she was getting ready to embarrass them by doing her shoulder shimmy. "Congratulations!"

"Thanks, mom." Sophie eyed her father. "I hope you're happy for me, too."

"Of course I am, my angel." Nixon smiled and wrapped his arms around her. "As long as you're happy, I'm happy." Here, he shifted his attention back to Max. "So, a cop marries into a motorcycle club." He shook his head with a laugh. "That doesn't really need more of a punch line. Welcome to the family, kiddo."

Max beamed at his soon-to-be father-in-law. "Thank you, Mr. Tyrell."

"You should get in the habit of calling me 'dad'."

"And why on *earth* would he do that?"

Sophie froze, recognizing the woman's voice. They all turned to the

Joneses. Max's hand found hers again; gave it a reassuring squeeze.

"'Cause I asked Sophie to be my wife, ma," Max responded reasonably.

Mabel's eyes remained on her son's, as if she was willing him to take the words back. Ronny and Rowena stepped forward to congratulate the engaged couple and introduce themselves to Jemma, Nixon and Connor. All the while, the Jones matriarch stood, glaring daggers.

An unbearable silence emerged in the group, and Sophie cringed inwardly. Was what would bring her the most joy really going to be met with such resistance? Surely, if her father could forgive Max for being in the police force, Mabel could forgive her for being white?

"I suppose congratulations are in order," Mabel muttered. "Let me see the ring."

With dread in the pit of her stomach, Sophie moved forward and showed her.

"Gorgeous," Mabel said, "my son has impeccable taste." Here, she fixed Sophie with a firm stare. "I know you think I'm against you because you're white, but that's not true."

"Right."

"When you have your first child, you'll understand. I raised that boy to be the kind, well-mannered man he is today. It's difficult to think that he's ready to turn to *another* woman to share his life with." Mabel looked away, crossing her arms over her chest. "No one will ever be good enough for my boy, but I trust his judgement, even if I'm not a fan of what you do for a living."

Sophie's eyebrows bunched together. "I didn't realize that living my dream was reason for concern."

Max coughed. "Soph—"

"No." She peered at his mother thoughtfully. "You're not the first to judge me, and you probably won't be the last. I made peace with that a long time ago. But you're the grandmother of the kids we plan to have, so you'll have to learn to respect my decisions." She motioned to the table. "Take a seat so we can all have a meal together."

As Mabel huffily did as she was bid, Max pressed a kiss to Sophie's temple. "Nicely done. I wouldn't be surprised if that changed her mind about you."

"Max." She held his face in her hands, somber. "I don't give a shit about anyone else's opinion. I'm in a relationship with *you*, not your family. And yes, they play a huge part in our lives, but they don't get to decide who *we* are.

That's my only condition going forward."

"Where do I sign?"

"You know exactly where," she murmured, giving him a quick kiss. "Let's get this dinner out the way so we can go home."

They joined their families, who were already chatting like old friends, and ordered bottles of bubbly to celebrate. Sophie knew that she'd chosen a man with the best qualities to spend the rest of her life with. They might still be in the phase of their love where everything had a rose-colored tint to it, but she had no doubt that they would stand strong when those lenses faded.

He'd wanted to get married to her even before they had sex. The bond they've forged since they met went deep and made her excited about their future.

I can't wait to tell Logan.

As she gazed at the people around her table, she hoped that Logan would learn that he was worthy of this kind of love. In her opinion, his decision to become a professional athlete proved that he was already halfway there.

CHAPTER SEVENTEEN

LUCA STARED AT her naked reflection, trying not to view each scar as a failure to protect herself. It's taken a long while for her to truly open up to Dr. McKauley, but it's been worth taking the leap. It was interesting to hear how psychological and physical trauma could affect one's life. Luca was determined to rise above it.

That said, she still struggled to accept her body. Who would ever love her?

Letting out a soft sigh, she reached for a pair of tattered, baggy jeans and a long-sleeved shirt. She rolled thick socks on and pushed her feet into leather biker boots. She braided her hair down her back, grabbed her backpack and headed downstairs.

She dropped the bag at the front door, striding to the kitchen where she could hear Cinnia and Byron talking. She paused at the threshold, like so many mornings before, smiling at their banter. It had been unusual at first, yet she's become used to the love between the two. Her interest was roused at the mention of Logan's name.

"He sounds exhausted," Cinnia remarked. "I'm worried he's not getting enough sleep because he's playing so often."

"He's getting used to it. It's part of his job."

"I suppose."

"I get it, babe. You want to go over there and take care of him."

"I just want him to be okay."

There was a brief silence and Luca suspected Byron was taking Cinnia in his arms. Although she didn't always understand it, she loved seeing them together. The Raptors MC has given Luca a new perspective on friendship and romance, but was she brave enough to want it for herself yet?

No, she sighed.

"He is okay," Byron murmured finally. "He's enjoying himself."

Luca cleared her throat before she walked in. "Morning."

"Morning," Cinnia smiled, stepping back from Byron's embrace.

"Hey, Luca." Byron pointed at her plate, which was already loaded with food. He and Cinnia were both great cooks, and she's been spoiled for choice ever since she was rescued from the side of the road. "Want me to add bacon?"

She considered that, mentally checking in with her body. She didn't always eat meat, but she craved it today. "Yes, please."

"Logan phoned earlier," Cinnia told her. "He says hi."

"Thanks."

She didn't understand why her heartrate often increased at the thought of him. They've been through so much: at first, she hadn't trusted him and, more recently, he hadn't trusted her. He had left before they could really remedy their fractured relationship, but they spoke via family video calls every once in a while, and sometimes she felt like they could be friends. Maybe not as close as she was with Jesse or Hallie but friends, nonetheless.

"I'm still battling with the time zones," Cinnia continued, pouring them each a cup of coffee. She only believed in buying the good stuff and has successfully converted Luca into the morning ritual.

"The only negative about his new life," Byron chuckled.

Luca thanked him for the streaks of bacon and dug in as soon as they joined her at the breakfast nook.

"How's prep for your next test going?" Cinnia asked.

"Good, thanks. I like math."

"A woman after my own heart."

Byron rolled his eyes. "Doesn't mean she'll follow in your footsteps, Cin."

"You're only saying that because she's definitely not following in yours."

Luca hid her grin behind a hand when they both looked at her. "No comment."

"Hmm, a life in PR, then," Cinnia said, playing along.

"I have time to sway you to the dark side, Luca."

A comfortable silence descended between them. Luca glanced at each of them. She's lived here for a year and honestly couldn't imagine her life without these two. She would've never known what it's like to have a healthy relationship with adults, had it not been for the Johannsons.

To a bigger extent, the Raptors community has also changed her view on motorcycle clubs. The Falcons was nowhere near as kind or supportive. She shuddered thinking about the life of constant fear she'd led there.

"I'm considering journalism," she offered.

Byron raised an eyebrow and Cinnia smiled. "Hanging out with Jesse has given you an appreciation for writing, huh?"

"Yeah, and I like that it's mostly about investigation. Research."

"The quiet appeals to you," Byron realized.

"Yes."

"You'll have to conduct interviews," Cinnia pointed out.

Luca winced. "I know. I hope Dr. McKauley can fix me by then."

Cinnia gently placed her hand on Luca's forearm. "There's nothing wrong with you."

Luca wished she could believe that. She balked at the idea of talking to strangers. To this day, she didn't know why she'd immediately trusted Logan, Cinnia and Jemma when they'd taken her in, especially after he introduced himself. He'd been her target, the one she had been instructed to isolate and trap for the Falcons to finish off, and yet his presence had been comforting. Nothing at all like the horrific picture of the Drummond bloodline that her father had painted.

"I think you'd be great at it, for what it's worth," Cinnia said. "Hey, why don't you volunteer for the school newspaper to get a feel for it?"

"Cin—"

"It's okay," Luca told Byron. Cinnia could overwhelm Luca sometimes, but this was a useful idea. "I'll ask today. I could use the practice."

Cinnia stuck her tongue out at Byron. "See? Not overbearing."

He shook his head with a laugh. "Ryan says you're doing well at the diner. I'm sure that'll help with your confidence."

"People are nice there," Luca agreed. "I like Ryan."

They finished their meal and Luca cleaned up, as has become habit. She went upstairs to brush her teeth, greeted Cinnia and followed Byron to the SUV. Once she was strapped into the passenger seat, she clasped her hands on her lap and wondered how best to approach what was on her mind.

"You know you can tell me anything," he commented, having noted her expectant silence.

She nodded. "It's still tough for me, sometimes."

"You're doing great, Luca. We're proud of your progress and glad that you trust us."

"I just feel like I should be doing more."

"You're sixteen. The only thing you should be doing is going to school. You chose to work part-time, even though you don't owe us anything."

That was what she couldn't quite comprehend: viewing what they did for her without any strings attached. The fact that they expected nothing in return for how good they were to her blew her mind. Her life used to be a constant wager, and she'd thought nothing came without a price. Sometimes she wondered when the other shoe will drop.

"I want to get my motorcycle license," she blurted out, half-stunned by her own audacity.

"I didn't know you like to ride."

"Riding is freedom."

Byron laughed under his breath, inclining his head. "Can't argue with that. You're of age, but it might be a struggle seeing as we don't have your birth certificate. I'll ask Teagan to look into it and we'll take it from there."

"Really?"

"Of course. What kind of bike would you like? Reade's working on a couple of classic Harleys that'll be easy for you to handle."

Her head was spinning. "I haven't thought that far."

"How about you ask Cin to take you to the workshop after school? See if there's something you like."

"Okay. Thank you, Byron."

"You're welcome." He brought the car to a halt in front of the school and turned to her. "You're so brave, Luca. I wish you could see that."

She gulped at the kindness in his eyes, not sure what to make of it. "I wish you were my father," she whispered. "I know that sounds pathetic, but—"

"It's not," he soothed. "Cin and I consider you our daughter. We might not have the same blood, but we'll move heaven and earth for you, Luca. You're part of our family."

Tears burned her eyes and she coughed self-consciously. "I'm scared they'll find me and take me away."

"I'm handling it. I won't let that happen."

She gazed at her hands, wiping her tears before they fell. "Thank you, Byron."

"You're welcome. Ah, there's Hallie. Ready for school?"

Nodding, she unclipped her seatbelt and opened the door. "Bye."

"Have a good day."

She slung her bag over her shoulder and shut the door, smoothing out her facial expression as best she could. Hallie was up ahead with Dane and her friends and, even though they were older than Luca, the twins have taken it upon themselves to keep Luca company at school.

"Hey," Hallie greeted, a slight furrow to her brow. Her long, silky black hair was in a messy bun, although the rest of her outfit was still kick-ass punk: leather pants, Pantera T-shirt and boots. She took after her aunt. "Everything okay?"

Luca dipped her chin, not yet trusting her voice not to waver when she spoke.

"Alright, then. Let's get you to class, young lady."

"Old lady," Dane corrected, not for the first time.

"She's got a young body."

"And an old soul."

"Pointing that out makes people feel weird."

"It's what I do, sis."

"That's what your ex said, yeah."

"Mature," Dane snorted.

Luca enjoyed their crosstalk. She wondered if she would've been the same with Logan, had they grown up together. She thought of him as a protective older brother, seeing as he'd rescued her. He had brought her into this amazing life. She'll always be grateful for that.

"You guys are hilarious," Kaylee, a girl who was shamelessly into Dane, laughed. She flicked her bleached blonde hair back. "I don't think you're weird."

"Your view is obscured by your hormones, my dear," Hallie teased.

Kaylee blushed. "What? Hallie!"

"I'm not that great," Dane said nonchalantly.

Sometimes Luca wondered if any of the girls at school appealed to him. Hallie was equally as picky. Luca has caught Hallie staring dreamily at Aurora, on the odd occasion Luca tagged along to Raptors social gatherings.

"Here we are, milady," Hallie announced, stopping in front of Luca's first class. "See you at break?"

Luca smiled. "Yes."

"Try not to outsmart your teachers," Hallie started.

"But if you do," Dane continued, equally theatrically, "make sure to go out in a blaze of glory."

I'll never understand twins, Luca thought as she watched them walk to their own class, their ever-present entourage in tow. Taking a deep breath, Luca went inside. She ignored the usual stares—she wasn't considered new anymore, but she hasn't made any other friends and that set her apart from the rest—and strode to her seat at the back of the class. She froze once she realized it was occupied already and a cold chill trickled down her spine at the smug face of the boy sitting there. It was someone who had terrorized her when she'd been part of the Falcons.

"Oh, were you going to sit here?" he asked, keeping his tone friendly to play to their audience. His light blue eyes, the eyes of a predator, gave more weight to his faux happy-go-lucky attitude. "I'm new. I don't know the rules yet."

She couldn't move. She was haunted by memories of his abuse. His father was Ian's VP and this boy... The apple didn't fall far from the tree.

Ashton patted the chair next to him. "Looks like there's enough space for both of us."

No!

As gripped by fear as she was, she refused to be anywhere near him. She had a choice this time.

She spun on her heel and went to sit at the open table closest to the door, feeling his gaze on her back. She got her books out, inwardly cursing herself for being smarter than other kids her age since that's the only reason why she was in *this* class, with older students. He never would've passed as a sixteen-year-old.

He's Jesse's age, though, she reminded herself. *How did he enroll at this school without the Raptors finding out?* Her stomach dropped. *How did he even get into town? Byron said they have eyes on the Falcons! Unless he was lying...?*

She was feeling lightheaded. There were only a handful of people she trusted with her whole being, and one of them was in her vicinity. She fumbled for her phone and opened the instant messaging app, typing: *"Please come get me."*

She didn't have to wait long for Cinnia's response: *"I'll be there in 10."*

The bell rang and the teacher began the class, getting everyone to focus. Luca sat staring at the numbers on the white board as if she wasn't fearing for her life, as if the man at the back of the room hadn't raped her. She shut her eyes firmly, willing those memories away. She couldn't afford to get swept up: she had to stay in the moment or risk—

"Luca Johannson, to reception."

Her salvation!

She hardly registered the murmur of the students behind her. She jammed her books into her bag and rushed out, her heart hammering against her ribcage. She thought she heard a commotion behind her but, in this state, it was impossible to know what was real and what not.

"Luca! Get back here!"

A sob tore past her lips and she felt like she was wading through water. She picked up the pace, sprinting to the administration office and only stopping when she nearly slammed into Cinnia, who deftly caught her.

"Luca? Oh my God! What's the matter?"

Luca chanced a peek over her shoulder, her knees weakening as soon as Ashton appeared in the doorway. He did a double take the second he spotted Cinnia, and bolted. "Please tell me you saw him," she wept in Cinnia's arms, past the point of caring if she saved face or not.

"I saw him," Cinnia confirmed, a steely edge to her voice. "Come on, let's go."

It was steady going, what with them both being on high alert, but they eventually got into Cinnia's car. Cinnia activated the hands-free kit and called Byron, and then she linked the fingers of one hand with Luca's.

"Babe? Is Luca okay?"

"There was a guy chasing her when I got there," Cinnia replied. She must've told him about Luca's message on the way over. "He looks too old to be in school. I have no idea how anyone let him in." She squeezed Luca's hand. "What's his name, Luca?"

"Ashton," she sniffed, "Ashton McCleod."

"Son of a bitch," Byron muttered, no doubt recognizing the surname. "I'm on it."

"Thanks, babe." Cinnia ended the call. "I'm so sorry, Luca. I don't know how they slipped past us. We have eyes everywhere."

"I'm so scared."

"I know. I've got you. You did the right thing by contacting me."

Luca clung to Cinnia like a lifeline, too afraid to look at the change in scenery in case she saw another familiar face intent on hurting her, or worse.

"I'm taking us to the club. It'll be safe there."

"Okay."

"We can punch some bags while we're there, if you're up to it."

That startled a laugh out of Luca. "Sounds good."

"There she is." Cinnia tucked a wayward lock of hair behind Luca's ear and smiled. "They don't have to control you, you know. You can choose to say 'fuck 'em' and live your life without fear."

Luca respected Cinnia's opinion, having heard what the woman has been through. She simply didn't know how to be that fearless.

Cinnia parked the car and they both got out, walking towards the clubhouse. A group of men were already gathered, clearly discussing tactics to protect Luca and the Raptors from the Falcons. Luca squirmed under their gazes, wondering if they blamed her for what's happening.

"It's going to be okay," Cinnia whispered, resting her arm on Luca's shoulders for a moment. She steered Luca towards her office. "Stay close, but feel free to do your own thing."

Luca nodded, drifting to the workshop. She relaxed once she saw Reade, remembering her conversation with Byron about motorcycles.

Reade was busy spray-painting the shell of a Harley, deftly maneuvering to add beautiful pearlescent shading. His grey hair was slicked back and the overalls he wore was branded: *Drummond Customs & Repairs*. He glanced up as she approached, flipping his visor to talk to her.

"Hello, lass."

She waved awkwardly and sat on a nearby bench. "Don't let me stop you. I like watching."

"See somethin' ye like?"

Gauging the available options, her gaze stopped on a silver '70s Harley lowrider. It's always been her favorite model. She felt a tingling on her palms, as if the handlebars were calling out to her.

Reade chuckled, putting down his equipment and wiping his hands. "Aye, tha's a good choice. A classic beauty." He strode towards it. "Ah'm nearly done. Come have a look."

Spellbound, she went closer. Her fingers slid along the smooth metal of the rear spoiler and onto the soft leather seat. She caught Reade gazing at her with a fond smile, and blushed. "Whose is it?"

"Ah gather it's yers, lass." He nodded when her eyes widened. "Byron called me after ye spoke to him about ridin'. Someone else had their eye on it, but Ah can make 'em somethin' different."

She shook her head. "I couldn't possibly—"

"Ye're a Raptor, Luca. Ah take care of ma own."

She bit her lip, knowing how stubborn members of this club were when it came to proving their loyalty. It was admirable: as if money has never been the motivating factor behind their actions. Reade could easily sell this Harley to a well-paying customer and make a fat profit, and yet he insisted on giving it to Luca for free. Because she belonged.

Emotions were welling up again and she refrained from blinking. "Thank you, Reade."

"Ye're welcome, lass. Any finishes ye'd like?"

She mulled that one over, taking the bike in. She traced a finger over an outer rounded edge of the seat. "Spirit, engraved here," she murmured. "It's my favorite movie."

Reade nodded as if that made complete sense, heading towards the accessories rack. He peered at the items, taking down a black jacket with short tassels on the sleeves and in a V-shape on the back. He pointed to the smooth patch that would cover her shoulder blades. "Spirit, along here? Under the crest?"

An excited smile bloomed on her face. She was amazed by how well he knew her: he'd picked up her obsession with Native American culture from one word. "Yes, please."

"This helmet?" he continued, gesturing to a silver shape worn by fighter pilots.

"Oh, I love that."

He grinned. "Happy to hear tha'. Would ye like to help?"

"Yes!" Luca clamped a hand over her mouth, giggling. She couldn't describe how happy she was, but it pleased her even more to see how touched he was by her response.

"C'mon, lass. Ah'll show ye how."

Luca only realized, when Cinnia called her over for lunch, that Reade had successfully distracted her from the disturbing incident at school for three full hours. She'd been totally engrossed in designing her own helmet and adding embellishments to her new jacket, and hadn't even noticed the time pass. He had gone so far as to teach her how to use the spray-paint gun.

"Having fun?" Cinnia asked, handing over a vegetable wrap.

"Uh-huh," Luca gushed. "Reade is so cool."

"I like your jacket."

"Thanks, me too."

Cinnia smiled as she watched Luca eat. Her facial expression turned pensive. "Do you think you'll stick around once you graduate?"

Luca chewed carefully, taken aback by the turn in conversation. They've never really discussed her future, other than what she might do after school.

"I'm only asking because I love you," Cinnia said quietly. She tucked her silver-streaked hair behind her ears, her emerald eyes guileless. "I get that you'll have your own life one day and I'm glad I get to take care of you until then. I was just hoping you'll still be here, somehow."

What an emotional day! Luca has been on the verge of tears at least four times. She chose her words carefully, wanting to be honest and clear. "I like this town," she started, "and I love the MC. I'd like to stay. I can't see myself being happy somewhere else. One day, I'd like to be patched in."

Cinnia reached for a napkin to dab at the corners of her eyes. "That makes me happy."

Byron appeared in the doorway, smiling tensely. "Hello, ladies."

"What's wrong?" Cinnia questioned.

"We found the McCleods." Here, he made eye contact with Luca. "They won't bother you again. I'm sorry about this morning."

Luca flinched. "Byron—"

"No, I need to say this." He walked closer, kneeling in front of her. "I dropped the ball, Luca. I swore to keep you safe and I—oomph!"

Luca had thrown her arms around him, hugging him tightly. She could sense the hesitation in his body while he slowly returned the embrace. She shut her eyes. "I don't blame you," she whispered. "I just got scared."

"I don't want you to ever feel that way again."

"I know." Tears were flowing freely now. "That's what makes you Hero."

Cinnia joined them, resting her head on top of Luca's. "I love you both so much."

The three of them remained like that, emotional but connected, until someone cleared their throat. Luca glanced up and frowned at the unfamiliar man, whose gaze was piercing.

"Didn't mean to interrupt," he said apologetically.

"What the hell are you doing here?" Byron asked, his tone unwelcoming. It wasn't like him to be downright hostile.

The man held his hands up. "I heard you still have a Falcons problem."

Byron rose to his feet, jaw clenched, and blocked Luca and Cinnia from the man's view. "It's not like that's ever bothered you before. Start talking, Eduardo."

"I didn't know about all of this until this morning," the man explained, as if he was somewhat fearful of Byron and yet also confident Byron wouldn't hurt him. "Guilietta's kept this from me for years because... well, she found out about me having an affair with Jasmine."

Luca's ears began ringing and she wasn't even aware of Cinnia catching her before she tipped over. Her dead mother's name echoed in her mind. She barely had any memories of her childhood, yet she recalled the beautiful woman Jasmine had been: olive skin, brown eyes and long, dark hair. She remembered Jasmine's kindness and big laugh.

She also remembered screams of mercy, of help...

When she came to, Cinnia had a damp cloth pressed to her forehead, her brows furrowed with worry. "Are you okay?" Cinnia murmured.

"I think so." Luca looked around the office. "What happened to Byron?"

Sighing deeply, Cinnia dropped the cloth and took both Luca's hands in hers. "There's no easy way to say this, so bear with me. Years ago, Byron was abducted. He met your mother while he was away. She was a sex worker for a cartel."

This wasn't news to Luca. She waited for the other shoe to drop.

"A couple of years after he came back, the new leader of the cartel came by his office. She asked him to take a woman and child into our protection." Cinnia swallowed thickly, her eyes brimming with tears. "It felt like a trap, like she would keep asking for favors if he gave in. He had so many scars from his time there, you have to understand... I told him to tell her no. He did."

The knot in Luca's stomach seemed to grow. Was she going to be sick? "Who was the woman and child?" she squawked, afraid of the answer.

"You and your mother."

There's the other shoe.

"As it turns out, Guilietta found out that Eddie cheated on her, way back when," Cinnia went on hurriedly. "She was so angry, she didn't lift a finger when Ian kidnapped Jasmine. He didn't know she was pregnant at the time... He was besotted with your mother. Obsessed. When you were born, he lost his mind because he could see you weren't his. That's when he became violent. Guilietta knew and didn't do anything, until one day when she saw you, battered and—" Her voice cracked and she took a moment to regain composure. "She felt bad. That's when she tried to get us to help. We said no. Jasmine died and Ian—"

"I know the rest," Luca muttered, ripping her hands away from Cinnia. "How long have you known?"

Cinnia's gaze dropped. "I only found out about your mother and Eddie a couple of minutes ago."

"And the rest?"

"Luca—"

"*How long?*" she demanded.

Cinnia cupped her elbows in her hands, sobbing. "About a month after we found you."

Luca stood up so fast the chair tipped over behind her.

"You were still healing, Luca! We didn't want to upset you!" Cinnia exclaimed reasonably.

"Everything that's happened to me could've been avoided!" Luca screamed. "All those times they beat me, *raped* me—"

"There's not a day that goes by that I don't regret saying no," Byron said quietly, having returned without being noticed.

He truly seemed contrite, but Luca was too hurt to give a damn about anyone else's feelings. "You only regret that because I'm your problem now!" She motioned to herself. "After you said no, you never gave 'the woman and child' another thought!"

They avoided her eyes, knowing she's right.

"No one fought for me!" Pent-up emotions boiled over. She had no control left. "You could've changed all of it, but you didn't! You left us there to rot!"

Unlike this morning around the breakfast table, the silence between them became loaded, heavy. Uncomfortable.

"What am I supposed to do with this information?" She felt like she was falling apart. "I have a father I've never met, and I live with people who could have changed my life for the better, sooner! What do I do? What's there for me to—" She broke off, shaking her head. "I've got to get out of here."

"Luca—"

"No!" she yelled, pushing past him and breaking into a run. She stumbled into objects, both human and machine, as she sprinted out of the workshop. Tears blurred her vision and she had no clue where she could go: she just had to get away. Away from all of this.

Oh God, even Logan must've known!

The shame was nearly debilitating. She was hysterical by the time she was stopped at the closed gate. "Let me through!"

Nixon held up his hands in defense. "I can't do that."

"Let me go!" she shrieked, her throat raw. She pushed him, frustrated that he didn't budge. He was a hulk of a man, but had a soft heart: why couldn't he pretend she was stronger? She punched his broad chest. "Nixon, let me go!"

"Luca," he cautioned, easily grabbing her wrists, "calm down."

"No!" Panic threatened to overwhelm her. Why did she have to pick a fight with *him*, of all people? He could hurt her! "Don't touch me!"

"Luca, relax, I'm—"

"No!"

He moved quickly, locking his arms around her in a stifling embrace. "Shh, girl. It's going to be okay. We're doing this for your own good, I promise. We're trying to protect you."

"P-please!" she howled. "Please let m-me go!"

He made soothing noises, stroking her hair, but never relinquished his grip, reminding her of the day Logan found her at the side of the road. She shuddered as she wept, wondering if she'll ever be put back together again.

Was she Humpty Dumpty? Broken from the start, broken until the end?

"I j-just w-w-want to leave!"

"Shh, girl, it's gonna be okay."

A painful prick on the side of her neck was the last thing she felt before she lost consciousness.

CHAPTER EIGHTEEN

THE BOTTLE OF whiskey taunted him from behind the counter. He had to find a way to be happy about the glass of water in his grip.

"All those times they beat me, raped me—"

Byron squeezed his eyes shut, but it did nothing to alleviate the pain. Foolishly, he had hoped Luca would never find out about the role he'd inadvertently played in her life. He should've known he was on borrowed time: he'd hardly been able to keep it under wraps for a year.

"She's still out," Jemma commented, pulling him back to the present. She got behind the bar to prepare herself a drink. "Poor girl."

"Yeah."

She rested her hand on his forearm. "Don't blame yourself, By."

"How can I not? Everything she said is true."

Knocking back a shot of tequila, she poured herself another. "For some reason, this makes me think of that philosophical question about the train tracks. Do you hit one person to save many, or many to save one?"

"The one thing I hate about philosophy is that it never resolves anything," he muttered.

"Of course it does," she insisted. "Damn it, By, the tequila I'm drinking could've killed someone before it ended up in my mouth. You could very well be a contributing factor to the destruction of rain forests because of the toilet paper you used to wipe your ass this morning! How were you supposed to know you'll be faced with—"

"That's how karma works," he reminded her.

She slammed her hand on the counter. "Snap out of it! You've done nothing wrong. You were trying to move on with your life. You couldn't have known."

He nodded to himself. "Logan said something similar once."

"He's a bright kid." Jemma smiled wryly. "I don't blame Luca for feeling hurt and betrayed. From her point of view, she could've been spared a shit ton of pain, and I get that. But I also don't blame you for being the reason for that. You did what was best for you and Cin, Byron. You *also* went through hell because of that chapter in your life. Two wrongs don't make a right, but you have a chance to be what Luca needs *now*."

He took a long drink of water, wishing it was something stronger. Even after all these years, he craved alcohol with an intensity that scared him. "The thing that hurts the most is that she hugged me for the first time," he whispered. "She loves Cin, but she's skittish around most people. I love her like a daughter, Jemma, and today she hugged me." He pinched the bridge of his nose, close to breaking down. "And then she found out I'm—"

"Stop," Jemma interrupted. "She trusted you once. She can do it again. You're worthy of her trust."

"Am I?"

"Absolutely."

He slowly got a hold of himself. He couldn't indulge in self-pity at the moment: there was a huge operation underway to catch Ian Mc-fucking-Dermot and Byron had to keep his wits about him.

As if on cue, Eddie sidled up to him. "You okay?"

"No."

"Well, I've got good news: the guys are at Ian's house. They'll let us know once they have him."

Byron nodded, staring at that whiskey.

"Fuck, I still can't believe I have a kid I never knew about," the man remarked.

"I don't believe that you never knew."

"You clearly don't remember how committed Guilietta can be to a certain role."

Byron clenched his jaw at the resulting memories. She had done things to him that were downright sadistic to prevent Georgie Warner from learning she was planning on betraying him. Eddie's alibi, as it were, was airtight. It didn't mean that Byron had to like it.

"Can't wait to kill that bastard."

"Get in line."

"Don't get in my way, Byron. I've got a bullet with his name on it for what he did to my daughter," Eddie argued.

"*I've* been taking care of her. *You* haven't even spoken to her!"

"*You're* the reason she even needed taking care of to begin with!"

Jemma reached over and slapped Eddie across the face. "Say that one more time, asshole. I dare you."

The tension in the room skyrocketed. Some of Eddie's men jumped to their feet, only to pause with their hands on their holsters when the bikers did the same. Byron gave his brothers a signal to stand down, turning to give Eddie his full attention.

Eddie touched his reddened cheek. "I'm sorry. I shouldn't take my anger at Guilietta out on you. She's really the reason for all of this."

"Spare me the bullshit," Byron snapped. He got up, feeling decades older than he was. "The only reason we're letting you stay is because we have a common goal. Once we've achieved it, you're gonna leave and never come back."

Tilting his chin up, Eddie challenged: "We'll let Luca decide where she wants to live when this is over."

Byron would never admit to this scum how much that pained him. He straightened his spine and strode to the hallway without another word. Cinnia was sitting on the floor outside the room Luca—who Jemma had sedated two hours ago—occupied, seeming haunted.

"Hey."

She didn't move. "Hey."

He took his place next to her, holding her hand. "I'm sorry."

"It's not your fault, babe. It's just..." She trailed off, sniffing.

"I know."

"She told me she wants to stay here, be a part of the club and—"

"I know." He kissed her fingers and shut his eyes.

"I want to kill him."

"Ian?"

"Eddie."

He barked a laugh, glancing at her. "Bloodthirsty."

She met his gaze, unflinching. "Yes."

His heart stuttered in his chest, as it so often did when he looked at her. This woman… She'd changed his views on life and love and, whenever he felt like he knew her as intimately as his own mind, she surprised him. He's already made peace with the fact that he wouldn't have enough time in his life to figure out her deepest secrets, but hell, he would try until his dying day.

"We're gonna get her back, Cin."

Those emerald orbs mesmerized him. "Promise?"

"I promise."

She breathed deeply and rested her head on his shoulder. "Good."

He must've drifted off, because he jolted awake when Nixon touched his shoulder. "What is it?" he whispered sleepily.

"Church," Nixon responded. He turned slightly, revealing Jemma behind him. "Can you look after Cin?"

"On it," she confirmed, swapping places with Byron.

Byron trailed behind his burly friend to the conference room, where most of the MC had gathered. Connor was at the head of the table with bags under his eyes. He'd probably rushed here right after his shift ended. Byron sank down on the open seat to Connor's left.

Eddie and one of his men crossed the threshold to lean against the wall. Teagan shut the door.

"Heard I missed quite a show," Connor said dryly.

Nixon snorted. "You could say that."

Connor quickly got serious, not having enough energy to keep faking good humor. "Ian is on his way. He's alive. So far, the truce holds," he said, giving Eddie a meaningful glance.

Eddie dipped his head in acknowledgement.

"I reached out to Terence." Haye shifted on his seat. "He's agreed to keep the Falcons in check over the next couple of weeks."

"The Falcons need to be dismantled," Byron insisted. "None of this bullshit will stop if they're still loyal and committed to their fucked-up vision."

"That's the plan," Connor remarked. "Terence will give them the choice to become Jackals once the dust is settled. The Jackals are closer, and we've never been interested in expanding to that side of the world. If the Falcons refuse and stir up shit, we'll have to step in."

"Hopefully, it won't come to that," Dane piped up. His ebony hair came down to his jaw, but he'd slicked it back. Although he didn't have the trademark green eyes of the Sloanes, there was no mistaking that he was Teagan's son and Cinnia's nephew. "Violence isn't as cool as it was in the past and I'd like to see us finally moving on from it."

"Aye," a few younger members agreed.

Byron gazed at the new generation, pride swelling in his chest despite Logan's notable absence. He knew this was exactly what his son wanted, too.

Ramsay Drummond had started the club and had had no qualms about breaking the law. Reade had tried to clean up his father's mess, but there had been too many bad habits for him to overcome. Brennan had given it a shot, too, only to die in the process. It was about time the Raptors MC got to enjoy the biker lifestyle without the accompanying drama.

Soon, his gut hinted.

"We'll deal with Ian when he arrives," Byron decided. When Connor opened his mouth to protest, Byron shook his head. "Trust me on this. The only way for you to get what you want is for your hands to be clean."

"They're not clean. We're still complicit," Connor pointed out.

"There's a difference between knowing who's pulling the trigger, and pulling the trigger yourself," Nixon muttered.

"Besides, *I'll* be killing the bastard." Eddie spread his arms theatrically. "The Raptors won't have blood on their hands at all. Problem solved."

"The fuck you will," Connor growled. "Logan will want—"

"To keep the spotlight off the club," Eddie interrupted, grinning broadly.

A silence descended as the Raptors exchanged glances.

They craved vengeance but, more than anything, they wanted one of their own to be safe and happy. Logan had given the title of Prez to Connor, yet he was still technically the MC's legacy, and now he had the kind of international career that ensured his name was always in the press. The club would do anything to keep his reputation clean.

"Fine," Connor relented.

Eddie seemed much too pleased with himself. "I'll arrange for my men to take him straight to our premises. You let me know if Terence needs help keeping the Falcons contained."

It went against the grain, but even Byron could see the logic. If they truly wanted the club to change, they had to start changing the choices they made. He was just wary of owing favors to a cartel again.

"We'll be in touch," Eddie said in departure, fixing Byron with a stare before stepping out of the room.

They sat in deafening silence, each waiting for the other to speak first. Connor, being the leader, bit the proverbial bullet: "What do we do about Luca? We can't keep her sedated forever."

Byron wished he knew. Simply thinking about her had his stomach in knots.

"Maybe she should stay with someone else for a while," Haye suggested. "She can move back in with us."

"Or maybe we should decide, *together*," Hallie announced as she sashayed inside, Jesse and Aurora hot on her heels. She leaned a hip against the table and crossed her arms over her chest, raising an eyebrow. It was sometimes difficult to believe that she wasn't Cinnia's daughter, because they had the same aura of sass about them. Then again, Piper could also be downright terrifying when she had a bone to pick with someone. "We all want the club to be different, so let the women be part of the decision-making process and we'll turn this ship around."

Dawn and Piper appeared at the door with proud, motherly smiles on their faces. Byron felt the corners of his lips tilting upwards and his spirits lifting from the interaction.

"If we're really doing this, we should all be present," Connor said. "My mom and Cinnia aren't here."

Teagan raised his hand in agreement. "Aye."

A broken chorus of "aye" followed as, one by one, the other men gave in to this new course of action. If anything, this proved how badly they all longed for a brighter, violence-free future. Byron wished Brennan could be here to witness it.

"You just had to be dramatic, huh?" Connor chuckled, getting to his feet and pulling Jesse closer.

"You just had to pull your heads out your own asses, huh?" she countered cheekily.

Byron burst out laughing, which set everyone else off. A few took that as their cue to leave the room, while others began brainstorming on everything that could change in the club. Byron's shoulders continued to shake with chuckles until his mood dipped and he started weeping. He covered his eyes as tears poured down his cheeks.

How will Luca ever forgive me? Can I blame her if she doesn't? Will she leave? Who will take care of her?

He didn't blame the others for not comforting him. There was only one person who could, and she'd been rendered unconscious for her own safety. In retrospect, that was probably going to count against them. She was emotionally volatile and had been injected against her will.

You had no other choice.

He wasn't so certain anymore: there was always a choice.

"Byron."

He raised his head, aware that his lips and chin were covered in snot.

Luca, her violet gaze red-rimmed and bleary, stood at the door with a blanket around her shoulders and a box of tissues in one hand. She headed towards him, took a seat, and placed them within reach.

Aware of her watching his every move, he blew his nose and dried his cheeks. He wasn't sure what her presence meant and refrained from asking, in case that would make her leave. He hadn't lied when he said he saw her as his daughter: he might not have wanted any children of his own, but he loved her as much as he loved Logan. He didn't want to imagine a world without her.

"I need to understand."

He winced. "I don't—"

"Please, Byron." She briefly hesitated. "What could've been so bad about saving me?"

"Absolutely nothing."

"Then why decide against it?"

He glanced to his left, his eyes landing on the numerous photos lining the wall: generations of bikers wearing leather and the Raptors MC patch. Their frozen smiles didn't hint at the violence they'd had to endure.

"I had to draw the line somewhere. You might not understand... I don't quite understand it myself, especially now." He sighed deeply. "I always put others' needs ahead of my own, thinking I needed to validate my existence that way. I suffered so much because of Guilietta that I didn't trust her motives. I was also abused and raped, Luca." He cautiously met her gaze. "While I was there, I didn't know if I was ever getting back to the club, to Cin and Logan. It doesn't excuse the fact that I said no to taking you and your mother in, but what I lived through contributed to that decision."

Her eyes were wide, and her mouth parted in shock.

"I figured she would let someone else take care of you. Fuck, I was so wrong. I can never tell you how sorry I am. If I could go back…" He trailed off, remembering his conversation with Logan. It seemed like a lifetime ago. "The truth is, I don't know if I would've chosen differently, as much as I might want to."

She absorbed that in her usual silence, peering at him. "I never thought I would be free. The girl I was then… She wouldn't have blamed you. She wouldn't have risked her life for someone else, either." Her odd purple eyes became watery. "I changed, though, because of you. I got to feel what it's like to belong somewhere. I got to meet people who really care about what happens to me. You're so different now, having taken me in, that it's difficult to imagine a version of you that wouldn't."

Holy fuck, that hurts.

"I only know what love and safety is because of you and Cin. I think that's why I know what betrayal is, too."

"Yeah, they tend to go hand in hand," he mumbled grimly.

"Did your family ever hurt you?"

"Yes."

She nibbled on her bottom lip for a moment. "Did you ever forgive them?"

"Eventually. My mom reached out a few months before she passed away to make amends." He gestured to their surroundings. "But mostly because of Cin and my brothers here, I found a new family. A supportive, forgiving family."

"If I wanted to leave, would you let me?"

"Yes, although I'll worry about you every day you're gone."

They sat staring at each other. Byron's anxiety was through the roof, and he had no idea how she could tolerate being this close to him, considering what he's done. He didn't have many regrets in life but, of them all, telling Giulietta to fuck off was his biggest one.

Go figure. That's the thing about life: only in retrospect do we get to see how our choices impacted our—and others'—experience. In the moment, it feels good or bad, but it's very rare that we immediately know why.

Byron knew that she understood now. He could see it in the set of her shoulders. If she'd been presented with the same, she might've made a similar decision. She'd wanted to judge him, *hate* him, but his reasoning changed her mind.

It gave him hope.

"I want to start over," Luca confessed. "When Logan rescued me, I was just so grateful to be safe that I made myself as small as possible. I didn't want to be an inconvenience to anyone. I chose the club, even when that led to Kristen..." She linked her fingers together: her nervous trait. "But I want to feel more secure. I want you and Cin to adopt me. I want to be Luca Johannson for real. It might seem like a moot point seeing as I'll be an adult soon, anyway, but I think it'll help me move past this."

His mind whirled at her declaration and a tear slipped past his defenses. "I'll make it happen. What else?"

"If I ever get married..." She smiled meekly. "Will you walk me down the aisle?"

"Jesus Christ, Luca." He was back to sobbing, although it was with relief this time. "Of course."

"Let's start over, then. No more lies."

"No more lies," he nodded.

She leaned forward to hug him.

He held her tightly, hoping that this was real because, if not, he would rather die than have her hate him again.

CHAPTER NINETEEN

BYRON KEPT HIS word: he and Cinnia were now legally her parents.

She had no clue how he had managed it, seeing as she didn't have a birth certificate. But Teagan, with his questionable tech savvy, had somehow made it happen. Frankly, she didn't need the details: it was enough that Byron had come through on his promise.

Looking back on it, Luca didn't know when exactly her hysteria had turned into understanding and, finally, acceptance.

It might have had something to do with seeing him utterly defeated, hunched over the boardroom table, crying his eyes out. Hearing his history, so similar to her own, but somehow more horrific because he's a man and society didn't believe that men could be raped or abused. She had never imagined that she could relate to a man, because they'd always been the reason for her pain.

Now, one of them was the reason for her healing.

She'd acknowledged and even empathized with the weight he carried on his shoulders. Byron wasn't selfish: for him to have chosen not to help her and her mother had been for his own sanity. Through his relationship with Cinnia and his brothers at the club, he got to make a new life. A *better* life.

Luca refused to be a victim, too. She was tired of living in fear.

7

From that moment on, she'd tackled her studies with determination. She not only wanted to make her new family proud, but to exceed her own expectations. She'd thrown herself into social situations that made her uncomfortable, even going so far as to join the cheerleading squad. Although she preferred the company of Jesse, Hallie and Dane, she made a few friends in her year. They often went shopping or to parties together and it became easier, the more she exposed herself to those scenarios, to relax around a large group of people.

The only thing she couldn't yet stand was the touch of a man. Boys were interested in her, but she didn't feel comfortable enough to be alone with one of them. Those psychological scars ran too deep.

From what she'd heard, the Falcons had been left rudderless without Ian McDermot. Kane, his right-hand man, had perished during the skirmish between the Raptors and Guilietta's cartel, and it had therefore been easy for the Jackals to take over their territory. The Raptors still kept an eye on Luca's whereabouts but, for the most part, the dark cloud that had hung over her head for so many years disappeared.

Eduardo Sequera had begrudgingly accepted her decision to become a Johannson. She'd met with him on three occasions to get to know him better and he'd vowed to protect her, in his own way. He was charming and funny and had kind eyes. Their close resemblance in appearance briefly consoled her: even though her mother was dead and gone, there was another side of her family that she'd never met. Endless possibilities awaited.

In the end, she simply couldn't envision being a part of the life he had to offer. Guilietta was too much of a loose cannon to be trusted. Eddie chose to stay with her only because he was terrified of what she'll do if he left. Luca didn't want fear to taint her life and told him that she would prefer to be with the Raptors.

He hadn't liked her decision, but he had respected it.

"What do you think of this one?"

Luca blinked out of her reverie and turned to Hallie, who was holding an Ajax jersey up. Luca wrinkled her nose at the crop top style. "I don't know. It's... revealing."

"Give me a break." Hallie rolled her eyes. "It's already difficult enough to find merchandise for his stupid team. Just take it."

"Only if you get one, too."

"Duh."

"*And* tell Aurora how you feel," Luca added, raising an eyebrow.

Hallie glared at her. "I regret telling you about that."

"No, you don't."

"No, I don't," Hallie agreed. She grabbed another jersey and headed for the till. "Let's go, Johannson."

Luca smirked as she followed. "I don't understand why you're not asking her out. You're out of school now."

"She just pisses me off."

"Then how do you know you like her?"

Hallie fell silent while paying for the jerseys. She only spoke again once they were outside, getting on their bikes. "There's more to her than what she shows everyone else. I've seen glimpses. I want to peel those layers back, be with the *real* her."

"And you don't think she's ready?"

"No." Hallie put her helmet on. "Let's go. The game starts in thirty."

Luca ignited *Spirit's* engine and followed Hallie to the club. It's been nearly two years since Logan had left for Ajax and, although these days they frequently spoke via video calls, she hasn't seen him in person in all that time. He was taking his decision to play ball for a living seriously and she had her own life here.

That said, she often dreamt of him and, lately, those dreams have become dirty.

She parked next to Hallie and they rushed to the warehouse, where Cinnia had arranged a large setup for everyone to watch the game. Luca happily waved at Jesse, who was sitting on Connor's lap.

"Hey!" Jesse greeted, jumping up to hug Luca. "Could you get it?"

"Yeah." Luca pulled a face. "It'll show my stomach."

"You can afford to show it, miss cheerleader." Jesse grabbed her hand. "Come on, let's get you changed."

The three of them went to the bathroom. Luca noticed Jesse was limping slightly and frowned. "Are you okay?"

Hallie snorted when Jesse blushed deeply. "Do you really want to know the answer to that question?"

"Oh!" Luca's eyes stretched wide in realization. "Another romp with Connor?"

"Can't keep my hands off him," Jesse mumbled, pushing her black-rimmed glasses up her nose. "He's... really good."

"How do you know for sure?" Hallie taunted, grinning. "He's your first."

"I knew what orgasms felt like before I slept with him. He gives me plenty."

"You just like playing 'hide the salami' too much, addict."

"It's more than a salami," Jesse said tartly.

"I keep telling you: I need evidence, or I'm going to keep thinking you're lying."

"And I keep telling *you*: this is how I keep the competition eliminated."

Luca busied herself with her shirt, trying not to seem too awkward. She loved hearing them talk about sex—they were so liberated and cavalier about it—but didn't know how to contribute. She knew rape and consensual sex were at opposite ends of the spectrum, but she couldn't fathom how having a naked man on top of her would ever feel good.

Would it be different with Logan?

She didn't know, yet she wanted to find out. She trusted that he wouldn't hurt her, but did he desire her?

A toilet flushed and Aurora stepped out of a cubicle. Her auburn hair was piled on top of her head in a messy bun, and she wore faded jeans and a checkered button-up shirt. She gazed at Hallie for a moment and Luca could have sworn she saw longing there.

Aurora had come out to her parents shortly after Logan and Connor had left for Amsterdam. Everyone had taken it in stride, even though some had been confused, given the way she'd pretended to be straight. Since then, she's changed her style to what *she* actually preferred: black tights, knee-high boots and flannel shirts.

And she's had a regular rotation of women, much to Hallie's dismay.

"Couldn't find a jersey?" Hallie asked, her eyes lingering on Aurora's curves.

"I'm not that much of a fan," Aurora shrugged as she washed her hands.

"Logan will be disappointed."

"Logan won't even know. Not everything in our lives revolves around him."

Luca and Jesse exchanged a knowing glance. This wasn't about Logan anymore. The tension in the room was palpable.

Another cubicle opened, revealing a tall blonde. She smiled at them as she stood next to Aurora. "You must be the girls I keep hearing about. I'm Malorie."

"Hallie, Jesse, Luca," Jesse greeted, gesturing to the three of them in turn. "Good to meet you."

"You too! It's so exciting, seeing the inside of the Raptors club. I've heard so much about it."

Hallie crossed her arms over her chest. With her leather pants, biker boots and long, black hair, she looked like someone who kicked ass and took names. The venom in her light brown eyes did nothing to soften her appearance. "Friend of yours, Ror?" she asked, her tone deceptively cheerful.

"Girlfriend, actually," Aurora replied, swiping her plump mouth with lip gloss. She made eye contact with Hallie. "Problem?"

Luca was afraid to breathe. She tugged at the baggy crop top and wished she could disappear.

"Why would there be?" Hallie asked. She gave Malorie a charming smile. "You are gorgeous. Too bad Rory snapped you up first."

Malorie flushed, tucking her hair behind her ears. "Thanks."

"I'm meeting someone here tonight, myself."

"You are?" Luca, Jesse and Aurora chorused in varying tones of curiosity.

"Yeah." Hallie turned to the mirror and pretended to care about what she looked like. "He's such a cool dude, actually. Really knows how to get me going." She smiled broadly and gave Aurora a light spank, jolting her. "You know what that's like, don't you, Ror?"

The four of them watched as Hallie left. Aurora was fuming.

"She seems really cool," Malorie remarked, oblivious to the underlying charge of emotion. "How do you know her?"

Aurora narrowed her eyes. "Family friend. Let's go, babe."

"Jeez," Jesse muttered once they were alone. "Those two are the worst."

"Why don't they just hook up already?" Luca wondered.

"Pride. Connor and I were similar, but not nearly as toxic." Jesse smiled. "You look good, by the way."

"Thanks. I'm trying not to think about it."

"Good." Jesse scrunched her wild curls. "Ready for the game?"

Ready to see Logan? is what she really meant.

Luca bit her lip and nodded. "Let's go."

It was absolute chaos in the main section of the warehouse. Many of the Raptors were running around, getting the food and drinks going and making sure everyone was comfortable. Luca sat with Jesse and Connor; Dane and his friends were close-by. Aurora and Malorie were making out, the former watching Hallie even while her lips were locked with another woman. To the untrained eye, Hallie was as cool as a cucumber, but Luca knew her well enough to see the hurt underneath.

Byron and Cinnia occupied the front row along with Reade, Mysie, Loraine, Jimmy, Teagan and Piper. The Tyrells were mingling with Haye, Dawn, Ryan and his girlfriend, Annabelle.

Luca spotted Hallie leave briefly, returning with a good-looking guy in tow. Luca didn't have to look to know Aurora was upset: the victorious set to Hallie's mouth was proof enough.

Why do people in love act like this?

The place was buzzing with excitement. Everyone was ready to watch their golden boy. They cheered when Logan's face appeared on the screen and Luca ignored the wild beating of her heart.

His jet-black hair was stylishly cut, and he's grown out his beard, which was lighter and had an auburn tint. The red and white of his jersey suited him, made him seem distinguished. He's performed really well at the club and there were rumors that the Netherlands wanted to draft him for the upcoming World Cup.

Those green eyes, though… Focused and intense. They sent shivers down her spine. He's the new face of DKNY and has peered at her from social media posts and billboards in a way that unsettled her. Excited her. Dr. McKauley has warned her about white knight syndrome.

Luca tried to rationalize her feelings—she's never really had a conversation with Logan about his likes and dislikes, for heaven's sake!—and yet he was the sole object of her fantasies. She didn't know if she would've felt any different about him if he wasn't drop-dead gorgeous.

The vibes she'd seen between him and women like Alyssa were off the charts, though. He probably didn't feel anything for Luca except brotherly love and, besides, she didn't want to *date* him.

She cheered when Ajax's captain scored an early goal, assisted by Logan. The two had an easy partnership that was often commented on by sports analysts. Logan might be a foreigner and one of the youngest players, but supporters loved him.

That's another thing she couldn't quite reconcile: his popularity. She's done her best to acclimatize to the life of a "normal" teenager, but she still preferred her own company and couldn't envision living the jet set life of a football player's girlfriend. To be constantly interrupted while having dinner or walking in public didn't sound appealing at all. She wouldn't learn to handle it, not even for him.

You're getting ahead of yourself again. He's probably not even into you!

Sophie joined them during halftime, still glowing even though her and Max have been engaged for nearly two years. She had hoped that her wedding, now only a few weeks away, would be intimate but, with the amount of people she and Max knew combined—not to mention pressure from Max's family— the guest list already topped two hundred. She'd asked Luca to be one of the bridesmaids, which was terrifying.

Alyssa was the maid of honor.

Considering the mixed feelings Luca had for Logan, she surprised herself when she learned that she actually liked Alyssa. They've spoken a few times while making arrangements for Sophie's upcoming bachelorette's party, and Alyssa's wisdom appealed to Luca. Cinnia also adored Alyssa in a way that suggested she wanted Alyssa, or someone like her, to be her daughter-in-law, and Luca could honestly see that happening. Alyssa had this aura of pure white light about her that was probably irresistible to Logan.

During one of their deep conversations, Alyssa had encouraged Luca to venture outside her comfort zone and learn who she was underneath the layers of childhood trauma and, because it's so similar to advice Dr. McKauley had given, Luca has taken it on as her motivation to improve her sense of self-worth. Despite all these positive traits to Alyssa's personality, though, Luca couldn't help but feel downright competitive considering how badly she wanted Logan's attention.

But you're not even sure you want him that way, remember?

Jesse has worked the situation into the storyline of her new book, calling it a "classic love triangle". Luca couldn't wait to read which woman the hero chose, since she's living vicariously through fictional characters for the time being. She didn't yet trust men enough to be around them *that* way.

Ajax won the game with a total of 2-1, leaving the Raptors to celebrate the only way they knew how: hard. Music was blaring from the speakers;

people were dancing or huddled around tables, laughing; kids entertained themselves by playing football outside, emulating the game they'd just watched. It was such a far cry from what Luca had experienced with the Falcons, that she took a moment to soak up the love these people had for one another.

She was chatting to Jesse on a bench near the parking lot when Alyssa arrived with her attractive boyfriend in tow. Her hair was long these days, down to her shoulders, and dyed lilac. She wore a floaty Bohemian dress with cowboy boots, and several necklaces of varying lengths and colors. Luca would never have the courage to wear something that stood out so much, but she couldn't imagine Alyssa ever donning plain outfits. The woman was born to stand out.

"Lys! Jake!" Jesse called out.

"Hey, ladies," Alyssa greeted warmly.

"Wow, this place is incredible," Jake murmured to himself, glancing around as if he's never seen the inside of a motorcycle club before. Similar to Malorie's reaction, actually. Luca sometimes forgot how foreign MC's must seem to regular folks.

"Sophie mentioned you might be dropping in," Jesse smiled, getting up to hug Alyssa. "It's good to see you."

"You too. We were watching the game at a pub and Jake's friends didn't want us to leave." Alyssa turned to him. "Sophie called, said it's an emergency, and Jake decided to tag along because he's never been here before."

"Only because I can't believe you guys actually know Logan Drummond," he smiled.

"Jake's got a bit of a crush," Alyssa laughed.

Luca watched the woman intently. There was only the barest hint of longing in her tone, one that Luca could recognize because she knew what it was like, too. She felt a pang of jealousy: she suspected that Alyssa has been as close to Logan as Luca dreamed of being. She had no idea why the two weren't together, though: Logan was a subject they always avoided broaching.

"Him and about five million women around the world," Jesse teased.

"Yeah, get in line, babe."

Jake chuckled good-naturedly as Sophie appeared, who seemed relieved that Alyssa was there. "You made it!"

"You sounded kinda hysterical over the phone," Alyssa murmured, embracing her friend. "Are you okay?"

"Max's mom is trying to take over the wedding again." Sophie grabbed Alyssa's hand. "Come on, we'll talk inside. I'm stealing your girlfriend, Jake. Lova ya, bye!"

Jesse shook her head with a smile while watching the two rush inside. "Not really giving me a reason to say yes to Connor."

"Has he been asking?"

Jake cleared his throat. "Before you girls get into that, do you know if Max is in there?"

"Yeah, he was at the bar, last time I checked." Jesse waited until they were alone again. "Connor's been hinting."

"Wow."

She sighed. "I think it's too soon."

"I don't. You've known each other since you were kids."

Jesse couldn't quite hide her excitement at the idea. "I just don't want to make a big fuss, you know? Maybe after Sophie's wedding, then."

"He's going to be extra goofy if you tell him that."

"Which is much better than how grumpy he used to get."

Luca grinned, waggling her eyebrows. "That's because you changed his life."

Shaking her head with a laugh, Jesse looked away. "It's still unbelievable, how happy we are. It's been better than I thought." She bumped her shoulder on Luca's. "Logan's going to visit soon. Are you ready for that?"

Luca thought about it, breathing deeply. "I'm looking forward to seeing him in person," she admitted quietly. "Trying not to focus on the rest. I don't want to have unrealistic expectations. He might have a girlfriend."

"That's fair," Jesse nodded, "or he might have a massive ego now. Nobody likes that."

"Connor has one."

Jesse blushed. "Yeah, don't remind me."

They sat in companionable silence, each wrapped in their own thoughts. Luca allowed herself to envision Logan's upcoming six-week visit. He would arrive, catch up with his friends and family and, once he's settled back in, spend more face-to-face time with her. They could go to—

For a second, she was stumped.

She wouldn't call them the best of friends, but they also weren't strangers.

What did they even have in common? They hardly ever spoke about books or movies. She didn't enjoy the things he did: rock-climbing, sports, crowds… The only thing that really pulled them together was Cinnia and Byron, and the club. They were technically stepsiblings now, as well, which made the prospect of them dating forbidden. Besides, she wasn't even sure if she wanted him, long-term…

They could figure it out over dinner!

Are you seriously saying the only thing you have in common is eating?! Why not breathing, while you're at it?

She nibbled on her bottom lip. Whenever they had video chats, they spoke about his life in Amsterdam or her experience at school. That's how their relationship had started: Logan sharing stories about his life in an attempt to get her to open up.

That doesn't mean we don't have anything in common, does it?

"I think you should make a move when he's here."

Luca was pulled back to the present. She glanced at Jesse with a frown.

"It'll be the easiest way to figure out if he's what you want," Jesse explained, shrugging. "If you don't take the chance, you'll always wonder."

"What if… he's not?"

"It won't change how I feel about either of you." Jesse had a kind smile on her face. "But what if he is?"

Luca swallowed past the lump in her throat, feeling dizzy and nauseated. She's already established that his lifestyle was not one she could—or wanted to—fit into. That didn't mean they couldn't find another way to be together, did it?

Jesse was right: Luca should take the chance, if only to know for sure.

PART III

THE MAN

CHAPTER TWENTY

HE HASN'T BEEN home in over two years. There was a time when the thought alone would've seemed impossible. His parents, friends and the club have been an integral part of his life, and he'd given up the safety and security to make his wildest dreams come true.

His life has been a scary and exhilarating emotional roller-coaster ever since. He has become Ajax's superstar player and a favorite among fans. A part of him couldn't believe how quickly his life has changed, or that he might be representing the Netherlands at the upcoming FIFA World Cup.

His team members had initially been reluctant to accept him, but had eventually come around, mostly thanks to the captain being a great leader. Logan's skills often led to sports journalists and bloggers comparing them, but Andries wasn't jealous or intimidated. Instead, he had shown Logan the ropes and offered his experience as a way for Logan to find his own footing in the lifestyle and industry.

Logan couldn't have asked for a better mentor.

Because football tournaments kept players busy enough year-round, Logan was pleasantly surprised that Ajax was willing to give him a six-week break. It coincided with Sophie's wedding: she had been about ready to scream bloody murder when it seemed like he wouldn't get the time off.

While they might not be as close as they once were, she was still one of his favorite people and he didn't want to disappoint her. For the rest of his break, he'll be visiting his parents and the MC. He was quite excited to see his hometown, and to reconnect with the people he'd grown up with.

Unfortunately, his flight got diverted due to bad weather, and he wasn't looking forward to the one-hour bus ride the airline had arranged for the affected passengers. Coupled with the constant chatter of the fangirl next to him, he was exhausted.

For a moment, he blamed Marcus, who had prodded Logan into accepting an endorsement deal with DKNY. The money and free products were fantastic, sure, but having his physique immortalized on billboards, websites and magazines around the world wasn't helping him dodge women. It was hard enough remaining celibate as things stood.

It hadn't been a conscious decision to not have sex anymore. He had simply taken his parents' advice to heart and put all his effort into making a success of his chosen career path, and so Alyssa remained the last woman he's been intimate with: that fraught meeting of flesh in an airport bathroom stall was seared to the back of his eyelids.

Logan briefly shut his eyes as he became immersed in memories of her. These days, they only spoke sporadically, mostly because she's been involved with another man for over a year. Logan couldn't stand it, although he did his best not to show that side of him. The times they've made love were still hotter than all his previous conquests combined, but the underlying energy that tied them together was impossible to release. He didn't know if he ever could.

He sighed with relief as the plane landed and counted down the minutes until the door opened, absently answering the fangirl's questions. He felt remarkably better by the time he entered the small airport building, grabbing his bag from the carousel and following the passengers to the awaiting bus outside.

"Logan!"

Glancing up, it took him an embarrassing amount of time to recognize his stepfather and good friend, only because he hadn't envisioned a familiar face at this airport. Both of them wearing jeans, a black T-shirt and a Raptors leather jacket, Byron grinned broadly as he strode over with Connor on his heels.

Logan's eyes burned with tears and he met Byron halfway, embracing him.

"Hey, punk," Byron chuckled, "rough flight?"

"You have no idea."

"We have some idea. That's why we came to get you," Connor quipped.

Logan stepped back to greet his former VP. They hugged wordlessly, patting each other on the back. Their time in Amsterdam had deepened their bond and, even if they hardly ever saw each other, they always answered phone calls and text messages.

Connor's dark blonde hair wasn't cut as short as in the past, the new style somehow adding a sparkle to his blue eyes. "I've missed you, man."

"I missed you." Logan turned to Byron. "Not that I'm complaining, but why're you guys here?"

"Called the airport when we saw the clouds rolling in, and they confirmed your flight will be diverted." Byron rested his arm on Logan's shoulder while they walked. "We figured you'd enjoy a proper ride into town."

"I doubt the weather's good to ride home in."

Connor grinned and gestured with an arm. "That's why we're going to have a boys' night *here*."

For the second time in as many minutes, Logan came to an abrupt halt. The entire original Raptors MC was parked in the drop-off area, complete with two prospects in the van. Logan lifted his hand to the left side of his chest, his heart aching at the sight. God, he's missed this!

"How...?" He trailed off and glanced at Byron. "How'd you get mom to agree?"

"Believe it or not, it was her idea. She said she'll be happy to monopolize your time for the rest of your stay."

"Sounds about right."

"I got one of the prospects to ride your bike here," Connor commented. "You can fall in behind me, seeing as you don't know where we're going."

Logan saluted his childhood friend. "Yes, Prez."

"Shut the fuck up, Lo," Connor said while rolling his eyes. He couldn't hide his proud smile, though. "Let's go."

The prospects loaded Logan's bags in the van while he straddled the Blackline. He took a moment to enjoy the feel of the beast between his legs; then he donned his helmet and started the engine.

"Welcome back, Logan!" the men chorused on their helmets' comms system.

"Thanks, guys. It's good to be back."

Connor pulled away from the curb and, one by one, they followed. Logan gazed at the environment along the way, feeling like a familiar stranger. Ever since he'd moved to Amsterdam, everything that had happened before seemed like it was a part of someone else's life. He was trying hard not to feel guilty for leaving in the first place.

The convoy of motorcycles arrived at a motel and one of the prospects went to reception to sort out their booking, while the rest of them loitered in the parking lot. Logan went to stand with Byron and Ryan.

"It's weird seeing you in person, for once," the chef remarked with a smile. "I'm so used to your face on a TV screen."

"Feels weird being here, and not on a football pitch." Logan rubbed the back of his neck. He loved his career, but the recognition that went along with it often made him uncomfortable, and he didn't like the people he grew up around looking at him like he was different. He wasn't. Right? "What's the plan, dad?"

"Well, you probably need a power nap. We're going to meet back here in two hours and then go out." Byron grinned broadly. "It's Max's bachelor's party."

Logan glanced around. "Where is he?"

"The prospects are gonna 'kidnap' him later," Ryan chuckled. "His friends are in on it, too."

"Oh boy. I'm surprised Sophie didn't give a list of things we're not allowed to do to Max."

"She did," Nixon said as he and Connor joined the three of them, having caught the last bit of the conversation. "She also knows we're not going to listen."

"It's not like we'll put him in danger," Connor added.

"Just a few strippers and lots of alcohol. The usual."

Logan shook his head with an amused expression at Nixon's deadpan delivery of that line. "I hope for your part Sophie's forgiving."

"Max would never fuck up his chances with her," Connor shrugged. "He's a good guy."

The prospect—*Henry*, Logan reminded himself, having read his nametag—returned and began handing out room keys to everyone.

Connor held a key up in victory. "You're bunking with me, bro."

Byron clapped Logan on the shoulder. "Go get some shut eye."

Grabbing their bags from the van, Logan followed Connor to their room. "It really is bizarre, having you here," Connor said as he retrieved two mini bottles of whiskey and handed one to Logan. "How've you been?"

Logan got comfortable on his bed and leaned his head back. "Honestly? I've been dreading this trip."

"Why?"

"I don't know." Logan stared at the bottle for a moment before taking a large sip. "I feel so far removed from everyone, not just geographically. I mean, I still don't know what happened with the Falcons."

Connor nodded, breaking eye contact. "We all decided it's best to give you a fresh start. We didn't want to bog you down with the details."

"Was it your suggestion, or dad's?"

"Mine." Connor grimaced. "Are you mad at me for that?"

Logan saw the earnest expression on his friend's face and sighed, shaking his head. "I would've done the same. You're good at this Prez gig."

"I'd like to think so. I enjoy it."

One piece of the weight he's been carrying loosened, and Logan smiled as he leaned forward to clink his bottle to Connor's. "So, mind clueing me in?"

"We found Ian, for starters." Connor kicked his shoes off and lay on his back, staring at the ceiling. "He had charisma, I'll give him that. It's like he was the leader of a cult or something. They were fiercely loyal to him."

"He *had* charisma?"

"He's gone now, if that's what you're asking. Him and his band of loyal assholes."

"Who did it?"

Connor clenched his jaw and took a large swig before answering: "Eddie Sequera. Turns out, he's Luca's real dad." When Logan's eyes widened, Connor sighed. "We voted to try a different approach. Included the women for once. We wanted everyone's hands clean this time around, especially yours."

"Fucking hell, I've missed out on everything, it seems. Dad didn't even tell me about Eddie" Logan finished his whiskey and went to the mini bar to grab another. "Do you ever think about this life we've inherited? I mean, *really* think about it?"

"I used to, all the damn time. But Lo?"

Logan's eyes connected with Connor's, who seemed uncharacteristically serious. "What?"

"You have to stop," Connor replied somberly. "It's enough. You've tormented yourself about things you can't change. I thought for sure that with you living your *real* dream in Amsterdam, you'll finally move on from the past. You've got to start looking forward to shit. Forgive yourself for moving on, and *move on*."

Logan blinked back the tears in his eyes, chuckling to relieve the tension. "Dr. Tyrell, what on earth has happened to you?"

"I became Prez, something my lineage was never prepared for." Connor grinned. "Plus, Jesse's pregnant, so I'm becoming philosophical."

"*What*?! Why haven't you said anything until now?"

"She doesn't know that I know. Everyone, including my girl, keeps forgetting I'm a fucking doctor and can recognize the signs." He laughed to himself. "She's probably waiting until after Sophie's wedding to break the news because she doesn't want to steal the spotlight or some shit, but she's three months along."

"Wow." Logan moved toward Connor to shake his hand. "Well done, you."

"Thanks. Now, have I answered enough of your questions for the time being? Can we take this fucking nap already?"

"Of course." Logan got into bed, turning on his side to look at Connor. "It's great to see you, Con."

"You too, Lo."

They drifted off with content smiles on their faces. Knowing that his family and friends were happy filled Logan with warmth, with hope. Connor was right: Logan should start living without reservation. Despite being halfway across the globe, he's been clinging to the past.

His dream started with the vibrant colors of the music festival he'd recently attended in Amsterdam.

"Remember when we were on that roof?"

He glanced to his left, his heart stuttering at the sight of Alyssa. Her lilac hair complemented the olive tone of her skin and made her soulful brown eyes appear like dark, sparkling gems. He swallowed, captivated.

"I think about it all the time," she smiled. "I've never felt that close to anyone."

"Same."

"I don't know what our future holds, Logan. I don't know how to stop loving you."

"Then don't."

She looked away, nibbling on her bottom lip. He envied her teeth. "There's something else that needs to happen, first."

He nodded, knowing she was right. "Soon."

Taking his hand in hers, she gazed up at him. "Soon."

Blinking, he was disappointed to find her gone. The colors were muted now, too, as if the light had been sucked out of them. He moved forward, slowly recognizing his childhood home in front of him. He opened the door, which revealed Luca in the entryway. Her bright smile nearly blinded him, and she jumped up to—

His alarm ripped through the vision, startling him awake. Logan sat up, rubbing his eyes as the dream faded. The number of times he's dreamt of Alyssa over the years… It's become unremarkable, standard, at this point. From past experience, it meant that she would send him a message in the near future.

His phone vibrated. Smirking, he picked it up to read her text.

"Heard you're going to be at the wedding. Nervous. Excited."

His thumbs tapped four times to spell "same", an echo of what he'd said in the dream.

"I'm still with Jake."

He rubbed his chest, where his heart was panging. It wasn't fun, loving someone as much as he loved her while knowing that she's got another life. A different life. *"Are you happy?"*

Her reply didn't come immediately. *"Yes."*

"I'm happy for you. I won't make things weird."

"It isn't you I'm worried about."

He chucked the phone to the side and went to the bathroom to splash his face with water. He stared at his reflection in the mirror. His life has forever changed, thanks to Ajax. He had to take Connor's advice and stop lingering in the past, even if that meant giving Alyssa up.

Easier said than done.

Connor was awake by the time Logan walked back into the room. His eyes were glued to his phone. "The prospects have kidnapped Max. We're meeting them at the club in twenty. Are you ready to go?"

"Aye, Prez."

"Shut the fuck up." Connor grinned as he stuffed his phone in the back pocket of his jeans and reached for his leather cut. "Come along then, golden boy."

Logan rolled his eyes and followed Connor out of the room. Most of the Raptors were already in the parking lot. Logan greeted a few of them before pulling Byron into another hug.

"Hey," Byron laughed, "you okay?"

"I'm great." Logan smiled broadly. "Let's party."

"There he is!" Connor cheered. He turned to the gang. "Guess what? Logan's back and he's ready to party!"

The men cheered and whistled, getting on their Harleys to rev their engines. They waited for Connor to take the lead and rode in convoy to the nightclub the Raptors had booked for the evening. They headed inside to the reserved tables. There wasn't much space left for other patrons.

A round of drinks was ordered and Logan settled in to enjoy this for what it was: a cultural tradition to celebrate Max's dying bachelor status. He caught up with old friends, all of whom he considered brothers, while they waited for the groom to arrive.

Henry was the one to hush them mere seconds before three other prospects burst into the club, looking like they were having trouble lugging Max's tall, muscular body towards the front.

"This is not going to end well for you!" Max hollered as he tried—and failed—to get out of his bonds. He had a black bag over his head and was probably scared shitless, not that he would ever show it. "I'm a cop, you hear me?! You've really fucked up!"

"Yeah, yeah," one of the prospects taunted, shoving Max into a seat. He gripped the one edge of the bag. "Tell that to my friends."

Max blinked furiously in the dim light once the bag was lifted off. It took him a while to realize that he was not in danger and that he was, in fact, surrounded by men who cared about him.

"You sons of bitches!" he yelled hoarsely, his booming laughter filling the room. "You motherfucking sons of bitches!"

Connor stepped forward and slapped Max on the shoulders before undoing his bonds. "Welcome to your bachelor party, bro!"

Max jumped up to give Connor a bear hug. "I should've known it was you!"

"But you didn't," Connor guffawed. "Man, you should've seen your face!"

Henry motioned to the DJ to start the music and get everyone another round. Logan was impressed with their planning and waited in line for Max to greet him.

"Jesus, even Logan Drummond is here," Max said, shaking Logan's hand.

"In my capacity as a friend. Congratulations, Max."

"Thanks, man. It means so much to Soph that you're going to be at the wedding."

"Of course, I wouldn't—"

"Gentlemen and reprobates!" Connor interrupted, having located a microphone. He leapt onto the stage while the men turned to look at him. "Now that Max is in on the joke and *before* we all get shitfaced, I'd like to say something to the groom."

"Oh boy," Max stage-whispered, causing a few laughs.

"Hush, you, this is more important than naming you firstborn after me," Connor teased. "Max, I'm so happy that Sophie's managed to find a decent man. I mean, you're a cop, but not everyone's perfect."

"Hear, hear!" the men cheered, drumming on nearby tables.

Connor motioned for them to settle down. "Seriously, though, you make my big sis very happy, and you've been amazing to the club. That's why we would formally like to welcome you into the Raptors MC."

Henry handed something to Connor, which Connor opened up to show everyone: it was a Raptors leather cut with "Copper" on the back.

"Max, with this, we officially recognize you as a brother!"

If Logan had thought they'd celebrated *his* return, it was nothing compared to the noise they made to welcome Max to the family. A part of him was jealous and felt left out, but the overriding emotion was joy. Life at the club had gone on without him, and that was better than the alternative.

Max jumped onto the stage to embrace Connor again, before stepping back to put the cut on. "Thank you, Prez."

"With that out of the way, let's get this party started! Whoo!" Connor yelled.

Drinks appeared as if by magic, the music began booming and women started gyrating on stage to entertain the men. Any hopes that Logan had to have heart to hearts with the people he's missed went out the window. Max getting patched in aside, this wasn't an evening meant for sentiment.

No, debauchery was on the menu.

For once, Logan didn't care that he was recognized by fans, even in this setting. He dutifully posed for pictures and accepted round after round of drinks. He didn't often get to let loose anymore and, although he already knew he was going to regret it in the morning, he faced the evening's activities head-on.

The party unfolded in flashes. Logan's never had a great tolerance for whiskey—it made him euphoric, horny, weepy, and then blackout drunk, in that order—but it was flowing, so how could he say no?

The men danced to classic rock songs, singing their hearts out. Logan and Byron broke into their air guitar routine as soon as *Living on a Prayer* started. Connor and Nixon, eager to outdo the father-and-son duo, did their own rendition of *Highway to Hell*. That encouraged many others to join the friendly competition and, to everyone's surprise, Ryan and Oscar won the impromptu dance battle with their fancy footwork to *Take on Me*.

It was inevitable, with so many beautiful women around, that the guys would eventually lose interest in rock music and segment into smaller groups to get special, individualized attention in return for hefty tips. This also clearly divided the room between happily married men, or soon-to-be, and those that wanted to chase tail.

Logan found himself in a private booth with three strippers grinding against each other to put on a show for him and Connor. The Prez was polite about their attention, but Logan could see he wasn't really interested in anything more. It made Logan proud to witness how devoted Connor was to Jesse, considering the man had been an absolute man-whore before they got together.

Like you were any better, once upon a time.

"Be careful, Lo, but enjoy."

Logan blinked, wondering when Connor had left. He was losing all sense of time and enjoying the ladies that stayed behind to make sure he was okay. One of them had Alyssa's build, bringing to mind their intimate evening in Amsterdam. He remembered how she'd looked like a female warrior angel claiming her mate, shining against the backdrop of the night sky.

He was not shocked that his next conscious memory consisted of being balls deep in the stripper. She was bent over the edge of the loveseat, her face reflected in the floor-to-ceiling mirrors of the room and contorted by pleasure. He rammed into her while her friend caressed his back.

"Ah, *fuck!*" the woman cried out, collapsing forward.

"Was it good, Angel?" The other one bent next to her friend, touching her cheek while gazing at Logan with lust. "Was his cock good?"

"Oh my God, yes."

Logan held the base of his appendage, absently noting he'd had enough common sense to put a condom on, before dropping into the open space on the loveseat. He'd just started enjoying the sex, damn it!

The friend left Angel's side to straddle Logan. She had oriental features and her long, black hair was silky to the touch. "Don't worry, gorgeous, I'll finish what Angel started."

He blissfully shut his eyes when she took him right to the hilt, riding him hard and fast. The feel of lips on his face, neck and chest elevated the sensations building inside of him. This was the first time that he's had sex in years: an orgy seemed fitting and if these beautiful women wanted to use him for their own pleasure, he would happily oblige.

"*Oh!*" the Asian woman moaned, her manicured nails pinching his pectorals. "Oh my God, that feels *so good!*"

Logan looked past her to see yet another woman, wearing a strap-on, taking the Asian woman in the ass while she bounced on Logan's dick. How many of them were in here? Five, six?

Doesn't matter, he thought with a grin. *All mine.*

The Asian woman came hard and was pulled off Logan by the strap-on wearer. He grabbed the back of the latter's head to kiss her, steering her to one of the other women. "Fuck her," he instructed as he reached for the discarded bottle of lube.

The woman wasted no time, clearly on the same page.

He squirted a generous amount of lubricant on his covered cock and her own crack, his thrust inside pushing the fake dick into the woman below. This whole scene was thrilling, dangerous and depraved. He couldn't get enough of it.

When he glanced to the left, he saw Angel being eaten out by two of the other strippers. Their bodies were toned and curvy, some surgically enhanced, and too fucking beautiful for words. Having this giant pile of women in the room with him did wonders for his ego: he didn't even care that he'll probably have a massive bill to settle later.

The two below him reached their own pinnacles and he pulled out, discarding the condom and grabbing another. He pointed to the next woman, a fiery redhead that looked vaguely familiar, and carefully balanced her on the back of the loveseat as he pushed his aching dick inside. Someone had already prepped her, which meant he easily slid home.

"Logan," she breathed in his ear as she clutched his shoulders.

For a second, he wondered if he knew her; then figured she must know who he is from watching football. He was ready to blow his load, but not before she came, so he took his time to get her there. They shuddered in each other's arms, and he gripped her ass to make sure he didn't lose his balance.

"That was fun," she giggled, keeping her legs wrapped around him. "The girls don't stand in line for just anyone, you know."

He pulled back slightly, trying to focus through his drunken haze, and froze. "Meghan."

"I was wondering if you'll recognize me."

He suddenly felt completely sober. He's just had sex with the one woman he had sworn he would never bed. "Fucking hell," he sneered, pulling out and chucking the used condom in the direction of the trash can. He tucked his privates back into his briefs and zipped his jeans up. "I don't believe this."

She sighed deeply, righting her glittery G-string and standing with her hands on her hips. "Don't freak out."

"Are you kidding me?"

"Logan—"

"I don't want to hear it."

He got his things, dumped way too much money on the side table by the door, and stormed out. The main room was virtually empty and, apart from a few members, it seemed as if the Raptors had left. How long had he been in that orgy?

The answer to his question was the bright sunrise outside. He blinked furiously while his eyes adjusted and rubbed his temples at the signs of a blooming migraine.

"Will you stop and listen to me, please?"

He glanced over his shoulder. Meghan had donned a robe and stood behind him with her arms crossed over her chest. "Did you try anything with him?"

"No, of course not." She tucked long, dyed locks behind her ears and

316

rolled her eyes when he gave her a disbelieving look. "I know, right? How on earth could Meghan Nolan grow up and get over her obsession with Byron Johannson?"

"Nolan?"

"I changed my last name right around the time I left home."

He let out a long breath. "Okay, I'll bite."

The hint of a smile touched her lips. She was a stunning woman: it was the reason he'd been attracted to her in the first place. The shrine she'd had of Byron, however, had quickly wiped any desire from his mind, way back when.

"My mom always spoke about your dad like he was the one that got away. It's messed up, actually, when you take into consideration how much she hated him. When I first saw him with my own eyes, a part of me hoped that I was somehow his daughter." She looked away. "But that's impossible because goody-two-shoes *mommy* would never cheat on dad, even though she hated him, too."

Logan shifted on his feet, intrigued.

"Mom and I have always been competitive and I figured, hey, *I* could probably get and keep Byron Johannson where she'd failed and yes, I know how crazy that sounds." Snorting, she added: "It took over a year of therapy for me to realize how stupid I was." Here, she gazed at him. "To realize how destructive I was. I'm really sorry, Logan. For everything. I never thought I'd get to say it in person." Her smile briefly landed. "I'm not sorry I finally got to have sex with you, though. I've always wondered what it would be like. You didn't disappoint."

"This is…" He trailed off, not sure how to continue. "It's a lot to take in. How did you end up here?"

"Well, I disowned my family and needed to pay the bills somehow." She shrugged nonchalantly. "Also, I'm not ready to commit to a relationship. I don't quite trust myself."

"That's a mature way of looking at it."

"No shit," she laughed. "Are we cool?"

"Yeah, we're cool."

"Good." She stood on tiptoes to peck his cheek. "Congrats on being such a shit-hot player, by the way. Always knew you had it in you."

"Thanks, Meghan." He gestured to her, sheepish. "You look fantastic."

"I know," she winked as she walked backward to the entrance. "See you around, or not."

He waved, completely thrown by the interaction. When Meghan had disappeared from view, he turned to his Harley and got on. If this was any indication of what being back in town was going to be like, he had a feeling he'll be excited to return to Amsterdam, Ajax and his new home.

"Best get on with it, then," he chuckled as he opened throttle.

CHAPTER TWENTY-ONE

SOPHIE'S WEDDING WAS sensational, from beginning to end.

The number of guests closely rivaled Byron and Cinnia's celebration, which was saying a lot, all things considered, and the total opposite of the small, intimate affair Sophie's always wanted. It was held at the same church and conference venue, too, which suggested to Logan that the Raptors were helping to foot the bill.

"I gave in to the pressure," she'd sighed a few days ago, when they had caught up over a cup of coffee. "His mother was becoming unbearable. Bless her, she really is great, but at the end of the day I'm getting what I want whether I have a big wedding or a small one."

"Good for you, Soph," he had grinned. "How does it feel, not being in control?"

"Shut up, you." She'd returned his smile, glowing beautifully. "This is it, Lo. I'm about to become a married woman."

"I'm very happy for you. You deserve it."

"Yeah, I do." Sophie had peered at him curiously, as if truly seeing him for the first time. "It's so weird, you being back here. You don't belong here anymore, you know?"

His heart had skipped a painful beat. "You think so?"

"I know so," she'd answered. "Don't get me wrong, we all miss you beyond words, but we know that it's for your highest good. That's what makes it bearable. Your face, whenever you're on the field... Damn, Lo, it's so clear you're doing what you love."

"I never really allowed myself to imagine what it would be like. Now that I'm living it, I can't come back for good."

"Glad to hear it." She had reached for his hand, giving it a squeeze. "Are you ready to see Alyssa?"

Back in the present, Logan knew that nothing could've prepared him for the sight of Alyssa on another man's arm.

She looked beautiful in a midnight blue, figure-hugging mini dress, her lilac hair in a respectable bun at the nape of her neck. He's never seen it so long before, and it suited her even better than the pixie cuts he was used to. The silver-studded platforms heels on her feet reminded him of her piercings, the symbols of her rebellious streak.

When those deep brown eyes connected with his, time stood still. How was it possible for her to have this effect on him, after everything? Why did every time feel like the first, and why was it so impossible to imagine a future without her?

She whispered something to Jake and then they were walking straight to Logan. He braced himself for impact, not sure what to expect.

"Logan," she greeted warmly.

"Alyssa."

A small eternity passed between their unblinking stares, broken by Jake's self-conscious cough.

"Man, it is so good meeting you in person," Jake said as he held his hand out to Logan. "I'm such a huge fan."

"Good to finally meet you, Jake." Logan's professional smile was in place while they shook hands. He did his best not to size the man up, seeing as his testosterone levels were spiking.

Jake came across as a chilled, surfer type. He was attractive and seemed as if nothing could faze him. Happy-go-lucky, like Alyssa was. On the surface, they were a good match. Underneath it all, however, Logan failed to see the depth that would keep them together, long-term.

That observation may be influenced by your jealousy.

"Wow, you've told him about me?" Jake asked Alyssa.

"Of course," she answered.

"Thanks, babe. Are you ready for the World Cup?"

"Not sure if I'm on the team yet, so I'm trying not to think about it."

"They would be stupid not to pick you! I mean, this last season you've been bloody brilliant and…"

Logan nodded politely as Jake rattled off Logan's latest statistics and accomplishments, unable to keep his eyes off Alyssa. He was relieved to note that she had a similar dilemma: it was the same kind of look they'd given each other at the airport, at the train station, at that café in—

"Logan!"

The spell was broken at the sound of Connor's shout. Logan glanced to the side to see the best man pushing through the crowd waiting outside of the church.

"It's time!" Connor announced once he stopped. He gave Alyssa a quick, sideways hug. "Hey, gorgeous. Jake, how's it hangin'?"

"All good, man," Jake laughed as he bumped his fist to Connor's. "See you out there!"

Connor basically dragged Logan to the front of the church. Logan was only an honorary groomsman and didn't really need to be a part of the festivities, but Sophie had insisted and, wanting to keep his bride happy, Max had conceded.

From this vantage point, Logan could see the guests as they began filling the church. A sense of déjà vu overcame him when he spotted Luca rushing down the aisle to sit next to Jesse. The lavender dress she wore highlighted the strange hue of her eyes and showed more skin than usual, although it still had a conservative neck and hemline.

She had been happy to see him, which he hadn't expected. She'd even jumped into his arms the second he'd stepped over the threshold. Now that the Falcons had been dealt with, it's as if a weight has lifted off her shoulders. His feelings for her were as visceral as they'd ever been, although her being on the cusp of eighteen wasn't helping him figure out if it was only lust or love: no matter what went on in his heart, he couldn't act on it. Plus, she was technically family.

Were these forbidden aspects part of the appeal? Or did he have real feelings for her?

"All rise," the officiant announced, snapping him back to the present.

The music began playing and the bridesmaids sashayed towards the front. Alyssa was the last of them, which explained the matching-colored dresses the ladies wore, although that's where the similarities ended: each garment was designed and tailored for the various body types of Sophie's friends. Logan suspected aunt Piper was behind that fashion choice.

And then, at long last, Sophie appeared.

She was elegant and graceful in a strapless, mermaid-style gown covered in delicate, creamy lace. Her blonde hair cascaded down her bare shoulders. She clutched a pink bouquet in front of her and took steady steps all the way to the altar, her gaze fixed on Max. Up close, Logan could see she'd opted for minimal makeup. Her blue eyes sparkled, framed by thick black lashes, and her lips were a soft pink.

Once upon a time, Logan had entertained the notion of being the man Sophie deserved. But now, watching true love unfold in front of him, he could finally see how right he'd been to insist on friendship, even when he'd been tempted to turn it into something more out of sheer loneliness. *This* was what he wanted for himself, too.

"You may be seated."

The ceremony went off without a hitch and included plenty of tearful, heartfelt moments. The bride and groom said, "I do", and then rushed outside to the sound of jubilant cheers. The guests trailed behind them, each trying to catch a glimpse of the happy couple, and eventually got into their cars or on their motorcycles to drive to the reception.

The expected program unfolded there: the parents of the bride and groom made anecdotes about their life going forward, the best man maid of honor, Connor and Alyssa, delivered speeches that were entertaining, and the couple opened the dance floor.

Logan sat next to his own mother, holding her hand. *One day soon, that will be me. I can feel it.*

Or it could be more wishful thinking on his part, considering he was single and the only romantic prospects he was interested in weren't viable.

He saw Alyssa sitting with Jake and rose to his feet. She looked up when he was about halfway to her, and those soulful eyes widened slightly. He could see the understanding light up her face and he fought a smile when she gave him a slight nod.

She knew what he was going to ask. Better yet, she wanted it.

"Oh hey," Jake smiled once he noticed Logan approach.

"Why aren't you two dancing?"

"It's not really our thing."

"Do you mind if I dance with Lys, Jake?"

"You good with that, babe?" Jake asked her. When she dipped her head, Jake's face brightened even more, if such a thing were possible. "Have fun, kids!"

Logan held out his hand, shivering once Alyssa's slid onto it. He hoped to God that he was keeping the excitement off his face and out of his posture while he led her to the dance floor. He held his breath as he turned to take her in his arms.

"I can't believe I'm letting you do this again," she teased.

He began swaying them to the beat, keeping as respectable of a distance between their bodies as his conscience would allow. "Face it, Betty: you've always wanted to dance with me."

"Busted."

"I'm curious," he murmured, glancing at Jake for a moment, "what *is* your thing? The two of you?"

"We bonded over aliens and conspiracy theories, actually."

"That checks out."

"Hey!" She smacked his chest with a laugh. Slowly, she became somber, staring up at him in open curiosity. "Are all the rumors about you and those supermodels true?"

"I haven't been with anyone since the airport." He winced, remembering. "Well, until a week ago."

She raised an eyebrow. "What happened a week ago?"

"Max's bachelor party."

"Why did you wait so long?"

"It wasn't on purpose. It… kinda worked out that way."

"So, you haven't been in a relationship?"

"No."

She let out a humorless laugh and broke eye contact. "That doesn't make me feel better."

"Why not?"

"I don't like thinking of you feeling lonely."

"I'm not." The next song was slower in tempo and Logan shifted his hand to the arch in her lower back. She hissed a breath, making him frown. "What?"

"I'm just so aware of you, all the time. It freaks me out."

He fell silent, inwardly knowing that he should've never asked her to dance, but not caring enough about the consequences. She leaned her head on his chest while they gently shuffled in the middle of the floor, mostly shielded by the other couples around them. It was as if they were sealed off from the rest of the world.

Logan savored the moment, inhaling her citrusy scent all the way to his core. He got the sense that this was only the beginning: their previous encounters were preludes but *this*, right here, was the start of their story. How it will unfold remained to be seen.

"Ladies and gentlemen, it's time for the throwing of the garter!"

The announcement cut into their private moment and Alyssa stepped to the side. Logan rubbed the back of his head as he turned to join the ritual. He wasn't a fan of some of the lewd jokes, especially considering there was family around, but he also wasn't going to judge Sophie and Max for choosing to go through with this.

Max got the garter off her slender leg—she did a great job hiding everything from the knee upward from prying eyes—and shifted to the men who'd gathered round. He pulled his arm back before slinging the garter into the crowd. He'd gone long, which was why it reached Logan, who was standing all the way at the back.

Logan blinked at the garter: hooked around the corsage pinned to his jacket. He hadn't caught it consciously or even voluntarily, but it confirmed his prediction that he would get married soon.

"There you have it, folks! The eligible bachelor and superstar athlete, Logan Drummond, is the next bull to the slaughter," the MC joked. "Now, let's see who his bride might be!"

If anything, that announcement incited the single ladies. They huddled together behind Sophie, who yelled funny quips while she prepared to throw.

Logan watched as if outside of himself. The bouquet lifted into the air in slow motion, travelling over desperate hands and landing in a set that had multiple silver rings stacked on long, delicate fingers. Hands that Logan knew all too well.

"The maid of honor herself, folks! Alyssa Edgar!"

Their eyes found each other's from across the floor. His heart stopped beating while he waited to see what she would do: laugh it off, or come to him?

Connor interrupted by bumping into Logan with a tipsy laugh. "Man, it's not fair! There shouldn't be any professionals when the garter is tossed!"

"If you wanted that thing off your sister so bad..." Dane trailed off with an edgy grin.

"Oh, come on! Don't be gross! I just want to marry my girl!"

"Then ask her, you idiot," Logan's cousin snorted. "There's no need to be so dramatic."

"It would've been romantic!"

"You should really think about why you're buying into all of these rituals, Con."

Logan zoned out the banter between his friend and cousin, looking around. He's lost sight of Alyssa but sensed that something was wrong. Jake was cracking jokes with a handful of men off to one side, oblivious to his girlfriend's exchange with Logan, or her departure.

"Excuse me," he muttered, heading out of the venue. The last time the two of them were here, she'd left: he couldn't let that happen again. He found her in the garden, standing at a large fountain and looking as if she was hyperventilating. His protective side kicked in as he rushed to her side. "Alyssa, are you okay?"

"No!" Her teary gaze met his with one hand pressed to her chest. The other clutched the bouquet. "I'm not okay, Logan! I feel like I'm dying."

"Do you want me to take you to the hospital?"

"*No!*" she exclaimed, shaking the flowers like they held the answers.

It dawned on him that she was working through the same conflicting emotions he was. He moved forward and placed his hands over the one she had on her heart, waiting for her to look at him.

"We're not in a hurry, Betty."

"W-we're not?"

"No, we have all the time in the world."

She sniffed as she tilted her head back. "I just... I don't know how this works. I don't know how to make this work for us."

"A long time ago, this girl I know told me she wanted to leave it up to fate."

"Did she?" Alyssa choked on a laugh. "She doesn't sound like she knows what the fuck she's talking about."

"She definitely does," he murmured, pulling her into his embrace.

She cried into his chest while locking her arms around him. "I love him, Logan."

"I know."

"It's not going to last."

"I know."

"I don't know what to do."

He closed his eyes and stroked her back, grateful that she was calming down. "You don't have to do anything, Betty. Just let it play out. Who knows? We may be wrong about us."

She gripped his jacket, as if afraid he would leave right now. "I don't want us to be."

"Then at least you know you'll always have a backup plan."

"I don't want you to be a backup plan, asshole!"

He chuckled, his chest vibrating against hers. "Fuck, Lys, I miss you every goddamn day."

"Logan," she sighed wistfully.

He bent to lean his forehead on hers. They stood like that, as close as two people could be with clothes on, until her sobs subsided and her body relaxed. He cupped her face in his hands and smiled.

"Feeling better?"

She nodded. "Thank you."

"Ready to go back?"

"Yeah."

Shrugging his jacket off, he draped it over her shoulders and walked next to her as they meandered to the venue. No one seemed to have noticed their brief disappearance, which was just as well. The last thing either of them needed was an inquisition.

She turned to him as they stopped at her table. "Soon," she promised.

A chill went down his spine as he echoed the word she'd spoken in that dream, a week ago. The same word she'd uttered now: "Soon."

He turned on his heel and strode to his family, vowing that he would have fun for the rest of the evening. He had a renewed sense of hope regarding Alyssa: he didn't know when their paths would cross again, only that they would.

And when they did, there would be no holding back.

CHAPTER TWENTY-TWO

LOGAN WAS OUT of breath and drenched as he walked into the house. He'd spent the last two hours out on a run: mostly to stay fit enough for the upcoming season, but also to shake off his hangover. The recent drinking at the bachelor's party and the wedding was not part of his new and improved lifestyle.

He headed to the kitchen for a bottle of water, clapping his dad on the back. "Morning, old man."

"Look who's talking, punk," Byron chuckled.

"Fair." He gulped down the contents of the bottle and grabbed another from the fridge. "It was a cool wedding, huh?"

"I'm surprised you even noticed. You were all up in Alyssa's business for most of it."

Logan rolled his eyes. "Hardly, but sure."

"What happened there, anyway? I saw you—"

Byron was interrupted by the ring of Logan's phone. Logan glanced at his watch and tapped on a wireless earphone to answer. "Andries, hey."

"Hi, Logan. I don't know what time it is over there. Has the wedding already happened?"

"Yeah, it was last night," Logan chuckled. "Is everything okay? What can

I do for you?"

"Well, I asked coach if I could be the one to tell you, and he agreed."

Logan paused, heart racing. "Tell me what?"

"You're on the FIFA team."

"So, when you said coach, you mean—"

"The one and only Petri Hollinger."

"Holy fucking shit!" Logan didn't care that his outburst attracted his father's raised eyebrows. "Are you for real?"

"I am," Andries laughed. "Marcus is probably emailing you as we speak."

Logan took his phone out of his pocket and tapped on the screen, his butterflies exploding once he saw Marcus' email confirming Andries' claims. "He already did."

"See? You're on the FIFA team. More than that: you're making your debut, my friend."

"Holy shit, wow." Logan couldn't really concentrate on the words on the screen, and the multiple incoming messages of congratulations from team members and new friends weren't helping. "Thanks for the call, Andries."

"Sure thing. We'll chat again later?"

"You bet. Bye."

Logan put the vibrating phone on the counter and turned to his father, who had unabashed curiosity in his eyes. "I made the Netherlands team for the World Cup."

"Oh my fuck, Logan!" Byron tightly embraced his son, laughing joyfully. "Well done, punk! Congratulations!" A scream from upstairs had them both pulling back in alarm, but once they heard Cinnia rushing down Byron relaxed. "She has your name set as a Google alert on her phone," he explained mere seconds before his wife burst into the kitchen.

"That's a bit terrifying," Logan muttered, thinking of some of the rumors she must've seen.

"Oh my God, oh my God," Cinnia chanted as she jumped into Logan's arms. She had thankfully donned a T-shirt and sweatpants before coming downstairs: her and Byron were known to sleep in the nude. "I can't believe it! I can't fucking believe it!"

"Jeez, thanks mom," he teased.

"I didn't mean it like that, boy!" She smacked his shoulder as she stood back on her own feet. "I just can't believe one of *us*—" She broke off once the waterworks started. "I'm so proud of you, Logan!"

He hugged her again. "Thank you."

"We *have* to celebrate this news!" She kissed his cheek and started checking something on her phone. "Looks like everyone already knows. Should we do a barbecue at the club?"

"Ma, calm down. I'm here for at least another four weeks."

Byron tilted his head to the side. "Will you have to go back earlier?"

"Maybe. I'll check with Marcus."

"Even more reason to do this as soon as possible," Cinnia insisted. "I'll get the girls to help out."

Logan sighed. "I know I can't stop you."

"Congratulations, Logan."

He spotted Luca hovering at the kitchen threshold and smiled. "Thanks, Luca."

"You're going to be even more famous now," she added, those violet eyes sparkling.

He rubbed the back of his neck, unintentionally catching a whiff of his armpits. He desperately needed a shower. "Not looking forward to that part." He touched his mother's shoulder. "Please don't go overboard with the celebration: people are still recovering from the wedding."

Byron snorted. "Like that's gonna stop her."

Cinnia narrowed her eyes. "Okay, I'll show you overboard."

Shaking his head with a laugh, Logan headed to the staircase, squeezing past Luca on the way. He thought he saw interest in her gaze, but that might just be his imagination. Besides, if he was going to try something with her, it definitely wouldn't happen with his parents around.

She's not eighteen yet. Let it go.

The shower was refreshing, exactly what he needed. He got dressed and returned to the kitchen to get breakfast, halting once he saw that Luca was manning the stove by herself.

"Where'd my parents go?" he asked.

"They went out for breakfast with Jemma and Nixon. I think it's a post-wedding type of thing," she shrugged. "Would you like some bacon and eggs?"

"Sounds great, thanks."

He checked his phone while he made a protein smoothie, giving Marcus' email his full attention. His manager had included a proposed schedule for the games Logan would be playing. He would be on the field for the first, which was both nerve-wracking and exciting.

Luca dished for them, and they sat down at the breakfast nook to eat.

"How's school going?" he asked conversationally.

"Fine. Cheering is keeping me busy."

He still couldn't believe she was a cheerleader. "How did that happen, by the way?"

"Dr. McKauley said it'll help with my trust issues," she responded, smiling wryly.

"Has it?"

"To an extent."

"That's great."

The sound of cutlery clinking against plates filled the silence, not that Logan minded. He was distracted by Marcus' comms. From the look of it, he'll have to fly back to Amsterdam two weeks earlier to start training with the Netherlands team. Andries was the captain there, as well, which is probably why he'd decided to give Logan a heads-up first.

This will change everything. Are you ready?

"I'm actually struggling with boys."

Logan froze, not certain that he'd heard correctly. "What?"

She sipped on her coffee, watching him intently. "The trust-thing. I'm good with the club and my friends, mom and dad… But it's tough with boys."

"In what way?"

"I can't seem to relax when I'm on a date," she admitted softly. "Dr. McKauley says it's normal, but I… I think there's something wrong with me."

"Luca, there isn't anything wrong with you."

"Then why can't I take it when a guy wants to hold my hand or… or kiss me?"

"You've had a rough past. It's going to take time. But isn't this something you'd rather chat to my mom about?"

"Gosh, no." She tucked her hair behind her ears with a soft laugh. "Mom's amazing, but she can be a bit…"

"Meddling?" he suggested when she trailed off.

She grimaced. "Does it make me a bad person for thinking that?"

"It makes you an observant person," he chuckled.

Her smile was absolutely breathtaking. "I've been meaning to talk to you about this. I know it's very presumptuous, but I..." She inhaled deeply. "I was wondering if you'd do to me what you've done to Nina."

His brain shut down, and he could do nothing but stare at her.

"You remember Nina, right?" Luca asked, incorrectly interpreting his silence. "The blonde girl that you... You know, the day after your—"

"I know who Nina is," he interjected, his tone clipped. He placed his hand over his mouth when she seemed to take offense at him being curt. "Sorry. Go on."

"Well, see, everyone my age is having sex."

What the fuck?!

He gulped down half of his smoothie, mostly to stall while he thought of something to say. Was this how his mom had felt, way back when *they'd* had this chat? "That doesn't mean you have to. You're not even eighteen yet, Luca. You still have time."

"I want to."

"Oh...kay. Why are you telling *me* this? Do you like someone?" He inwardly cursed her silence when she only inclined her head. She seemed to have lost her nerve. "What's the problem, then?"

"I don't want to ruin things."

"What makes you think you will?"

"When boys take me out, I keep wondering when they'll—" She broke off abruptly, and took a while to gather herself. "Will they hit me? Will they rape me? Will I deserve it?"

Logan leaned forward, maintaining eye contact. "Any decent man won't, but I understand why you think that. What happened to you... No one should ever have to go through that. You don't deserve being treated that way."

"I want to be over it."

"Sweetheart, I don't know if you will ever be one hundred percent over it. You know that my mom was beaten up by a bunch of men, and I know there are times when she relives those memories. The first step is letting someone in and taking a leap of faith. More often than not, you'll be rewarded."

"That's why I'm talking to you."

He tilted his head to the side, waiting for her to finish. Was this going where he suspected it would?

"Will you help me?" She hesitated briefly. "I think something like what you did with Nina will work."

"Luca—"

"Only if you want to," she interrupted quickly. "If you don't, well, do you know someone who would?"

How was this happening for a second time? Had the situation with Fitz and Nina prepared Logan for this moment? Or did he give off some sort of vibe that made people want to use his BDSM knowledge? Use *him*?

Alyssa doesn't, a voice reminded him.

"Why are you pushing this?"

"I want to have sex and enjoy it. I want to feel a man's hands on my body and not get flashbacks to what others have done to me. I don't want to be broken."

He let out a short breath and raked his fingers through his hair. "Why me, Luca?"

She lifted her shoulders, as if the answer was obvious. "I trust you."

Rendered speechless, he continued to ogle her as if she's grown a second head. He couldn't believe that this was happening. Before he'd met Alyssa, he might've jumped at the opportunity to have sex with Luca. Heck, he had often fantasized about this very conversation!

She's young. She doesn't need to make this decision now. Plus, she's your stepsister now!

"That's huge," he said finally.

"I can't imagine doing this with someone else, Logan. Please say yes."

"There's a lot of planning that goes into a BDSM relationship, Luca."

"I know, I did research."

That momentarily took the wind out of his sails. He tried a different angle: "You'll have to submit completely."

"I can try. Does that mean you'll do it?"

Fuck yes!

"I..." He reached for the smoothie again. What should he say in this situation? "Can I think about it?"

"Of course." Luca smiled broadly, which lit up her entire face. "If you agree, can we do it before you leave for the World Cup?"

Jesus fucking Christ, he thought, wishing that his parents were here to stop this madness. Wishing that he'd already said yes so he could bend her over this table and fuck her silly.

"If it's still what you want, by then," he said finally.

"Thanks for considering it, Logan." She turned shy, knocking his defenses down when she added: "And for not making me feel messed up."

"You're not, Luca." He briefly rested his hand on hers, setting off sparks in his bloodstream. "You should never feel ashamed of your desires." He tilted his head, teasing. "Unless they're malicious, of course."

She burst out laughing. "Yeah, I think I know what *not* to do."

Her laughter happened so rarely that he sat staring at her, enthralled. He's always hoped that she would evolve into a confident woman, and it was remarkable seeing her blossom. He might've been living a completely different life for the last two years, but that didn't mean that he was a different person. He still wanted her.

Badly, his sex drive piped up.

Clearing her throat, she asked: "Why would you do this?"

He got to his feet, eager to take a ride to clear his head. "I don't trust a random stranger to do right by you."

"Right." With a frown, she followed suit, staring at her feet. "So it's not because you... I mean, do you find me attractive?"

There were layers to Luca's question and, to set her mind at ease, he decided to lay it all on the line. "You're a beautiful girl, Luca, and I am attracted to you, but I'm worried that you're too young for this. That you should wait for someone you love."

"I do love you, Logan."

His lungs ceased functioning and, once again, he was convinced this was a dream.

"I consider you a good friend," she went on. "I wouldn't have asked if I didn't."

Friend.

He shook himself and nodded, breaking eye contact. "I'll let you know when... You know." Feeling awkward as hell, he basically fled to the front door, grabbing the keys to the Blackline. His breathing didn't quite return to normal until he was on the road, the steady vibrations of the motorcycle calming him.

What the fuck just happened?

In the span of one conversation, he got everything he's ever wanted from

Luca. It's something that could change his life forever—and *would,* hers—and alter the probability of being with Alyssa. Already, he could sense other possibilities grow.

Slow down.

Luca was almost done with high school, which meant that she was probably ready to move somewhere else to further her studies. What if she came to live with him, and enrolled at the University of Amsterdam? He could pull a few strings to get her in. He wasn't the biggest celebrity, but his success at Ajax must mean something.

Slow down!

Or they could try long-distance dating at first, if Amsterdam is too much too soon for her. So far, it's not like he's been tempted by the women that threw themselves at him all the time. If not for Max's bachelor party, Alyssa would've remained the last woman he'd had sex with, and—

Logan, slow the fuck down!

He snapped out of his thoughts, realizing that he was way over the speed limit, and applied brakes. Riding while this distracted would only lead to trouble. He had to get it together before he forced himself out of the FIFA World Cup.

You're getting ahead of yourself, a voice he's come to associate with Brennan warned him. *Take it one moment at a time. There are no guarantees.*

With that internal pep talk behind him, he decided to take a ride out to the Raptors' picnic point. He always thought more clearly when he was surrounded by nature, and he hasn't been to the lake since he got back.

It was just as beautiful as he remembered.

He sat at the water's edge for hours, meditating and staring at his surroundings. His mother phoned at around lunch time to find out where he was, and he promised that he would be back long before the celebrations started at the clubhouse. On his way home, he stopped for a healthy meal at a diner that was owned by Ryan.

He was the only one in the house when he got back. He changed into exercise clothes and went to the gym, eager to continue his usual routine. He spoke to a few of his team members along the way, glad that most of them were happy for him. Secretly he was a bit concerned being at FIFA so young, but he had to trust that the Petri Hollinger knew what he was doing.

When he was back in his childhood bedroom, he caught up on emails and the new contract that needed to be signed. Marcus had thankfully already gone through it and tagged the places that needed his attention, but Logan asked Byron to read it as well, just in case.

"It's pretty standard," Byron concluded once he finished. "There are severe restrictions to prevent injuries before and during the Cup, which is understandable. And whatever campaigns your sponsors want to do during this time need to be run by them first."

Logan nodded. "That is standard."

"It's a lot of money, Lo." Byron shook his head with a laugh as he handed Logan's laptop back. "It boggles the brain."

"I guess football's a pretty big deal overseas," Logan teased. He lifted a shoulder in faux nonchalance. "It's fitting, seeing as I'll only be able to play for about fifteen years."

"Have you considered some of the investments I sent you?"

"Yeah, there are a few that will fit my 'brand', as Marcus calls it. After the Cup, I want to start buying property."

"I think the Cup is going to bring other clubs to your doorstep."

"For now, I'm happy to stay at Ajax."

"Even when Everton gives you a better offer?"

Logan hesitated. Moments like these, he could barely believe that this was his life. When did he get so lucky?

You worked your fucking ass off. You deserve it.

"I might reconsider then, but I'm not going to count my chickens before they hatch."

Cinnia appeared in the doorway. "Ready to go?"

"Just about," Byron chuckled as he got up. "Logan needs to celebrate how rich being in the World Cup is going to make him."

"I worry about that ego," Cinnia remarked, patting Logan on the cheek when he passed.

Logan burst out laughing. "You'll keep me in check, momma."

"You better believe it."

Luca joined them in the driveway, and they all got into the SUV to drive to the club. Logan sat at the front with Byron, trying to ignore that Luca was right behind him. He could feel the sexual tension pulse between them. In that moment, his decision was made.

The number of vehicles at *Drummond's Customs & Repairs* blew Logan's mind, especially considering Sophie's wedding had been the day before. The Raptors were showing up to support him: it was incredibly touching.

He walked into the warehouse first, overwhelmed by the congratulations, love and warmth that everyone sent his way. He wasn't surprised when they started chanting for him to give a speech, and jumped on a nearby table to elevate himself so that he could see them all.

"Two years ago, this seemed like a pipe dream," Logan started, tears burning his eyes. "I left here an absolute wreck, thinking that I've made a mistake. I'm a Drummond, you know? My place should be here."

His gaze landed on his grandparents. The pride in their facial expressions choked him up.

"Every day, even now, it seems inevitable that I'll lose everything I've worked for. I sometimes feel like such an imposter when I'm on the field. I feel like one right now, talking to you. I wonder if I can even call myself a Raptor anymore." He caught Connor's eye and smiled. "But your Prez reminded me that I'll always be part of this family, no matter what. That's what pushes me every time I feel like giving up: your support is what drives me. Thank you so much for being here!"

They erupted in cheers and whistles as he jumped down to hug or shake hands with each of them. He soaked up the praise and spent the next hour making sure he was available to every person that wanted to wish him good luck.

At the end of the long line was Luca, beaming at him. She wore tight black jeans and a baggy *Nirvana* crop top. Her dark hair was tucked over one shoulder, down to her waist. That bronze hue to her skin made her seem like she was glowing from within, and those eyes...

She was impossibly beautiful. A siren.

Mine, for however long she'll have me.

He grabbed her hand and marched away from the festivities, from the constant surveillance. He led her into a storeroom, shutting the door behind him and flicking the lights on.

"Are you okay?" she asked, eyes wide.

"What's your safe word?"

"Snow." Her ready answer confirmed that she has, indeed, researched the BDSM lifestyle.

"Do you know what your limits are?"

She swallowed thickly. "Does this mean you'll do it?"

"Yes, if that's what you want."

She took a step closer to him. "I don't know what my limits are, yet. Can't I just tell you when I'm uncomfortable?"

"Fair enough. Are you on birth control?"

"Yes."

"Are you clean?"

"Jemma did all sorts of tests when you found me, and they all came back negative. I haven't been with anyone since."

He flexed his fingers before he began circling her, feeling like a predator sizing up its prey. He noted that she was fidgeting nervously and wondered if it was because she's excited or concerned. Facing her again, he lifted his hand to her cheek and waited to see how she'll react.

Other than her lips parting, she didn't balk: a far cry from when he'd found her.

"Luca," Logan murmured, tilting her chin up to kiss her. She gasped as her mouth returned his passion. He thrust his tongue inside, over two years' worth of hunger taking the steer. He wanted to fuck her until she screamed.

Not tonight.

He became aware of her palms pressing against his chest and pulled back to gaze at her. He half-expected to hear the safe word. When it didn't happen, he warned: "I'm going to push you, Luca. By the time I'm through with you, you won't remember the bad things. When I do *this*—" His hands gripped her ass and pulled her closer. "—you'll know it's because I want to fuck you *with* your consent. You'll even want me to."

Her body went rigid as she squirmed to get out of his embrace.

He could see the panic in her eyes, but she needed to learn to trust him on a sexual level if this had any chance of working. "Let go, Luca." Squeezing her eyes shut, she strained her arms to keep him at bay, but he stood his ground. He shifted his mouth to her ear. "Sweetheart, let go."

She went from one extreme to the next, her arms passively dropping to her sides like she expected the worst. When he didn't move, she peeked at him.

"Good girl," he praised, a smile twitching at the corners of his mouth. He massaged her ass with one hand and tilted her head back with the other. "If you keep this up, you'll get a reward."

His lips touched her neck, exploring the length of it. She trembled as his tongue joined in, licking his way up and down her skin. He sensed her knees weakening when he began nibbling and used the hand on her ass to steady her, slowly turning to push her against a nearby storage rack.

She moved her head to the side, the softest noise coming out of her mouth.

He slithered the hand clutching the back of her head lower, to the dip of her waist, to shift underneath the crop top. His fingers stroked her stomach while his mouth continued to tease her neck and then, inch by inch, went further up. He anchored her against the rack by grinding his crotch into her stomach, while getting both his hands on her tits.

She inhaled sharply when he impatiently pulled her bra cups down to tweak her hard nipples. "Oh!"

"Oh?" he repeated, rubbing his thumbs over the peaks. "Do you like that, Luca?"

"Yes."

Fuck, hearing that made him so hard. But he knew he wasn't going to get his fill: tonight, it was all about her.

He lifted her shirt over her head and stared at her full breasts in his hands. "You're so sexy, sweetheart." He pushed them together and bent to get his mouth on her nipples, sucking and biting each one in turn. He halted when she grabbed the back of his head. "Let go, Luca. Hold onto the shelf."

Shivering, she obeyed.

Pleased, he continued giving her tits attention, loving the way her skin became reddened, and how her inhibitions began lowering. While sucking one of her nipples, he dropped his hands to the button of her jeans to unzip them. She jerked when his hand pushed beneath her panties, and he nipped her tit in response.

"Ah!" she panted, her hips rocking ever so slightly.

He smiled against her flesh when he felt that her bush was trimmed neatly: she'd probably shaved not long after he said he would consider doing this. His fingertips painstakingly slowly traveled down her seam, before parting her labia.

She was soaked through already.

"Hmm, such a naughty girl," he growled as he raised his head to look into her eyes. All the while, his fingertips took turns pressing against her entrance, one after the other. "Your pussy is so wet, Luca. Have you ever been wet before?"

She bit her full bottom lip and nodded, her cheeks going red.

"When?"

"Sometimes, when I think of you, I get... wet."

He pushed the first knuckle of his forefinger into her, chuckling darkly when she gasped again. "When do you think of me?"

"When I'm alone."

"Really?" His finger slipped deeper inside. "What do you do when you're alone and you think of me?"

She blinked at him. "Do?"

"Yes, Luca, *do*." He went in all the way, wishing it was his cock, before retreating to add a second finger. He wondered if she was even aware that her hips were getting more aggressive in their quest to seek friction. "Do you touch yourself when you think of me?"

"No," she whimpered.

"Next time you're alone and you think of me, you're going to take off all your clothes." He bit the side of her neck and soothed the sting with his tongue, his fingers vigorously fucking her. "You're going to get on the bed, spread your legs and touch yourself like this." He pushed his thumb against her clit, drawing circles on that sensitive bundle of nerves. "Do you hear me?"

"Y-yes."

"Will you touch yourself like this?" Logan asked, squeezing her nipple with his free hand. She was so close: did she know? "And think of me fucking you while you do?"

"Yes!" she cried out.

Logan crushed their mouths together, kissing her while she exploded. The feel of her clenching around his fingers drove him wild. He leaned back to gaze into her fluttering eyes. "Have you ever had an orgasm before?"

Luca shook her head in answer, panting.

"I'm honored to be your first." He lifted the fingers that had brought her pleasure to his mouth, licking up her cream. "You taste really good. I can't wait to bury my face in your pussy."

"You say such dirty things," she breathed.

"Stay tuned." He winked at her while he zipped her up, righted her bra and reached for the discarded top.

She took it with a frown. "Didn't you want to…?"

"That was a lot of fun for me, Luca," he replied, pressing his lips to her forehead. "Are you okay?"

Nodding, she pulled the shirt over her head.

"Good. I'm not sure when next we'll be able to do this, what with school and both of us staying at home, but at least you know what to expect."

"Thank you, Logan, for… teaching me."

He gave her a tight smile, reminded that she only saw him as a friend. "This is just the beginning."

CHAPTER TWENTY-THREE

FOR THE NEXT week, Logan could only focus on two things: training for the FIFA World Cup and getting Luca alone.

If his parents noticed the untoward, lecherous looks exchanged between Logan and Luca, they didn't mention anything. He tried to convince himself that it wasn't so bad, being attracted to someone who wasn't yet eighteen. Someone who'd been gang raped just two years ago. Someone who was technically his stepsister.

That technicality only seemed to heighten his desire. Besides, she wasn't biologically related to any of them, and he couldn't be placed in the same category as a groomer because he hasn't been around to do something so cruel. She'd consented to his attention; in fact, she was the driving force of this dirty, exciting affair.

The familiar obsession was reignited, and his mind did crazy acrobatics to make the situation okay.

With her still being in school and both of them living with his parents, they didn't get many chances to themselves. When they did, he made it all about her, mostly to figure out how she liked to be kissed, touched. He focused on her erogenous zones, only satisfied when she whimpered and made a mess of his fingers or face. He aimed to see her eyes glazed over and didn't stop until that happened.

He wasn't as successful hiding from his friends.

Connor and Dane were making an effort to keep Logan motivated and physically on track for the World Cup, even though they found it difficult to keep up with his advanced exercise regime. They were out on a run one morning when Dane noticed that Logan was distracted.

"Luca?" Dane asked in that matter of fact, straight-to-the-point way of his.

Logan huffed out a breath and slowed his trot. "I don't know what you're talking about."

Dane shook his head. "She's always had this effect on you."

Connor snorted, but kept quiet, which pissed him off. "Is there something you want to say to my face, Prez?"

"You have a deeper connection than this with someone else, remember?"

Turning away from them, Logan clenched his jaw. "She's with Jake."

"What?" Connor blinked. "No, you—"

"Con, back up," Dane warned, exchanging a look with Connor before he came to a standstill next to Logan. They were silent for a while, catching their breaths. "Look, cuz, you can do what you want with whomever consents—"

"Thanks," Logan said sarcastically.

"—but just stay grounded," Dane went on. "Don't get obsessed."

Logan recalled his conversation with his gran, years ago, when she'd explained Brennan's single-mindedness where Cinnia had been concerned. Logan knew he had a tendency to act like his biological father in that regard and did his best to balance it with the lessons Byron had taught him.

Dane clapped Logan on the back. "You need to let this play out or you'll always wonder about her and fuck up any chance you have at happiness with someone else. But don't forget who you are in the process."

"And who am I?"

"Logan Bean Drummond, superstar athlete and okay-looking man," Connor piped up, only half-kidding. He smiled broadly when Logan rolled his eyes. "For real, though, you know who you are by now, so just remember that when you're balls-deep in Luca."

"Fuck, Tyrell," Dane muttered, "your pep talk sucks."

"It's still way better than yours, Sloane," Connor chuckled. "You've got it bad for Misty, after all."

Logan was eager to change the subject. "Who's Misty?"

"One of my patients."

Raising an eyebrow at Dane's red cheeks, Logan said: "Tell me more."

The three of them broke into a jog again and Dane did what he could to bring Logan up to speed. His cousin's romantic interest was a girl with a bad heart and an upcoming operation. Connor, her surgeon—and broadening his role to love guru—believed that Dane and Misty were destined.

Logan listened raptly, even as his mind wandered back to Luca. He was grateful for their advice on the matter, but didn't feel like they understood how badly he wanted this to work. He would do just about anything. That's why he found himself making a booking at the fanciest hotel in town later that day.

By the time his mother arrived home, he'd already devised the perfect way to get Luca alone.

"Hey, my boy," Cinnia greeted as she came to sit with him in the living room. "What did you get up to today?"

"Training," he shrugged, eyes fixed on the screen: he was watching a Netherlands match on mute. Although he was used to playing with Andries, the rest of the team were signed to other clubs, and he only knew them socially. He wanted to be fully prepared by the time he got back. "Research."

She shook her head with a soft laugh. "God, that orange is going to look hideous on you."

He chuckled, inwardly agreeing. "I'm going out, by the way. I'll probably sleep over."

"Makes sense: it's Friday. Can you give Luca a ride?"

Careful to keep his facial expression appropriately curious, he asked: "Where to?"

"She's got a party at one of her friends' houses."

It worked, he thought smugly. "Sure. What time?"

His mother checked her watch. "She said she needs to be there in half an hour."

"Okay." He switched the TV off and turned to Cinnia. "Are you and dad making it a date night, now that the kids are out the house?"

She grinned, her emerald-colored eyes sparkling. "You know what? We might just."

"It's really cool that you still feel that way about each other."

"Your dad's my best friend," Cinnia smiled.

Alyssa's mine.

He cleared his throat to distract himself from that line of thinking. "Well, let me go get ready so we can get out of your hair." He kissed his mother's cheek and made his way upstairs. He was about to enter his childhood room when Luca stepped out of the bathroom with a towel wrapped around her.

She bit her bottom lip, her eyes going wide at the sight of him.

His cock became hard just looking at her. Her hair was damp, and that bronze skin glistened from the shower. So far, it seemed she was dutifully following the instructions he'd sent to her phone.

His ears strained as he listened for his mother's movements: it sounded like she was in the kitchen. Logan crossed the distance to Luca and pushed her against the wall, tilting her chin up to claim her mouth. His free hand went under the towel to cup her pussy, and he growled under his breath when he felt smooth skin. She had shaven, like he'd asked.

"I'm fucking you tonight," he whispered against her lips as he stared into her violet eyes. "Tell me now if you want that."

"I want that."

"Good." He gave her a chaste kiss and stepped back. "Go get dressed." He turned on his heel and walked to his bedroom, immediately reaching for the bag he'd packed in preparation to make sure he had everything: condoms, lubricant, rope, some sex toys and a blindfold. He added a set of clothes for the morning, as well as his toiletry bag, and then headed downstairs.

His phone rang as he was shrugging his Raptors leather jacket on, and he checked his watch before answering. "Marcus, hey."

"How's it going? I checked your stats, and you made good time today. Coach is impressed by your dedication."

"I don't want to fuck up my chances." His heart skipped a beat. "Did I?"

"Of course not," Marcus chuckled. "They're eager to get you started. I know you've already cut your trip short, but is there any chance you can come through next week? There are a few formalities and events that you need to attend."

His head was spinning at the thought of making Luca fall for him in an even shorter time frame. "Sure, I'll be there whenever I'm needed."

"Okay, I'll amend your booking and send through the details."

"Thanks, Marcus."

"Enjoy what time you have left there, kid."

Logan hung up and closed his eyes, thinking: *it'll have to be enough. I'll show her how good we can be together. She'll come around.*

"Logan? Ready to go?"

Snapping out of his spiraling thoughts, he glanced up at Luca, who stood at the foot of the stairs. "Yeah."

"Cool." She smiled, taking his breath away, and turned to call over her shoulder. "Bye, mom!"

"Have fun, kids!" Cinnia hollered from the kitchen.

Oh, we will.

Logan held the door open for Luca and watched her hips sway to the Blackline, which was parked in the driveway. He secured their bags in the side panniers and mounted, shivering at the feel of her lithe body getting on behind him. He ignited the engine and backed out, breathing easier once they were on the open road.

This is really happening. Finally.

The hotel was a bustle of activity when they arrived. He was recognized in the foyer and told Luca to go ahead with his credit card while he signed autographs and posed for photos. The longer he was detained, the more people realized who he was, and it took a full seven minutes before he could break away to the elevators, where Luca stood.

She looked at him as they waited for the doors to open. It was absolute torture not being able to take her hand, but they couldn't risk any photographs leaking of them together.

They stepped into an elevator, and he let out a puff of air once the doors closed, sealing them inside. Alone.

"That was… overwhelming," she remarked.

"Are you okay?"

"Yeah, just rattled. Your life is invasive."

"Sorry. Every sport has its injuries."

"Literally," she giggled.

They got out on the top floor and walked to one of the bigger suites at the end of the hallway. Logan scanned the key card, and she went in ahead of him. His adrenaline kicked in once the door clicked shut.

"What now?" she asked.

He took her in from head to toe: she'd played up the high school party act and was wearing tight jeans, a slightly more revealing top than usual and ankle boots. Her makeup was minimal but striking, and she'd braided her long hair over one shoulder.

He had to rein in the urge to pounce. Instead, he walked to the living room and placed their bags on one of the couches. "Take off your clothes."

Seeming nervous, she started with her shoes. She hesitated only briefly once her jeans dropped to the floor, quickly shedding the rest as if she was afraid to lose her nerve. She straightened her spine and bravely met his eyes once she stood in all her naked glory.

Christ almighty.

Her scars have faded to faint white lines on her arms, legs and back, and were the only signs of imperfections. She was beautiful, from head to toe. Logan didn't think she knew what power she held over him. Over men, in general.

"Go get on the bed," he said hoarsely, grabbing a few things from his bag after she disappeared.

Get it together, Logan. Make this good for her.

He marched into the room with a carefully controlled mask, placing the items on one of the side tables and then taking off his jacket, shirt and shoes. He noticed her dark nipples were erect.

"Cold?"

"A little."

"Don't worry, sweetheart. I'll get you warmed up in no time. Arms over your head."

She raised them, wriggling when he began twining the rope around her wrists. He tied it to the headboard, tugging a few times to ensure she couldn't get loose.

"Do you remember your safe word?"

"Snow," she nodded.

"Good girl." He moved around to the other items, aware of her gaze on him. "What?"

"N-nothing."

He clicked his tongue. "This doesn't work if you don't tell me everything you're thinking and feeling."

She swallowed and stared at his collarbones. "You look... hot."

"Yeah?" He grinned, touched by that admission. "Can't wait to hear you beg me to put my cock in you." He briefly clutched his covered package, satisfied when her gaze dipped to the strained material. "And once I'm in your pussy, you're going to beg me to fuck you again, and again, and *again*."

Her knees pressed together. "That's so… filthy."

"I know. Open your legs, Luca."

She shook her head. "I can't."

"Yes, you can. If you don't, I'll flip you around and spank you."

She slowly parted her thighs, gasping when he helped her along by pinning her knees to the bed. "Logan!"

He bent his head and closed his mouth over her dripping sex. "Hmm, so wet, sweetheart," he murmured.

"Ah!"

Unlike the previous times, they didn't have to worry about keeping it down. Logan's tongue swiped over every part of her pussy, licking up her essence until she began twitching. He rolled it over her clit and jabbed it into her hole. He laughed wickedly as her hips sought more friction.

"Stop moving," he warned.

"Logan, please!"

"Please what, sweetheart?"

She stubbornly kept her mouth shut.

"Fine by me." He returned to his open-mouth adoration of her pussy, while reaching for the bullet vibrator he'd purchased earlier. He pushed it inside and held her legs open when she began fighting him. "Don't move." He sat up, pinning her down with his knees. "Time to play."

"But—"

"Sounds like you want a spanking, after all." He pointed to the nightstand. "I can always tie you up completely, Luca, but it's more fun when you control yourself. Think you can do that?"

Hesitantly, she nodded.

"Let's test you." He pressed a button on the remote to start the vibrator and her back arched in invitation. He shook his head in faux disappointment. "You'll have to do better than that."

"Please, Logan!"

"Unless you're begging me to fuck you, I don't want to hear it."

Her breathing became labored as soon as his mouth latched onto a breast. He set the vibrator to a randomized setting, put the remote down and gave her lush breasts his full attention: licking, sucking and biting her nipples. He could feel the tension coil in her body from the effort of staying still, from her impending orgasm.

"Think you can cum like this, sweetheart?" He pinched both nipples and pulled them hard, shifting his mouth back to her weeping pussy to lick her like she was his favorite delicacy. When his hands moved from her breasts to grip her ass, causing her to arch into his face, he felt her let go.

"Oh God!" she panted.

"Scream *my* name."

"*Logan!*"

He sat back on his hunches, watching her come undone. "That's it. So beautiful." He turned the vibrations off and reached between her legs to tug at the string of the vibrator. He chucked it over his shoulder, slipping a finger into her. "Hmm, so slippery. So ready."

She whimpered when he added another and massaged her inner walls. Her eyes crossed as he curled those digits upward, which had her moving wantonly.

"Naughty," he commented, using his other hand to anchor her hips to the bed. His fingers continued their leisurely exploration of her pussy. "Are you ready to beg?"

She nodded, crying out in disappointment when he removed his fingers.

"Doesn't sound like it."

"Please, Logan," she whispered.

Tilting his head to the side, he regarded her. "What do you want, sweetheart?"

Other than a huff of breath, she didn't say anything.

"If you can't ask for it, we're done here."

"No!" she exclaimed, a terrified edge to her voice. "Please!"

His fingers went back inside. "Is this all you want from me?"

"No!"

"Then what do you *want*, Luca?"

"Your cock!"

"Now we're getting somewhere." He stroked a swollen nipple as her reward. "Where do you want my cock, hmm?" He touched her mouth. "Here?" He grabbed a breast. "Here?" His fingers pressed on her G-spot again. "Here?" They slipped out, venturing to the puckered hole of her anus.

"Or here?"

Sheer panic entered her gaze. "No!"

"Nowhere?"

"No!"

"Then where?" He unzipped his jeans to free his aching dick. "Maybe it'll help if you see it." Her eyes nearly popped out of her skull at the sight of him, and he was sure she was going to scream *Snow!* When she didn't, he stroked his erection while carefully watching her face for any sign of distress.

"I want your cock in my pussy."

Goddamn!

"I never thought I'd hear 'pussy' from your lips, naughty girl."

"Sorry."

"Don't apologize, sweetheart. You know what you have to do." Logan grinned. "Beg."

"Logan, please put your cock in me," she pleaded, spreading her legs in invitation. "*Please!*"

He quickly sheathed his cock and shifted closer, angling it at her entrance. "That's how you get what you want from me," he informed her huskily. In one, smooth thrust, he went right to the hilt and stilled, anticipating her reaction.

She shrieked at the invasion, no doubt remembering the last time a man was inside her.

He pressed up on his elbows. "Look at me."

Her tearful gaze met his.

"It's me." He touched the side of her face. "You want me, remember? You asked for this."

It took a few moments, but her breathing evened out. She wriggled under him and gasped, tilting her head back. "Please, please, please!"

"Please what?"

"*Please fuck me!*"

He let out a relieved sigh. "Gladly."

Luca moaned every time he retreated and slid back in, and Logan lost himself. She wrapped her legs around his waist, her heels pressing on his ass, and arched when he put his mouth on her neck.

He could barely stand it. "Move." He buried his face in her hair, his lips next to her ear. "Fuck me back!"

She obeyed, rocking against him. "Harder, Logan," she panted.

Fuck!

He did as she asked, pounding into her like a man possessed. He bottomed out, ramming against her cervix. If it hurt, she didn't say. The fact that she was repeating his name like a mantra had him right at the edge, and he reached between them to finger her clit.

"*Logan!*"

She unraveled and he followed shortly after.

Fucking hell, he thought, chest heaving with exertion. It was nothing close to being with Alyssa, but sublime in its own way and much better than he'd imagined. *How am I ever going to recover?*

Once his breathing became regular again, he pulled out and stared at her peaceful, sleeping face.

He smiled to himself and got up to go to the bathroom. He splashed his skin with water and dried his body with a towel, before wetting a facecloth to clean her up. He pulled his jeans on and took a walk to the minibar in the living room. He only allowed himself to bask in what's happened after he gulped down a bottle of water.

"Jesus," he whispered to himself, "I just fucked my stepsister."

Do you care?

He chuckled, shaking his head. Was he losing his mind again? "Not at all."

CHAPTER TWENTY-FOUR

LUCA WAS ADDICTIVE, and Logan fell hard.

Gone from his mind were the warnings from his gran, his friends, and his cousin. Gone were his own misgivings. Heck, he even forgot to worry about his impending trip back to the Netherlands, now only a few days away, or his dreams about to come true at the World Cup. He was too consumed by the fantasies he could indulge with her.

They spent every moment they had free together and became regulars at the hotel. They had to find creative ways to evade the constant group of photographers in the lobby, although they managed to keep both their reputations clean.

She wasn't a fan of crowds, but she would get used to the fans. He knew she cared about him and that she wouldn't make him choose her over his career. They were both young, with their whole lives ahead of them: by the time he asked her to marry him, she would be a bona fide WAG.

Although he did his best to keep their burgeoning relationship a secret, he wasn't surprised when his stepdad pulled him aside one day with a clenched jaw. "So, you and Luca?"

"Yeah," Logan said happily.

"I guess this was inevitable." Byron rubbed his temples for a moment. "I don't like that it's interfering with school, Lo."

"It's not, dad. I'm helping her study."

"Sure."

"Look, I know it's weird—"

"No shit! She's my daughter now, and you're my son. How am I meant to react?"

Logan took a moment to consider what Byron was saying. "Do you want us to stop? Is this you or mom talking?"

"It's us both, Logan. And we don't know what the better option is here. We just want you to be careful."

He softened. "We are, dad."

"I meant *you*," Byron insisted. "The way you're acting… It's not healthy."

"What do you mean?"

"I mean that there is a world beyond Luca. You remember that, right?"

Logan frowned. "Of course."

"Maybe you should ask her what she wants. You're leaving in two days."

His heart clenched painfully. "Yeah, I know. I'm dreading it."

Byron tilted his head to the side, barely concealing his shock. "Surely you mean you're excited? This is the opportunity of a lifetime."

"That part is exciting, yes."

"Okay, good." Byron placed his hand on Logan's shoulder. "We know you'll make the right choice. We're just worried, you know?"

Logan pretended he did, but he was too far gone to realize what they were trying to warn him against. Everything finally felt right, like the stars and planets have aligned for his benefit. Why would he purposefully stop the momentum?

He went to pick Luca up from school, his hormones going into overdrive at the sight of her. Wearing her trademark punk outfit, it was difficult to believe that she was the captain of the cheerleading squad, although her lithe body hinted at her active lifestyle.

He hardly noticed the curious or appreciative looks he received from other girls: his sole focus was on Luca. It didn't matter that he was a local celebrity, or that his Raptors cut always turned heads.

She smiled when she spotted him. She hugged her friends in farewell and made her way over, getting on the Harley behind him. "Hey."

"Hi," he greeted, handing her helmet over.

"What are we doing today?"

He grinned. "Each other."

She burst out laughing while she secured the helmet. "Smooth."

"I try."

He pulled away from the curb, loving the way her arms wrapped around his waist and her weight leaned into him. For a brief moment, he allowed himself to fantasize about their life together: he could get a Harley in Amsterdam, and they could go on a tour through Europe.

He ignored the part of him that knew that was nothing but a pipedream. He hardly ever had time off, as the football league lasted year-round, and somehow a Harley didn't fit into his new world.

Doesn't matter, he decided, *I can make it fit.*

He pulled into the hotel parking lot, and they crossed the lobby to the elevators one by one. He greeted the local journalists that made a habit of staking out the place in the hopes of catching him doing illicit things.

If only they knew...

Once they were alone in the steel box and he'd pressed the button for the penthouse suite, he pushed her against the wall and sealed his mouth on hers, swallowing her gasp of surprise.

The ride was too short for him to get too grabby, but he happily took note of her red-tinted cheeks before they stepped out.

"I guess no more talking?" she asked, a little breathless once she dropped her school bag by the door of his room.

He didn't answer. Instead, he tugged her towards the jacuzzi. He bent to open the taps and start the jets, and then turned back to Luca.

God, she's so beautiful.

Her ebony hair was braided, as usual; her bronze skin glowed and somehow emphasized the odd color of her eyes. In contrast, she wore a black tank top under a translucent blouse, with whitewashed abraded jeans and biker boots. She was so punk, like she's ready to fight anyone intending her harm.

The complete opposite of the day they'd met.

"Strip," he ordered, his voice thick. She was too perfect. He wanted to taint her, somehow, make her naughty. Depraved. Debauched. He didn't quite understand this compulsion—

It's obsession.

—but it was primal, and he gave in to it every time.

Once she stood naked before him, all common sense flew out the window. The only thing he knew for certain was that his cock had to be in her, as many times as possible.

"Take my clothes off," was his next instruction.

Her eyes widened slightly, but she did as he asked, starting with his jacket. He stepped out of his shoes at the same time she pulled his shirt over his head, her fingertips brushing his skin and setting off sparks that inflamed his desire. She dropped to her knees to unbuckle his belt, her violet gaze briefly flicking up to his. As if to say: "Is this where you want me?"

Fucking hell, he thought, clenching his teeth with the effort of keeping still while she carefully pulled his pants down to the floor. She came back for his underwear and, excruciatingly slowly, dragged it over his rock-hard dick. She stayed there, in the submissive pose, with her eyes on his feet.

The power he felt in this position would surely kill him.

Logan left her there, going to the main bedroom to fetch lube and a few toys. Then he returned and shifted his attention to the jacuzzi, which was nearly full now. He tested the water before getting in, placing the items on the edge.

"Come here, sweetheart."

Without hesitation, Luca followed suit.

"Turn around."

He waited for her to comply before plastering the front of his body to the back of hers. One of his hands gripped her hip while the other wrapped around her neck, his fingers tilting her head towards him. His mouth captured hers in a hungry kiss, and he savored her answering whimper.

With his cock between her ass cheeks, he sat back with her on his lap and hooked her legs over his. He spread her wide and, with their mouths sealed and tongues dueling, began stroking her exposed pussy. His other hand slipped down from her neck to her tits, squeezing them greedily.

Her hips started rocking, hesitantly at first. When she realized he wasn't going to punish her for it, she became more daring: teasing his cock with the undulations. He pinched a nipple and her clit at the same time, something he's learned she loved, and she broke the kiss on a loud gasp.

"Please, Logan!"

"Please what, sweetheart?"

"Please fuck me!"

"Yeah?" He pushed two fingers deep into her pussy. "Like that?"

"N-no," she stammered, "I want your cock."

"Ah, I see." He lifted her off him and moved forward to position her on her knees, on the edge of the seat. With her ass perched high, he couldn't resist giving one of her cheeks a spank.

"What was that for?" she panted.

"I don't need a reason: this ass is mine." Reaching for a condom, he slipped one on and added a generous squirt of lube, which he rubbed over his cock and her pussy. Her well-trained restraint meant that she didn't wiggle her hips to get more friction, and for a second Logan was overcome with anger.

Will this be the rest of my life? Doing all the work? No spontaneity, no reciprocity… Just sheer dominance, all the time?

"Logan, please. I need you."

Her voice pulled him back from that train of thought, and he lined his cock up to her entrance. Closing his eyes to get back into the zone, he slid all the way home and shuddered.

This could be my reality, forever.

He fucked her as aggressively as she begged for it, bent over the side of the jacuzzi as she was. When she came on a wail, he flipped her around and buried his face in her chest while he pounded into her, hoping to forget the scent of citrus and flash of lilac-colored hair. Luca's body, as rigid and closed off as it could sometimes be, always welcomed him.

They recovered in the warm, bubbling water, and talked about an upcoming football game where she will be cheering. He wouldn't be able to watch her, not with his upcoming departure to the most watched football tournament in the world. He left the discussion open-ended in the hopes that she would ask to join him.

Why would she? She might think you're only in this for the sex.

When she didn't pick up what he put down, he pulled her into his arms and kissed her. Those plump lips pressing against his were like an addiction; her tongue like the salve to an open wound. He still held out hope for a great, lifechanging love, and he wouldn't be surprised if Luca was The One.

You're hardly twenty-one, with your whole life ahead of you. Why would this happen now?

That didn't mean it couldn't, right? To have someone by his side while he soared to new career highs and, in turn, being by *hers* as she came into her own. Surely that wasn't so farfetched?

He was becoming increasingly frustrated with his line of thinking while he held such a beautiful woman. Why couldn't he accept this for what it was: a good time between two consenting adults? It didn't have to be anything more at the moment. They were both still young.

And so he pinned her down and had his way with her, basking in her answering moans of delight. Her body, so pliant and obedient, served as a direct connection to ecstasy. He was one lucky son of a bitch to have her.

Later that night, he and Luca were on the couch, watching a movie. She was cuddled into his side with her hand on his chest, and he savored the feel of her so close to him. Whenever he thought of how skittish she used to be, how averse to physical contact, he felt honored that she chose to be more open with him.

It's enough. For now, this is enough.

"I can't believe it's almost time for you to go," she murmured tiredly.

His heart skipped a beat, cautiously optimistic that she'd brought it up. Perhaps she'd needed a moment to absorb their earlier conversation, first. "Yeah," he sighed, stroking her bare arm. He inhaled the clean scent of her ebony hair, barely paying attention to the moving images on the screen while he waited. For what, he didn't know.

"It's been fun having you around again. Like old times."

"Except with sex."

She giggled. "Yeah."

He mentally debated whether to voice what's been on his mind since they became intimate. He didn't want to pressure her but, at the same time, he didn't want to miss his chance.

"This doesn't have to be the end of us... hanging out." He winced at that term. He might be young, but he hated the thought of not committing to someone. He was too much of a romantic.

"Aren't you going to be busy in the next two days?"

She'd misunderstood. "No. I mean yes, I will be..." *Deep breaths, Logan.* "You could come with me. To the World Cup."

Her body tensed. "What?"

"We could keep hanging out like this and—" He broke off when she cleared her throat and sat up, reaching for a nearby robe. Frowning, he asked: "Luca? What's wrong?"

She avoided his gaze.

"Sweetheart? Talk to me."

"I have to finish school, Logan."

"Yeah, you can join me when you graduate. In Amsterdam." Her silence was unnerving, which meant that he couldn't stop babbling. He suddenly felt very vulnerable, being in the nude, and followed her example of putting on a robe. "They have fantastic universities, with many competitive—"

"Logan, stop."

"What? Why won't you look at me?"

Her hands clenched at her sides, and she inhaled deeply before she made eye contact again. "My life is here."

"But you're thinking of studying."

"Remotely," she confirmed. "I want to be here, with the club, and get patched in. I've been working at the diner and I really enjoy it. Ryan's already said, if all goes well, I might even become an assistant manager until I get a job as a journalist."

Shit.

That took the wind out of his sails. Logan stood, wishing she would come back to him, close the distance between them. He hasn't felt this far removed from her since that first day, when he'd found her battered and bruised while rock-climbing.

"I thought…" He trailed off, not sure how to finish that sentence without sounding like a lovesick fool. She flinched and it shattered his delusion: he *was* the lovesick fool! "You just wanted me for the sex?"

She gazed at him seriously for a heartbreaking amount of time. "Logan, I can never be anything more to you."

"Why do you say that?"

"We don't want the same things."

"Do you even know what I want?"

"I watch people," she nodded. "I've always known you like me… like *that*. For a while, I thought I liked you back, but I can never be what you want and you're a fool if you can't see it."

He stared at her, completely thrown.

"You have this incredible, fast-paced life, and I'm so happy you get to live your dream. But it's not *my* dream, Logan. For most of my life I didn't even know that it was possible *to* dream!" She spread her arms with an apologetic look on her face. "After everything that's happened to me, I want a simple life. I love this town, the club, and the people here. *This* is where I want to be."

"You might change your mind."

"Yes, I might, but that doesn't mean you should wait for me. I don't want you to. I would never forgive myself for holding you back, if you did."

He swallowed past the lump in his throat. "You're saying you don't love me."

"Are you kidding? I *do* love you!" She gave him a half-smile. "I told you that you're one of my closest friends. You've seen me at my absolute worst, and you haven't once judged me."

There's that word again: friends. I'm such an idiot.

"You want a big family one day. I can't give you that." She clasped her hands in front of her. "Even if I wanted kids, which I don't, the doctors say I can't have them. I... I'm damaged from..." She swallowed and looked away. "The abuse."

Just like your mother.

He shook his head to get rid of that thought. "We could adopt."

"You're not hearing me. I don't *want* kids."

He rubbed his forehead and moved to the minibar to grab a bottle of whiskey. The abrupt turn in their conversation—all *his* doing—has thrown him entirely off his axis. They've gone from blissful cuddling to the end of the road awfully fast.

The sting of the alcohol cleared his brain fog, if only a little.

She was right: he kept looking for a way to twist her words to suit the picture in his mind, and to convince her that they belonged together. He had been too sure of himself, completely ignoring the signs and possibility that she might feel differently.

"I'll always be grateful for the role you played in saving me from the Falcons," she murmured, sounding like she was right behind him. "At first, I thought that I was in love with you. Why wouldn't I be? You're an amazing man: you're kind, generous, intelligent, driven. Attractive. The whole damn package. I wanted to try this, to see if it's really love that I feel for you." Her touch was gentle on his back, intended to be reassuring. "I trust you, which is why I asked you to help me with intimacy. If we had to go on chemistry alone, I'm sure that we would be great together but, in the end, we don't have the same values or goals. I'm sorry that the sex confused everything."

He closed his eyes, utterly crushed. She embraced him from behind, her arms locking around his waist. He placed his hands on hers, ignoring the cold drops of his tears on his skin.

Why are you so tethered to the past?

Connor, of all people, had tried to warn him. So had Dane, and Byron. They'd noticed something he'd been oblivious to, because he had desperately wanted it to work with Luca. He couldn't have Alyssa—she was with Jake— and so Luca could be the one, right?

She was your consolation prize, then?

No, he wouldn't have used her. They did enjoy each other's company, and they had great chemistry, as she'd rightly pointed out. They could be good together, but…

It's not the kind of love I want.

The last two weeks played through his head, his mind searching for the any indication that he could have what he preferred. That she *did* want a life with him, she simply didn't know it yet. But the picture was off from the beginning: he'd just been too determined to fully see it.

You can't make her love you. That'll make you the same as the assholes that chose on her behalf. She's moved on, psychologically, and can decide whatever future she wants. If that doesn't include you in the way you want it… tough luck.

"I'm sorry."

"It's okay," he mumbled, not really meaning it. He moved away, wiping his tears, and said: "Grab your things. I'll take you home."

"Logan—"

"I'm going to get dressed and then I'll meet you downstairs," he interjected. He hurriedly pulled on the clothes she'd taken off him in the jacuzzi room, feeling lightheaded. His ears were ringing.

You tried, that's all that matters.

He made sure he had his phone and wallet before heading for the main door. He was dazed as he walked to the elevator, to the lobby, to the parking lot outside. He stopped at his Blackline, feeling so absolutely removed from everything it represented that he had no idea who he was anymore.

You're Logan Bean Drummond, superstar athlete, Connor's voice reminded him from the past.

You're my son, Brennan told him in the present. *You know who you are and what you want. It was never this. You can't be half-in, half-out of this new path you've chosen. You need to embrace it all to get what you want.*

He wished he knew what the future had in store for him! He'd taken a leap of faith with football, seeing as it had never formed part of his original plan, and it seemed like he would have to take the same approach to love.

Now you're getting it.

"Logan!"

He straddled the Harley, the rumble of the engine drowning out whatever else she was about to say. She reluctantly settled in behind him and he shot off into the night, the wind ruffling his helmet-free hair.

Being on the open road made him realize with a shock that he wasn't actually angry, or even heartbroken. He's known, deep down, that his time with Luca would be temporary. He'd felt it the second the plane landed: this wasn't his home anymore. He was nothing more than a tourist, visiting his old life.

Once he pulled into the driveway at his parents' house, he cut the engine and waited for Luca to dismount. He looked at her, truly seeing her for the first time. She was beautiful, smart, capable. And completely her own person.

"I'm sorry if I scared you," he said.

She gave him a watery smile. "Thank you." She held out his leather cut and duffle bag. "You left this in the hotel room."

He took the bag but left the Raptors regalia in her possession. "I don't need that anymore."

Reading between the lines, she inclined her head. "You're leaving."

"Yes."

"At least say goodbye to mom and dad."

He checked the side pocket of the duffle for his passport and shook his head. "I'll call them from the airport."

"Logan—"

He silenced her with a swift, sideways hug. "Bye, Luca."

She sighed. "Bye, Logan. Good luck with everything."

"You, too."

He waited until she was safely inside the house before he sped away. He only noticed he was smiling broadly halfway towards the airport. It felt as if the final weight, one he hadn't known he'd still been carrying, has lifted from his shoulders. This time, leaving town wasn't as terrifying as before, because he finally knew, with absolute certainty, that he was making the right decision.

Chapter Twenty-Five

IF HE'D THOUGHT the Ajax fans were loud, it was nothing compared to this. Logan stood in the tunnel, absorbing the roar of the crowd with a racing heart. It was a moment that he'd never thought was possible, growing up. And now, this was his life?!

You love every second of it.

His parents were in the VIP box with other players' families. They'd been hurt, but understanding, when he had left town without saying goodbye. He'd called his mom as soon as he had landed safely in Amsterdam, and she had reprimanded him for a few minutes before getting down to business.

"So, Luca."

He'd looked around the airport to avoid her emerald gaze glaring at him from the screen. "Yes?"

"I wish you'd have come to me before you decided on that, I would've told you it's a bad idea."

"I know, mom."

"You *don't* know, Logan! Stand still and look at me!" She'd waited until he obeyed before continuing. "I love both you and Luca, but you were never going to be good for each other." At his frown, she nodded. "Not even if you'd stayed behind. There is attraction between you, yes, and some sort of bond that you can't always explain, but that doesn't mean that you should be together."

"I don't understand."

"No shit," she had laughed. "I feel like I don't often understand it, either. What you feel for Luca… It's similar to how I felt about Brennan. Don't get me wrong, I will always love him and I don't regret one moment, but I never gave *my* life and *my* desires a chance until he was gone. He was part of so many childhood memories. And now that I'm older, I wonder what kind of man I would've ended up with if I'd *really* given my life in the city a shot. If it hadn't been out of spite, and I hadn't let him drag me back."

Logan had taken a while to absorb what she was saying. He'd bitten his lip, not sure if he should tell her what's on his mind. Then he had inhaled sharply and plunged ahead: "There was a moment when I realized Luca is a lot like you."

Instead of taking offense, Cinnia had nodded as if she'd known the same thing. "Very much like me. It's part of the reason why I hoped you two would go your separate ways. She's my daughter, Logan, and I want her to explore life on her own terms, too." She smiled slightly. "You both deserve someone who expands your lives, not someone who keeps you small."

Alyssa.

He had briefly shut his eyes. "Thank you, momma."

"You should come to me more often. I give great advice."

Chuckling, he'd said: "I'm sorry I forgot that about you."

With all forgiven, he'd arranged to get the three of them to the World Cup. Luca had politely declined, since she was more comfortable in the crowds she knew than new ones. That had inadvertently confirmed that it was a good thing they weren't romantic: he would've held himself back for fear of triggering her anxiety, and potentially missed out on so much in life.

She needed someone who could explore the world at her pace, but he wanted a partner that wasn't afraid to jump into the unknown or put herself out there, and live life to the fullest *with* him.

And so that became what he focused on whenever he meditated.

Back in the present moment, he marched onto the football pitch with the rest of his team. There were large sections of orange in the crowd, broken up by parts of yellow: they were playing against Ghana. Logan didn't expect it to be easy because Ghana was a great team and they've had an incredible season leading up to the Cup.

Their national anthems played, one after the other, and then the teams took their sides and waited for the whistle. Logan was making his debut in the very first game: fresh legs to hopefully get them to the top sixteen, where the more experienced players were scheduled to take over.

The whistle pierced through the rumble of the supporters, and the match kicked off.

While he played, Logan couldn't help but draw parallels between his high school experiences and his career. Although the stakes were similar, playing for the Netherlands elevated it to a new level: a whole nation depended on their success. And facing off against the best athletes in the world made it tough to uphold their expectations. Five minutes before halftime, they scored their first goal, assisted by Logan. He hardly heard the thunderous cheers of the crowd since the team was crashing together to celebrate and exchange congratulations.

In the second half, there was pressure to both maintain their lead over Ghana, and to widen the margin by scoring again, but their opponents had upped their defenses and finding a gap wasn't easy. Even when it was more of a challenge, Logan soaked in every moment. He had no way of knowing if he would play in another tournament.

The ball landed at his feet, and he sensed Andries to his left.

As if in slow motion, he began dribbling towards the goal, successfully bypassing the first opponent that tried to block him. He wouldn't have the same luck with the second, so he passed the ball to Andries.

His captain dodged two Ghanian players while Logan ran to an open spot, and then kicked the ball ahead of Logan.

Heart beating wildly, Logan sprinted forward, got the ball under control, aimed at the top-right corner of the box, and kicked. Hoping and praying he wasn't offside...

The ball skated past the goalie's glove and the net rippled at the impact, the referee's whistle confirming that it was a legitimate goal. Logan was overcome with emotion as his team nearly tackled him to the ground, the deafening sound of the Netherlands supporters echoing in his ears.

Their team managed to keep the score 2-0 by the time the match ended. They shook the hands of the talented Ghanian players and made their way to the locker room to hear from coach Petri. After, they all took a refreshing shower and Andries headed out to the press room to discuss the match.

Logan and the rest of the team made their way to the VIP box to mingle with loved ones and rich fans. He came to an abrupt halt when he spotted a familiar face standing next to his parents: there was only a hint of purple in her otherwise blonde hair.

"Fucking hell, punk!" Byron exclaimed as he rushed over to hug Logan. "That was perfection!"

"Well done, my boy!" Cinnia cried, joining the embrace.

Logan could barely focus on them with Alyssa standing mere meters away.

Cinnia pulled back and noticed that he was distracted. She smiled in that way that showed she'd been sneaky-but-brilliant. "I couldn't let your third ticket go to waste, so I asked Lys if she wanted to tag along."

He cleared his throat. "Great idea."

Byron and Cinnia exchanged knowing glances. "We're gonna go grab a drink at the bar," he said as they moved away.

Alyssa stared at him while nibbling on her lower lip. When the silence became nearly unbearable, she blurted: "I shouldn't have come."

"No!" Snapping out of his mental haze, he stepped forward to take her hands in his. "I'm glad you're here."

"Really?"

"Of course. It's so good to see you." He quirked a smile and then let go of her, although it felt wrong. "If I'd known in advance, I would've arranged another ticket for Jake."

She raised an eyebrow. "You really would've, huh?"

He glanced over his shoulder at his parents, not surprised that they were failing at pretending not to ogle him and Alyssa. "Am I not getting the joke, or something?"

"Jake and I broke up."

That brought his gaze back to hers.

"About a week after the wedding, actually," Alyssa went on. "It just… happened. One second we were having a good time with friends, and the next we both decided we're not what we want anymore."

Logan thought back and swore under his breath: Connor and Dane had known but hadn't mentioned anything! "Was it because of us?"

She shook her head. "Not directly. I mean, seeing you made me reevaluate our relationship, but we didn't break up because of that. We just… didn't want the same things, when it came down to it."

"I can relate."

"You and Luca?"

"Yeah." This time, when Logan looked at his parents, they grinned back goofily. He felt like he could simultaneously punch and hug them for keeping this a secret. "How much did they tell you?"

"Only that you tried." Alyssa rested her hand on his forearm to get his attention. "I was hoping you would fill in the blanks."

They shared one of those life-altering moments again, as if they could reach to the core of each other's essence. Logan realized that being in her presence gave him the same rush and sense of belonging he got from playing ball: both were things he's always wanted, but never could envision as a kid.

"Do you want to go somewhere?"

"Don't you have social duties here? You're a superstar after that goal."

He took her hand in his, sliding his fingers between hers. "That can wait."

She fought against a smile, not quite succeeding. "Okay."

Without a word to anyone else—he would deal with the consequences later, if there were any—he led her out of the VIP box, down the passage and into an elevator. Only once they were sealed inside did he face her again.

"Lys, I—"

She grabbed his lapel and pulled him down for a kiss.

That first touch of her lips on his made him feel like everything was right in the world. It excited him beyond measure, overwhelmed him as much as that goal had done. Strengthened him. Liberated him.

The *ping* of the elevator arriving on the ground floor interrupted them. As the doors parted, excited chatter filled the air.

"Are we doing this properly, then? No more messing around?"

"Yes," he answered, sticking his hand out to catch the door before it closed, "no more messing around."

Inhaling, she dipped her head. "Let's go, superstar."

As they walked towards the exit, it didn't take long for him to be recognized by those who were loitering in the hope of seeing their favorite athletes. The first fan tipped off the rest and, within seconds, Logan was swarmed. Because he's spent years in Amsterdam, he kept up with the rapid-fire Dutch around him while he signed autographs and posed for photos. He accepted the awe and praise with a warm smile, inwardly knowing that they only cheered when things were going well.

Alyssa was by his side, seeming unperturbed.

"Is this your girlfriend?" someone asked, having noticed her.

His answer was a simple yes. Their excitement doubled, but Logan kept pushing until, finally, he and Alyssa had worked their way through the crowd. They made a beeline for the closest taxi and got onto the backseat.

"Girlfriend, huh?"

"If that's what you want?" He leered at her, grinning broadly. "Quickly followed by fiancée, and then wife?"

She burst out laughing. "Fucking hell, Beanie."

"Hey, you're Logan Drummond!" the taxi driver declared in accented English. "Your goal was incredible!"

"Thank you." Logan asked the driver to take them to a restaurant close to the hotel where he was staying. He turned back to Alyssa, waiting for her to pick up the conversation where they'd left off.

"Well, you did catch that garter belt."

"And you caught the bouquet."

"It's tradition."

"Fate, even." He twirled a strand of her hair, now shoulder-length, around his finger. "I like the color."

"Figured I could get away with looking boring on the outside."

"Smashing, sexy, gorgeous. Beautiful." Logan inched closer to her lips, eager for another taste. "Never boring."

Her belly laugh was muffled by his kiss. Their tongues glided together, enticing one another. Reigniting the searing passion they've shared in the past. She threw her arms around his shoulders, and he held the back of her head, content with making out for the rest of the night. There was no rush: they had the rest of their lives to get more intimate.

The taxi stopped and they separated with flushed cheeks. Logan swiped his card, adding a generous tip, before getting out and guiding Alyssa across the street to the restaurant. It was packed to the rafters but, after recognizing Logan, the maître-d got them a secluded booth at the back.

There were perks to being famous, but also downsides, as was made evident by the many gazes on their backs while they moved further into the restaurant. Once they were seated, he only had eyes for Alyssa.

"It's really good to see you, Betty," he murmured. "I'm glad you came."

"Me too. Everything was sold out by the time I realized I should get here to share this experience with you in some way." She laughed softly. "I was so happy when your mom phoned to tell me about the spare ticket. On the flight over, she mentioned that you had tried with Luca, and then I thought I was making a mistake in thinking you're ready. I nearly turned back."

"I'm glad you didn't."

Their conversation was momentarily interrupted by the waiter. They ordered drinks and entrees—Logan sticking to still water and healthy food, as per his contract with the team—and he resumed when they were alone again.

"For a while, I was obsessed..." He remembered the primal need to dominate, to *own*, and hardly related to that side of him. "It wasn't so much about what she wanted, long-term, but what I could have if I persuaded her. I turned into my father, for a second. At least, the entitled part that everyone's told me about."

"And then what happened?"

"Luca was more grounded about the whole thing than I was. She's grown a lot, over the years."

Alyssa smiled. "Luca's great. We interacted a few times leading up to Sophie's wedding, and I admire her resilience."

"Yeah, me too." He shrugged. "At the end of the day, she was right: we don't want the same things. She can't have kids, which is something I desperately want. I know what it's like to grow up as an only child, and I want better for my kids."

"Funnily enough, Jake and I broke up for the same reason. Although we had loads in common, we don't have the same goals and values. I know what it's like to be alone, growing up. He has a brother and sister and, because of how full his upbringing was, doesn't see the point in having kids."

"I'm both sorry and happy it didn't work out for you. You two looked good together."

"Ditto."

The waiter brought their drinks and appetizers, but for a full minute they did nothing but stare at each other.

"I was always sure about *us*, Lys. Where the thrill of the chase drew me to other girls, you've always thrilled me just by being with me, by me *not* having to chase."

"Those fucking shrooms," she remarked dryly, shaking her head.

"It goes back to the minute we met, and you know it."

"You're right," she nodded. "You make me believe that forever is possible with one person."

He reached for her hand and gave it a squeeze. "Forever will be good for us."

"I agree."

"I know it won't always be easy." Logan gave the other people in the restaurant a sideways glance. "But I think we're honest enough with each other to give this a real shot."

She inclined her head, smiling. "They don't scare me. The only thing that scares me is *not* trying."

With that settled, he began quizzing her about her blog, and what's been happening in her life since they last saw each other. She hasn't been posting on social media as much, so he was delighted to hear about her recent travels to Peru. She'd used it as an opportunity to realign with her life's mission: having adventures.

"Adventure isn't just about putting on a backpack and exploring the world. I believe adventure can be something simple, like becoming a wife or a mother, or building a business."

Listening to her saying so many things that he wholeheartedly agreed with, he pondered the many clichés surrounding the concept of romantic love:

Some would say to marry your best friend, someone who you're compatible with and shares your values. Others, that opposites attract.

Some argue that love is meant to be fun; others, that love is meant to push your buttons to help you grow.

Some believe that chemistry leads to lasting love; others point out that long-lasting attraction should spring from comfort, stability.

To him, it was more important to forge his own path and find his own way in life, and in love. His parents had set a solid foundation and they've shown him the best parts of a reciprocal relationship, but that didn't mean he had to repeat the cycles of the past. He had the responsibility to choose his fate and leave behind a different legacy.

After their meal, they took a stroll in a park nearby to continue their conversation about life, love, the universe, and everything else. He loved the way her mind worked and how she challenged some of his beliefs, and she found his take on these topics insightful. He admired her strong sense of self: she'd gone through many ups and downs to figure out who she was and what her ambitions were, but she knew that even that could change in future.

They reached the end of the trail and stopped, facing each other.

He tucked her hair behind her ears. "I'd like to invite you to my room, but I don't want you to feel pressure to do anything."

Alyssa grinned naughtily. "Why would I feel pressure? We've never done it in a bed."

He burst out laughing. "Fair enough." He grabbed her hand and, with a renewed sense of urgency, led her to his hotel room. He was most excited about falling asleep next to her: that's only ever happened once, on the rooftop in Amsterdam, but she'd left before he had woken up.

"Can I take a shower?" she asked, tugging at her clothes. "It's been a long day."

"Go for it."

She bit her lip for a moment. "Do you want to join me?"

"I thought you'd never ask." He pulled her into his arms and kissed her. They shed their clothes as they stumbled to the ensuite. He reached into the shower to get the water going while his hands traced her body, loving the way she explored his in turn.

They stepped under the spray and washed up with teasing strokes. He watched the makeup coming off her face and thought, *so damn beautiful.* His gaze took a long, unhurried journey over her toned body. Glistening nipple rings. Trimmed pubic hair under which, if memory served, another stud resided.

"I just realized I've never seen you naked while sober. Not bad at all, Beanie."

He raised an eyebrow and shut the tap. "You had a glass of wine tonight. And we both know you've stared at my DKNY ads."

She playfully smacked his chest, laughing. "Watch that ego, superstar!"

"Let's continue this chat on the bed," he said, passing a towel.

"Is doing it against the wall too boring for you, all the sudden?"

"Oh, I'll have plenty of opportunities for that." He threw her over his shoulder, relishing in her surprised yelp, and walked to the bed, where he unceremoniously dumped her.

"I thought you wanted to chat?"

He spread her legs and parted her lower lips, satisfied at the sight of her piercing. He was about to have so much fun. "Chat away."

"But—*oh*!"

Her fingers delved into his damp hair as he began licking her pussy. Her taste was a throwback to that night in Amsterdam. He nudged the stud with the tip of his tongue, over and over again, to drag needy moans from her. He pushed two fingers into her warmth, flattening his tongue against her clit when she rocked her hips.

He hummed his approval against her slick flesh when she cried out his name, and reached up to cup a breast with his free hand. Her hand covered his, showing him how she liked to be touched. He could sense her body's tension coiling, getting ready to explode, and increased the intensity of his tongue's swipes over her studded clit.

She unraveled beautifully. "Yes, *Logan*!"

Only with Alyssa is this not a power play. Only with her do I get to be myself.

Propelled by the need to become one, he shifted up to swallow her whimpers with a kiss and pushed his cock into her pussy. They moved together as if they've done it a thousand times before, but it felt new and exciting all the same. She wrapped her legs around his waist, causing him to go deeper, and he gripped her ass to tilt her hips up, changing the angle.

Her short nails dug into his back, and she arched against him when another orgasm pulled her under. He followed shortly after, collapsing on top of her.

"Oh my God," she panted, "is the bed better than the wall, or what?"

"Better than the roof and an airport toilet, too," Logan chuckled. He braced over her on his forearms, careful to remain inside her, and kissed her eyebrow. "I love you, Alyssa."

She beamed at him. "I love you."

When she clenched around his dick, he hardened and whatever they were about to say took a backseat. They made love until his phone's reminder to get some shut eye went off somewhere in the room, where he'd discarded his jeans earlier. They fell asleep in each other's arms, and he once again dreamt that he was surrounded by the most brilliant cocoon of light.

When his alarm sliced through the dream, the light was still there as he opened his eyes.

CHAPTER TWENTY-SIX

THE NEXT TWO weeks would live on in his memory forever.

Between matches, dating Alyssa publicly and entertaining his parents, Logan's cup was near to overflowing. He understood that life wouldn't always be this jam-packed with events, but he was enjoying every busy moment.

He hadn't been in too much trouble for skipping out with her, although his team teased him incessantly for committing to a serious relationship so young. He took it with a pinch of salt: even if he hadn't matured faster due to his upbringing, he would still make decisions aligned with his desires. And if it didn't work out, well, at least he'd tried!

The team was performing exceptionally well, and Logan was the talk of the football world. Despite the match against Brazil resulting in a draw, the Netherlands were on a clear path to the quarterfinals.

Every free moment he had, he used to explore Spain with Alyssa and his parents. They visited many sites, museums and restaurants as a family, and Logan often thought how amazing it was that Alyssa slotted in so easily. It didn't take long for Cinnia to start talking about wedding plans and, although it was too soon, Logan and Alyssa didn't discourage her.

Byron picked up on this and, on one particular outing, walked ahead with Logan to have a man-to-man conversation. "When are you asking her?"

Logan shrugged, gazing at their surroundings. "I have to get a ring first."

"Is she moving in with you?"

"Yeah, she's coming with me to Amsterdam."

Byron nodded to himself. "You're lucky to have this so early in your life."

"Not what everyone else seems to think," Logan chuckled.

"Fuck what they think." Byron winked when Logan gave him a look. "Rather regret something you did, than something you didn't." One corner of his mouth tilted up. "And, for what it's worth, I think you're an excellent match."

"But fuck what you think, right?"

Byron burst out laughing, letting the swearing slide. "Exactly."

"I am glad you approve, although I would've gone ahead anyway." Logan glanced over his shoulder at his girlfriend, who was sharing a joke with his mother. "I've always loved her."

"I can relate to that," his stepfather sighed, draping an arm over Logan's shoulders. "You are an absolute goner, punk."

Logan didn't deny it, but he did feel a sense of relief that this time around he wasn't consumed by obsession. Instead, his romance with Alyssa was appealing to his adventurous side: the one that liked dangling off the edge of a cliff. Best of all, she would be joining him on those types of activities.

At night, they explored the ways they could drive each other wild with desire, and the ways to satiate urges quickly. If Logan hadn't been so committed to his career, he might've succumbed to frequent sex marathons into the early hours, but thankfully Alyssa wasn't complaining about his dedication to his craft.

The quarterfinal match against the World Cup hosts arrived much too soon, and Logan was benched because the coach wanted his legs fresh if the team went through to the semi-finals. Logan sat at the side of the pitch for every nail-biting second, wishing he could help his teammates.

Spain's playing was phenomenal, and they had the Netherlands scrambling to keep up. Thanks to fancy block work from Dieter, the Netherlands' goalie, Spain couldn't score. The match ended in another draw for Logan's team, but the hosts had lost a previous match, which meant Logan would be playing in the semi-final. And with one of the best teams in the world out of the running, the Netherlands stood a real chance.

He didn't want to get too optimistic, because he knew it could change at any moment, but fuck, did it feel good to keep progressing! How was anything ever going to compare to his first World Cup experience?

That evening, he celebrated with the boys.

They weren't allowed to drink alcohol or take drugs, but that didn't mean they couldn't get up to a whole bunch of fun. They started at a karaoke bar, singing tone-deaf versions of classic songs by Queen, Elton John and Bon Jovi. After that, they went for dinner at a prestigious restaurant, having to pose for several photos once they were recognized. They ended up at a nightclub, dancing until the early hours.

Logan had to fend off advances from women, but he wasn't the only one. He could never really understand the appeal of professional athletes, although his teammates were not complaining about the attention: several of them left with multiple women on their arms. He might've been jealous if he wasn't deeply in love.

Alyssa was fast asleep when he eventually entered their shared hotel room, his ears still ringing from the club's loud music. He took a quick shower to wash the stench off before crawling into bed. Like him, she slept in the nude, and he couldn't stop his hands from roaming.

"Betty," he whispered, turning her on her back.

"Hmm," she mumbled tiredly. She squinted at him. "You're back."

"I am." He bent over to catch a pierced nipple between his teeth, tugging gently.

"Have fun?"

"Loads." Logan's hands fondled her breasts while his mouth alternated between the two peaks: sucking, licking, biting. He was encouraged by her fingers locking on his hair, to keep his head there. "Missed you."

"I can tell." Her knee brushed his aching dick before she reached down to grip it. She stroked, slowly at first. "Hmm, so nice."

"That feels so good, Lys."

"I know what'll feel better." She pushed against his shoulder, and he rolled them around. Settling between his legs, she lowered her mouth to his cock and began swallowing it down.

"Alyssa, fuck," he moaned, gripping the back of her head in case she decided to stop. "Yes!"

She undulated her tongue against the tip, swirling around it, and pumped him with her hand while she sucked his cock deeper. She was drooling all over it, making each touch a slippery, wet mess. He wanted her to keep going, to finish him off, while also wishing she'll replace her mouth with her pussy.

She must've picked up on the latter mental cue because the next moment she was straddling his hips and working her way down his shaft.

"Ah, you're so wet," he gasped, holding her hips in case she changed her mind.

"Logan," she whimpered as she began to move.

"Don't stop."

"Never."

The view was remarkable. Her lean body bounced on top of him, taking him so deep. She was touching herself while she rode him, too, squeezing her breasts, pulling her nipples, flicking her pierced clit... He was spellbound and knew he wouldn't last long.

"Lys," he warned.

She leaned forward, hands on his chest, to grind against his pubic bone. Her dark brown eyes connected with his and her cheeks went red as she got closer to the edge. His name became her mantra that, with every thrust, she repeated.

He sat up and gripped her ass harder, almost aggressively pulling her onto his dick. He wanted to drive as deep as possible, to touch a part of her no one else will ever reach. His mouth latched onto the side of her neck, where he nipped at her sensitive skin.

"Lys, you better soak my cock," he grunted.

"I'm gonna," she promised, picking up the pace. "You coming?"

"Ah, fuck." He shut his eyes, her breathy tone and the feel of her slick pussy driving him past the point of no return. "Alyssa!"

"Logan!" she cried out, nearly crushing his face to her chest when she exploded.

He unloaded deep inside her, feeling her pulse around his dick. They stayed like that, clinging to each other, for what felt like ages while they came down from the high. He pressed sloppy kisses to her neck and shoulder, the exhaustion hitting him hard.

She tilted his chin up with a lazy smile. "Congrats on the win, superstar."

He gave her ass a playful smack. "Oh, I scored, alright."

"Cheesy, Beanie," she laughed. "Time for bed?"

Reluctantly letting her move away, he dropped back onto the pillows.

"Only if you cuddle the fuck out of me."

"As you command."

He drifted off into a dreamless sleep to the sound of her teasing laugh. His phone's ringtone broke through the abyss, and he groaned as he got up to look for it. It was in his pile of clothes in the bathroom.

"Marcus?" he croaked in answer.

"Ah, you're awake now. I've been trying for hours."

"Sorry." Logan rubbed his eyes as he shuffled back to the bedroom to peek out of the curtains. It was nighttime already. "Wild party."

"No alcohol though, right?"

"Or drugs," he confirmed.

"Good, we can't afford a scandal right now."

"What makes you say that?"

"It's Everton. They want you."

A different kind of ringing sounded in his ears while he absorbed that information. His favorite team wanted… *him*? "You must be joking."

"No jokes. I was on a video call with their manager earlier," Marcus went on, barely concealing the excitement in his tone. "He's sent the deal over, and Logan, it's good: five years with an option to renew for a further three. Loads of zeroes."

"Holy shit," Logan whispered, unable to believe his ears. Were the gods having a laugh? Was this for real?

"I know you've enjoyed your time at Ajax, but this is what you've always wanted, right?"

"Fuck yes."

"Think on it and get back to me. You don't have to decide right now. If you say yes, they want you to start in two months."

"Fucking hell." Logan turned at the sound of the door opening, feeling more grounded at the sight of his girlfriend entering the room. "Okay, let me just get through the semis first."

"Good. We'll talk soon."

She dropped her bag on the bed and sashayed to him as he hung up. Her newly bleached hair was piled on top of her head. "Everything okay?" she asked by way of greeting, wrapping her arms around his waist.

He touched the side of her face for a moment, in awe of the way everything in his life was aligning. A few months ago, he'd thought the greatest thing that would ever happen to him was playing in the FIFA World Cup!

"Everton sent a deal to Marcus. They want me on the team."

Her jaw dropped. "What?! Beanie, that's *amazing!*"

"Yeah, I know." His mind was racing. "It would be more central for you, living in the UK while still traveling for your blog."

Nodding, she embraced him tightly. "For sure, but can we talk about what a big deal this is for *you?*"

He chuckled, closing his eyes and inhaling her citrusy scent. "It's pretty big."

"*Huge!* I'm so proud of you."

"Thanks." He kissed her temple, his body beginning to respond to her proximity. "What did you get up to today?"

"Went shopping with your mom," she replied as she took a step back, a knowing glint in her eyes. "I got you something, but it's not as cool as the Everton deal."

"Let me decide. Show me."

She rummaged in her bag and retrieved a palm-sized, square box. She handed it over, her nerves palpable. "When I saw it, I had to buy it for you because... Well, you'll see."

Flipping the lid open, he froze. Against a white satin cushion lay a tungsten chain necklace, with a pendant about the size of a coin: a geometric-inspired design of a mushroom.

"No way," he breathed.

"Right? I couldn't believe my eyes when I—"

"Lys, I love this. I love *you.*" He pulled her into his arms and kissed her deeply, steering her towards the bed while his hands worked at getting her clothes off so that she could be as naked as he was. "Marry me."

She gasped when he cupped her bare pussy. "Logan—"

"Please, Alyssa." His mouth sealed over hers for a long moment while his fingers played with her clit. His tongue mimicked the movements of what his cock would do soon, plunging into her mouth and coaxing her to respond. "Will you marry me?"

"I already—" She arched against him as he slipped two fingers inside. "I told you I would!"

"I'm serious."

"Me too," she moaned, moving her hips and clutching his shoulders. "No more messing around, remember?"

With a growl, he flipped her onto her stomach and tilted her ass up. He held the base of his dick as he began pushing into her tight pussy. "Love you," he grunted, "forever."

She gripped the covers, exclaiming his name when he finally bottomed out. "Oh my God, *move!*"

He obeyed, thrusting into her. He loved that she always gave it back to him as eagerly and openly. He loved the feel of her pussy squeezing his cock while he brought them both to new heights. He *loved* the sight of her facial expression changing as she got closer to the edge.

And he absolutely fucking *loved* the sounds she made when she reached orgasm.

An urgent knock on the door stopped him from unloading and, with great reluctance, he pulled out. He kissed her shoulder, tucked her under the covers and went to check who it was, careful to hide his nudity behind the wood.

Andries gave him a sheepish smile. "Sorry to, ah, interrupt." He coughed to clear his throat. "We need to get to the bus. We're leaving in five."

Logan swore under his breath. "Of course. I'll be right there." He shut the door and turned to Alyssa, who was beautiful in her afterglow. "What time is your flight?"

"Only later tonight. I'm going to the airport with your parents."

"Okay." He touched his lips to her forehead. "I need to get going." He winked. "We'll finish this in Barcelona."

She laughed, stretching lazily. "Can't wait."

Logan hurriedly packed his things and, before he said goodbye, put the necklace on. The chain was long, and the mushroom pendant rested against his breastbone. *Fitting,* he thought, *on the beating of my heart.*

Rushing to the bus, he blushed deeply at the teasing that ensued. He wasn't the last one on board, but everyone had guessed what kept him. Once they were all accounted for, they were off to the semifinals.

The next two days went by in a blur: he hardly had any time for himself. Because the World Cup was close to wrapping up, every team member had to avail themselves for press interviews and, due to his "stellar performance"—according to some journalists—he was singled out.

He's never particularly liked having the spotlight on him, which was probably a remnant of having to keep secrets for the club, but he understood that it came with the territory and did his best to position the team in a good light.

Each practice was riddled with tension, excitement and a touch of panic. Getting to this part of the tournament was a feat in and of itself: they've come so far, and they were so close to the finish line. Logan didn't want to get too optimistic, but even he couldn't deny that they had a one in four chance of taking home the trophy.

Just be in the moment, the voice he associated with Brennan reminded him, time and time again. *All you have is this moment.*

As much as he wanted to spend more quality time with Alyssa, he slept alone to make sure he got uninterrupted rest. He took his commitment to this life seriously.

The morning of the match against Germany felt unlike any he's ever experienced. The team jogged and ate together, and ran through their drills one last time. Petri gave them an encouraging speech in the locker room and, before they knew it, it was kickoff time.

The crowd was wild, the raucous cheering deafening. But when that whistle blew, silence descended over him: all that mattered was the ball.

He and Andries nearly scored a goal in the first half, but the German goalie was the best in the world for a reason, although the Netherlands' counterpart was able to hold his own during the first forty-seven minutes. The score was 0-0.

Petri urged them to start focusing, to become more aggressive, as they wouldn't want to go into extra time or, heaven forbid, penalty shoot-outs. Logically, they all knew this to be true, but the talks during halftime could only do so much to prepare them for the real game. Sadly, by the end of the second half, neither team had scored.

Logan and some of the others who'd played since the first second of the game—heck, the first *match* of the tournament—were fatigued, but agreed that it would be best to save substitutions for the last fifteen minutes of extra time. This meant that, should the game get to penalties, only the freshest legs would be kicking. It also meant that Logan's focus wasn't as sharp as it was in the beginning of the match.

When a German player purposefully tripped him, he twisted his ankle before going down, hearing a sickening tear over the noise of the crowd.

Fuck, I can't get up!

He tried not to panic as he held his shin, too scared to touch his throbbing foot. He didn't much care for players that faked injuries—called "taking a dive"—in the hopes of scoring an advantage and had promised he would never succumb to that pressure.

But this was different. This was *pain.*

"Logan!" Andries' concerned face hovered above him. "Are you okay?"

No, was what he'd meant to reply. A strangled sound was all that came out.

"Fuck!"

There was a commotion on the field, not that Logan could pay much attention to it. The crowd was booing; the referee blew a whistle, and then they were cheering again. Voices closer to him were nearly shouting to be heard.

The pain wasn't subsiding.

Medics kneeled beside him and started asking questions, which he hoped he was answering coherently. They determined it would be best for them to support him as he hobbled off the pitch, because it didn't sound like he had a concussion or a neck injury, and wouldn't it set the fans at ease?

For the fans, Logan thought darkly, allowing them to pull him into a seated position and then onto his good foot. He took a moment to find his balance, peeking at the chanting crowd. In their own way, they *did* care about what happened to him.

A genuine smile cracked on his face, and he clapped to show them that he would survive. Impossibly, they cheered louder than before. Then, clenching his jaw, he leaned against the medics for support while they led him away from the game. He could only imagine what the commentators were saying: he'll be immortalized in the highlights reel, for sure.

Like you weren't going to be anyway, given what you've accomplished here.

Petri ran over, his eyebrows drawing together. "That bad?"

Logan nodded. "Sorry, coach."

"Are you kidding? You were great out there." Petri briefly rested his hand on Logan's shoulder. "Go get that checked out. I need to get back to it."

The game resumed while Logan was steered to the stadium's First Aid room, where physicians were already waiting. They confirmed that he's torn his Achilles tendon, just as he'd secretly feared. Although he wished it hadn't happened, that he could've somehow remained invincible, there was not much else he could do but succumb to their treatment.

"Logan!"

That drew his attention to the doorway, where his parents and Alyssa had burst through. Cinnia reached him first, the lines of a mother's worry on her forehead.

"You should be watching the rest of the game," he said teasingly.

"Fuck the game," she muttered. "What happened?"

"Tore my Achilles tendon, no big deal."

Byron's eyes stretched and Alyssa drew in a sharp breath as she took his hand.

"Don't worry, guys." He smiled through the tears. "This won't be the end."

Cinnia inclined her head. "Damn right it won't. You're going to let this heal and get back in the game."

"Yeah."

His gaze shifted to his fiancée: her soulful brown eyes had the distinct ability to calm him, and now wasn't any different. In the grander scheme of things, an injury like this was inevitable. The timing sucked but, thankfully, it wasn't insurmountable.

The Netherlands lost 3-2 during the penalty shoot-outs. With this much love and support in his life, Logan still felt like he was leaving a winner.

CHAPTER TWENTY-SEVEN

LOGAN'S GAZE BURNED like green fires while he stared at himself in the mirror. His reflection was focused, formidable and excited. Dressed in a tailored designer tuxedo that accentuated his build and coloring, he could already imagine the headlines in online newspapers, magazines and social media alike.

He didn't give a fuck what they thought.

It's been a whirlwind since his injury at the FIFA World Cup and subsequent start at Everton. Logan had healed very well because he stuck to the physiotherapist's strict list of warm-up exercises, and he had mostly been welcomed by English fans. His fellow teammates were not as friendly as those at Ajax had been at first, although it hadn't stayed that way. Some of them were here today.

I'm getting married.

His mirror image smiled happily. He had no idea how his mother and Alyssa had pulled this off so quickly, but it helped that he had a bit of celebrity that could be leveraged to secure a large venue. They simply knew too many people to keep the wedding small: as much as he didn't want a fuss, that was exactly what they were getting.

And besides, they *had* to get married: she was expecting twins.

Mirror Logan's smile broadened as he remembered the night she'd broken the news. She'd seemed nervous when she came out of the ensuite at their penthouse apartment in Liverpool, wearing nothing but his Everton jersey. She had joined him on the bed and rested her hand on his arm to get his attention.

"I have to tell you something," she'd said quietly.

His mind had immediately jumped to worst case scenarios at her tone, preparing retorts in case it had something to do with breaking off their engagement, but he'd stopped himself from saying anything and instead waited for the punch line.

She'd nibbled on her bottom lip. "I'm pregnant."

Thank the gods!

Logan had been absolutely blown away by the news, laughing as he cupped her face in his hands to kiss her forehead. "Fuck, that's incredible! Really?"

"You're happy about this?"

"Aren't you?"

"I don't know…" Alyssa had trailed off, glancing away. "Logan, we're so young."

"So?"

"You just started at Everton."

"So?"

"The wedding's three months away."

"And?"

"What do you mean, *and*? Don't you think this is too soon?"

"No, I don't." He had eyed her seriously. "Do you?"

She had gazed at him for a long moment, the worry slowly fading from her facial expression. "Not really. I swear I didn't do this on purpose."

"Is *that* what you're freaking out about?" Shifting her onto his lap, he'd stroked her thighs while he looked up at her. "Betty, no more messing around. I don't care if it's now or later in life, as long as we have a family together. I don't care if you have a bump at the wedding. I don't care what people think."

Alyssa had let out a long breath and smiled. "Good, 'cause I think I'm two months along."

He had pulled her into his arms for a passionate kiss that turned into tender lovemaking. She'd been on birth control and still fallen pregnant, which suggested that their babies were eager to be here. So what if they were both under the age of twenty-five? They would figure it out together.

"There are so many photographers staking out this wedding, it's insane," Connor said in awe, bringing Logan back to the present. "I don't know how you get used to it."

"I'm not," Logan chuckled. "I try to ignore them."

"It's all you can do," Andries agreed.

"It's a good thing Logan's the famous one, 'cause you would've let it go to your head," Fitz teased.

Connor shrugged, not denying it, and straightened his bowtie. More than ever, he looked like the male protagonist of Jesse's book series in that suit: like he was an undercover special agent with a Navy Seal background.

Byron entered the room, dashing in Tom Ford. "It's time, Lo."

Logan nodded excitedly, following the men down a corridor that led to the front of the aisle. They were in a beautiful Catholic cathedral, and for a moment Logan got distracted by the architecture while he mused a life that could've been.

If he hadn't met Alyssa, who would he have married? Luca? Someone else? Would they have been happy? Would he have made a good architect? A decent Prez to the club?

Doesn't matter now, Brennan's voice reminded him from somewhere. *You chose a different path, and you're better off for it.*

If he'd thought that the World Cup had been eventful, what with making his debut and finally getting a real chance with Alyssa, it's been nothing compared to the months that followed.

Connor and Jesse got married mere weeks after the semifinals. As Connor's best man, Logan had to hobble along in a moon boot while his childhood friend said his vows. Jesse had been nearly six months pregnant at the time, positively glowing as she said "I do".

He and Alyssa had had brief moments to catch up with loved ones before they flew back to England to move into their new place. Ajax had been sad to see him go, but the friends he'd made there were for life, and he had taken the competitive jibes they made in stride.

Between their own wedding arrangements, his new start at Everton, settling into their condo and her pregnancy, Logan had no idea how they've made it to the Big Day unscathed, but he was thrilled to spend the rest of his life with such a kick-ass partner in crime.

"All rise."

The five hundred guests fell silent as they stood up and turned. They were all taken aback by the song Alyssa has chosen for her bridesmaids: *Another One Bites the Dust* by Queen. Logan wasn't the only one grinning as, one by one, they sashayed down the aisle to the bass-driven beat. Wearing gorgeous light pink gowns designed by Versace, a highly pregnant Jesse was followed by Alyssa's fellow bloggers, Mia and Kayla, and her maid of honor, Sophie.

He dipped his head at the latter, who gave him a bright smile in return. She had been his best friend and introduction to sex, before their paths split in different directions. She was also the reason he got to meet the woman he's about to marry, way back when, and he'll always have a place in his heart for her.

A silence descended over the church as everyone eagerly waited for the bride: none more eager than Logan. He let out a delighted laugh once Elvis Presley's voice crooned from the speakers. *Can't Help Falling in Love* was the perfect song to describe their relationship.

He held his breath when she appeared, feeling like the whole world has ceased to exist except for the two of them. He remembered having a brief vision years ago, when he'd been the best man at his father's wedding, about Alyssa in a wedding gown, but nothing could ever be as striking as reality.

Her ivory-colored dress was designed by Vera Wang and wrapped perfectly around her toned physique. She was five months pregnant now, but the high waist and A-line skirt gave no hint of her belly. Her face was hidden by a veil.

Logan got swept up by the music as she walked closer on her father's arm. Falling for her had been completely beyond his control and their timing has always seemed off, yet their connection hasn't wavered over the years: it grew stronger with every breath. By the time she arrived in front of him, he had tears in his eyes.

Her father, Dustin, lifted the veil and kissed her cheek with a tender expression on his face. Then he nodded to Logan, before taking his place in the pews next to her mom, Felicity.

Logan's gaze connected with Alyssa's. Her makeup was tastefully done, merely emphasizing the warmth of her brown eyes, and fullness of her pink mouth. She'd dyed her hair a darker shade of golden blonde, which somehow made her skin glow even more. She smiled tearfully and whispered that she loved him.

Taken by her beauty and the moment, he cupped her face in his hands and kissed her. He didn't hear the gasps or chuckles from the priest and their guests. All that mattered was the feel, smell and taste of her.

"I love you, too," he murmured on her lips as he pulled away.

"Naughty, Beanie," she giggled with rosy cheeks. "That comes *after*."

He pecked her again and straightened, turning to the priest.

"You may be seated," the man said, shaking his head with a laugh. At least he had a good sense of humor. "Dearly beloved, we are gathered here today to witness the union of Logan Bean Drummond and Alyssa Bethany Edgar in holy matrimony."

Although they weren't religious, they saw the ceremony for what it was: a way to publicly affirm and celebrate their love. They had therefore decided to get married in traditional fashion. It added a certain weight and gravitas to the day that made them both feel more secure, and it involved their family and friends. The community that will be holding them accountable.

Connor handed over the ring at the appropriate time, and Logan held Alyssa's left hand while he slipped it on. "With this ring, I thee wed," he winked, eliciting another giggle from her. They'd agreed to have a dramatic opening to their vows. "Betty, you made me a man. You showed me that life doesn't have to be difficult, that I'm in control of my destiny. And every day, you've inspired me to make my own way. Your support over the last couple of months has blown my mind. I'm happy that we're here, finally, and look forward to spending the rest of my life loving you."

Alyssa dabbed the tears from her eyes and whispered thanks to Sophie, who'd quickly reached over to give her the ring and a tissue. Alyssa's trembling hand held Logan's as she pushed the wedding band onto his finger.

"With this ring, I thee wed. Beanie, I've loved you from the moment we met, although you couldn't make me admit that before now." She smiled when he laughed. "I've been so proud and strong, and yet you've shown me that it's okay when I'm not. That I still have value, even when I'm vulnerable. Watching you become who you are today has been one heck of a ride, but I wouldn't have it any other way. You push me to be better, to seek adventure, and I love you for that. I'm excited to go on this wild journey with you."

"With the power vested in me by the Church of England, I now pronounce you husband and wife. You may resume the kissing."

Logan chuckled as he pulled Alyssa closer to the seal the deal. This time, he was more controlled and cognizant of their guests and kept it appropriate.

"Ladies and gentlemen, Logan and Alyssa Drummond!"

They broke apart and made their way down the aisle, passing their loved ones. Luca stood with Cinnia and, although Logan's heart skipped a beat at the sight of her—she remained a beautiful young woman—it didn't carry the accompanying hormonal charge or sense of possession he'd known before.

Small flowers showered down on them as they hurried to the awaiting car, and the cheers of their guests cut off once they were tucked inside. He turned to his wife, unsurprised to see that she was emotional. He touched her cheek and kissed her forehead.

"You okay?"

"Yeah, I just can't believe this is real," she sniffed. "It feels like it's been a long time coming."

He held her. "It has."

"Or maybe it's just because I'm fat and pregnant."

His shoulders shook as he laughed. "You're only one of those things."

She leaned back to stared at him. Even though her makeup was smudged from her tears, he didn't think she's ever looked more stunning. When her hand slid up from his chest to his neck and she breathed his name, he knew what she needed because it burned within him, too.

Their lips met with heat.

His hand dove under her gown at the same time she shifted to straddle his lap. Her kisses were hungry, arousing beyond belief, and she gripped the back of his neck when he began teasing her pussy through the lacy G-string she wore. It wasn't long before he felt the effect he had on her: heady, in and of itself.

With quick maneuvering, he freed his cock and notched it at her entrance. "Take me, wife."

Alyssa whimpered, wide-eyed as she worked her way down his shaft. Her eyelids fluttered once he was sheathed, and she gripped his shoulders. "Oh my God, Logan."

"Move," he gritted out, the moment already intense enough to make him mindless with arousal. "Alyssa, *move.*"

She either didn't hear him or was being defiant, because the leisurely way she rode him contrasted with the need she'd expressed minutes ago. "Logan," she mumbled, throwing her head back.

He shut his eyes, mentally transported to that night on the roof when his whole life had changed. Her turquoise-tinted mohawk messy from his grabby hands, her lips swollen; nipple piercings glistening… Light emanating from her skin. Her breathy moans as he'd taken her again, and again, and *again*… She'd been a formidable angel, claiming her soul mate.

Her pussy clenched, bringing him back to the present, and he watched this version of her doing the exact same thing.

Growling, he gripped her ass under the sophisticated dress she wore and forced her to move faster. He basked in her surprised yelp while he ground his cock into her, deeper and deeper.

She made eye contact again, her face flushed in pleasure, and her lips parted. "Logan!"

He felt the pulses that confirmed her release, and shivered as they pulled him under, too. He wouldn't be surprised if his fingertips left marks on her ass from holding her so tightly.

She leaned her forehead against his. "I love you."

"I love you," he panted, in awe of their connection. Slowly, his hands moved forward to her touch her rounded stomach: he was so grateful for this woman. "Thank you for meeting me at the World Cup."

She burst out laughing. "Thank you for waiting for me."

He glanced to his right, noting that the car has stopped. "Guess it's time to get back out there."

She squeezed his semi, grinning when he twitched in response. "I guess."

Pressing a kiss to the corner of her mouth, he whispered: "We'll have plenty of time for that, later."

"We kinda have forever now."

"Exactly."

She dismounted and they straightened their clothes. Logan made sure they were both presentable before exiting the vehicle first, since this wedding has attracted the paparazzi and he didn't want to put her in a compromising position. Thankfully, the windows were tinted, or the press would've seen quite a show!

He helped her out of the car to the sound of cheers. The guests have already arrived at the country manor Alyssa had fallen in love with. She didn't know it yet, but this wasn't only their reception venue: his offer to purchase had been accepted early this morning.

It would be the perfect place to raise their family.

Alyssa's makeup artist rushed over to fix their faces, and for the next two hours they were directed this way and that by the photographers and videographers. Their family and friends joined them for snaps but were otherwise being entertained inside the manor. Due to their extensive guest list and, to a lesser extent, Logan's celebrity status, their day wasn't as short and sweet as they'd hoped.

Eventually, they were allowed to join the festivities.

They sat at the main table and endured the retelling of childhood stories and inside jokes by parents and friends. They opened the dance floor, their family and bridal party following suit. At some point, Logan even danced with Felicity.

"It's so good to see her this happy," Alyssa's mom smiled, gazing at Alyssa, who was dancing with her father. "I didn't think I'd ever get to see it."

"How so?" Logan asked, curious.

"She was always headstrong and independent. Aloof, even. I didn't realize that she was interested in conventional commitment until you two got engaged. She was never this serious about Jake."

He knew that Alyssa's relationship with her parents was strained, and suspected it was due to miscommunication. While he longed to repair it, he wouldn't interfere.

"I'm glad I get to make her happy."

And so the conversations went with every dance partner. It was seen as a moment to gush over the wedding or newlyweds, or to catch up. His mother monopolized his time for longer than the rest, as expected.

"You're going to be a dad soon," Cinnia murmured, her green eyes swimming in tears. "You're your own man now."

He pecked her cheek. "Thanks to you and dad."

"We just pointed you in the right direction, my boy."

"You always do that."

She frowned. "Do what?"

"Deflect my compliments." He raised an eyebrow with a slight smile. "Can't you just accept that you're an awesome mom, and I have all of this because of you?"

Blushing slightly, she wiped her tears as they fell. "Thank you, Logan. It always felt touch and go. I know I can be overbearing."

"I think you found your freedom through granting me mine."

"Yeah, you're probably right, but don't sound like such a wise ass."

He chuckled. "Love you too, momma."

The food was incredible and the three-tier cake absolutely delicious. Both he and Alyssa had changed into more comfortable outfits by the time they were smashing cake on each other's faces, playing into the rituals even more. He remembered questioning these activities at Sophie's wedding. Now that the shoe was on the other foot, he was having a blast.

Connor and Jesse left early. She was highly pregnant and dead on her feet. Sophie and Max weren't far behind, even though she was the maid of honor and technically supposed to stay until the very end.

"I love you, Drummonds, but not that much," she quipped as she hugged them each in turn.

Alyssa laughed, squeezing Sophie. "Go make those babies, guys."

"Oh, we will," she vowed, tugging a chuckling Max to their car. "Thanks for paying for the hotel, Lo!"

Logan waved, twining his arm around Alyssa's waist as they turned back to the massive house. "So, I have a surprise for you."

"Yeah?"

He gestured towards the manor. "This is ours."

A frown brought her eyebrows together. "What do you mean?"

"I bought it. It's not that far away from the city, and I think it's more appropriate for raising a family. And I know you love it."

She gaped at him. "Appropriate for raising a…? How many kids do you want, twelve?"

"That's a football team, plus a substitute."

Smacking his shoulder, she exclaimed: "You bought this?!" When he nodded, she threw her arms around him. "But it's going to be impossible to keep clean!"

"I'll let you figure out those details. You did grow up in a house like this, after all. Besides, if all else fails, we can always turn it into a travel destination."

"We will *not* be doing that." She kissed his cheek as she dropped back onto her feet, beaming up at him. "Thank you, husband."

He could feel himself glowing at the new endearment. "Let's get back to it, wife."

Many guests began trickling out: it was getting late and not everyone was prepared to party into the early hours. The official end to the celebration was a display of fireworks in the backyard.

Alyssa's hand was clutching his as she leaned into him, seeming as content as he felt. He knew it wouldn't always be easy, but he was blessed to be married to the only woman he could ever fully be himself with.

INTERLUDE—2—ALYSSA

SHE'S ALWAYS BEEN proud of her strength.

It was one of the few things she could claim as her own: something her parents' wealth had nothing to do with. To this day, they couldn't understand what drove her to be so independent and self-sufficient; why she insisted on working when she was the daughter of a family with old money and married to a football superstar.

She often didn't understand it herself, but her life would've been very different if she'd accepted what she's been given.

As a young girl, Alyssa hadn't fit in with her snobbish peers at private school. She had been too adventurous and "out there" and had seen her fellow students as carbon copies of their parents. She'd quickly come to the conclusion that she'd rather become a fully formed person in her own right.

She'd met Emile and his band of misfits at a hockey camp, and they'd kept in contact once they realized they were from the same town. They'd been inseparable, constantly on the lookout for the next exciting activity to try. It wasn't long before they had settled on rock-climbing, where she'd met Sophie and, eventually, Logan.

When Emile passed away, Alyssa had been devastated, nearly inconsolable. But she'd seen it as even more of a wake-up call: he had lived a carefree life, never once balking at the call to adventure, and she'd decided to continue that philosophy.

Her family's opinions on her lifestyle quickly became less important than her own happiness. The more adventures she embarked on, the more she felt comfortable in her own skin. She had traveled to incredible and obscure places, made friends from all walks of life—people who hadn't been raised with silver spoons in their mouths—and through it all she hadn't lost sight of who she was.

Yes, she prided herself in her strength. But damn, she felt *weak* whenever she clapped eyes on Logan Bean Drummond.

The man was perfection, from head to toe: a foot taller, lean like the professional athlete he was, pale skin, those green eyes that got tinged with ice whenever he was angry or turned on, dark hair and a naughty mouth... And he made her laugh until she couldn't breathe. His mind fascinated her; she loved listening to him talk. She had been putty in his hands from day one.

It hadn't been easy falling for someone who'd been infatuated with another woman. Alyssa's connection to him had been instant and intense, and yet she'd also seen how he felt about Luca. Their three-year age gap wasn't that significant, yet he'd only been eighteen at the time. He had been struggling with his identity; Alyssa had recognized the signs and stepped away of her own accord, although it had broken her heart to let him go. And every time they'd run into each other, it had left her more hung up on him.

Now, four years into marriage and a set of twins later, she still couldn't believe how their life has changed. They were incredible, like she's always suspected they would be, even if they were by no means perfect. He was one of her favorite people, and staunchest supporters.

He's going to knock and ask what's wrong if you don't snap out of it, she thought, staring at her reflection.

She washed and dried her hands, turning to the side to eye this version of Alyssa Bethany Drummond. Her bump was small, like the first time, but that wouldn't last long. Just like before, they had a two-for-one deal. Both of their families had a long history of twins, so she wasn't that surprised, but *four* kids... She and Logan were overachievers!

The first pregnancy had been a surprise because he'd knocked her up even though she'd been using contraception. His reaction to the news had been the opposite of hers: euphoric, while she'd been terrified. True to form, he'd given her the time she needed to mentally get on board.

Alyssa often mused how weddings had formed the basis of their relationship. First his parents', followed by Sophie's, and then Connor and Jesse's a few weeks after the World Cup. Each of these events had deeply impacted Logan and Alyssa, reinforcing what they viewed as the ultimate commitment in life, until they had tied the knot themselves.

Stroking the rounded part of her stomach, a soft smile curved her mouth upwards. She was four months along and happy their dream of having a big family was being realized. It was a departure from her and Logan's only-child upbringings, but an adventure they've taken on together.

Their two boys had arrived three weeks earlier than expected and, although she'd hoped to give birth naturally, they were delivered via emergency C-section. They named Calvin James after Cinnia's father, and Lincoln Reade after Brennan's. At nearly four years old, they were the lights of her life even when they drove her crazy, which was often: she was surrounded by men!

There was a knock on the door. "Betty, you okay?"

She fought a smile as she walked towards his voice. "Yeah, I'm great."

Logan's green gaze took her in. "You look beautiful." He reached for her tummy and grinned. "Can't wait to meet these two."

"Me too, if only to skip over the next couple of months."

"Mom's asked if they can keep Cal and Linc for another night. Apparently, they're having a ton of fun."

She wrinkled her nose. "I don't know. I miss them."

"So do I, but it does mean we can have more uninterrupted sexy time."

Bursting into giggles when he pressed her to him, she quipped: "You, Beanie, are getting a vasectomy."

"You're already pregnant."

"Nah-uh, you promised."

"Which is why my appointment's next week." He bent his head to nuzzle the base of her neck. "Are you saying you don't want sexy time?"

She shivered, clutching his shirt. She doubted it was possible to grow tired of him. "I'm saying you should make me want it."

"Oh *really*," he murmured, his fingers sliding into her long hair. "Does that mean we're skipping the game?"

The Jackals were in town for the annual match against the Raptors and, because Logan was on a rare two-week break, he could play with the men who'd shaped him into the person he was today. He and Alyssa had decided the best way to spend his time off would be here, with their family. Years ago, he'd purchased a house three blocks away from where he'd grown up, which was where they were currently staying.

"Would that be… bad?" she teased, standing on tiptoes and angling her mouth to his earlobe, which she captured with her teeth.

"The guys will never forgive me."

Her hands slipped under his shirt, exploring his back. "That sounds like a you-problem."

He tilted her chin up and kissed her deeply, his fingers locking on her hair while he anchored her to the wall with his hips. She loved the way his erection pressed against her rounded stomach, serving as a reminder that he only had eyes for her. Moaning, her hand dipped into his shorts to take a hold of the reason why she was pregnant.

"Alyssa," he hissed when she began pumping. "Jesus, do you want this to be over before it begins?"

She pouted. "I thought you're in a hurry."

"I don't want to finish in your hand." He hiked her skirt up and cupped her core, groaning once he felt she wasn't covered. "No panties?"

"Damn, I forgot."

"Love your pregnancy brain." Two fingers pushed into her damp channel. "Keep forgetting all about underwear."

"Logan!"

"That's my name, Betty."

She would've rolled her eyes if he hadn't distracted her by rubbing her G-spot. "Stop being a dick," she whimpered.

"But you love my dick," he chuckled.

Before she could formulate a huffy response, he dropped to his knees to lick her pussy without stopping the vigorous way his fingers rubbed her.

"Going to miss this piercing," he mumbled on her clit, his teeth clamping on one end of the silver bar and tugging.

Her knees felt like they were made of jelly. If he kept at it, she was going to end up slithering to the floor in a puddle. "Logan!"

"You're so wet, Alyssa. It must mean you like me."

"I would if you—*Ah*!" He'd nipped that sensitive bundle of nerves! "Did you just *bite* me?"

"Did you just like it?"

She could've lied and said no, but her hands were clutching his head and she was rocking into his face, which meant she didn't have much of an argument. No one's ever eaten her out like Logan. His tongue, teeth and fingers turned her into a moaning mess. She was so close! If he'd simply flick her clit a few more times—

"Alyssa, are you going to soak my hand?"

—then she would unravel. "Yes," she panted.

"Do you promise?"

Two more, she thought blissfully, *I need two more licks!* "Yes!"

He sighed contentedly. "Cum for me, baby mama."

She would've smacked the back of his head, had her body not done exactly what he commanded. She trembled at the intensity of her orgasm, shutting her eyes. He's confessed on a previous occasion that he's only ever had such carefree sex with her and that she's the only one he didn't want to dominate and control, therefore she allowed his wisecracks. She secretly adored them: anything that separated her from the many women he's bedded was fine by her.

His lips brushed hers, giving her a taste of her own essence. "You kept your promise: my hand is soaked." He hooked one of her legs over his hip and withdrew his fingers. When the tip of his cock pressed on her entrance, he said: "Look at me, Alyssa."

Eyelids fluttering open, she met his interesting blue-green gaze. They changed color when he was angry or aroused. "I love you."

"Do you want more?"

"Yes," she replied as she bucked against him, frustrated that he resisted. "Logan!" He laughed softly and pitched forward, filling her with another inch. It made her overly aware of how much his cock stretched her. "Logan, please!"

"More?"

"Yes!" she begged.

He complied, going in a *little* deeper. "Like that?"

Letting out a frustrated moan, she demanded: "Fuck me!"

His eyes darkened. "Hot damn," he said as he rammed inside, to the hilt.

She clung to his shoulders as he thrust into her, moving her hips to help him set a pace that had them both gasping for breath. Her pussy greedily clenched around his cock, and she loved the tormented grunt he gave in response. She giggled: he was not going to last much longer.

"Think you've got this?"

"Know I do," she countered. Her back bowed when his finger circled her anus. "Logan!"

"This is why I wanted you to soak my hand."

She screamed in pleasure as that digit pushed in, instantly toppling over the edge.

"Fuck, you're beautiful when you cum," he whispered reverently. He carried her to the bed, their favorite place to have sex. Once he was braced over her, he began pushing inside again. "I love you, Alyssa."

Her brain has turned to mush, as it so often did when he made love to her, and all she could do was kiss him while their bodies moved together. She hated that they weren't naked, since she longed to feel his smooth skin on hers. Then again, his cock moving in and out of her slick core was a welcome diversion.

When he reached orgasm, she was right behind him. He collapsed on top of her, and she stroked his hair while they basked in the afterglow. "Every time is like that night on the roof, and somehow a million times better."

"I know," she smiled.

He raised his head. "Ready to get going?"

"Yeah, let's."

He pulled out, got up and righted his clothes, before holding his hand out to help her up. "Meet you downstairs?"

"Sure."

She headed to the ensuite to splash her face with cold water and wipe away the liquid trickling down her inner thighs. She remembered underwear this time, and slipped her feet into comfortable loafers before walking downstairs.

She found him in the kitchen, where he was packing her favorite juice and a couple of bottles of water into a cooler bag. He draped his arm over her shoulders as they sauntered into the garage, kissing her temple before he opened the passenger door of the SUV for her.

"Ever the gentleman."

"I know what I have to do if I want to keep getting into your panties," he teased. "You know, on the rare occasion you wear them."

Rolling her eyes with a laugh, she pressed the button for the garage door.

He started the engine and easily reversed, looking hot as fuck in his Raptors uniform. It somehow suited him better than the Everton colors.

"Have you told your parents about the babies yet?"

His question took her off guard. She gazed out the window. "No, why should I? They haven't made much of an effort with Cal and Linc."

"To be fair, we live half a world away."

"Don't be fair: they're mega rich. They can go where they want, when they want."

"I don't think you're going to like what I'm about to say."

She narrowed her eyes. "Spit it out."

He glanced at her, a worried set to his mouth. "Well, you haven't really invited them to visit. Maybe they're respecting your boundaries and don't want to show up unannounced."

She opened her mouth to retort, and then shut it when she realized he was right. It wasn't always nice when he called out her bullshit, but she appreciated that he didn't tiptoe around her feelings.

"Good point."

"Write down the date and time, ladies and gentlemen."

"Milk this for all it's worth, while you can."

He grinned. "Oh, I will."

They continued the verbal banter until he pulled into the parking lot at the sports field. There weren't that many open spots available, but Byron and Cinnia must've arranged for Logan to park next to their car.

"Remember when we were in Amsterdam, talking about kids?"

He turned the ignition off and smiled, inclining his head. "Yeah, I'll never forget the way you looked at me, as if you knew I was going to knock you up one day."

"I don't know how I knew that. But I'm glad we're here."

He stroked her cheek with the back of his hand, a contemplative look on his face. "It's been—"

Bang!

Connor slapped Logan's window, causing them both to jump in fright. "Come on, lovebirds! We've got a game to win!"

Alyssa placed a hand over her wildly beating heart. "Sometimes, I want to wring his neck."

"You're not the only one," Logan muttered. He opened his door and stepped out. "Impeccable timing as always, Prez."

She didn't hear Connor's witty retort, but waved at Jesse, who was tugging her daughter along. "I don't know how you stay sane with him."

Jesse giggled and hugged Alyssa. "He's a loveable asshole."

"How are you, Brigitte?" Alyssa asked, kneeling in front of the gorgeous, if shy, five-year-old.

"She's in another one of her moods," Jesse sighed when no answer was forthcoming. "She and her brother had a fight."

"Where is Liam?"

"With my mom and Sophie. Brig insisted on tagging along."

Alyssa smiled when Brigitte pressed a small hand to her baby bump. "Good to see you too, Brig."

"Babe!" Connor interrupted the moment. "Time to go!"

The five of them meandered to the bleachers, although the men split off halfway to convene with the rest of the team. Jesse and Alyssa chatted until they spotted the Raptors women.

"Get ready for chaos," Alyssa whispered, which made Jesse giggle.

"Lys! Look, boys, there's your mommy!"

Her heart leapt with joy at the sight of her sons with their gran, and she rushed forward to hug them. They were nearly identical with their light skin and dark hair. Their similarities ended with their eyes: Lincoln had her brown, but Calvin had one amber and one green.

They clung to her neck, and she kissed each of their cheeks. "Did you miss me? I missed you!"

"Granny made us lasagna," Lincoln declared proudly.

"Oh, really?"

"Yes, and then Bobby Brown farted," Calvin nodded.

Alyssa pressed her lips together so she wouldn't laugh. Their utterings were so damn cute. She straightened, taking each of their hands, and walked to her mother-in-law. "Thanks for taking such good care of them."

"Are you kidding? They're the best!" Cinnia gave Alyssa a sideways hug. "I wish they could stay forever."

"They would be spoiled beyond measure."

Cinnia batted her eyelashes. "You know me so well."

They merged with the rest of the group, Alyssa greeting each one of them in turn. Part of her wondered what her life would've been like if her and

Logan still lived here, although she wouldn't really change a thing. They had phenomenal experiences together that she couldn't imagine trading for a simpler, more conventional life.

Aurora and Hallie seemed to be going strong, even though it had apparently taken them a while to get into a healthy rhythm. They had no plans to get married, but were saving up to do a jet setting tour around the world. Hallie had even contacted Alyssa for traveling tips. Even Dane had found love with one of Connor's patients, Misty: they were set to get married in a few months.

Jesse was a devoted wife to Connor, and mindful mother to her two redheaded kids, Brigitte and Liam. She'd recently struck a lucrative book deal after years of honing her craft, and there were even rumors that the series will be adapted onto film.

Sophie and Max were going from strength to strength. Her dance studio was thriving due to regular collaborations with budding artists, and Max had been promoted at the precinct. They had three kids together: Topher, Celine and Matthew.

These were all things that her and Logan have missed out on, and yet no one resented them for it. In fact, every reunion picked up where they'd left off.

"Hey, ladies, how's it going?"

Everyone's eyes shifted to the latest addition.

Luca smiled with a warmth that had been lacking in her teenage years. She was wearing a long-sleeved, translucent black shirt with a crop top underneath, along with trademark abraded jeans and black boots. Her dark hair was braided over one shoulder, and her face without any makeup. She'd donned a cap to keep the sun out of her violet eyes.

Alyssa was once again struck by Luca's beauty. She could see why Logan—not to mention a horde of other men—had been drawn to her. Despite their past, though, Alyssa had nothing but appreciation for the woman. She'd helped Logan grow up.

"You made it!" Cinnia nearly tackled Luca to the ground. "I've missed you so much!"

Luca returned the hug with open joy. "Told you I'll be here, mom."

The women took turns greeting Luca, failing to notice the man standing off to one side until, all hugged out, Luca reached for his hand. A second hush fell over the group while they perused this newcomer. His dark hair was even longer than Luca's, and he gave off the appearance of someone who enjoyed heavy metal music.

"Ladies, this is Ethan," Luca introduced him. She chewed on her bottom lip for a second, exchanging a glance with him. "My boyfriend."

Cinnia gasped, her eyes filling with tears, as if she'd never thought this day would come but was relieved it had, all the same. "It's a pleasure to meet you, Ethan." She briefly embraced the man, and then fondly touched the side of Luca's face. "Please, join us! I want to hear *everything* about your trip!"

Alyssa paid rapt attention to Luca and Ethan's recollection of how they'd met on Luca's latest assignment. She was proud of Luca for putting herself out there, given her history. They had a calm energy about them that gave the impression that they were taking things slowly, which was exactly what Luca needed. Ethan was a beautiful soul.

A whistle interrupted their story, and everyone's focus turned to the pitch. Luca kissed Ethan's cheek, eliciting a collective sigh from the Raptors women, and then she moved to sit next to Alyssa.

"Hi," she greeted again, this time giving Alyssa her full attention.

"I'm so happy for you, girl. Congratulations."

"Thanks. I've thought of you a lot ever since I met him. I wondered what you'll think, since you're so perceptive and considering what you told me. You know, about finding myself."

"It looks like you have."

"I'm getting there," Luca nodded. "It's liberating."

"I can imagine." She bumped her shoulder to Luca's. "Logan will be glad to see you."

"I'm nervous about that." Luca rubbed her legs and glanced at Ethan, who was answering Cinnia's probing questions into his past with grace. "I don't know how to handle them in the same space."

"Welcome to my world," Alyssa chuckled.

Luca seemed bewildered. "Oh my gosh, Lys—"

"You and I are cool." Alyssa squeezed Luca's hand. "You have a place in Logan's life and, by extension, mine."

"Good to know." Her eyes dipped to Alyssa's abdomen and back up again. "I don't mean to pry, but are you pregnant?"

"Yes, four months. Twins, *again*."

"Oh wow, that's so amazing! Logan's always wanted a big family."

"And Ethan?"

"He knows it's not something I can have or even want, and he's happy with that."

"That's awesome, Luca. I'm glad you found someone."

"Me too. He makes me feel like I'm part of something bigger."

Alyssa knew what that was like. The man running circles around the rest on that pitch was the reason why she believed in forever, and why she would continue to seek adventures: for her, for him, their children and extended family.

He's right, though: you need to make peace with your parents.

And she would start with that as soon as this game was finished.

Chapter Twenty-Eight

LOGAN TURNED ON his side to stare at the woman next to him.

She was fast asleep, her waist-length brown hair spread on the pillow. Her lush mouth was parted slightly, bringing to mind the countless times she's laughed, yelled, and brought him pleasure. The sheet had shifted down to her ribs in the night, exposing the swells of her breasts, which stirred his arousal.

Waking up with the woman he loved was his definition of happiness.

Usually, he was out on his morning run by now. She joined him whenever she could but, because she was such a hands-on mother and the kids tended to rise at the crack of dawn, she didn't often get the chance. By the time he'd get back, the five of them would already be busy in the kitchen, where he'd fall in to help with breakfast before heading out to train at Everton FC.

Today, they could sleep in: it was Christmas.

Their parents and his grandparents had arrived at their manor in the Liverpool countryside two days ago, and they all took turns looking after and entertaining the kids. With the bedrooms soundproofed—a necessity when you're the father of two sets of twins—he could only imagine the commotion going on downstairs.

He moved closer to Alyssa, tugging the sheet further down. She'd gone for a breast lift a year ago and there was only the slightest scarring left around her piercing-free nipples. She had a few stretchmarks on her hips from carrying their kids, though her tanned skin was otherwise blemish free. The small C-section line on her lower stomach always made his heart expand with love.

In his eyes, she was absolute perfection.

The sheet stopped mid-thigh and he gazed at her trimmed pussy. During the last pregnancy, she'd decided to remove her piercings once and for all. They had made it their combined mission to prove she could still reach orgasm, seeing as she'd originally got the one on her clit to enhance her pleasure. He had been relieved when they succeeded the first time, and it had got significantly easier from there.

Her athleticism was identical to what it had been the day he met her. He'd been supportive of her decision to "fix her boobs", although he hadn't initially seen the need for it. She had reminded him it was for *her* more than anything else, and he had stopped trying to change her mind from there.

He traced one of her collarbones with his fingertip, following it to the center of her chest. It roamed to her left breast where, in a spiraling motion, it edged closer and closer to her nipple. By the time it reached its target, that peak was puckered, and he added another finger to squeeze. Even after nine years of marriage, his desire for her hasn't been sated, and he took immense pleasure in making her feel good.

Alyssa twitched in her sleep.

His hand slid down the side of her waist to her hip, where it turned diagonally towards her mound. He pressed his mouth to her shoulder while his fingers lightly stroked over her seam, back and forth.

"Hmm."

Taking that as encouragement, he leaned over her and wrapped his lips around the nipple he'd abandoned earlier. He wedged his knee between her legs while his tongue rolled over the curve of her breast and he sucked the peak, hard.

"Oh!" she gasped, finally waking.

He quickly licked two of his fingers before parting her lower lips and playing with her clit. "Morning," he murmured against her other breast.

She gripped his hair. "Hey."

"Want to make the most of the quiet."

"Good idea."

He chuckled, loving that she was just as insatiable. They had made love in the shower the night before, and it's not like they didn't have quickies whenever they got a moment to themselves, but here they were getting it on *again*. Granted, it wasn't always easy what with their busy careers and four kids, but sex was an important factor in their relationship that they prioritized, as frequently as possible.

Her pussy was getting nice and wet, so he shifted down to tease it with his mouth.

"Logan."

That moan washed over him, by far his favorite sound in the world: the quiet, wistful, reverent tone gave him more chills than the cheering of thousands of football fans ever could.

He licked her from entrance to clit and back again. He fucked her with his tongue and sucked that sensitive bundle of nerves. He stretched her with his fingers, angling the tips up to attack her G-spot. She rocked underneath him, faster and faster, and exploded with his name on her lips.

He thrust his cock all the way inside, his skin tingling when she scraped her nails across his back to settle on his shoulder blades. He kissed her deeply—fuck morning breath—and her tongue twining with his made his toes curl. They moved together like well-oiled machines, pushing and pulling, and he only allowed himself to unload after she got her second fill.

Her wet kisses on his neck were heavenly. She bit his earlobe and whispered: "I love you."

"Merry Christmas, Betty." Logan smiled wickedly. "Your first present consists of five orgasms."

Brows furrowing, she protested: "But I only had two."

"Exactly." His cock was hardening inside her, and he retreated his hips a little before ramming to the hilt. "That's why we're not out of bed yet."

"Beanie," she whimpered, arching against him. "Oh my god, you feel so good."

He hooked her legs over his shoulders to change the angle, spreading her wide while he pounded into her. She gripped his ass to keep him at it. Her fingers did such a good job massaging his cheeks that he had to fight not to get pulled under by the tide.

"Lys," he warned.

Her answer was a naughty giggle.

With a growl, he sat back on his hunches, careful not to slip out of her tight warmth. His arm curled around her legs, keeping them together and braced against one of his shoulders, and he held her immobile while he went even deeper.

"Logan!" she cried.

He fucked her sweetly, but firmly, until she screamed the pleasure of her third orgasm. He pulled out, breathing fast, and dropped onto the mattress. "Get on top of me."

"Bossy," she noted in that breathy tone that indicated she couldn't remember her own name. She followed his instruction, all the same, her long hair tumbling over her chest as she notched his hard length.

"Obedient," he teased as his thumb pressed against her swollen clit. Her pussy was absolutely drenched, which drove his arousal higher.

"Only 'cause I love your cock."

She rode him leisurely at first, prolonging the sensations flowing through them both. Inevitably, her pace became nearly frantic as she rushed to the pinnacle in the hopes of getting him there first.

With a clenched jaw and a massive amount of self-control, he managed to stay on the edge even with her pussy pulsing around his cock a fourth time. Alyssa collapsed on top of him, panting heavily and mumbling an apology.

He stroked her spine and kissed the top of her head. "Shh, it's okay. Just enjoy the moment."

They stayed like that, connected on more than just the sexual level, for a long while. She eventually sat up to gaze at him, tucking her hair behind her ears. She smiled, dazed: with her flushed cheeks, she took his breath away.

"Merry Christmas, Beanie."

He twirled a lock of hair around his fingers. "Let's go get cleaned up."

They headed to the ensuite on shaky legs, wetting washcloths to wipe away sweat and the evidence of their lovemaking. They were side-by-side, brushing their teeth and giving each other heated looks via the mirror, when his cock stirred again.

She saw the shift in his facial expression and her gaze dipped below. When she made eye contact again, he could see she wanted it just as badly. After so many years together, they knew every tick and tell but, instead of it becoming boring, it made them more excited to exploit and explore.

They rinsed their mouths and embraced, kissing fervently while they fondled each other. He was torn between hoisting her up on the edge of the counter and flipping her around to fuck her from behind. He caught their reflection and, with a grunt, his decision was made.

He bent her over the edge, tilted her hips up and shoved his cock inside, intently watching her mouth part on a gasp. Those deep brown eyes stayed on his face, though his green ones locked on her mirror image. His hands cupped her breasts and tweaked her nipples while he thrust into her, over and over again.

God help him, he could never get enough of this. With Alyssa he had learned the definition of making love and, while their coupling varied from slow and sweet to hot and heavy, he couldn't imagine how he'd had such meaningless encounters as an adolescent.

You've got to experience the lows to appreciate the highs…

"Logan!" she exclaimed, slapping a palm on the mirror to steady herself.

He leaned forward to cover her hand with his own, tilting his head to her ear to whisper: "You look so fucking hot, Lys. Can't wait to feel you coming all over my cock. Are you gonna give it to me?"

She bit her lip, seeming pained while he enticed her with dirty talk. Her fingers twitched under his and she went rigid for a moment. And then her body convulsed as she came undone.

Logan saw that silver aura around her again: the warrior light that had first burst from her skin one steamy night on a rooftop. It tackled him over the edge and his grip tightened on her hip as he erupted.

They waited while their breathing evened out, staring lovingly at each other. He dropped a kiss on top of her head and eased out of her body, giving her round ass a playful spank. "That's five."

She burst out laughing. "Thank you, superstar." She reached for a brush to untangle her hair. "Do you think your mom's cooking breakfast?"

"Only if she beat *your* mom to it."

Shaking her head with another laugh, Alyssa grabbed the discarded washcloth to clean herself up again.

She'd reached a compromise with her parents shortly before Taron and Ava were born, and Logan had agreed to giving them Edgar second names: Kevin and Katherine, respectively. Since then, their relationship has greatly improved, to the point that Dustin and Felicity didn't miss out on any family events.

Felicity and Cinnia had hit it off, although they had a healthy competition going where cooking was concerned. They were both exceptional in the kitchen, and he was wise enough not to commit to a definitive answer when it came to the "who won?" question.

He and Alyssa got dressed and, hand-in-hand, ventured downstairs.

Logan had kept the apartment in Liverpool for when training or a home game ran late, but spent as many evenings as he could with Alyssa and the kids. He continued to play for Everton, although many English and greater European clubs have attempted to buy out his contract.

Because he had switched to a British premiere league team, he'd had the opportunity to represent England in two FIFA tournaments. In the last one, they'd made it all the way to the finals under his captaincy. Logan hoped that he would still be fit and good enough to play in another World Cup and that his team would win. Now that he was nearing thirty, though, the odds of keeping up with younger players were starting to dwindle.

Be that as it may, he remained a firm fan favorite, and the many endorsements that Marcus has secured over the years have allowed Logan to provide for his family and make investments, mostly in property, that have paid off well. Logan's main concern was building a legacy that would last long after he stopped playing football, although he was careful not to spoil his children too much.

He and Alyssa wanted them to understand the value of hard work.

Her blog had evolved into her own travel agency, which she managed from home. She'd insisted on being involved in their children's formative years. Frankly, Logan couldn't see that changing anytime soon and, as long as she was happy, he didn't really mind. Her degree in physiotherapy hadn't been for nothing, since she loved helping Logan with any injury or discomfort he picked up from being an athlete, but she'd long since decided not to pursue it professionally.

They found the men and their kids in the living room. As always, Logan's heart swelled with pride at the sight of the two pairs.

Calvin was patiently helping Ava open one of her presents. As the eldest, he's taken it upon himself to ensure everyone's safety and, with Ava being the lastborn and only girl among the boys, she was doubly protected.

Lincoln, Dustin and Byron played FIFA on the Xbox, while Taron made clay figurines with Logan's grandfathers, Reade and Jimmy. Taron loved crafting things with his hands, while Lincoln excelled at football. Logan had a feeling Linc would be an even better player than him one day, but has vowed he wouldn't pressure his children into anything.

Like him, they will get to choose their own fate.

"Morning," Alyssa greeted everyone.

A broken chorus of "morning" filled the room.

"Mummy, look!" Taron said happily, showing off his attempt at a clay elephant.

"Good job, my boy," she praised, going to him.

Logan went around shaking hands with the men, giving his kids a squeeze in turn, and settled with Calvin and Ava. With her auburn hair and ice blue eyes, there was no mistaking that she was Brennan's granddaughter.

"Daddy, Cal got me a mermaid!" Ava declared as she waved the doll. "Her hair's like mine!"

"How cool?" He kissed Calvin's forehead while beaming at his daughter. He didn't have favorites, but he knew he wasn't the only man in this house that would give up his life to defend Ava. "What did you get him?"

She smiled proudly, pointing. "That watch he wanted."

Calvin raised his wrist, a sardonic grin on his face. He'd figured out last year that Alyssa and Logan were behind purchasing gifts, but he was a team player and wouldn't spoil it for the other three.

"Wow, buddy," Logan winked. Calvin's mismatched eyes fascinated Logan to no end: as if his son had received both his and Alyssa's coloring, but with an amber twist. "It looks good on you."

"Thanks, dad."

Alyssa snuck out of the room at some point, probably to help the rest of the ladies in the kitchen, while Logan got to talking with the other adults. There were a few notable absences.

Luca and Ethan couldn't make it, as they were busy ticking off a mutual bucket list item: climbing Mount Kilimanjaro. They'd had a commitment ceremony two years ago—their version of a wedding—and seemed to be going strong. Logan was happy that she was living a full and rich life with someone she loved.

Connor was spending the holidays back home with Jesse and their kids at Dawn and Haye's, along with Jemma, Nixon, Aurora, Hallie, Sophie and the rest of their family. Even Dane and Misty had opted for a "chilled Christmas with the crazies". With Aurora and Hallie's tempers in the mix, Logan wasn't surprised by Dane's term to describe them.

Uncle Teagan and aunt Piper were on their second honeymoon. After years of back and forth, they'd decided to recommit to each other, to both Dane and Hallie's—not to mention Cinnia's—relief.

There were many other loved ones scattered around the globe that had sent video messages from their destinations: Fitz and Nina, kissing under the Eiffel tower; Andries and his family in the Netherlands; Tessa and her latest girlfriend, Emma, on a motorcycle tour back home; Logan's Everton teammates in tropical places like Bora Bora, Thailand and Mauritius.

All in all, Logan was grateful for the many people in his life, and especially grateful that they were healthy and happy.

"Breakfast is ready!" Loraine yelled down the hallway.

It took nearly ten minutes for everyone to settle in the large dining hall. Alyssa only ever used this room when family visited: the table could comfortably sit twenty people and reminded Logan of scenes from movies based on Jane Austen novels. He'd teased her for succumbing to her parents' grandiose style—she'd inherited her portion of Edgar money when she turned thirty, two years ago—until she had rightly pointed out that he didn't need an underground garage containing five sports cars and three Harleys, did he?

Logan, at the head of the table, cast a glance over his family.

These moments made every ache in his body worth it. Being surrounded by loved ones and providing them with a good meal were two things he was immensely proud to do. Sharing it with the woman who held his heart… Well, he couldn't imagine a better life.

Dustin tapped a spoon against his glass of orange juice to get everyone's attention and rose to his feet. He chuckled when Alyssa groaned theatrically. "Don't worry, I won't take long."

"I hope not," she said sweetly.

Felicity hid her giggle behind her hand.

"I just wanted to say thank you, to you and Logan, for opening your home to the rest of us again this year," Dustin told her. "When you were younger, your mother and I didn't understand your need to break away from our traditions or—"

"Dad, you say this *every* year," Alyssa interjected.

"Because it's important," he insisted. "We came from strict families, ourselves, and weren't allowed to question the status quo. You didn't wait for permission to break away and, Lys, I can never thank you enough for following your heart." Tears glistened in his eyes. "I don't think we would've ever been this close if you hadn't. And I'm grateful, every day, that we are."

Logan smiled as he watched Alyssa jump up to hug her father. When he'd met Alyssa and they'd started their romance, this had been a rare sight. These days, it was fairly common, but no less special.

"And *I* just want to say that Felicity upped her game with breakfast," Cinnia piped up as she began dishing for her parents. "These eggs look amazing."

"Aye, Ah cannae wait to try," Reade agreed.

"Thanks, Cin. Couldn't have done it without you," Felicity said.

"Dig in, everyone!" Alyssa urged them, having stepped away from her father and wiped her tears. She busied herself with the kids, making sure they had enough on their plate. At some point, she must've sensed Logan's gaze on her because she paused and made eye contact.

I love you, he mouthed.

She winked in response.

Breakfast was long and loud, bringing to mind the Raptors MC shindigs of the past. Logan sometimes missed the smell of grease, rubber and gasoline that hung around the warehouse of *Drummonds Customs & Repairs*; the sound of drunken male bonding booming over excited female chatter.

After the meal, they all helped clean up. Cinnia and Felicity were already talking about how to set the table for lunch—with a stomach this full, Logan had no idea how they could think about eating again—while everyone else scattered throughout the house to chat, have a nap, or play.

Logan went to the enclosed patio, staring at the snowy landscape outside: a complete juxtaposition to the environment where he'd grown up, and yet an ingrained part of his life today. Warmth settled in his chest a moment before he sensed a familiar presence.

You're lucky, my boy. All is well.

"Bren is here."

Logan glanced over his shoulder at his gran and held his arm out to her. Mysie shuffled over to him, and they stood together: three generations of their bloodline, although only two were in physical form.

"He's so proud of you," she whispered. "Your grandfather and I, too."

"Thanks, gran." He dropped a kiss on her wild grey hair. She was getting up there in age but was healthy and strong. *Still crazy*, he thought with a chuckle.

She poked him in his ribs. "I heard that. You're not too old for a spanking, you know."

"Hey, I'm a professional athlete now."

"You're a brat, is what you are."

His laugh echoed in the room. "I'm not in danger of becoming one with you people around."

"Good, no one likes a showoff."

"Look who's talking, Mrs. I-Can-Tell-The-Future."

"I *can*, sure, but I don't like to: it's much more fun watching you all suffer."

"Gran! That's not very nice."

"I've never been nice."

They began making their way back inside, exchanging quips along the way, and met everyone in the living room. Ava launched herself into Logan's arms while Taron tugged him in the direction of the Christmas tree to open more presents. Byron and Cinnia got Lincoln's massive gift from the back of the tree; Jimmy and Loraine were sitting with Calvin at the coffee table, assembling the five-hundred-piece puzzle he'd wanted; Felicity, Dustin, Reade and Mysie helped Alyssa pour tea for everyone.

Brennan had it right: Logan *was* lucky.

As a child and young man, he'd been so unsure of his identity and destiny, yet now he lived with a full heart. He was a son, grandson and cousin; a husband, lover and best friend; a father and mentor. A leader, in his own right.

And in that way, he was a Drummond, through and through.

413

EPILOGUE

HE HEARD THE bullets tearing through his skin, and instantly knew that it was over.

He should've listened to his gut, to *Byron's* gut, but he's always been too goddamn stubborn for his own good. He'd thought sheer willpower alone could change his fate, and perhaps in some ways that was true.

But he had only succeeded in prolonging the inevitable.

His mother had warned him this day would come: that somehow he would go before his time, should he insist on being with Cinnia. He didn't always understand how Mysie knew these things, although a part of him did, too. Maybe that's why things have always felt primal with Cinnia. Unavoidable.

In another life, he might've given up on the notion of marrying her, making her *his*. He could have met someone better, had a different life, and stuck around longer. They would have had a family, without all the conception drama, and he would have taught his sons how to play football and protected his daughters against men who weren't good enough for them.

Did that mean he had regrets?

No.

He could never regret following his heart and bringing Cinnia back to him. He had changed his ways and become a better man, because of her. They had made it through hell together, and they'd been blessed with Logan.

No regrets.

Byron was saying something, shifting him on the Blackline and fiddling with his belt. He wasn't really paying attention: there was too much pain ripping through him. He trusted Byron to do what's right. He was the Hero, after all.

He blinked in and out of consciousness, not knowing what was real and what wasn't. Time ceased to have any meaning or relevance.

Sometimes, he caught glimpses of Cinnia and Byron falling deeper in love. Byron comforting her, and Cinnia succumbing to the urge to take their friendship to the next level. They were keeping it secret from the club while they played house and raised Logan, but they couldn't hide that underlying energy that's always connected them.

He hadn't been blind to it, yet he knew they wouldn't act on it while he was alive.

Does that mean I'm dead?

Sometimes, he was shown flashes of Byron suffering at the hands of a man and woman, one more sadistic than the other. Byron was drugged out of his mind and being used for sex, struggling through an immense amount of physical and mental torture to get back to the club. To Cinnia, and to Logan. Sometimes he and Byron got to talk, although the conversations generally didn't last long and the advice he gave didn't always make sense to his conscious mind.

Am I conscious?

He could sometimes detect an ominous beeping—one he identified as a hospital monitor from the number of times he'd visited Cinnia after her attack—and at other times, complete and blissful silence.

I am dead, he realized.

He thought he saw Logan questioning his identity. From this place, he knew he couldn't help his son, but he reached out anyway. It didn't always work because Logan was mentally too confused for him to break through. He had to watch as Logan repeated the same mistakes he'd made: losing his virginity too soon, chasing skirts all over town, turning sex into a power play...

A woman with different hair colors—sometimes orange and yellow, other times blue or pink, or even blonde—could change it all. Did Logan see it?

No, he's too torn between his choices: one keeps him home and happy, but the other will truly fulfil him if he dares to take the leap.

The girl with the violet eyes, the one that tempted Logan to repeat a family cycle he wasn't even fully aware of, finally set him on the right path. She broke Logan's heart, which caused him to break free of everything that's held him back. All the guilt for wanting a different life, and the shame for not feeling like he belonged, gave way to his soul's true desires.

If he'd had breath in this other place, he would've let it out in relief.

He couldn't have changed his own path because he'd been too hardheaded and, frankly, unaware. But his son was more perceptive. Perhaps the very fact that Logan had been an unusual conception and birth set him apart from the Drummonds that came before him.

What brought him peace was seeing Logan, fully-grown and playing football for Everton. Not only because Everton had been *his* favorite team, but because of the joy Logan experienced every time he set foot on the pitch. That version of events involved a deeply loving, albeit simplistic relationship with a woman—her hair was a natural brown now—and four kids. A house filled with noise and laughter, the opposite of Logan's own upbringing. A life centered around love, commitment and family, without the danger and violence of previous generations. Without the responsibility of the Raptors Motorcycle Club.

He saw his mother with Logan, on the morning of a white Christmas, and felt such love for, and deep connection to, them both. He was comforted by their acknowledgement of his presence and although he never felt lonely in this place, it made him feel less adrift.

This version of Logan was at peace.

And if this was the end, as Brennan assumed it was, isn't that all a father could wish for his child?

THE END

Author's Note

THIS BOOK HAS been a long time coming. Logan's story had seemed destined for a specific ending when I started writing, but the vision kept shifting and it took an immense amount of grit for me to see it through.

I cannot thank you enough for your patience.

Personal identity is such an onion-layered topic: there are many reasons why we feel the way we feel and do what we do. Many times, they are little-known or unconscious decisions based on our thoughts and beliefs about ourselves and our place in the world. If nothing else, I hope that you were able to empathize with Logan while he figured out his own, unique journey, even when it deviated from the overall Raptors theme.

In my own life, I have had to go through a similar journey to discover what I truly needed versus what I *believed* I wanted. And although my books are meant to have sexy moments that make you wish for your own Logan—or Byron, or Brennan, or anyone!—I always try to inject deeper meaning in these chapters to simulate that discovery process. I can only hope that you have found the value in that.

And no, this won't be the last Raptors MC novel ever, so go to my website to find other books from this universe: www.rudelleo.com